THE LOW ROAD

Also by A. D. Scott

North Sea Requiem
Beneath the Abbey Wall
A Double Death on the Black Isle
A Small Death in the Great Glen

WITHDRAWN

THE LOW ROAD

A Novel

A. D. Scott

ATRIA PAPERBACK

New York   London   Toronto   Sydney   New Delhi

ATRIA PAPERBACK
A Division of Simon & Schuster, Inc.
1230 Avenue of the America
New York, NY 10020

Copyright © 2014 by A. D. Scott

First Atria Paperback edition September 2014

ATRIA PAPERBACK and colophon are trademarks of Simon & Schuster, Inc.

For information about special discounts for bulk purchases, please contact Simon & Schuster Special Sales at 1-866-506-1949 or business@simonandschuster.com.

The Simon & Schuster Speakers Bureau can bring authors to your live event. For more information or to book an event, contact the Simon & Schuster Speakers Bureau at 1-866-248-3049 or visit our website at www.simonspeakers.com.

Cover design © Richard Yoo Design

Manufactured in the United States of America

10   9   8   7   6   5   4   3   2   1

Library of Congress Cataloging-in-Publication Data

Scott, A. D.
    The low road / by A. D. Scott. — First Atria paperback edition.
        pages   cm
    1. Journalists—Scotland—Fiction. I. Title.
    PR9619.4.S35L69   2014
    823'.92—dc23

                                        2014005047

ISBN 978-1-4767-5616-5
ISBN 978-1-4767-5617-2 (ebook)

For Elka Ray

By yon bonnie banks and by yon bonnie braes,
On the steep, steep side of Ben Lomond,
Where me an' my true love were ever wont to gae,
By the bonnie, bonnie banks o' Loch Lomond.
Oh ye'll tak the high road,
An' I'll tak the low road . . .

—Traditional

PROLOGUE

~

He shuddered as he got off the bus outside the main gate of the former Duke Street Prison. There was a *give up all hope* air about the prison gateway and the crenellated castle structure above. The main archway and two minor arches either side were bricked up, derelict and dirty-soot-darkened bleak; the ending of more than a century of punishment had neither reformed nor inhibited the crime that flourished in the poverty of the city. That the prison was in keeping with his mission was a thought he preferred not to think about.

He turned in to the street leading to the flat of his old friends and slowly climbed between tenement terraces; here large families shared one- or at most two-roomed flats, with a communal stairway and often communal outside lavatory. The walk was a slow struggle, as he'd forgotten how steep the brae was.

He couldn't recall when he had last visited the family, when they had all been together: the father (his friend and colleague), two boys, and Mrs. McAllister, a woman he had always had a sneaking fancy for, her being so pretty and bright and a great cook. He had a bad feeling that the last time he'd visited had been for one or other of the funerals that left a widow with one son.

He was not impatient as he waited for her to answer the door; at their age he well knew how long it took to rise from the armchair and shuffle down the hallway to the door. Looking around in the half-light of the close, feeling the chill of stone walls and the draft coming down the dark staircase from the top landing, four floors up, he fancied he could feel the high-summer June warmth from outside in the street drain out through his Sunday shoes onto the slate flagstones.

He knocked.

"Who is it?"

Her voice was not as he remembered it—more an old crow than the linnet of years ago. "It's Gerald Dochery, Mrs. McAllister."

She opened the door. Even with the light behind her it was a surprise. *My God she's aged,* he thought. Then he remembered, *Me too.*

She neither smiled nor seemed surprised. "Come in." And she turned and walked down the hallway, expecting him to follow. The wallpaper was faded. The light that came from high up in the hall ceiling, filtered through a lampshade that had been installed a week after her honeymoon, was as washed out as her hair. The flat smelled of old people, but that Mr. Dochery did not notice, as he smelled the same.

Then he recalled, *It's been nearly fifteen years since we last met—at her husband's funeral.*

Both knew he would not visit without a reason and delayed what they sensed would be a difficult conversation. They chatted on the usual—weather, health, the infrequency of buses. After tea and a finger of shortbread, which he himself had made—baking being his hobby since his wife died—he told Mrs. McAllister why he was here.

"There's this man frae the Highlands. I'm told he's a friend of your John. Needs help so he does."

She gave no indication, but the spoken and the unspoken—that Mr. Gerald Dochery was bringing trouble to her door—was now confirmed.

"And what would the man's name be?"

"Jimmy McPhee."

The name meant nothing to her. "Where can he be found?"

"Last I heard he was Barlinnie Prison. Now . . ." He shrugged.

He knew that in this city a man could easily disappear: in the slums of the Gorbals, in the derelict areas of the Clydeside docks and warehouses, and in former merchant buildings. A merchant city, a high-Victorian homage to tobacco and cotton and slavery, the city was streets and terraces and private enclaves of former wealth and glory, interspersed with ruination more usual in bombed-out Europe than in the Great Britain of 1959.

"I wouldn't be bothering you, missus, if it wasn't that this McPhee character is in danger of his life. And the man likely to do him harm is ma son, Wee Gerry."

She looked at him. Saw his age. His pain. "I'll let John know."

"Good enough, missus." He knew he could hope for no more.

They said their goodbyes as though it would be their last meeting in this realm.

As she shut the door she wished Mr. Dochery had not come. *Trouble,* she thought, *the last thing ma John needs is more trouble.*

ONE

~

The letter arrived two weeks after his fiancée, Joanne Ross, was released from hospital. McAllister read it and put it aside. *Mother doesn't know that Jimmy McPhee is more than capable of looking after himself,* was his reasoning.

Then two weeks later, at the offices of the *Highland Gazette* where he was editor, a note, in a plain brown envelope, was delivered by hand. It read, *Meet me at seven tomorrow in the snug bar.* The writing was rounded school-pupil-in-fourth-form script. He had no doubt whom it was from, even if he hadn't caught a glimpse of a redheaded young man loping off down the Wynd to the High Street like a lurcher ambling behind a Traveler's caravan.

It was an appointment he knew he had to keep. There was too much history between himself and the matriarch of the McPhee family.

"McAllister." Jenny McPhee acknowledged his presence, and with a left jerk of her head, indicated he should sit. A glass of whisky was brought in by a middle-aged barman with no memorable features whatsoever, and a white linen tea towel over his shoulder with what looked like someone's brain matter encrusted on one end.

McAllister forced himself not to shudder, as the man wiped the none too clean glass with it.

Though he was thinking *Jenny's buying, what does she want?* he knew better than to ask. He waited. After the second round, and after the Highland ritual of asking after family health and happiness was observed, he watched Jenny stare into the light-peat-colored liquid, swirling it around the glass, releasing the scent of heather and peat and high summer on the moorland.

He was fascinated by this woman. Seeing her examine the whisky, another image came to him, the image of an old Gypsy woman near Seville, looking deep into a crystal ball, shuddering at what she saw, before throwing her shawl, a bright yellow embroidered shawl, over the offending image. And not long after, Madrid fell to General Franco's forces.

They were of the same age, the Gypsy woman and Jenny, but Jenny McPhee was a Highland Traveler, not Romany, and although their ways were similar, their antecedents were completely different. For McAllister, however, a powerful woman was always beguiling, no matter her age or tribe.

"Our Jimmy."

The name shook McAllister from his dwam. He hadn't seen Jimmy McPhee, her second son and right-hand man, for some time, but the recollection of the letter from his mother made him listen carefully. And look more closely at the woman sitting opposite.

She's not herself, he thought. Her hair was mostly white in that bleached-out, slightly yellow way of former redheads. Her skin, always dark from years traveling in a horse-drawn caravan, was now not just the color of a walnut, but the texture also. And her coal-black buttons of eyes had equally dark rings underneath.

He felt that somehow the fierceness of Jenny McPhee had been tamed, much as the ponies and horses, beloved by the Traveling people, were tamed and trained by her son Jimmy.

Having made her decision, she sighed and her mouth tightened; asking an outsider for help was not something she did lightly, but this outsider was from the city, it was in his bones. Plus she thought he would still have contacts from his former job in the city newspaper. "Jimmy," she started, "he's gone missing. Glasgow was the last place he was seen—about four weeks since. Not that I'd normally worry, but he's due back here weeks ago—has to get the horses ready for the Black Isle Show. It takes months to get them in condition—an' he's never missed a show since he was a bairn—since he was in the womb even."

He felt she knew more than she was telling. Then so was he. She had her shawl clutched around her as though she was feeling the chill of one of those long summer nights where the light evaporated for a few hours yet was never completely dark. But it was mild. Balmy even. Except Jenny McPhee seemed cold, and McAllister knew that feeling too well.

"I phoned Barlinnie Prison after I got your message," he said. "He did thirty days for breach of the peace but was released two weeks ago." From the look on her face he immediately knew he should have told her. And paid heed to his mother's warning.

"And how did you know he was there?" Jenny was not perturbed that her son had been in prison, but she was not pleased McAllister knew and hadn't told her.

"My mother wrote to me. An old friend of our family mentioned something of Jimmy's whereabouts."

"You should have told me!" But her anger died as swiftly as it arrived. "Sorry. You've had your fair share o' troubles yerself."

She knew what had happened to Joanne Ross his fiancée; she had visited the hospital once, and visited at McAllister's house twice. And Jenny McPhee was well aware how long it could take to recover from a blow to the head, days in a coma, locked up in a cellar by a volatile madwoman. *It's a wonder she survived,* Joanne's mother-in-law had told her, even as she fussed over a tinker woman's visiting the house and McAllister's allowing the visitor into the sitting room.

Jenny had heard the rumors of perhaps permanent brain

damage to Joanne. Even now, six weeks after the rescue, there was no firm verdict as to whether she would recover completely. But she had always thought Joanne Ross was a woman of strength—a strength Joanne herself did not recognize.

McAllister acknowledged the older woman's ire. Leaving a message in this public house, which she was rumored to own, would have taken him no effort. "I apologize, I didn't want to embarrass you."

She waved a hand as though cooling porridge. "One o' ma sons in the gaol for a few days . . ." The slight shrug of her shoulders and gesture said it all. "Oor Jimmy no' coming home to see to the horses, that's different."

Jenny McPhee knew in her bones, mostly in her solar plexus, when danger threatened. A life on the road, the treatment of Traveling peoples through the centuries, and the weather made Scottish tinkers a wary, superstitious lot. And suspicion of outsiders, who could never know their ways, or their language, had kept them alive, if not healthy. Jenny and Jimmy McPhee's relationship with McAllister might seem a friendship to outsiders, but both sides were aware it was far more, and far less. There was respect. And the acknowledgment that they could never be close. On McAllister's part, he was never sure what drew him to Jimmy McPhee. *Perhaps I'm just a romantic*, he thought.

Jenny knew better; she recognized a fascination with violence in McAllister, knew it came from the streets he grew up in. And in an unformed way, she knew men like McAllister, forever chaffing at the conformity of his chosen life, romanticized the Traveling peoples, not seeing that their life too was confined, by weather, the law, antagonistic townsfolk. And now, in the twilight of the old ways—settled life in houses, cottages, and council schemes—their millennia-old way of life was ending.

McAllister apologized again. "I'm sorry, I should have been in touch before now. Tomorrow I'll make a few phone calls, see if I can find out more." He was trying not to check the time, but he knew he should be back home. Joanne was not up to making the cocoa, reading the story to Jean, her younger daughter, and putting the girls to bed.

"It might be best if you go to Glasgow." It was a challenge. She was looking into his eyes, daring him to refuse.

Yes, he thought as he returned her stare, *she does know what she's asking of me, so it must be serious.* "Let's wait and see. But I'll ask around, contact old colleagues, try to track Jimmy down."

"Aye, you do that." She was still staring into his face as she said it. He looked away first. There was a loud shout from the bar next door, the banging of a door, then sudden quiet, before the usual barroom murmur recommenced.

"Give Joanne my regards," Jenny said, releasing him.

Driving home across the river, the late sun hovering in the west made the water glint like whisky in a glass held up for the traditional toast, *Slàinte*.

He had acquired an affection for the town, and its inhabitants, and chastised himself for not being more appreciative. It was undeniably attractive: the castle looming high above the river, the handsome Town House, the mixed eighteenth- and nineteenth-century architecture with some buildings dating back to the seventeenth century and earlier still intact. As he drove past and admired, he thought, *Yes, this is a bonnie place*—but for a well-traveled and well-educated man like himself it could be boring, parochial even, a county, a country, with one foot still firmly in the prewar era.

The meeting with Jenny McPhee had also revived what he had been trying to quash—the overwhelming sense of helplessness he felt when confronted with Joanne's condition. He had never known fear as paralyzing as the fear of losing her. He had never known rage as powerful as the rage he felt on discovering it was one of their own, the former *Gazette* advertising manager, who had been responsible for Joanne's imprisonment. And now he was ashamed of his need for normality, his need to escape the troupe of doctors and nurses and police and friends and parents-in-law who visited his home, stayed for tea, chatted, smiled, forcing a cheer that fooled no one, disturbing the peace and the quiet and the anonymity that he so cherished.

But Joanne was alive. They were about to be married. He would no longer be pitied as a middle-aged bachelor, at the mercy of every war widow in town. One of his mother's favorite sayings popped into his head: *Count your blessings,* she'd tell him. But he had been too young and too arrogant in his affected persona of escaped-from-the-slums-now-star-journalist to hear the wisdom in the platitude. Or was it a hymn? A Sunday-school song, perhaps? Having lost religion, he wasn't sure.

He changed gears down to second to drive the last steep slope to the district where he had lived since arriving from the city to revamp an ailing local newspaper. The absence of life on the tree-lined streets depressed him. *Not like Glasgow,* he thought. *On a summer's night like this, the women will be sitting on doorsteps, on walls, out the back green, chatting, laughing, yelling at the bairns running wild, playing cowboys and Indians. Or skipping with a length of clothesline. The chip shop will be busy. And the men will be down the pub.*

He knew Joanne could never understand his fascination for the dirty, decrepit city, long past its glory days of the Victorian Merchant City era. Though still magnificent, it was the people, his clan, his tribe, that he loved the most. He smiled when she described the thick air, dirty with traffic fumes. He knew she hated the constant noise and shouts and fights. He once asked her if she had had firsthand experience of the city violence and had laughed when she'd said, *No, but I've read about it.* From Edinburgh folk, most likely, he'd replied before telling her of the journalists' axiom: Never let the truth get in the way of a good story.

When he came home, he found Annie, almost twelve, the daughter of his fiancée, in the sitting room. She said, "Mum's asleep," and told him her wee sister, Jean, two and a half years younger, was also asleep.

Seeing the girl now comfortably nestled on the sofa with a book, an empty cocoa mug on the floor beside her, McAllister did not think to tell her to go to bed. He too found the long white nights unsettling: a time out of time; not light, not dark, the midnight dim seemed like the light of a half-remembered dream, all color washed out, the outlines of mountain, river, loch, and sea blurred, yet distinct—and time felt suspended.

McAllister started to talk. Quietly, he began telling her of his day at the *Gazette.*

She told him she'd like to work in a newspaper. "Or be a writer," she added.

He believed her. He told her to do one or the other, telling her journalism can ruin an aspiring writer. They discussed the house—Joanne wanted to move to somewhere new, or back to her own wee prefab, changing her mind daily. Annie said she wanted to stay in this house. She liked the attic, where she could hide out and read without her sister or grandmother interrupting. She liked the old wood-burning kitchen stove, and it was a short walk to the academy, where she was certain to win a place when the eleven-plus exams results were announced.

"I might have to go to Glasgow for a few days," he told her. "I've a few things to sort out."

"You're not going to leave us, McAllister?" Annie asked.

He heard her anxiety and he hated her father for what he had done to his family. No matter how many in society accepted it as the norm, for McAllister domestic violence was never, ever, no matter the circumstances, acceptable. "My mother wrote to me. I need to see her. I'm also on a mission to try to persuade Mother to come here to visit. To meet you all." He was disappointed in himself for telling a half-truth, something he'd sworn he'd never do. *But*, he thought, *the story belongs to Jenny McPhee.*

"Good enough," Annie said in imitation of her grandmother. "Go over a weekend. Granny Ross can be here with Mum, and Granddad will take me and Jean out to the pictures."

He knew the timing was wrong. And leaving felt cowardly. But from the moment the thought had formed, he knew he needed to breathe the air of Glasgow. He needed to be where no one knew him or his situation. He needed respite.

"Good enough," he said back at her.

Annie smiled, then, putting the marker in her book, she stood. "Night-night, McAllister. And don't feel bad about leaving us for a few days, we'll be fine."

He tried to settle back into the novel he'd been reading on and off for a week but unable to concentrate on. The benediction from a child had made him feel guilty. And the phrase would not go away, *She's not herself*, running around his brain, a thought chasing a thought turning to dread: *What if she's never herself again? What if Joanne is never again the woman I love, the woman I wanted to spend the rest of my life with?* There was only one place those fears would dissolve—the bottom of a whisky glass. So, tonight, as on so many nights recently, he reached for the decanter.

Thelonious Monk was at the piano, the book was by Kingsley Amis, the whisky from Aberlour. He'd been sitting sipping, reading, dreaming for almost two hours when he became aware of a shadow flitting through into the room.

"McAllister." Annie's voice was a whisper, and in a flannelette nightgown, the color washed out to an indeterminate shade of porridge, she seemed more phantom than child. Her hair, very short and looking as though she had taken the scissors to it herself—which she had—emphasized her blue-green eyes, giving her a resemblance to an Edwardian illustrator's idea of a pixie or elf. Her long, lanky body spoiled the image, the resemblance being more that of an adolescent giraffe.

"I can't sleep," Annie said, not looking at him, running her hand over her hair, massaging her skull, or her brain, a habit he found endearing. "It's Mum." She paused, searching for the words, but nothing in her vocabulary could express what she felt. "She's not herself."

He was shaken to hear the phrase repeated back to him; he was certain he had never said it aloud. In the pause while he composed an answer to the girl, the clock struck eleven. Eleven in the evening in this town was "ungodly."

"Your mum has had a terrible experience. It takes time to get over something like that." He immediately regretted the clichés. Annie deserved better.

"I know."

She was quiet for a moment and as he watched her absorb the information, he caught a glimpse of the girl's intelligence, and resilience, and suspected this would always save her.

"I know it was terrible," she repeated, "but Mum is not getting better." She knew adults were not perfect—she'd learned that early from her father. But she expected more from McAllister. He should have noticed.

And he was not himself either. But unable to recognize why. All he knew was that he had never known loneliness until he had fallen in love with Joanne Ross.

In his need for solitude, if even for a few hours, he'd taken to staying up late into the night. After years on the evening desk of a national newspaper, his body rhythms were set for the early hours of the morning with the music playing quietly, the fire banked up even though it was midsummer, his book, the decanter of whisky, and a pack of Passing Clouds cigarettes at hand, this quiet was a now rare delight.

Annie looked at him again. For a fraction of a second he felt himself being appraised. And again he felt he was failing her, and her mother. He had not seen, or chosen not to see, that the Joanne he loved, whose face and voice and laughter he carried in his head, was not the compliant, puzzled woman he had watched that morning in the garden. He saw her on a stripy deck chair in the sunshine, looking around with a nervous twist to the head, and commenting—to no one in particular—how the flock of cotton-wool clouds were forming and re-forming in an attempt at blocking out the sun, and failing. "Look," she was saying, shielding her eyes with one hand, "look at the clouds. They're like sheep. And those wispy ones, they're like thistledown."

Annie looked at him, waiting for more. Then she understood that he was as afraid as she was that her mother might never be her old self again, that was something he, too, was terrified of. "'Night," she muttered, and went back up to bed.

He listened but didn't hear the girl creep up the stairs. When he heard her door close, he shut his eyes. How to explain to a child the evil that had almost killed her mother, how to diminish the horror of the three days Joanne had been locked up in the dark with a head wound or tell her that, when rescued, she'd been given little chance of survival without serious brain damage by the surgeon and doctors—that was McAllister's quandary.

His head felt heavy, his shoulders tight, and running around his brain, like the repeat refrain from the backing singers of a particularly annoying song of the doo-wop variety on the radio, the phrase kept repeating, *She's not herself, She's not herself.*

◆　◆　◆

Next morning, McAllister walked to the *Highland Gazette* office. When he climbed the spiral stone staircase to the reporters' room, he found the others already there, seated around the long narrow table that almost filled the room. The far end of the table was territory the deputy editor Don McLeod had not visited in at least forty years; squeezing past colleagues and chairs and overlarge typewriters was beyond a round person like himself, so he reigned at the head of the table. Wreathed in cigarette smoke, his stomach spilling beyond the circumference of his high wooden chair, and with his wee red editing pencil tucked behind his ear, he resembled a potentate from *Tales of the Arabian Nights*.

He looked up at the tyrant, as he called it, the wall clock, ruler of the newsroom. It was ten minutes to nine in the morning, early for journalists, and even though today was deadline day, and unusually early for McAllister, Don said nothing, because nothing was normal these days.

"What's happening?" McAllister asked, glancing at the layout spread over the table.

"Not much," Don answered.

"Thank goodness," Rob McLean said. With Joanne Ross sick, he was their one and only reporter. "Sheepdog trials is enough excitement for me right now." Quiet felt good; school prize-giving ceremonies, ferry cancellations, and Loch Ness Monster sightings were all the excitement he wanted.

This was not what an editor of a newspaper wanted to hear, but they had had enough of front-page headlines featuring death and damnation. Rob most of all.

"Advertising is steady," Frankie Urquhart, the newly appointed advertising salesman and Rob's best friend, said. "No surprises there." Everyone felt relieved at that except Frankie. He wanted a full-page ad from somewhere, anywhere, to prove that at twenty-four, he was old enough to be promoted to the position of advertising manager.

"I'm thinking I'll go to Glasgow on Thursday. Back Sunday night," McAllister told them.

"Oh, aye?" Don McLeod looked up at him.

Perhaps he meant nothing by his question, but McAllister felt the need to justify himself. "Aye, my mother has written to me. I should go see her. It's been too long . . ."

He knew he was overstating his case. Knew his mother was not bothered if he visited or not—as long as he wrote regularly, she was content to live in solitude with only the noises of neighbors in the communal close for company. Why he did not mention Jenny and Jimmy McPhee, and their troubles, to a man he trusted, a man who knew more than he about the McPhees and the inhabitants of the town and county and Highlands and Islands, he did not know.

"I'll call in and see Joanne when you're away," was all his deputy said before turning to the layout for the next day's edition. "Now where the hell is thon eejit of a photographer? I need the photos of the academy's sports meeting."

And so the day went on. And so another deadline on the *Highland Gazette* was met. And on Thursday morning, after a cooked breakfast with Joanne and the girls, McAllister went in to the office, reviewed the edition, saw to some paperwork, signed off on the accounts, then walked to the train station.

As he took his seat in the first-class compartment, hoping for solitude or at least a minimum of conversation, and as the train began the long slow climb over the pass of Drumochter, he admitted his need of a break from work, from the Highland town he had come to, to bring the *Gazette* from the nineteenth century to 1958. That he could also be running away from the woman he was about to marry, the woman who was *not herself*, he buried deep down in a dark place, hoping his conscience could not reach that far.

Two

The train arrived at Glasgow's Central Station early Thursday evening. As the passengers disembarked he noticed the hesitant first-time-away-from-the-Highlands families, couples perhaps on holiday, solitary young men and women leaving home in search of work, all hesitant, looking around or upwards through the high vaulted ceiling where, even two hundred miles south and in the heart of the city, it was still bright daylight—just not their evening light; it was city light—grey, dense, and hostile.

McAllister walked through the Victorian cathedral to engineering into streets that had been built with the spoils of empire. Street upon street. Terrace upon terrace, parks, public houses, museums, art galleries—all were products of this once prosperous city, this proud product of an empire few could ever imagine would vanish.

And few of those proud Georgian and Victorian merchants could have imagined that a century later, grime would turn their buildings dark, bombs would obliterate warehouses, shipyards, and engineering works, and poverty would overrun their model housing tenements built for workers.

For the people of Glasgow, one thing that never changed was the fierce loyalty to their city. *There's Scotland, then there's Glasgow,* was the saying, and the natives were Glaswegians first. And foremost.

McAllister hesitated, then turned towards the street and the bus stop. Taking a taxi to his mother's home would invite comments from the neighbors. "Come up in the world, has he?" Or, "Soon be too good for the like o' us." His mother hated that. To live an anonymous life was all she wished for.

Along George Street, past the great edifice of the Glasgow council offices, and the statues in George Square, the bus lurched past the Duke Street gaol to his stop at the foot of the brae. As he tuned in to the passengers on the bus, the voices, the patter, he began to feel lighter, Glaswegian again. Then it was a climb up the oh so familiar streets, walked every day for his last six years of schooling in another part of the city. Before turning towards his mother's ground-floor tenement flat, his childhood home, he paused to catch his breath and look for changes. To his left was the ancient bulk of the cathedral with tombstones and the monuments and stone angels in all their glory strewn throughout the graveyard, memorials of those who had brought the wealth of the colonies and the profits of the clipper trade to Glasgow. That kirkyard had been his favorite playground, and he doubted much would have changed. *Just a few more graves.*

He let himself in, calling out, "Mother, it's me," even though no one else would have a key. The sound of the wireless came faintly from the kitchen, the one room his mother permanently inhabited. He suspected she would sleep there if a bed could be fitted in.

"Hello." He smiled at her. Patted her arm. This was as much affection as they ever allowed themselves.

"You should have written. There's nothing in the larder." It sounded harsh. It wasn't meant to be. They were not people who had much in the way of an emotional vocabulary.

"I only decided to come down yesterday. Besides, with the chip shop just up the street, no need to cook."

"All the same . . ." she started. But from the way she stood, from the way she reached for the kettle and the tea caddy, with movements more spritely than the last time he had visited, he knew she was pleased. He saw that she was wearing a tweed skirt and a twinset and was happy that even for sitting solitary in her kitchen listening to the wireless, knitting, she had dressed. It hadn't always been so; for many long years, almost twenty, after the death of his younger brother, his mother hadn't often found the energy to get out of slippers and a dressing gown, far less visit her remaining son in his new home in the Highlands.

They drank their tea. She asked about his work, and the fiancée she'd never met.

He lied, telling his mother Joanne was getting better every day. He told her of Joanne's girls, Annie and Jean, his soon-to-be stepdaughters. He painted a cheery picture of the Highland town, its river, its weather, and its inhabitants.

His mother liked that. Although she had never been that far north, like all Scottish city dwellers, she had a romantic notion of the Highlands, the clans, the history. And Bonnie Prince Charlie.

Nothing was said about the letter. McAllister did not mention he had paid it no heed. She did not mention she had been asking for help.

"Another pot o' tea?" she asked, it being her firm belief that the longer the journey, the more tea needed to recover.

"How about I fetch some fish suppers?" he asked.

"I'm sorry," she replied. "If I'd known I'd've . . ."

"Not to worry, our local has the best fish and chips in Glasgow"—by *Glasgow* he meant the universe.

"Nothing for me," she said, but he bought an extra fish anyway, hoping to persuade her to eat at least a half of it—which she did. They had a cup of cocoa, said their good-nights, then she went to bed, leaving him to listen to the news on the wireless and make his bed with the clean sheets she had left out. In the morning they'd speak of why he was here.

All was as ever between them, and McAllister slept a long deep sleep untroubled by nightmares for the first time in a long time.

At breakfast he let her boil him an egg, and he ate it with soldiers of toast—just as he had when a boy, when they could afford eggs; salted oatmeal porridge had been the childhood staple breakfast, eggs a Sunday treat.

"I'm off to the *Herald* this morning, catch up with everyone," he told her. "But whilst I'm here I'd like to talk to Mr. Dochery, see if I can find out what's troubling him?"

"I've been thinking on that." Mrs. McAllister sighed, shaking her head slightly. "I'm no' sure you should be getting involved. You've enough troubles o' your own."

"Joanne will be fine." He was saying what he only half believed. "Mr. Dochery was Dad's friend . . ." He was not going to mention Jimmy McPhee. "And wasn't he best man at your wedding?"

"Right enough." She was acknowledging that Mr. Gerald Dochery had the right to ask a favor, the first ever in over fifty years of their acquaintance. "I'll see if I can get a message to him."

How the message would be delivered he didn't ask, but McAllister remembered the notes wee boys, himself included, would run with from neighbor to neighbor, a farthing, or with luck a halfpenny, waiting for them when they returned. What the going rate was these days he didn't know, but he knew it would be at least sixpence, plus, in Mr. Dochery's case, the price of a bus fare or two.

"Well, well, well, the teuchtar comes to town." Sandy Marshall was grinning as he used the disrespectful term for Highlanders. But he was allowed to be disrespectful; he and McAllister had been firm friends since, as seventeen-year-olds, they had started their careers as copyboys on the same newspaper, the *Herald*. "I suppose you need a favor. Or have you seen the light and come home to civilization?"

"Both." McAllister shook the proffered hand, sat down in the visitor's chair, and after Sandy Marshall waved away McAllister's preferred Passing Clouds and took a Player's for himself, both men lit their cigarettes.

McAllister blew the smoke towards the ceiling, observing his friend through narrowed eyes. Sandy had put on weight, and his hair and his skin made him look prosperous and as sleek as a well-fed seal in the zoo.

"Still smoking thon Fenian brand, I see." Sandy pointed to the packet of Passing Clouds on the desk.

"Aye. And still a Celtic supporter through and through."

"I'd be careful where you shout that from these days," Sandy told him. "There's even more trouble about than usual." He pushed a copy of that morning's newspaper towards him.

McAllister took it. Front page, large headlines, and an article spilling onto page five told it all: the razor gangs had claimed another victim. One dead, two injured, three or more escaped, and the grass on Glasgow Green still stained red, no doubt. "Same old gang violence?" he asked. "I thought most of that had been cleaned up."

"Aye, it's much better than the old days, but this is gangs, or so the police are saying. But one o' my reporters doesn't think so. She says it's a turf war—who controls what areas, who collects the brown paper bag after the pubs close, after the billiard halls shut, the protection money from the stallholders at the Barrows, the garages, the boxing clubs—all the usual stuff. And"—it was Sandy's turn to blow smoke towards the ceiling—"I'm inclined to believe her."

"Her?"

"One Mary Ballantyne, a distant relation of the great journalist Thomas Ballantyne no less, and a real looker in a bluestocking kinda way." Sandy grinned. "I'd introduce you, but aren't you as good as wed?"

McAllister ignored the comment. He knew, as did any journalist in Scotland, of the great nineteenth-century editor and publisher, but to find his female relative writing front-page crime stories nearly eighty years later was intriguing.

"How can a woman come up with information on the gangs? Surely it's dangerous?"

"Aye. It is. I've warned her off, and she keeps coming back with more. I've another reporter backing her up, but no one comes close when it comes to accurate, timely reporting. She's a woman on her way up. *Manchester Guardian*, like her forebear, is her next stop, so she says."

Now McAllister was intrigued. "So maybe she'd have contacts at Barlinnie Prison?" he asked.

"More than likely." Sandy looked up at a large clock placed in the center of the wall opposite the editor's desk that every editor, past and present, knew must be obeyed. "She'll be in in half an hour. I'll introduce you. In the meantime . . ." He waved at the clock hands ticking down the minutes to deadline.

"I'll hunker down in a corner of the newsroom, if I may?"

"Aye. I owe you after the last story you shared. It must have been hard to write up a vicious crime story concerning your own fiancée." Sandy said no more, sensing that a discussion of the events involving the *Gazette* reporter Joanne Ross was not welcome. *Not yet, anyhow,* he thought, *if ever; a man for keeping his own council is John McAllister.*

◆　◆　◆

McAllister was at a borrowed desk in the newsroom, considering who amongst his former contacts might know of Jimmy McPhee, when a young woman, small, wiry, with long hair the color of sloe berries, strode into the newsroom and took a notebook from the desk next to his.

"You new here?" she asked. She looked closely at him.

He saw aqua-blue Celtic eyes, similar to wee Jean's china doll's eyes, the painted staring ones that gave him the creeps.

She saw a middle-aged man, handsome in a raddled way, with navy-blue eyes, and black hair now greying at the temples, looking back.

He held her stare, amused that she was obviously calculating if he was someone she needed to know.

"I used to work here a few years back," he told her. "John McAllister."

"Mary Ballantyne."

"I've heard about you," they said in unison. She laughed.

"You first," he said.

"Our esteemed editor told me of you, and I like the stories you send from up in the wilds. Sorry about the spot of bother your reporter had to endure."

Spot of bother was not how he would have put it. But he didn't elaborate. "Goes with the job."

"Tell me about it." Her voice was posh Scottish. Her confidence also. She was clearly the product of a private girls' school. But there was a touch of a Highland accent, not Edinburgh.

"I was wondering if you could help me track down someone from the Highlands. Jimmy McPhee, last heard of doing thirty days in Barlinnie, now released."

"I know the name . . ." Her eyes opened a fraction wider as a recollection popped up. "He's a tinker, is he?"

"His mother would prefer the term Traveler."

"This is Scotland, McAllister. Not likely they'll ever get the respect of 'Traveler.'" She was giving it some thought. "I've heard that name recently, but I can't remember where. I'll ask around."

"I'm here today and tomorrow. Leave on Sunday."

"Right. Good to meet you, McAllister." And she was off, waving off his call of "Thanks," walking past the subs' desk, where she stopped for a brief word before swinging a leather bag with a long strap over her shoulder and, with nary a look back, making her way out the door where she had just come in.

"So you've met the star reporter," a voice said from across the room. "Make the most of it, she won't be here amongst us mere plebs for long." There was a bitterness in the man's voice that McAllister put down to jealously or unrequited love. A glance at the man and his beer belly made him change his mind on the second option.

"Reporter, is she?" McAllister asked, knowing the answer.

"Chief crime reporter, according to her," was the reply. "And her no' that long out of university. Has all the right connections is why," he said to an unasked question. "And I don't mean street connections. More wi' the top brass, if you get ma drift, her family being who they are."

The phone on his desk started to ring. McAllister knew it wouldn't be for him but answered regardless, wanting no more conversation with the fellow. He was right, so he transferred the call back to the switchboard, feeling bad that he hadn't called Joanne. He knew he should but reasoned he had only been away one night and the conversation was too private to have with the radar-eared journalist listening in. *I'll call her from the phone box later on*, he promised himself.

Guilt assuaged, he made his way to the newspaper library and archives. He put in the request for all recent editions dealing with gangland activity.

"Can you no' narrow it down a bit?" a peevish wee moorhen of a man asked.

"Recent stories from Mary Ballantyne, say, the last six months?" McAllister suggested.

"I'll make that front pages, then, else you'll be here aa' day."

Two hours later, McAllister had a pub lunch of pie and peas with his former editor and friend. McAllister made a comment about what the world was coming to when a pub served food. Sandy agreed it did not go down well with the purists, and both agreed that the world was indeed changing. Rapidly.

In the late afternoon on the now busy editorial floor, McAllister sat at the desk, once more engrossed in the many articles written by Mary Ballantyne. He admired her writing, as well as her research. He knew from the stories that she must have contacts in the police as well as amongst the criminal fraternity.

"You still here?" It was said with a laugh.

He looked up. Same ice-blue eyes, same blue-black hair, same grin greeted him.

"It seems your Jimmy McPhee was indeed in the Bar L. He did his thirty days, was released, and no one's heard of him since."

"Thanks."

"So what's the story, McAllister? One of my contacts says there's a reward out for information on this McPhee fellow."

A current of cold ran down McAllister's spine. "Reward?"

Mary Ballantyne looked at him, and in that look he saw she was older than her years. A few years out of university she might be, but she'd been around.

"Maybe not reward, but it will be 'considered a favor' if news of him is passed on." Her voice went hard. "Is there something you're not telling me?"

He understood. Sharing information went two ways, and she had done her share.

"Maybe nothing, but . . . An old family friend, he came to see my mother, wanting my help. Seems his son might be involved in . . ." He couldn't think how to phrase it without slighting his childhood friend. "Might be on the wrong side of the law." He saw her eyebrows, eyebrows the shape of arched bows, raised in a *what else* question. "Mr. Dochery . . ."

"Gerry Dochery?"

"The father. Do you know him?" He was wondering if she had the second sight.

"Gerry Dochery, the son, is one of the hardest hard men in this city of hard men."

"Oh."

"Right. Oh. This calls for a drink."

Once again Mary Ballantyne surprised him. She led him not to the local journalists' hangout but to a discreet cocktail bar in the square where the Stock Exchange building took up central position, roads on three sides, the outward, columned, moneyed facade looking towards George Square, the side opposite the bar facing the Athenaeum, home of the colleges of music and drama. The bar was in the basement of a grand early-Victorian building and was all soft lighting and soft seats. The clientele wore suits, and McAllister suspected that smoking black Sobranie cigarettes would not be out of place.

"No self-respecting journalist would be seen dead here," she said as he brought the drinks—whisky with a dash of water for her, neat for him.

Looking around, he agreed; it was all city types, moneyed, or intellectuals, definitely not moneyed, but with style.

She took one of his proffered cigarettes, not noticing or not commenting on the sweetish taste of the tobacco. She started to speak without filling him in on the current state of the gang wars of Glasgow. *He's from Dennistoun, he will know*, was her thinking.

"This past year it's been more than tribal, religious stuff," she said. "Only not everyone believes me. The police certainly don't. Or, more likely, don't want to know—easier to pass it off as the usual nutters. The name Gerry Dochery has been heard around for a while, but in this last year even more so. He has his own men, but he's also an enforcer for hire. Only trouble is no one knows, or if they do know aren't telling, who it is he's enforcing for. I've been investigating for the past six months, and I'm no nearer finding the name of the head man of this particular gang than when I started. But whoever he is, he's a right evil bastard." She said all this without sipping her drink, without puffing her cigarette, without looking anywhere but straight at him.

McAllister could feel the force of her concentration, hear her intellect and, yes, her courage; it was a brave or foolhardy person who mined the blackness for information on Glasgow's criminal fraternity. Slashing a face open with a cutthroat razor was just for starters when someone was found asking too many questions, or even suspected of it.

"What particular area are they working on?"

"All the contracts for the slum clearance, the new housing schemes, the rebuilding of the city."

"That's huge."

She nodded. "Aye, it is." She looked at him. She'd shown hers, it was his turn. "So. What do you have on Gerry Dochery?"

"Mr. Dochery, the father, was my dad's best friend. Wee Gerry . . ."

She ignored the sobriquet, knowing "wee" meant either he was huge or the son, and in this case both.

"We grew up together. His dad and mine were firemen at the same station. We stood out, both being tall, and we sort of looked out for each other. Gerry's mum died when he was wee, so my mother helped out when she could. Once, on the Fair Fortnight, we all went on holiday together, to Millport. When we were boys, we hung around the fire station, always trying to cadge a shot at pretending to drive the engine, or sliding down the pole. You know." He paused. Tried the whisky. Was pleased at how good it was. She was waiting, and again he knew she was good; a good reporter knew how to listen.

"I won a scholarship to Glasgow High School, escaping the Jesuits, escaping Dennistoun," he told her. In this he was telling her which side of the Glasgow divide, religious and social, he'd been born into. "Gerry went on to the local, but he left at thirteen." He did not have to explain how decisive a rent in a friendship that meant, especially for boys from a hard, harsh neighborhood like Dennistoun. "We never really met up much after that. But when my father, and all on his engine, were killed in the Clydeside Blitz, Mr. Dochery, a good man, kept an eye on my mother, as I was too busy being the big-shot journalist."

McAllister surprised himself by saying that, but it was the truth, and something about Mary demanded the truth.

"And this McPhee fellow, he a friend of yours?"

"Kind of." He was nodding his head slightly as he tried to sum up his relationship with Jimmy McPhee. "Let's say there's a mutual respect. For him and his mother."

She understood. The Traveling people were a part of Scottish folklore, past and present. Having grown up in the country near Perth she knew the farms and fruit growers could never harvest the crops without the tinkers. She also knew that the Travelers were too different, too separate in their language, their way of life, ever to form close relationships with outsiders. She also knew well the widespread prejudice against them.

"McAllister, I'll do what I can to help you find your tinker friend, but if Gerry Dochery, or whoever he's working for, finds him first, it will be nasty."

They both took a good mouthful of whisky to swallow that thought.

"Maybe you should ask your old pal Gerry yourself."

"Maybe." He was reluctant.

She sensed it. "Keep me in the picture. Here's my home number if anything comes up."

The way she said this, he knew he would regret it if he ever crossed her. He nodded, asked her if she wanted another drink. She did. He fetched them.

They toasted crime and punishment. She asked about his time in the war in Spain, teasing him by saying she'd studied his reporting in modern history at university. She wanted to know about Paris after the liberation. He told her of the artists and writers he'd met. Of the cafés and art galleries and music venues he'd frequented.

She told him of her very proper family, her father dying in Thai-Burma railway as a prisoner of war of the Japanese, her isolated childhood in a freezing, almost derelict, castle in Perthshire, her even harsher isolation in a girls' school where the pupils were expected to study hard but not too hard, the principal purpose of their education being to marry well.

Not once did the twenty-year age difference, and the class divide, and her being at the start of her career and him beginning to feel in the twilight of his, make any difference to their ability to talk and talk and talk.

It was closing time before he knew it.

"See you around," Mary said as they parted on the pavement outside the bar. Without a wave or a thanks, she was gone up the street. From a distance her small figure looked as though she was speed-skating.

And he hadn't phoned Joanne. And now it was too late.

It was Saturday morning, two days since he'd left, before he made the phone call to Joanne. He'd bought the Saturday papers, and then found that the local newsagent cum corner shop no longer stocked his brand of cigarettes.

"You've been away that long," Mr. Cruickshank reminded him.

When McAllister asked for change for the phone, the newsagent scolded him, saying, "Wi' you now living in the back o' beyond, the least you can do is put in a phone for your auld ma."

McAllister agreed. "If you can persuade her to have one put in, I'd be delighted to pay."

They grinned; this was a man who had known McAllister, a man who, with his wife, had kept an eye on his mother through wartime and widowhood and the death of her son. He teased, "Seein' it's yerself . . ." and counted out florins and pennies to the value of ten shillings.

McAllister went to the call box on the corner that did not smell of urine, it being the newsagent's wife's contribution to the community to sluice it out every morning.

Annie answered the phone. "Why didn't you call last night? We were waiting."

He took no offence at being lectured by a child, feeling he deserved it.

"Sorry. I got caught up with some colleagues." He knew his excuse was pathetic. "How's your mum?"

"No change." There was a clear sigh from the phone receiver. "Wait a minute, I'll get her."

"I've lost my book, and I can't decide if we should have fish or a nice bit of lamb for dinner . . ." He winced at the lack of a "hello" or "how are you?" or acknowledgment that he was not at home.

"Maybe you could stop by the butcher on St. Steven's Brae," she continued.

He heard Annie's voice call out, "Mum, McAllister is in Glasgow."

"Sorry, sorry, you're not here, are you?" Joanne's voice trailed away. Her voice was light and sweet and breathy, and it terrified him. It was as though there was no substance to her. As though she were a glass with no contents.

"I'll be back tomorrow," he said. "Can I bring you anything? Books? Magazines?"

"You come back safe," she said, "that's enough."

"Are you well? Are the girls well? Is everyone looking after you?"

"You've only been gone a night." She hadn't noticed it had been two. "I know, bring me music, Scottish music. See if that new singer I heard on the wireless, Moira Anderson, has made any records. Or that singer on the television, Kenneth McKellar."

Not to his taste, he loathed *The White Heather Club*, now Joanne's favorite program, but he said, "I'll go shopping today."

"I have to go now, the roses need watering. 'Bye, McAllister." And she was gone.

Gone before he had a chance to reply, a chance to connect with the once laughing, teasing, woman he loved. He was left holding the receiver and wishing that candid news of Joanne's health, her state of mind, would mysteriously transmit through the ether, reassuring him all was well. Or otherwise. He thought of calling back. He didn't. He considered calling the *Gazette* and asking Don McLeod his opinion. But didn't. He left the call box, knowing that only thirty-six hours had passed. It seemed so much more.

The miles between himself and his fiancée were not the only distance between them. He accepted this as a consequence of her injuries. His fading enthusiasm for the post of editor of a local newspaper, in a place so foreign to a Glaswegian it might as well be Iceland, was not a new sensation. But never before was it so plain.

Unable to resolve his unease, he did not wait for a bus. Instead, in unusually clear sunshine, he strode out for the *Herald* office. The light showed just how shabby the city was; the coal-smoke-encrusted sandstone facings of the elegant but intimidating architecture around George Square seemed more pigeon-splatted than he remembered. The empty spaces around Queen Street train station, where a stray wartime bomb had fallen, were bright with fireweed. And all around, morning traffic was building up, and the crowds on the pavements were moving quickly, in and out, shoppers busy shopping, before the Saturday noon closing time.

He made his way down Buchanan Street, between the substantial buildings with ornate doorways and foyers with carved stonework around the windows of the upper floors invisible to the passer-by. The offices of the law firms and businessmen and insurance companies loomed over the street, turning it into a canyon of late eighteenth- and nineteenth-century architecture.

He first stopped at the tobacconist he knew kept his brand. That done, he visited his favorite record and sheet music shop. He bought jazz for himself, the requested Moira Anderson for Joanne and, on a whim, also bought her a new recording of Beethoven's *Pastoral* Symphony.

Once more at his borrowed desk, he realized he should have bought something for the girls. Books, he decided. He was on his way out when he ran into Mary.

"Where're you off to?" she asked.

"To the bookshop to buy presents for the girls." Why he left out that they were his fiancée's daughters he didn't know. But he was aware of being equivocal.

"How old are they?"

"Nine and eleven and a half."

"I'll come with you. I'm good at choosing presents for girls." She was remembering all the birthday presents from relatives who always underestimated her intelligence. "Besides, any excuse to spend time in a bookshop . . ." She laughed.

They made their way up to Sauchihall Street. He told her he hadn't heard from Mr. Gerald Dochery senior. She told him she hadn't any news either. Neither of them mentioned the previous evening.

McAllister chose the books, Mary added some colored pencils and notebooks and a writing set with pretty kittens on it for Jean.

"Perfect for a nine-year-old girl," she told him. For Annie she'd selected a journal in red leather with a gold-colored lock and key and matching gold trim. It was expensive. He didn't mind.

"There's no dates in this, so she can start her journal anytime," Mary said.

He was surprised to see that she had chosen for herself a novel by Ian Fleming. The lurid book cover, the author, and content were not at all to his taste. He offered to pay for the book. She refused. Purchases paid for, she turned to him, and as the sun caught her hair he was reminded of a raven's wing.

"If I hear anything of Jimmy McPhee I'll leave a message for you at the *Herald*. And remember, I want to know immediately if Mr. Dochery, father or son, contacts you. You've got my home number."

"I promise."

She smiled, and then was gone, walking up the steep slope to

Garnethill and the Art College without a break in her stride. It reminded him of the difference in their ages.

That evening, after cooking fish in milk with mashed potatoes for his mother, and not knowing what to do with himself on his last night in the city, other than drink, he went to the Cosmo Art Cinema to see an Italian film. The cinema was packed with students, and he found the subtitles hard to read, but he enjoyed it. A stray thought that he would have enjoyed it even more if Mary Ballantyne were with him he dismissed.

Leaving the cinema, the white-light night carried a sense of the Highlands, the air, the water, the mountains shadowing the horizon, but not the scent. And on the walk back past the pubs, the hum of the city, the dirt, the trams and buses and taxis, the shouts and the singing of the well inebriated, the murmurs of lovers as they kissed before parting—home to their parents and overlarge families filling every space in the too small tenement buildings—he could feel the city worming its way under his skin, reclaiming him. *You're Glaswegian, McAllister, and don't you forget it.*

THREE

Yesterday, without any expectations, his mother had suggested he come to early-morning mass. Hearing her moving about the kitchen, McAllister surprised himself by getting up, quickly dressing and joining her over her single cup of tea, as she would be taking communion.

"I'll come with you," he said.

The small nod was all the approval she'd show, but as they walked down the hill she allowed him to link her arm through his. For the first time in many years, if not a lifetime, he felt a connection with this distant woman who was his mother.

He sat at the back of the church, an observer, a former Christian. Nothing in the service made him consider changing his nonbelief. But he enjoyed the sense of community, enjoyed his mother's presence there on the wooden pew next to him. Since meeting and loving Joanne Ross he had begun to understand what family meant to most people—not that he regarded himself as most people; his sense of himself as a freethinking Scottish intellectual had set him apart from his family. He was, he hoped, now wiser, able to mock his former, youthful, self-importance.

They walked back, nodding to neighbors and fellow parishioners. Many were curious and not a few astonished to see John McAllister coming out of the church with neither a funeral nor a wedding being celebrated.

"Oh, it's yerself, John," one man acknowledged.

"Aye. Fine day," McAllister replied, racking his brains for the man's name and not finding it.

"'Morning, Mrs. McAllister," said a short round woman dressed entirely in black, a faded browning black, as though her clothes had been made from blackout curtains left over from the war.

A couple, middle-aged, *my age*, he thought, the woman with childbearing rounded stomach and hair more grey than birth-blond, smiled, saying, "Great to see you, John. How you doing, Mrs. McAllister?"

"Fine," he and his mother replied.

"Well, here's a surprise," said two women, obviously sisters, as they were as well matched as a pair of bookends. Again he couldn't place them.

"The McCrossan sisters," his mother quietly informed him when they were out of earshot.

This he found hard to take in, as he remembered them as stunning, and remembered how he had fancied both of them, flirting with them at church socials, which, when still at school, his father had forced him to attend. *To please your mother*, his dad had said, the emotional blackmail usually working—that and the chance to be in the presence of the McCrossan girls.

Outside the tenement, McAllister could feel his tummy rumbling. He was holding his mother's elbow, steering her over the broken flagstones, when a man came towards them out of the gloom of the close entrance. In the bright light of a sunshiny June day, he could not make out who it was. A neighbor, he would have thought—if he had given it a thought; he was busy thinking of breakfast, for he could almost smell the bacon frying in the pan, and he would make the ten-o'clock train back to the Highlands.

"Is that you, Gerry?" His mother was peering up at the large man standing in front of her blocking her way. "What are you doing here?"

"Hello, Mrs. McAllister. I was wanting a word wi' your John."

McAllister examined the man who was keeping to the shadow just under the archway as though coming into daylight might damage him, much as light would damage a vampire. Gerry Dochery was the spitting image of his father when he was in his forties, the time McAllister remembered the older man best. But McAllister felt that the resemblance was surface only; his father's friend had been cheerful, always ready with a joke and a laugh, always including the children in his smiles. This younger version was desolation personified with a side serving of malice.

This Gerry, "Wee Gerry," at well over six feet tall, and looking like half of that wide, was carved from granite, and his obsidian eyes, which were fixed on his former childhood friend, were as animated as the stone itself. A folded cutthroat razor was keeking from the top pocket of his black suit, worn with a matching black shirt. *Used to be black was only for funerals and existentialists,* McAllister thought, then suppressed a smile, mocking himself for being so pretentious.

"Something funny, McAllister?" Gerry Dochery had a high voice, not in the least in keeping with his hard-man image.

"Not at all, Gerry . . . just pleased to see an old childhood pal."

Gerry Dochery said nothing, not willing to pursue the subject in front of Mrs. McAllister.

The razor was an unseemly declaration of his trade. McAllister didn't immediately see that. His mother did.

"I can't be standing about for all the neighbors to see," Mrs. McAllister said. "Come on, John, Gerry, I'll put the kettle on." She bustled down the close and had the door unlocked and open before either of them could find excuses to refuse her.

"Thanks all the same, but I have to be going." Gerry Dochery tried his best to get out of the offer of hospitality, but Mrs. McAllister was firm.

"You'll do no such thing, Wee Gerry." She was off down the hallway to the kitchen, not checking they were following her, knowing they would. She took off her coat, kept on her hat, put the kettle on, told her son to fetch the milk and the bacon from the outside meat safe. "A cup of tea with old friends," she said, looking directly at him so Gerry had to look away. "Surely you've time for that."

And she didn't like what she saw, and she too looked away. His father's pronouncement that his son was lost to him now made sense. Remembering the times she had fed the boy, wiped his nose, cleaned him up when he fell off a high wall, carefully picking out the tiny stones stuck in the flesh of his knees and palms before dabbing the wounds in iodine, made her look again to see if there was anything of that lad left.

He caught her eye. Seeing himself as she saw him—an altogether different Gerry—made him flush. And angry. But he knew he had to swallow it if he was to find out what he needed to know.

It was the strangest of tea ceremonies, the three of them in the sitting room—it was Sunday, after all.

She was using her best china wedding service, which she kept for visitors. "How's your father?" she asked Gerry as she handed him a cup and saucer.

"He's fine, thank you for asking, Mrs. McAllister."

"He says he hasn't seen much of you these past years," she said.

"You know how it is," Gerry replied. "You must miss seeing your John an' all," he countered, the reproach clear.

"Aye. But he writes me a right lovely letter. Regularly." She bent over the table. "More tea, Gerry?"

He handed back the teacup and saucer, terrified; the saucer was as thin as ice, and the handle of the cup too small for his sausage fingers. *Funny he should be so clumsy*, McAllister was thinking, *he's known as a razor artist, able to carve the deepest and most damaging scar in exactly the right part of the face for maximum effect.*

"Remember how, when you were wee, you used to call ma husband Uncle John?" Mrs. McAllister was relentless; a rat in a trap had more chance than Gerry. "Aye," she continued, "one time—I think it was when we were all going for a day trip doon the water thon Fair Fortnight—you said, *Thank you, Mr. McAllister*, when he bought youse both an ice cream, and ma husband, he says, 'Call me Uncle John.' And I said, 'Call me Mrs. McAllister.' "

They all laughed more heartily than the remark warranted.

Round three to my mother, McAllister thought. He was enjoying the performance, but anxious about his train. It was clear to him his mother knew why Wee Gerry was here, and clear he would have to stay until his mother was ready to release the visitor. *To have the razor keeking out his pocket*, McAllister was thinking, *attempting to intimidate me, or show off, wrong move in front of my mother.*

"Well, it was nice o' you to visit, Gerry," Mrs. McAllister relented. "I'll no' keep you—this being Sunday, you'll be wanting to visit your father." Nodding her head in benediction, she finished, "Give him ma best." And Gerry Dochery was dismissed.

McAllister saw him out. They said little. But at the door McAllister held out his hand, and Gerry did not refuse.

"Good to see you, Ger. Any time you're up for a drink, call me at the *Herald* or leave a message there. It'll get to me."

McAllister knew he was looking at a man who had visited with the intention of doing damage. But something seemed to have shifted in the carapace of Gerry Dochery; his sense of invincibility now cracked with a hairline fracture. Or perhaps it was sheer embarrassment, the same as when, as young boys, they had been caught standing on the high wall of the Acropolis cemetery having a weeing competition onto a grave below. A woman had appeared, looked up at them before they had time to run, and shaking her head she went to lay flowers at the foot of the tombstone splashed with urine.

"I won't harm you, John," Gerry told him, "but I can't say the same about your friend."

It was then that McAllister realized he was right—harming him had been his former friend's intention. "About my friend, where . . ."

But Wee Gerry Dochery was off down the street without acknowledging the question. McAllister knew there was no point in chasing after him, in asking more; Gerry Dochery, childhood friend, had crossed a line long since and would not, could not, come back.

As he walked back towards the kitchen, he could smell bacon frying. The clock in the sitting room struck ten. He had missed the train.

"Sit yerself down," his mother said. "And you can make yerself useful by buttering the rolls."

After the full Scottish breakfast of bacon, eggs, black pudding, and fried tattie scones, he thought he and his mother would talk about Gerry's visit. Not so.

When he tried to broach the subject, all she said was, "Best leave it, Son, no use stirring up trouble." She stood. "I'll make a fresh pot."

"Not for me, I've missed my train. I need go to the station and book a sleeper. Then I need to let Joanne know I won't be back till the morning."

"Aye. You do that. And give the lass ma best."

"I will." He looked at her. She gave her usual tight wee smile. And suddenly, whether it was because of his living away in the Highlands, or because Joanne had prized open his I'm-a-buttoned-up-Scottish-male persona, he saw his mother anew; he saw the woman who had lost her husband, a fireman, in the horror of the wartime Clydeside Blitz; a woman who had buried her second son when, at sixteen, he had drowned himself in the River Clyde; a woman who had kept a family together through years of poverty, always encouraging her sons to break free of the Glasgow slums through education.

She caught his expression. "What are you doing, grinning to yerself?" She smiled back.

"Remembering how you used to make me sit at this kitchen table and never let me up until I'd done my homework. Years after, I discovered you'd asked my teacher to set me extra work."

"Aye, and look where it got you. You have a great job. And you own your own house."

"I would never be where I am now without you pushing me."

She turned away but not before he caught her smile. "Get away with you. Go sort out thon ticket else you miss another train."

He was glad he had acknowledged her insistence on his studying. And so was his mother. As he left the house, he was thinking, *It's too bad my education has made us strangers to each other.*

He was about to walk to Central Station, but a tram came by and he jumped on. As it rattled its way down George Street, he knew he should also call Mary as promised, letting her know he'd met up with Gerry Dochery. Her number was in his notebook under MB. Somehow writing her full name had not seemed wise. *Not that I'm hiding anything,* he told himself. *I enjoy her company much as I enjoy the company of Rob McLean on the* Gazette—*another person going places, another person twenty years younger than myself.*

He changed his train ticket, paid the supplement for the sleeper, then decided to call from the phone box outside the station.

"Hello." Again it was Annie who answered.

"Not at Sunday school?" he asked, putting what he hoped was a smile into his voice.

"No. And you're not on the train."

"I missed it. Too busy chatting to my mother to notice the time." There was a silence to that. "But don't worry, I'll be on the overnight train and see you in the morning."

"I don't care. It's Mum who worries when you're not here."

She was being deliberately rude, and there was nothing he could say because she was right. "Can I speak to your mother?"

The sound of the receiver being put down was loud, and he saw he was short of florins for the call. He put in his remaining change and pressed the button, hoping it would be enough. There was a wait of about two minutes before the sound of someone breathing like the sigh of wind in pine trees came down the line.

"Hello? Is that you, McAllister?" Her voice, timid, hesitant, was so unlike the Joanne he'd fallen in love with.

"I am so sorry, I missed the train, I'll . . ."

"Are you coming back? Will you be here soon?"

"Of course I'm coming back. I'll be home in the morning. Promise. I've already got my ticket. I'm . . . I've just got a couple of things to see to. I'm staying with my mother . . ." He knew he was blethering. "How are you? How are you feeling?"

"I love midsummer. It's never really dark. I like that. Last night a full moon came up just as the sun was going down. It was beautiful."

"Has the doctor been by? What did he say?" McAllister was feeling he no longer knew how to talk to her. He didn't know how to reassure her. Not without being with her, holding her.

"Come home soon, McAllister."

"I will and I'll . . ." The pips started. "I'll be back in the morning and . . ." He was shouting over the beeping counting down the seconds. "I'll . . ." But they were cut off.

He swore under his breath. He strode towards the newsstand to ask for change, then stopped, turned around, and made for the

Herald building. The newsroom was always open, Sundays being no exception. He had calmed down by the time he reached his temporary desk to call Joanne again, and have a proper conversation.

Without quite knowing how, he found himself saying, "Hello Mary? It's McAllister."

He had no intention of taking out his notebook. Looking up MB. Calling. He would have sworn he dialed by accident. A typewriter was sitting plumb in the middle of the desk—he could have left her a message. All this ran through his head in less than a second in real time.

"You're up bright and early for a Sunday." It was after eleven o'clock, but he remembered what an unearthly hour that was for a news reporter used to midnight deadlines.

"I had a visit from Wee Gerry Dochery." He was trying to sound professional. He didn't succeed. He wanted to see her. To chat. To laugh. To forget.

"Where are you?" she asked.

"The *Herald*."

"Meet me in Blythswood Square. The north side, in the middle. Give me half an hour." And she was gone.

He had to wait twenty minutes for the bus, it being Sunday, and was five minutes late. He stood on the pavement outside the black iron railings of the square park, under the full *prima verdi* canopy of trees. The sky behind the three-story Georgian terraces was an almost painful and very unlikely shade of deep blue. *This looks more Madrid than Glasgow*, was his immediate thought.

What were once family homes of the wealthy were now mostly offices for solicitors, dentists, or doctors, or converted into flats. Many of the basements, once the kitchens and servant quarters, were now flats, often rented by students who didn't mind the gloom or the damp. However, a few of the terraced houses remained intact, residences of the rich old-moneyed citizens of the city.

He saw Mary emerge from one of the homes. As she was locking the large door behind her, he could see no sign of the numerous bells that would indicate multiple occupancy. She looked across, saw him, waved, and came towards him in her usual setting-out-on-an-adventure stride.

"I'm desperate for breakfast," she said. "There's a great hole-in-the-wall café near the taxi stand at the back of Queen Street station."

"I've just come from that direction."

"Aye? I heard you're a Dennistoun boy."

He grinned. Before he had time to ask her whom she'd heard that from she was jumping off the pavement into the street shouting, "Taxi."

He marveled as a taxi appeared from nowhere, thinking she was the kind of woman for whom taxis mysteriously materialized when no one else could find one.

The café was indeed a hole-in-the-wall, and showing signs it had been busy early in the morning and was now in the lull between trains. They ordered mugs of tea, bacon rolls—two for Mary—and ate in silence. When Mary ordered a second tea, they both lit up, Mary again filching one of McAllister's Passing Clouds.

"You like those, do you?" he asked, indicating the pale pink packet. "An acquired taste, I'm told."

"I'm trying not to smoke, but I take whatever is on offer."

He laughed. It felt good to laugh. There had not been enough laughs recently.

"So," she said, blowing smoke towards what he thought were dark patches on the ceiling, only to realize they were congregations of flies, lazing in the heat of the fumes from the chip fryer.

"So," he started, "after mass . . ." He saw the arched eyebrows, the ones that looked as though they had been brushed on but weren't, rise. "To please my mother," he explained. "I lost all religion in Spain—somewhere between Madrid and Barcelona." He flicked the ash off his cigarette into the tin lid that served as an ashtray. "Gerry Dochery paid me a visit. My mother . . ."

"What?"

He smiled at her reaction. He described for her in ample detail the embarrassment—for both him and Gerry—of his mother's insisting Gerry come in for tea, of his mother's reminding Gerry of the family connection, of his mother's more than hinting that Gerry should visit his father. He finished by relaying Gerry's warning, word for word, as it was imprinted on his brain; Gerry Dochery knew of Jimmy McPhee, of that he had no doubt, and Gerry Dochery, or whoever he was working for, wished Jimmy harm.

"So you think it's Gerry Dochery out to get your friend Jimmy McPhee. Why?"

McAllister had no answer. "Search me."

Mary was leaning back in the chair—a posture McAllister was prone to using—staring at the fly-clouded ceiling. "Gerry Dochery doesn't do the dirty work, he has men for that, but I've heard he takes contracts. So maybe this is business, not personal." She stubbed out a half-smoked cigarette and contorted her mouth as though disgusted with the taste. "Tell me about this McPhee fellow."

He wasn't sure where to begin. Travelers and middle-class, middle-aged men like himself seldom had close friendships with the likes of Jimmy McPhee. Professional relationships—yes. But his relationship with Jimmy? Good reporters had to have good sources. Mary obviously had. Was that what Jimmy McPhee was? He couldn't answer his own questions. So he started by lighting another cigarette and telling her about Jenny McPhee, Jimmy's mother, Traveler, singer, matriarch, a woman said to have the second sight, a woman feared, respected, and a woman never to be underestimated. He told her of the Travelers' encampment, his respect for Jenny McPhee, his helping her in the past, and vice versa. "And Jimmy, her second son, is her right-hand man."

Mary was listening intently, and from her face he could see she understood his fascination with Jenny McPhee. "Would all this"—she waved her hand in a circle encompassing not just the table, the café, but the whole of Glasgow—"would it be to do with the Highland tinkers? A clan dispute? A blood feud?"

"No. If that was it, Jenny would have sorted it out herself. I've been thinking, why ask me? And I feel it has to do with this city. Jimmy lived here once, occasionally on the wrong side of the law, but nothing serious. He was a boxer in his youth, going places, so I hear . . ."

"Jimmy McPhee! I knew I knew the name. I saw him once when he was one of the young hopefuls of that Gorbals boxing club."

"How come you went to a boxing match? You couldn't have been more than a bairn." The surprise on McAllister's face was evident.

"My father was a fan. But a Marquis of Queensberry rules boxing fan. He took me to a couple of matches at the Kelvin Hall. That was before the war. And you're right, I was nine. When my mother found out she was furious." She was grinning at the memory.

It was only when a gaggle of bus drivers came in together looking for a table that McAllister glanced at the clock. An hour had passed.

"Listen," he said, "I'm catching the overnight train but have the afternoon free. Fancy a trip to the Art Gallery?"

"You sound like my dad. He thought every Sunday should be spent at a museum or the Art Gallery." She saw him flinch but didn't apologize. He was, after all, old enough to be her father.

"My mother is the same. I'm going anyhow. I have the afternoon free and I want to see the Salvador Dalí *Christ of St. John of the Cross.*"

"It's a brilliant painting, McAllister, you don't have to be religious to appreciate it."

Her private-schoolgirl-prim-and-proper voice made him look at her to see if she was teasing. She wasn't. The chasm between them in age, in education, in class, was clear. He almost changed his mind about the invitation. She sensed his hesitation.

"Tell you what, McAllister, it's rare we have such days of sunshine. Let's wander through Kelvingrove Park. We can decide about the Art Gallery after."

So they did. They walked. They talked. They laughed. They shared Glasgow childhood stories until the sun was at three o'clock. They took a quick trip into the Art Gallery, admired the painting before being hustled out by the attendants a minute before closing time. They parted, him to have supper with his mother before the train, her to do the same.

"Yes," she had said earlier, "still in my childhood home, still with my mother. We rub along no problem and it's rent free—a real bonus on a cadet's wages."

"You're still a cadet?" He was more than surprised.

"Aye, but finished this autumn." She didn't elaborate on her late start in journalism, her abandonment of her career in law, and the subsequent fights with her mother. "See you, McAllister," Mary said in farewell.

"Mind how you go . . ." He stopped himself. No need to warn her of the big bad bogymen of the city; she already knew. And besides, he was not her father.

Four

As McAllister turned in to the street of his mother's flat, he noticed that the hum of the city was lower than usual by a decibel or so; it acknowledged it was the Sabbath. However, he knew that the great cathedral would be awake; Sunday was when it came into its glory, accepting its rightful place as the center of Christian lives. To a heathen like McAllister, the quiet weekdays were preferable. Then the ancient building offered a refuge from the city, a place for contemplation and silence.

The train to the Highlands left in two hours. He knew he should call Joanne. *I need to call now. She's not at her best in the evenings.* He knew darkness still scared her half to death; most afternoons she would sleep, but be up and bright for afternoon tea. *It's still light until eleven, even midnight, at this time of year, thank goodness.* He knew he should be there, sleeping beside her, holding her when the nightmares left her shaking, sobbing, incoherent, but terrified her daughters would hear her cries, wake up, and be distressed by their mother's horror of the dark. Yet something was stopping him. And he had no idea what.

"McLean household," he heard Rob say as he was connected and the coins dropped into the box below with a thunk.

"McAllister here."

"You're in a call box. Where?" Rob was concerned, knowing McAllister should be on a train somewhere on the Grampian plateau.

"I'm taking the sleeper. I'll be in in the morning. Listen"—he cut across the sound of Rob starting to say something—"will you pop up to see Joanne? I spoke to her but . . . I'm sure she's fine, it's just . . ." Rob was not helping. McAllister felt the silence as a reprimand. "I missed the train. It couldn't be helped. Could you make sure she's doing all right?"

Rob said, "Why can't you call her?"

"I will again before the train leaves. It's just I'd like you to check up on her . . . you know, a friendly face . . ." He was blethering. And he sensed Rob thought so too.

"I'll drive over now. By the way, you're sounding very Glaswegian."

That threw McAllister. He didn't know what to make of the remark. "I'll be back in the morning. But start the Monday news meeting without me."

"Fine. See you in the morn—"

The pips went. His money had run out. Again. This time McAllister didn't mind.

He and his mother had their usual taciturn farewell, she treating him as though he came by every other day, and would see him next day, next week, next year, time making no difference.

"No news of your friend?" was all she asked about the reason for his visit.

"None." He was certain Jimmy could look after himself but was glad he had come to Glasgow. The thawing in his relationship with his mother was enough reason to be pleased; any other reasons to be cheerful he didn't acknowledge.

"Aye, well, no news is good news. I made you some sandwiches." She handed him an old tartan shortbread tin, her declaration of love. "And there's a fresh gingerbread an' all."

He swallowed and nodded his head. This trip, they came as near to talking as they'd ever had. Perhaps it was his attending mass, perhaps the visit from Gerry Dochery; his mother had been livelier than in years.

"Next time I visit it'll be to bring you up to the Highlands," he told her as they stood in the doorway unsure whether to touch.

"We'll see."

This was a major concession. He put one arm around her, gave her a quick squeeze, and left before she could see his eyes filling.

At the station, he called his house. Annie answered. "Rob's here. He told us you'll be back in the morning. Mum's fine with that. I'll tell her you called." She put the phone down.

Instead of being angry at the girl's decision not to call her mother, he was relieved. He found conversations with the not-quite-finding-the-words Joanne hard but reminded himself, *she'll be fine soon, and there's no need to leave her again. Jimmy McPhee can look after himself.* He walked across the station concourse. From the loudspeaker came the announcement of his train, and under his breath, as though repeating a prayer, he muttered. "She'll be fine."

The morning air was Highland air, crisp and clear with an undercurrent of what felt like static electricity. McAllister hadn't slept well; the sleeper beds were not built for a man over six feet tall.

He took a taxi. He would normally walk home, but the thought of the steep brae up to his home was daunting, as his back felt as though he was carrying a hundredweight sack of potatoes, not a small overnight bag. Plus the thought of bumping into people who recognized him—though he often had no idea who they were—and asking him questions about Joanne, the *Gazette*, and the price of coal, made a taxi the best, but more cowardly, option.

Arriving at his front gate, he saw the house and garden as a stranger might. Or a man returning from a long journey abroad, or a war. He saw the low wall where once there had been iron railings, handsome no doubt, now long gone, collected and melted to supply metal for armaments in that first war in 1914, the war to end all wars. He saw the nondescript shrubs, the funereal cypress, the front porch with the black-and-white checkerboard tiles and the solid dark green front door, painted to match the cypress, the stained glass windows shining, gleaming brass knocker and handle. The door was standing ajar.

He groaned. *Visitors, just what I don't need.*

"Hello, I'm back," he called out. "Home," he added.

"Hello," an unknown woman's voice called out. "We're in here."

He turned in to the sitting room, leaving his bag in the hallway. A short woman in a nurse's uniform was standing by the sofa. Joanne was sitting there, feet up, still in a dressing gown but, judging from the damp ends, her hair freshly washed.

"Nurse Davis helped me wash my hair." She was beaming at the nurse, not at him.

"Och, well, I have to check on the wound, make sure there's no swelling, so I might as well wash your hair while we're at it." The nurse was busy packing her Gladstone bag as she spoke. "Your fiancée is doing right well, sir."

He didn't reply, being too distracted, taking in the sight of his Joanne, who was smiling, pleased at the compliment, and looking like a wee girl who, after a long illness, was accustomed to others telling her what to do.

"Nurse Davis and the doctor say I'll be right as rain in no time." She smiled again. He thought she was waiting for his approval also.

"I'm sure Nurse is right." He was forcing himself to sound cheerful, as he was not at all certain. *She's not herself.*

"I'll let maself out. Cheery-bye for now." And the nurse was gone.

He sat on the sofa, pushing her legs gently to give himself more room. He took her hand. "I've missed you," he told her. He meant it in so many more ways than he could express.

"I missed you." She was truly herself as she said this. She took his hand in both of hers. "I've been lonely for you and . . ."

"Hello. Is that you, Mr. McAllister?" It was Joanne's mother-in-law, Mrs. Ross. She came into the room in her hat and coat, but with the coat unbuttoned to expose the flowered overall cum pinny she habitually wore, except to go to church.

She looked over the tableau on the sofa—Joanne had dropped McAllister's hand the moment she heard her ex-mother-in-law. Mrs. Ross examined them as though searching for signs that all was well, or not, then nodding, said, "I'll put the kettle on. Bacon and eggs ready in five minutes, Mr. McAllister."

When she was gone Joanne smiled and whispered, "That's you told. I'm sure she thinks there's no real food to be had in the city of sin."

"Don't worry, my mother saw to it I had a regular fry-up for breakfast yesterday." He didn't mention Gerry Dochery.

"A change from coffee and a cigarette then."

He laughed. He felt better, felt he had been mistaken. *She's on the mend.*

"The other night"—she was leaning back on the arm of the sofa, holding the dressing gown tightly to her—"my father came into my room asking why I hadn't said my prayers."

McAllister stiffened. Her father was dead. He had hoped his malign authority over his daughter had ended with six feet of earth shoveled over his coffin.

"I said, 'Yes, Father, I have.'" Her voice was that of a child. "He said I hadn't said them properly. I got out of bed and kneeled down and started to pray. I must have knocked the cord of the bedside light. It went out. It was pitch black and I panicked and was crying and my father said it was my punishment, said that I would always be in the dark because of my sins."

She was crying. Silently. Tears washing her face, turning her nose pink. She seemed oblivious to the salty stream. But her hands, which had dropped to her lap, were still clasped in prayer, holding the memory of her father's wrath.

McAllister leaned towards her, about to hold her when Granny Ross came in.

"What's this all about?" She was across the room, taking a hankie from her cardigan pocket, a man-size white linen square he recognized as his own. She was wiping Joanne's eyes as though she were her granddaughter, not an adult. "Blow your nose. Then go and wash your face. Breakfast is on the table."

"I've had mine," Joanne said.

"Aye, a wee piece o' toast. That'll no' put meat on your bones. You'll have a boiled egg and this time you'll finish it." Mrs. Ross turned, gave a tight-lipped half smile at McAllister.

It came to him in a flash; Mrs. Ross was enjoying being in charge. Relishing the role of nurse and housekeeper to her former daughter-in-law and grandchildren.

No, he told himself, *don't be so uncharitable. She's just pleased she can help the woman who was the daughter she never had, the woman whom her son had had the good fortune to marry and the misfortune to lose, he being one of those men who regarded a woman as a possession, enforcing her obedience with his fists.*

"We'd better do as we're told." The old mischievous Joanne partially reappeared. "Off you go, McAllister. I know how much you hate cold eggs."

When Joanne joined them in the kitchen, she was dressed, but her dress was hanging off a skeletal frame. Her hair, falling forward to hide the shaven part of her skull where the operation had been performed, was shiny and sweet-smelling but no longer the thick luxurious former "mane"—her word for her hair. Illness had made her head molt, the long hairs strewn across cushions and bedding and clothing.

"I have to go in to the office," he told them when he finished his breakfast with the customary cigarette, "but I'll be back at lunchtime. Then I thought we might go shopping."

"Shopping?" Joanne looked at him in amazement. Then at Mrs. Ross, who shrugged. Neither had ever known McAllister to shop. He ordered his clothes from a tailor in Glasgow, which were delivered once a year in a large parcel, everything being exactly the same as the previous model.

"It's summer," he declared as though they hadn't noticed the sun coming in through the open kitchen door, the violent blue heavens above the distant Ben Wyvis, and a nearer, but distant, outline of the Black Isle filling the kitchen windows. A scent of fresh-cut grass and a rare warm wind came up through the long garden that stretched down to a high stone wall and a drop over a cliff to the town and Eastgate below. It was soothing. Delightful. Even McAllister felt the spell.

"It's summer," he repeated, "and I am going to buy you a summer dress. Maybe two if you're good." He teased.

"But the girls need . . ." Joanne was shifting in her chair as though sitting on horsehair, not a gingham cushion. Going shopping for herself was not something she did. Her treadle sewing machine was her wardrobe mistress.

"Wheesht, the girls are a' right. You go and get yerself a nice treat," Granny Ross told her. "You deserve it."

Leaving the house, this time walking, McAllister headed down the hill and found himself fearful of what awaited him at the *Gazette*. The lift he had experienced as Joanne smiled at him, saying, "I'd like that," in answer to his suggestion that they go shopping, had evaporated and left behind a mild discomfort, much like indigestion.

In this newspaper, this town, this Highland community, he knew the news before it was written. It went something like this: arguments in council over health services; disagreements over road-widening plans; discussions on raising council rates; a cat down a well and the gallant rescue; the Boy Scouts' bob-a-job week; the Salvation Army's blankets-for-homeless-servicemen drive. These, and variations thereof, were stories that were the grist of everyday journalism on a local newspaper—stories that bored him, if not to tears, then to whisky.

He had transformed the *Highland Gazette*. Radically. Changed it from broadsheet to tabloid, pursued investigative journalism when it was warranted, altered the layout, instituted new columns, introduced photographs, introduced a sports section, and, the biggest change of all, banned advertising on the front page.

There had been resistance from some, but approval from most of the readers; the increased advertising revenue reflected that. There had been difficult times, especially when the staff of the *Gazette* had become involved in the stories they were investigating, yet the newspaper had been published, every deadline reached, every copy distributed, read, and digested and argued over—although it had been a close call on occasion.

And now, all was back to normal. He knew, as editor, he was needed but not absolutely necessary. The *Gazette* would continue for another ninety-odd years with or without Mr. John McAllister—so he was telling himself as he climbed Castle Wynd, turning right to another Monday at the office, albeit three hours late.

"It's yourself," Don McLeod greeted him as he came into the reporters' room.

There was no answer to that. And none expected. "Anything I should know?" McAllister asked.

"You've only been gone three days and one o' them the Sabbath," Don reminded him. "How was Glasgow?" He was watching his colleague, looking to see if there was anything amiss, but unable, for once, to read the editor.

"My mother's a lot brighter than I've seen her in years."

"Any news of Jimmy?"

"He did thirty days in Barlinnie—the usual, a drunken brawl . . ."

Don McLeod raised his eyebrows at that; in his experience Jimmy McPhee was not a drunk, the former boxer keeping himself fit, drinking sparingly. Money lending, illegal gambling, boxing, that and more he knew Jimmy to be involved in. But drinking and brawling?

"He was released and hasn't been seen since."

"Right." Don said no more, but McAllister could see he wasn't convinced the matter was ended. Later McAllister would wonder why he hadn't mentioned the reward out for information on Jimmy's whereabouts. It wasn't deliberate, but he was uncomfortable talking about the trip to the city.

"You'd better let Jenny McPhee know, but aye, Jimmy's well able to look after himself." Don glanced again at the provisional layout. There was nothing needing McAllister's attention. "Maybe you could knock up a few editorials so I've always got one handy."

"Fine," McAllister replied. "I'll write a note to Jenny, then do a couple of think pieces before I leave—I'm taking Joanne shopping," he explained.

"Good idea" was all the reply he got, Don busy taking his wee red pencil to some correspondent's article, leaving very little of the original story.

McAllister walked across the landing to his office, shut the door, rolled three sheets of paper, alternating with sheets of blue carbon copy paper, into his typewriter. He wanted to shut himself away from company at the communal high desk of the reporters' room, but again, for reasons he couldn't fathom.

He flexed his fingers and was about to start, then stopped. What kind of journalism is it where you can write the editorial weeks in advance? He despaired of a newspaper where the stories were so predictable. He wanted the adrenaline of a city desk, but knew those days were gone. He lit a cigarette. He leaned back until the chair was at a dangerous angle. *No, it's far too early for a dram.* Ignoring his inner mother, he went to the filing cabinet, took out the bottle and a crystal tumbler, poured at least half a gill, and sipped. It changed nothing.

He put the bottle and the dirty glass back into the drawer and went into the reporters' room. It was empty. No sign of his deputy nor Rob McLean, chief and only real reporter, nor Hector Bain, photographer and all-round nuisance. And Frankie Urquhart, the advertising manager and Rob's old school chum, bright young man-about-town and cheerful soul, was nowhere to be seen.

He walked down the semi-spiral stone staircase.

Only Fiona, the *Gazette* secretary, was where she should be, manning the reception desk and switchboard.

"Where's everyone?" he asked.

"Out," she replied. The phone rang. "If you'll excuse me, Mr. McAllister . . ." She picked up the receiver. "*Highland Gazette*, how may I help you?"

I can see I'm not needed, he was thinking as he hailed a taxi on the High Street. Arriving home, he asked the driver to wait while he fetched Joanne.

"A taxi?" she said when she saw it. "What an extravagance." But she didn't mean it. She knew he saw taxis as an everyday form of public transport, not the only-in-emergencies necessity she always regarded them as.

They emerged in front of the wide stone edifice. In the large plate-glass windows of the only department store in the Highlands were poised mannequins, some showing the latest but one year late compared to London fashions. Other models showed the best-selling tweed skirts and lambswool twinsets. Once through the double swing doors with gleaming brass handles, they took the wide carpeted sweep of stairs to the ladies' section. As they headed towards a rack of summer dresses, they were waylaid by a shop assistant dressed in the black uniform and the overheavy makeup that seemed to be a requisite for assistants in this establishment.

"Can I help, Madame? Are you looking for something in particular?"

The woman came too close, sizing Joanne up, mentally calculating whether there would be a good commission from this customer. And clearly deciding not.

McAllister felt Joanne shrink into her already much thinner frame. "We're fine, thanks," he said. "I'll call if we need your help."

Realizing that the man would be paying, the woman took Joanne by the elbow, steering her towards the more expensive clothing section.

"I think you'll find something to suit over here," she said in her put-on best posh Edinburgh accent. "These would look lovely on Madame."

The "Madame" came out as "Modom," and it was all McAllister could do not to laugh at the preposterous woman but, seeing how nervous she was making Joanne, he once more intervened. Pointing to a white summer dress with a rounded neckline and no sleeves, and large scarlet poppies and lime-green leaves printed on a full skirt, he said, "I like this one."

Joanne turned, saw it, and smiled. "It's lovely."

"A little young for Madame, don't you think? This one is perfect. The latest style from London." She held up another cotton frock, this one with cap sleeves, buttons down the front, a slightly flared skirt. A nice dress, in a subtle print in shades of blue and lavender.

Nice for a respectable middle-aged-matron-of-the-town dress, he was thinking, then realized the woman had steered Joanne into the dressing room.

"Hold on," he called out and took the summer poppy-strewn sundress from the rack, handing it to Joanne. When she emerged it was not the white with scarlet poppies she was wearing, but the dress in many shades of blue.

It fitted well; the fabric was practical, the length right, the buttons delicate. But it did nothing for her; it made Joanne look like any other woman of the town. She looked at herself in the mirror. He had no idea what she was seeing, but she said, "I'll take it."

"And the other one? Try it on," he suggested.

"If I was ten years younger maybe." She smiled—a faint weary smile.

Oh, my love—he looked away, scared she might read his thoughts—*since when did you think like that?*

That evening, after supper, after Mrs. Ross senior had gone home, and after the girls had done their homework, they were all sitting around reading or, in Jean's case, drawing with her new pencil set McAllister had brought from Glasgow, when Joanne said, "McAllister bought me a dress."

"Can I see it, Mum?" Jean asked.

"It's upstairs on my bed."

Jean ran upstairs, brought it down, saying, "I like the material, it's lovely and soft."

Annie looked at it, picked it up, and held it against herself.

McAllister was taken aback to see how tall she was growing, how soon she would be near her mother's height.

"Granny Ross will approve." And with that Annie put the dress on the sofa and went back to her book.

Joanne agreed. "It's lovely. And just right for church."

McAllister agreed. Just right for church.

It was late, after eleven. The house was quiet, Joanne and the girls in bed. McAllister was reading, the decanter of whisky on a table beside his chair. He heard the sound of the letterbox flap. And the sound of footsteps receding quickly. He put down the book and went to the front door. Picking up a piece of folded paper, he took it into the sitting room and the light.

It was printed on lined notepaper. *Tomorrow night. Six o'clock sharp. The bar.* He knew it was from Jenny McPhee. He knew he would be there.

Next evening, McAllister drove across the Black Bridge, noticing that at low tide and with an unusual lack of rain, the river was low. On the pebbled beach at the bend of the river where the fishermen kept the salmon cobles and where he had first kissed Joanne, the shore was wider and broader than usual. Stones and rounded smooth boulders—never having been exposed to the air before—were now a dull green, not the bright beech-leaf-green normally seen through the running river.

A drought in the Highlands, he thought, *that'll be the day.*

The road to the ferry led to the meeting place, the pub rumored to belong to Jenny McPhee. Not that she had ever admitted this. Not that anyone was ever able to prove it. He parked outside with five minutes in hand. He knew his car would be safe because this pub, the most notorious in the area, if not the Highlands, was hallowed ground. No one would voluntarily cross the McPhees.

The sun, still high in the sky even at this hour, shone on the stark edifice of a superbly unattractive blockhouse, doing it no favors. This building was a creature of the night. Daylight revealed rough concrete, badly laid tiles, high dirty windows. To McAllister, everything about the building was saying, *Despair all ye who enter herein.*

Jenny was sitting in the snug bar, where he knew she would be. She checked the clock.

"Right on time," she said.

"I'd be too scared not to be after your note."

She nodded in satisfaction. "I'll no' keep you. You'll be wanting to get home to Joanne and the girls," she started.

She definitely has the second sight, he thought.

She had her coat on, buttoned up. Her hat, the one that belonged on a scarecrow, was pulled down on the forehead hiding her face, partially. *She's looking old*, was his next thought, *or is it scared?*

"So what did you find out in Glasgow?" She knew that if he'd found Jimmy he would have come straight out with it.

"Not much," he began. He was not offered a drink. She didn't indicate a chair. Seeing that this was the way of it, he gave his account of the trip to Glasgow as though he was in the witness stand.

"He did his thirty days. Was released. A reporter at the *Herald* told me she'd heard there are people looking for Jimmy. She doesn't know who, but she's investigating." He refrained from lighting a cigarette, even though he needed one. This was not a friendly meeting; this was an interview.

"A man I knew as a boy came looking for me to warn me off," McAllister continued.

That made Jenny look up. "And?"

"This man, he didn't mention Jimmy's name, 'my friend' is what he said, and . . ."

"His name?"

"Gerry Dochery."

Jenny was shaking her head, indicating she had never heard of him.

"He's well known, runs protection rackets, though sometimes he'll take a contract, so I was told, but I couldn't find out how, or if, he is connected to Jimmy." He knew he wasn't being completely honest but then again, he was reasoning, Gerry Dochery only mentioned "my friend."

"So," Jenny said after taking a sip of a clear, peat-smelling drink, obviously an Islay malt. "So," she said again slower this time, "what do we do now? Have you an idea where to look for him?" She knew that if Jimmy were hiding, he'd be hard to trace. If not impossible.

"Not really. Mary Ballantyne, the reporter at the *Herald*, she has a better chance than most of finding Jimmy."

"Tell her there's some money in it for her."

"I don't think that will make a difference. Mary is in it . . ."

"For herself."

He'd meant her career. But maybe "herself" was more honest.

Jenny sighed. "Aye, a woman needs to be tough to get on in a man's world." She was looking into the depths of her glass as though it held the secret to her son's whereabouts. Then looking at him with her black-currant eyes, she said, "But you'll help this Mary woman when you're back down to the city to find ma Jimmy."

"I've a newspaper to run and family to . . ."

"Mr. McAllister, the McPhee family befriended you. If Jimmy needs you, you'll be there." This was said not as a threat, just a certainty. Friendship with a non-Traveler was not given lightly— if ever. "And your Joanne, she'll recover." This too was said with absolute certainty. "She's stronger than you think. She survived thon no-good husband o' hers, didn't she? Kicked him out? That lass has spirit." Jenny was waving his concerns away in a gesture that, not for the first time, made McAllister marvel at her resemblance to the Queen Mother. She continued, "And didn't Donal McLeod run the newspaper for years before you came up here wi' your fancy new ways? You owe us, McAllister. Go to Glasgow. Find our Jimmy."

"I'm sorry. I can't. Joanne . . . I can't leave her." He met her stare. And shivered. For all the legends and gossip about this woman, Jenny McPhee, head of her clan, rumored to have the second sight, also rumored to be a witch, he had seen only her courage, her fortitude. Never before had he felt someone look right through him to the bone, and look away, leaving him feeling he had failed the inspection.

"So be it," she said, "but if you change your mind . . ."

"I can't."

Walking down the pathway to his house McAllister felt light-headed, and for once it was not whisky. He had been shaken by the way Jenny had gazed, seemingly into the depth of his being. And a suspicion was sprouting; there was more to Jimmy's disappearance than she was telling, and if she didn't want him to know what or why he was in trouble, he would never find out.

The sound of recorded voices and canned laughter came down the hallway from the dining room, now the girls' domain. The dining table had disappeared under the spread of artwork, pots of poster paint, paintbrushes, crayons, fabric, pots of glue, and red lentils. The television on top of the china cabinet, which now housed Jean's dolls, was on, the volume loud.

McAllister asked, "Done your homework?"

"I don't have any," Jean replied. "I'm too young." She turned back to the obviously American show that had her mesmerized.

Annie looked up from rug, where she was sprawled with the journal from Glasgow open on the floor. She had a pen in one hand, and with the left arm she was shielding the page, anxious that, even at across the large room, he might read her writing.

"Mum's upstairs. She wanted a lie-down," Annie told him.

He went to the kitchen, made tea, took a cup upstairs to Joanne.

"Knock, knock," he said to the half-open door. But when he went in, she was asleep. Her fear of the dark often made her sit up all night, lights illuminating every nook and cranny of the house. But the summer nights were a scant five hours long. *Thankfully*, he thought. The doctor, on a home visit, had said when McAllister mentioned this, "Give her time." So he did. But it distressed him nonetheless.

He put the cup down on the bedside table and leaned down to touch her hair. She didn't stir. He watched her sleeping. She looked herself when asleep; that was the Joanne he wanted back so badly, it was an ache in his chest. He felt powerless. And most of all he felt trapped. He was certain he could not live the rest of his life with an invalid. *Too selfish, too stuck in my ways, too used to living life to suit myself, too old to change*, he admitted to himself. Yet he knew he would never abandon her.

He went downstairs and made cocoa for the girls.

They went to bed themselves, Annie saying she would tell Jean a story. She hadn't told anyone and had sworn Jean to secrecy, but Annie was writing stories, trying them out on her sister, and if her sister stayed awake until the end of the tale, she would transcribe it into a notebook. From now on, she had decided, the best stories would go into her new journal.

It was mid-evening, and once again McAllister was alone with his whisky and a book. He was reluctant to put on a record, half listening for Joanne, half worried she might have a nightmare and he might miss her cries.

He fell into a reverie; not a nightmare, not a dwam, more a

fantasy. He was back in the city, in a tall room with deep casement windows overlooking a square, much like Blythswood Square. There was the sound of a piano being played, Brahms, he fancied. There was a woman, indistinct yet familiar, the identity not yet revealed. He had a newspaper on his lap, a whisky in hand, and he was reading a page five in-depth analysis of some current topic, again not revealed, but he knew he had written it.

"Are you awake?"

The voice startled him.

Joanne was standing in the doorway, holding her arms around herself as though she was cold.

He smiled. "Come and sit down. Can I get you tea, a drink?"

"Later. First tell me about Jenny. How is she? Did you reassure her Jimmy can look after himself? Tell me all about it."

Since the attack, and the possibility of brain damage not yet clear, he wasn't certain how much he should tell her. The specialist had warned that worry was bad for her. He'd told her that, and she had been furious.

"McAllister. I had a horrific experience. I was hit on the head, locked up in the dark, I nearly died, but I'm alive. And I'm very, very grateful. These spells I have, they will pass. I have to believe that." She looked at him, and her eyes shone bright with the intensity of her resolve. "But one thing, McAllister: I always know when you try to hide bad news from me, and when you do, I'm scared it's about my health. All of you—you, the doctor, my mother-in-law—think it best to keep things from me, but it's not. I hate it."

He smiled and nodded. "Sorry. I'll do my best."

"Just treat me as though everything is normal . . . which it will be soon."

Looking at her, at her ghostly skin, her wrist bones sharp knobs on stick-thin arms, the dark shadows under her eyes, and the gingerly way she moved, he knew that was not possible. And the lapses in memory, the searching for simple words, the way she seemed unable to concentrate for more than half a minute on any simple task like reading the newspaper, that worried him most of all.

But he did as asked and told her of Jenny's concern that Jimmy hadn't returned home to prepare the horses for the Black Isle Show.

"And all you found out was that he did time in Barlinnie?" she asked when he finished.

He thought of lying, then remembered her plea. "No. A childhood friend came to see me at my mother's flat to warn me off." He told her about Gerry Dochery, but not of his reputation, only saying he was a petty criminal. She seemed to believe him.

He finished by telling her his mother would come north for their wedding, and she seemed satisfied. And not once did he mention Mary Ballantyne.

"I'd love that cup of tea now," she said. "And would you put on one of my new records?"

He selected Kenneth McKellar. He took the record out of the cover, put it on the turntable, and aligned the needle, letting it gently drop into the grooves. The young tenor's voice, sweet yet strong, floated across the room.

> Ae fond kiss and then we sever,
> Ae fareweel, alas, for ever . . .

McAllister could not bear to hear any more. He fled to the kitchen and busied himself with the kettle, the teapot, and a plate of shortbread. No longer could he hear the melody, but the words, he knew them by heart.

Had we never loved sae kindly,
Had we never loved sae blindly,
Never met—or never parted,
We had ne'er been broken-hearted.

He rejoined Joanne in the sitting room to pass the evening chatting quietly, with long silences, mostly comfortable; Joanne had the knack of sitting, saying and doing nothing, seemingly content. He put on more music, the *Pastoral Symphony.* Anything but "Ae Fond Kiss." And nothing more was said about tinkers or criminals or health. Or the future.

FIVE

Wednesdays at the *Gazette* were busy. Seldom frantically busy—this was a local newspaper in a small town—the stories were subbed, set by the typesetters picking out the type with tweezers, checked again by Don McLeod, reading upside down and back to front as easily as he did normal type. The spaces for the advertising and the articles set, there were sometimes gaps; these adjustments Don made on the stone. But not many changes; with over forty years' experience, he knew how much space a story would take with only an *and* or a *then* to be deleted or the font size of a headline changed. The *Gazette* would be published on time and, much to McAllister's chagrin, the most-read column was "Births, Deaths and Marriages," or, in newspaper parlance, "Hatched, Matched and Dispatched."

Between five o'clock and seven in the evening on deadline day, Don was up and down the stone stairs—the only exercise he ever took, several times an hour. He seldom answered the phone in the reporters' room—that had been Joanne's job. This afternoon, the phone wouldn't stop. He picked it up to shut it up. A voice yelled loud enough for him to hear even though the receiver was only halfway to his ear.

"McAllister, answer the bloody phone!"

"Now what would you be wanting with our esteemed editor?" Don asked. Rob McLean looked across the desk at Don and, seeing his expression of part amusement, part exasperation, assumed it was someone they knew.

"It's bloody important."

"And who might you be, Miss Important?"

"Mary Ballantyne, crime reporter, *Glasgow Herald*."

"Wait a wee moment, Miss . . ."

McAllister walked into the room.

Don laid the receiver on the table. "It's yer girlfriend from Glasgow," he said and slipped off his stool to go back down to the stone. He heard no protest at his joke. But he did catch a glimpse of McAllister's face.

He's looking guilty, Don thought. And halfway down the stairs he was shaking his head, thinking, *For the love of the Wee Man, that's all we need.*

Now Rob was curious, and was trying to listen in as McAllister took up the receiver.

"McAllister. Oh, hello. No. I haven't seen today's *Herald*. Really?" He listened intently as Mary told him the gist of the newspaper article. "And you're sure there's a connection between this man and Jimmy McPhee?" He listened for a minute more, then said, "Of course. I'll let her know. And Mary . . . be careful." McAllister was not being condescending when he said this; the new development was disturbing.

Now Rob was really interested. Even though the editor's back was turned, Rob could feel the tension. "Bad news?" he asked.

"Aye. But not our bad news." He went to his office, needing time to think. He knew Joanne and the girls were not expecting him home until late. But still he felt he should call.

"Hello." Again it was Annie.

"Everything fine?"

"Why wouldn't it be?"

A surge of exasperation made him snap. "Annie, I'm calling to make sure your mother is okay."

"Mum is in the kitchen with Granny. If I get her to the phone she'll wonder if something's wrong."

He knew she was right. "I'll be back later than I thought, so don't wait up for me."

"I'll let Mum know." And the girl hung up.

He was furious. He knew he had no right to be. He knew she was scared, afraid her mother would never be the same and, with the wisdom of an ancient, the child was protecting her.

From him? came a fleeting thought. *No, stop imagining things.*

He reached for the phone, took a deep breath, and dialed the *Herald.* He asked to be put through to the editorial floor.

The phone rang out again. "Is Mary Ballantyne there?" he asked.

"She's out."

"Can I leave . . ." *a message,* he was about to say to the dial tone. He knew it must be that man, the one who loathed Mary, bitter that she gave him no attention—or had stolen his thunder. Whatever the excuse, McAllister thought him totally unprofessional. He was about to redial and ask for Sandy Marshall, then thought better of it.

"*Glasgow Herald.*"

"Can I leave a message for Mary Ballantyne?"

"Certainly, sir. Can I have your number?"

"It's John McAllister. Tell her I'll be in Glasgow tomorrow night."

"I'll give her the message. Nice to hear from you, Mr. McAllister."

As he hung up he was smiling. *Not forgotten, then.* Then he jerked back in his chair. *Why did I do that?* He had had no intention of returning to Glasgow. *Jimmy can look after himself.* But he knew he would go.

He waited until he heard the presses rolling. Even from three floors up and even though the machinery was entombed in a carved-out rock cave of a room, the noise was loud, the vibration slight but noticeable.

When McAllister was in the office, Don was in the habit of joining him for a celebratory drink. *Another edition put to bed,* Don would say, and McAllister would open the filing cabinet and bring out the good whisky, the one they kept for themselves, not visitors.

He poured. Don came in and sat in the visitor's chair. McAllister passed him a tumbler of one of his favorite whiskies, a Glenfarclas. They drank. No toast, only a silent raising of the glasses.

"Any problems?" he asked his deputy.

"None."

"There might be a problem—in Glasgow." He wasn't looking at Don as he said this. Instead his eye was following the whisky as he swirled it around the glass, creating a vortex, releasing a scent of heather and moorland and loneliness. He'd always thought Scotland's national drink a duality—comfort yet pain. Much like the stories of this nation, he once wrote in his younger, more pretentious, days.

"Jimmy McPhee was apparently hiding out in a boxing club in the Gorbals. Last night the building was torched. It's badly damaged and a body was found . . ." He saw Don's eyes widen. "No, not Jimmy. It was the owner, Jimmy's old trainer from the prewar days."

Don, shaking his head as he considered the development, said, "Bad news indeed."

McAllister was grateful. He had no need to explain why he was involved. Don knew McAllister was obliged to help Jenny McPhee any way he could, if she asked for help. And she had.

It's just the way o' it, he would have said if asked to explain the Highland etiquette of obligation, hospitality, those invisible bonds that tied you to your friends, your neighbors—even strangers; the Good Samaritan would have recognized the Highland code.

"An anonymous caller phoned the *Herald* with a message for Mary Ballantyne. Someone is looking for Jimmy, they said, and next time, he won't be so lucky."

"And Jenny McPhee, she still wants you to find him?"

"Find him, bring him home . . ."

"That's if he wants to come home." Don took a sip of the whisky. He rolled it around his mouth before swallowing it in obvious appreciation at such fine malt. "The last thing you should be doing right now is getting involved with criminals, especially in Glasgow." He did not need to explain why.

McAllister said nothing.

"Do you know why Jimmy's wanted?"

"No, I don't know who wants him, or why." McAllister did not add, *And I didn't ask.* "I know this man Gerry Dochery is involved somehow, and he's a hard man . . ."

Don knew what that meant. A hard man in a city of hard men was a gangster in any other parlance.

"We grew up together. He came to my mother's house looking for me. He warned me off, but indicated there would be no mercy for Jimmy."

It took a silence and a refill before Don gave his verdict. "Best be off down south, then. It'll never go away, so get it sorted out as fast as you can."

"Joanne, the girls . . ."

"Talk to Elsie Ross. Have her move in. She's lived through two wars. She'll no' like it but she knows it's what men do—go off on dangerous errands against the barbarians, the Huns, all that, and she knows what women do . . . sit at home and wait."

McAllister had forgotten that Granny Ross had a Christian name—Elsie. She was Granny Ross to everyone in the household, including Joanne. "And the *Gazette*?" he asked.

"We'll manage." Don was firm, giving McAllister no choice.

"Jenny McPhee?"

"I'll talk to Jenny. I'll tell her you'll give it one last try. But if you canny find him . . ."

McAllister nodded, grateful that Don was releasing him from the responsibility of making decisions.

"Don't be away too long." Don looked at McAllister, a man young enough to be his son, trying to make light of the task. "I've been promised first dance with the bride, after the groom, of course, so we need you back in one piece."

McAllister stared at him.

"Your wedding. July. Or have you forgotten?"

He couldn't look at Don. "I hope Joanne will be well enough by then." He said no more, guilty at blaming her for his uncertainty.

"She will."

After Don left, McAllister stayed in his office, and another dram, another bout of guilt later, he knew he should go home. He would go to Glasgow. He had to. The obligations to the McPhees went too deep. If asked, he could not explain his attachment to Jenny and her son. Fascination, even. He knew it was likely a romantic notion that they, the Traveling people, were the true Scots, the remnant of the indigenous tribe of Iron Age metalworkers roaming the land for thousands of years. Sir Walter Scott and his writings were too florid for McAllister's taste, yet he recognized a similar romanticism in himself.

"*Breathes there the man with soul so dead . . .*" A poem he had often mocked, but in coming to the Highlands he now recognized the wellspring of the verses.

On the slow walk home through the long gloaming, he tried all he could to banish the many reasons for leaving the town for his city: trepidation at what marriage with a ready-made family would entail, boredom with a local paper editorship, never again being on a challenging and exciting newspaper writing stories read by tens of thousands.

And much as he didn't want to admit it, there was the thought of once more working with Mary Ballantyne. Her voice, her way of staring into his eyes, listening with all her body, from her he wanted the acknowledgment that he had once been *somebody*. He had been John McAllister, renowned war correspondent, the newspaper's man in Europe mixing with writers and philosophers and photographers and musicians, covering everything from Berlin to Paris to Rome and Madrid. Now he was a middle-aged man in a small town on a local newspaper, a pillar of the community, about to marry, about to lose his independence. And lonely.

The next morning did not start well.

Granny Ross normally came to the house after the girls had left for school. Today she was an hour early—something about needing to be at an important Women's Guild meeting in the church hall.

McAllister was sitting at the table with Joanne, explaining his reasons for leaving once more for Glasgow. The girls were in and out, asking for more toast, or where their schoolbags were, Jean wanting Joanne to tie ribbons to her pigtails, and Annie wanting her mother to whiten her school plimsolls. On being told by her grandmother to do it herself, she started complaining that if no one would help her she would be late for school.

Mrs. Ross was listening in to McAllister's conversation, darting from sink to pantry to cooker to sink, interjecting with a commentary on Joanne's health and the need for McAllister to stay at home.

"I can't be expected to do everything," she was muttering to no one, as no one was interested. "I've ma own life to lead and a husband to see to."

"Hopefully it will be sorted out quickly and I won't have to go back again," McAllister finished.

Joanne smiled. "You can be back in time for tea tomorrow. Betsy Buchanan—sorry, Ross—is coming round with the new baby. I said you'd be here to say hello."

Betsy Buchanan, as everyone still called her, was the former advertising manager at the *Gazette*, Bill Ross's new wife, and Granny Ross's new daughter-in-law. Even after marrying Joanne's former husband, they remained friends. When she discovered the affair, Joanne had confessed to McAllister that she was grateful to Betsy. "Betsy is good for Bill," she'd told him. "That makes my life much easier."

"Say hello from me," he said. He reached across and took her hand. "I won't be back until Sunday. Monday morning at the latest."

She nodded, then looked at him, her eyes liquid dark like those of a wee mouse cornered by a cat. "You will come back, won't you?" It was an echo of Annie's question less than a week ago.

"Annie, Jean, get a move on. You'll be late for school," Granny Ross snapped, her voice like a whip crack.

Jean jumped. She did not know what was happening, but she felt the tension.

Annie glared. McAllister was leaving her mum. Again.

"Of course I'll be back." He still had Joanne's hand in his and could feel her trembling. "But this is something I have to do."

"Schoolbags. Now," Granny Ross ordered. Some things, most things in her opinion, should not be discussed in front of children, particularly her eldest grandchild.

"I'll be back as soon as I can. Promise. And I'll try to persuade my mother to come back with me," McAllister continued. "She said she'd come for the wedding but I'd like her to get to know you before that."

"I'd like that." She was smiling, but it was a faint nervous twitch of the mouth, not the full-lips-and-cheeks-wide smile of a former Joanne.

The trust, the love that radiated from her made him ashamed. He knew that the trouble with a lie, even a partial lie, was that it was corrosive. It made everything dirty. It spread and soiled and tainted every part of a conversation. It made fissures in a relationship that could be covered but never mended.

Jean came between them, kissed her mother, and said, "Cheerio, McAllister, see you soon."

Annie stood in the doorway and said, "See you Sunday night, McAllister," daring him not to be back by then.

The front door slammed. They were gone.

Joanne said, "I'm going out to the garden."

He was uncertain if she wanted to be in the garden or not be in his company. "I'll join you in a minute." Alone with Granny Ross, he started, "Mrs. Ross . . ."

Something in his tone made her squint her eyes at him. "Aa' ye?" she drew out the word to a question.

"I know it's a lot to ask, but would you be able to stay here over the weekend, until Monday?"

"If needs be, of course I will. They're my family."

He suspected from the way she was standing, facing him square on, that she was not happy with his decision. *Or is it something else?* he wondered.

"Mrs. Ross, I'd like to pay you to be our housekeeper—you're here every day, and most weekends, and you deserve payment."

"Please don't insult me, Mr. McAllister. Joanne is like a daughter to me. And I'll remind you that those girls are my grandchildren." She turned towards the sink and began clattering the dishes so loudly he feared the crockery would crack. "I'll be here as long as I'm wanted. You can count on that."

He had the good sense to say no more. "Thank you, Mrs. Ross, I'm sorry if I offended you."

"Just be back when you promised. Monday morning. That should give you enough time to do whatever it is needs doing."

"I will. And thank you again."

There was no reply.

He went to the garden. Joanne was in the deck chair doing nothing. He hugged her goodbye.

"See you very soon," he said.

"Aye, I hope so." She closed her eyes against the sun and didn't open them until she heard the back door open, then shut. Then she closed her eyes again. "I'm as scared as you, McAllister," she said to no one in particular. "I made a disastrous choice the first time around, so I'm just as scared as you."

Six

He arrived in Glasgow seven hours later and went straight to the *Herald*. Mary was at her desk.

"Oh, hello," she said, looking up, "the editor wants you." Then she continued typing.

Sandy Marshall was busy with proof pages, marking this, running a pencil through that. "Take a seat, I'll be with you in a sec." He turned to the sub-editor. "This'll do, and make sure you up the font on the headline."

When the sub left, Sandy turned back to McAllister. "Good to see you again." He pushed the proof pages of an article towards McAllister. "This whole gang thing is blowing up, and you're our lead to Gerry Dochery. Can I second you for a week or so to work with Mary on the story?"

McAllister dropped into the chair across the desk from his old friend. They were more than colleagues, they had been cadets together, had grown up from full-of-themselves cocky young men to fully fledged journalists before their paths separated, McAllister to cover the Spanish Civil War, Sandy Marshall into some never quite explained position in the army dealing with information.

Misinformation, Sandy had once said. But that was all he'd ever shared.

"I know you have commitments up north," Sandy started, "but this story is big. And Mary is convinced it goes beyond plain old gangster territory disputes. Plus there is the mystery as to why your tinker friend's name keeps cropping up."

"Mary suggested I become involved?"

"No, this is me asking for a favor."

McAllister reached for a cigarette. *A favor*, he thought, *that's what brought me down here in the first place.* But he was interested. More than that, he was beginning to feel the thrill of a big story about to break. "How long will it take?"

Sandy laughed. "You know better than that . . . it takes as long as it takes."

"A week. No more." Elated at the opportunity, yet guilty, *how am I going to explain a week away?* McAllister couldn't believe he'd agreed so readily.

"Done." The editor reached for the phone. "Mary, join us in my office, will you?" He lit a cigarette. "Don't say I said this, but keep an eye on her. She's mixing with some right evil souls and she . . ."

"And she—meaning me, I suppose—can look after herself." Mary flopped into the chair next to McAllister.

He could see she was exhausted. He saw that her hair had lost its luster and her clothes were grubby.

She caught him looking. "I've been poking around the remains of the boxing gym and haven't been home. I need a bath, I need a hair wash—my clothes stink of fire—but later. You can sit across the room if you can't take the smell." She reached across for her editor's cigarettes. McAllister offered his lighter. She accepted, then asked, "So, you on board?"

"He is," Sandy answered.

"What do you want me to do?" McAllister asked.

"Talk to Wee Gerry Dochery," Mary answered.

"Why would Gerry talk to me?"

It was a rhetorical question. He and Sandy Marshall understood the implications—if Gerry Dochery talked, he would be signing his own execution warrant. Mary understood, but in an intellectual sense. She'd walked the streets and alleyways; she'd stood in the sawdust and blood of a Saturday night at a pub in the slums. But her name gave her protection; connections as high up as advocates and chief constables and peers of the realm, not to mention her late father's regimental colleagues. The gangsters were not stupid; they knew what harming her would bring down on the community.

Mary was impatient. Her legs, not quite touching the floor, making her look like the shrunken Alice in Wonderland, were swinging in a steady rhythm. "I don't know, he's your pal. Can't you persuade him to talk for old times' sake? Blackmail him? You know the man, we don't. All I do know is that this fire was an attempt to kill your Highland friend. And it succeeded in killing his former coach, a harmless old boxer, a man who was minding his own business, running a decent club, and encouraging a lot o' the young lads to find a legitimate way of venting their violence—in the ring."

"You know the Jimmy McPhee connection for certain?" McAllister saw her flush and look away. He recognized her ambition; he'd trained enough cadet reporters. He also knew that the training emphasized that speculation has no place in a journalist's repertoire. Facts, facts, and at least two sources to confirm those facts, were what he'd drummed into the overeager trainees.

"A very reliable source told me McPhee was hiding out in the gym, had been since he was released from Barlinnie . . ."

"So if someone is after him, why would Jimmy stay around the city?" McAllister was thinking aloud, not expecting an answer.

"Search me." Mary had thought this over and had no answers, and that annoyed her.

"So someone set fire to the place to flush him out?"

"No, McAllister. Someone tied up Old Man Laird, removed what was left of his teeth, and some of his fingers, then they set fire to the gym, with him still in it, alive." She saw the editor and McAllister look away; even they were distressed by the description, or perhaps distressed by the cold way she laid out the story. "The doctor who attended the deceased is hoping his heart gave out first, as they only removed three fingers. But . . ."

"If that's correct—the heart giving out first—it's manslaughter. If not, it's murder," Sandy Marshall spoke quietly. This was the first he'd heard of the torture. "That's why we need to contact Gerry Dochery before more deaths occur."

"More murders, you mean." Mary was not one to let a euphemism pass.

McAllister sighed. "I said I'm in. I meant it. Let me go home first. Let my mother know I'm here. I'll be back in an hour or so." McAllister stood. "See you."

As he left, he heard Sandy asking Mary, "When will you hear if it was his heart or the fire?"

"Don't know. Everything's speculation and . . ."

McAllister left them to it. He knew what a front-page murder entailed. He knew the adrenaline rush of pursuing a story, composing it, fact-checking, subbing, checking with the lawyers if need be, and having everything finished before deadline—deadline in a big daily newspaper being absolute. He knew he wanted to be in on this, if only one more time, before the anonymity of life as editor in a local Highland newspaper swallowed him up.

Twenty past eight was nearing his mother's bedtime.

Mrs. McAllister gave no hint of surprise at his unannounced arrival—twice in two weeks, once more than in previous years. She made tea, saying little until fifteen minutes later he said he had to get back to the *Herald*.

"Does this have to do with Wee Gerry?" she asked.

"Indirectly." He was fudging the truth, but she was not fooled. "I want to speak to him, that's all."

"I'm right sorry I wrote you yon letter." She shook her head, sadness leaking out from her voice into her shoulders. "John, Gerry is lost to us. Has been for a long while, poor soul. But I can see it must be important, if you've left your Joanne alone, not to say your job. I'll write to Mr. Dochery. *Maybe* he can help you with Wee Gerry." The way she said "maybe," full of doubt, said she was not hopeful.

He knew Mr. Gerry Dochery senior was a good man, but didn't think he would help; it would mean betraying his son. Then he realized he had no other way of finding Gerry. Out of contact with his previous informants, he wasn't certain he'd be welcome back in his old haunts in the Tollcross, and Maryhill, and some of less salubrious areas of the Gorbals—if there were any salubrious areas, which he doubted. He knew the inner-city areas of desolate streets, and back lanes, and poverty. The Broomielaw, stretching along the banks of the Clyde, better known for public houses than trees, was now almost foreign territory. But he had to find Jimmy. He'd promised.

"If you would write, I'd be grateful," he told his mother.

"I'll ask him to come here on a visit. No more. The man has enough troubles, what with Gerry and . . . and all that. He needs to know he still has friends . . ." She was waving her hand around, encompassing the whole city.

"Thanks, Mother."

"Aye, and the sooner this is sorted the sooner you can go home to your new family."

"And you can come north. Meet Joanne and the girls."

"Maybe."

He left, knowing *maybe* was a fraction from a yes. He should have been elated; he'd been trying for three years to persuade her to make the trip. Instead he felt his conscience settle in the pit of his stomach, reminding him of his misgivings. *A new life, a ready-made family, I hope I'm up to it.*

"Get a grip, McAllister," he muttered as he swung himself onto the bus platform, the pole sticky from previous passengers.

"If that's a prayer, I'll let you off at the cathedral, will I?" the clippie asked.

"The pub's mair likely to gie ye an answer," an old wag said as he stood beside McAllister, waiting to alight at the next stop.

McAllister smiled. This was Glasgow, home to a thousand comedians, and counting. He was back.

He ran up the steps of the *Herald* building to the swing doors, looking and feeling like a man on a mission. On the news floor he settled in at the desk. Happy. Enthused. Everyone was busy, too busy to notice him, although one of the subs gave him a wave and the six months' pregnant man across the way glanced up, then ignored him.

Mary's desk was empty, and he didn't ask. He rolled in the copy paper, interlayered with carbon sheets, flexed his fingers, took a deep in-breath of newsprint-soaked air, and, with a cigarette drooping from left of center in his mouth, he squeezed his eyes half shut and started to type. No notes; he knew what he was doing. *Give me background, context,* was all Sandy had said.

The typewriter was newer than the ones at the *Gazette*, whose machines felt like they had been installed in the heyday of industrial Victorian Scotland. Ash dropped onto his lap unnoticed. Only when he felt his lips burn did he put out the cigarette, then review the article. Poverty, slums, empty bomb sites, drink, endless children, shared outside toilets . . . No, he thought, *delete that, who would believe the poor deserve to have indoor plumbing?*

If someone from the *Gazette* could see him, they would not

recognize this man, a man possessed. At forty-six years of age, he felt the cozy job as editor of a local paper marked the twilight of a once illustrious career. Here, at this desk, on this newspaper, surrounded by the crème de la crème of the country's journalists, he was John McAllister, crime reporter, columnist. Somebody.

Writing the story, he could feel the pavements, the cobbled alleyways, smell the buses, the trams, the underground, hear the city, every element of it vibrating just below audible level. He felt like Lazarus as he relived, through his words, a night in the pubs around Tollcross with stumbling drunks at the "unco" stage, the hesitant, not quite ready for a fight stage, but with fists raised, dancing a drunken weave around your opponent, doing the "Glasgow jive."

He could smell the centuries of spilt beer and whisky as he typed, see the walls and ceilings so discolored from tobacco and open fires that there was no telling the original shade, but he guessed white, as whitewash—"distemper," in Scottish parlance—was the cheapest paint.

With every "ping" of the return carriage, the adrenaline surged. Half an hour to go and the article was almost finished. He knew it was good. He knew he was only revealing what everyone knew; the activities of the gangs accepted as much as the weather, causing comment and irate letters to the editor only when the violence was in plain sight of churchgoers of the smarter suburbs—the ones likely to write to the city councilors and the newspaper.

But to see it in print, spelt out for the rest of the country—even the English—to read, that was different, might require action from the city fathers, or at least a reaction. For a short while.

He glanced at the clock, a quick revision and it would be ready with ten minutes to spare. He smiled to himself as he edited the copy.

I'll never get away with "unco," he thought. Sub-editors everywhere, including Don McLeod back in the Highlands, would have their pencil through it. "Uncoordinated," he was about to type. Mildly drunk was what he should have put. *No poetry to that,* he told himself. And left it in.

He called across the room for the copyboy, decided against another cigarette, putting on his hat and coat instead. He glanced around. No Mary. *Ah well, we won't know if it's murder or manslaughter until after the postmortem.* He left the newsroom to another night, another edition. Exhilarated.

Coming down the steps, he turned up his coat collar against an almost rain. Being Glaswegian, he did not classify the light spray of non-puddle-forming precipitation as rain, no matter how penetrating the soft mist. When he reached the entrance to the communal close of his boyhood home, he removed his hat to shake the moisture out, and discovered the rain for what it was: deceptive, hat- and coat-penetrating, typical of the west of Scotland. He was shaking his coat before going into the flat when a voice came out from the alcove below the stairs.

"Hey mister, 're you McAllister?"

In the dim of the forty-watt lightbulb the girl looked eight but was more likely to be twelve, with the stunted growth and rickets that still blighted the poor of the city.

"Who wants to know?"

"A man said ye'll gie me half a crown if I tell ye summut."

McAllister knew that a sixpence would have been promised, perhaps a threepence. He gave her a half crown.

She screwed up her face, then recited, "He said to say you ken his mother. She's caa'd Jenny." She watched McAllister to see if he recognized the name and when he nodded she continued, "Tell McAllister I'm goin' across the waater. Stopping at the place where they study the fishes." She finished, saying, "That's all he telt me tae tell you," and she was gone in a flash of off-white summer dress, no coat, no proper shoes, only plimsolls.

"Thanks," he called out, but she didn't hear.

Surely it was 'doon the waater'—a boat down the Clyde, he was thinking. Not that Jimmy McPhee, a Highlander, would have said it in that dialect—this was a purely Glasgow expression describing the steamboat trip down the river into the Firth of Clyde, making for one of the seaside destinations like Rothsay or Dunoon. Then again, Jimmy had lived in Glasgow as a young man, did his boxing training here. *Where they study the fishes*—McAllister puzzled over it, made no sense of it, before deciding he needed help.

The phone box smelled of fish and chips and urine. The receiver was sticky. He only had a florin, no pennies. It was nearing midnight. The switchboard was closed, but the sub's desk was taking calls.

"Herald."

"John McAllister here. Is Mary Ballantyne around?"

"Mary, it's for you."

He heard a silence as the call was transferred.

"Ballantyne," was all she said.

"McAllister," he replied, amused at her adoption of a very male sobriquet.

"Uh-huh?"

"Tomorrow night. Fancy a visit to some boxing clubs?"

"Are you asking me on a date, then?"

He could hear her smile, but the question perturbed him. "My mother promised to contact Gerry Dochery senior, and I think a visit to some of the deceased's friends is in order."

"I'll be in late morning. Say midday? See you then, McAllister."

And she was gone. And he was left holding the receiver, the dial tone loud in the still, late night. And he was feeling foolish. Why he hadn't mentioned the message from Jimmy he didn't know. *Holding it back to impress her in person, are you?* his conscience asked.

As he walked back to the flat another thought nagged him. *A week,* Sandy had asked. *How could he stay away a whole week?* But he knew he was committed. Telling Joanne, dealing with the disapproval of his soon to be stepdaughter, his mother, Granny Ross, Don McLeod, all at the *Gazette,* that he would deal with—tomorrow.

His last thought as he fell asleep in his boyhood room, the one he had shared with his wee brother, the one who went to "sleep with the fishes," was of Joanne, the time he had keeked through the sitting room window and watched her as she danced to a record of Elvis, totally unaware she had an audience; this was the Joanne he had fallen in love with. This was the Joanne who was now absent. He was terrified she would never return. And afraid his cowardice would delay his own return. Maybe forever.

SEVEN

❦

Next morning McAllister was up early to fetch the newspaper from the corner shop. When he came back his mother had the frying pan in action. He knew there was no point in protesting that coffee and a cigarette was all he needed. Coffee was unheard of in this part of Glasgow, singling you out as a misfit or pretentious or both. Not that those words would be used; a much more vulgar expression, in a strong Glasgow accent, came to mind and made him smile.

"You still buying your rashers from the butcher in Maryhill?" he asked as he tucked into the perfectly cooked bacon.

"Aye, and I still go to Tommy McPhee for ma fish."

He knew he might be an adult, but Mother's rules applied—no reading a newspaper at the table.

She refilled his cup, the tarlike tea having the same caffeine hit as an espresso. "What are you on the day?"

"Still looking for my friend."

"I posted a note to Mr. Dochery last night. He should get it in the second post o' the day." There was no change of expression in his mother's face, or voice, but the disapproval was clear from the way she put the kettle on the stove, with a clang of metal upon metal.

"Thank you."

"I don't want thanks. An' I hope you have a good reason for getting involved with Wee Gerry Dochery. The man is long lost, especially to his father. An' you're no longer a lad trying to make a name for yerself. You have responsibilities." As she turned away, he knew she was interfering only because she was scared for him. "I'll help you this once—as much for Mr. Dochery, poor soul, as for you. But I'll no' help you any further."

She left him to finish his breakfast, although two eggs, three rashers of best Ayrshire bacon, the butcher's own black pudding, and his mother's tattie scones were almost beyond him. But he ate it all to please her.

He pushed his chair back. Taking the plate to the sink, he began to run water for the washing up. That brought his mother back in a hurry.

"Away and read your paper. It's a woman's job washing up."

He smiled at that, wondering what Mary would say to that. And Joanne.

He sat in the bow window with the newspaper, keeping an eye on the street for strangers. The front-page headline was direct: "Gangs Claim Another Victim." How Sandy could be certain he didn't know, but he must have the evidence to print such a headline.

The story told it all. Sources in the police, the fire brigade, the procurator fiscal's office, all said the same. Fire deliberately started; the boxing club previously threatened by person or persons unknown. Who had threatened the club owner, and for what reasons, no one was sure. And at least one other former boxer had received the same warning, so his premises were temporarily out of business. The information of the threats had come via an anonymous tip to the *Herald*. McAllister guessed from the wording—*a call was placed to a senior crime reporter*—that Mary had taken the call.

He turned to his own copy and was pleased to see the subs had touched it minimally. He'd also been given a byline. That he hadn't expected. He was reading the editorial, a piece bemoaning the crime statistics, when the realization hit him. The byline—Jimmy would know he was here. And Gerry. And all on the *Gazette*.

Joanne would see the paper, as the *Herald* was delivered to his home. He remembered as soon as he awoke he needed to call them. But he had procrastinated and now it was nine o'clock. The newspaper would be there. He went for his hat, told his mother, "I'll see you when I see you, but don't cook for me," and left to use the phone at the newspaper.

There were few people in the newsroom. Most would start to drift in around lunchtime.

A copyboy—girl actually, but that didn't change the title— asked, "Can I get you anything, Mr. McAllister?" She was another one with that eager look he saw in Mary Ballantyne.

"Aye," he said, "twenty Passing Clouds." He showed her the packet and told her where to buy them, then gave her the money, almost adding, *And keep the sixpence change for yourself*, as she seemed so ridiculously young.

No one was around. He picked up the phone and dialed.

"*Highland Gazette*, how may I help you?"

The pleasure at hearing the soft sibilant Highland voice startled him. "Hello, Fiona, McAllister here."

"Hello, Mr. McAllister, how are you?" He could hear the pleasure in her voice.

"I'm fine, thanks. Is Mr. McLeod about?"

"No, but Rob is here." She transferred the call to the reporters' room. As he waited for Rob to pick up, knowing he would answer only if there was no one else to take the call, he felt uneasy. He would have to explain he would be away for a week and preferred it was not to Rob, his junior reporter. *Definitely no more than a week. If I don't find Jimmy in that time, so be it.* He was so busy reassuring himself, he didn't notice Rob saying, "*Gazette*. Hello?"

"McAllister."

"Not McAllister the hotshot columnist?"

"No, McAllister the small-town editor." It came out more bitter than he meant. "I need to speak to Don."

"Leave a number. I'll get him to call you back."

"He can reach me at the *Herald* until noon."

Rob whistled. "Definitely the big time."

McAllister ignored him. "Have you seen Joanne?"

"No, but I promised I'd call round there tonight."

"Thanks. I'll talk to you soon." He hung up, not wanting any more questions from Rob. Or teasing. Rob had a good nose for a story, and he'd want to know what was so important that McAllister needed to be in the city.

He knew now was a good time to speak to Joanne. He would not have to hear the doubt from Annie. And Rob would be with her in the evening for company, for her to talk to, for her to ask Rob the questions that he didn't have the answers to, and for Rob in his bright joking way to reassure her. Making her laugh—he seemed to have lost the knack.

He dialed. The phone rang out. There was no answer. He tried again. Again no answer.

The girl came back with his cigarettes and change. He still had two left in the packet on the desk. He offered her one. She accepted. He gave her a light, and when she started coughing, he said, "You don't smoke, do you?"

"No, but I'm trying to learn. Makes me look older."

He grinned as it all came flooding back. First a copy kid, then a cadet, then a junior reporter, five years in all. Then, and only if you were very good, and lucky, and if the right story came at the right time, and if you cultivated the right contacts, and kept the sub-editors sweet, and kept on the right side of the cynical hard-drinking old journalists who had seen it all, only then might you get somewhere, especially if your starting place was the *Herald*. If none of the stars aligned, you'd end up on a local newspaper, in whichever small town you'd originally left to make your name in the big city. A newspaper like the *Highland Gazette*.

"Empty." Mary had appeared, picked up the cigarette packet, and shook it. Throwing it at a bin and missing, she ignored it, saying, "I'll die if I don't get a some coffee down me."

"If we go to Seraphini's I might just offer you a cigarette," he said; waving an unopened packet at her.

"You're on." She laughed.

The café was not far, but it was still a brisk walk. He remembered coming here after his return from Europe, when he craved the sound of any language other than Glaswegian.

"It's yerself, McAllister," the still round but greatly reduced owner, Marco, said as he and Mary walked into the warmth and fug and chatter.

That Marco and his brother and father had been interned for the duration of Italy's alliance with Hitler, McAllister knew. How it had reduced the man formally known as "Romeo" he hadn't given much thought to. But the sight of him, with little of his hair left, and a distinctive stoop, and his hands, hands that had once been roughened by no more than guitar strings, showed the effects of years of hard labor on a farm or a quarry or whatever menial duty the interned prisoners had been assigned, reminded McAllister how much the Italians of Scotland had suffered. It made no difference that they were mostly second- or third-generation Italian Scots who had brought coffee and ice cream, art, music, and vitality to many a small town in their adopted homeland; they were classified as enemy aliens, interned on the Isle of Man along with many Jewish people, and also other longtime citizens in Great Britain, including some of German heritage.

They took a tiny table covered with a red-and white-checkered oilcloth, then ordered.

"What's happening?" Mary asked after she had thrown back the first espresso in one gulp, then signaled for a second.

"I had an emissary from Jimmy visit me last night . . ." He saw her stare and knew she was about to say, *Why didn't you tell me?* so he quickly continued, "A wee girl, she brought a message and . . ."

"That means Jimmy McPhee knows where you live."

He hadn't thought of that. And he hadn't given thought to Gerry Dochery knowing where he lived, and that he was there, at home, with his mother, and writing about the gangs.

"Jimmy didn't identify himself, but he told the child his mother's name so I'd know it was from him. *'I'm going across the water. Stopping at the place where they study the fishes,'* that was the message." He didn't have to explain to Mary that "stopping" meant staying. She was Scottish enough in spite of her accent to know that. "Maybe he meant *'doon the water,'* but not being local . . ."

"No, he meant 'across,'" Mary said. "The island of Cumbrae in the Firth of Clyde has a marine biology station in the only town there—Millport. Across—he means by ferry."

"Of course!" He felt stupid for forgetting. "But why Millport?"

"Maybe he knows someone there. Maybe he thinks he'll be safe hiding in plain sight amongst the holidaymakers. The Fair Fortnight is their busiest weeks."

"A few times, on Fair Fortnights, when my wee brother and my dad were alive, we went to Millport. Lots of families in the fire brigade did. One time Gerry and his dad came with us."

"Your brother?"

"Long story."

She looked at him, saw he was not going to elaborate, and didn't push. Mary Ballantyne was certain she would find out. One day. "Right. Let's go. It's probably too late to catch the last ferry across, but first thing in the morning . . ."

"You can't come."

"And who's going to stop me?" She stood. She slung her bag over her shoulder. "I'm off to work. You go get the train tickets for Largs. First class. It's holiday time so the train will be booked out."

"Not first class to Largs it won't."

"There's a big race meeting tomorrow. All the trains to Ayrshire will be busy. Or have you forgotten everything about your homeland?" She was grinning as she left, waving cheerio to Marco. And she left McAllister with the bill.

Racing at Ayr. That reminded him of Don McLeod, a horse-racing fanatic. And Joanne. He must phone. He must call before evening or he'd miss Don. If not he'd have to phone home and answer to an eleven-and-a-half-year-old.

First the train tickets, then I'll call.

He didn't. When he got to the *Herald*, return tickets safely in his wallet, the breaking story blew everything out of his mind.

"The boxing coach was alive when the firemen reached him. He died of multiple burns," Mary told him as he came into the newsroom.

The brutal way she said this he recognized as distress. "So it's murder."

"Aye. It's murder." She squinted up at him, the unnatural blue of her eyes bright with anger. "So we're still on for tonight?" She saw him stare. "A tour of the boxing clubs? Or is it too dangerous for you?"

He laughed out loud. He needed her levity to take away the horror of death by fire. Some heads turned towards them, saw it was Mary, and went back to their task of keeping the citizens informed of the dark side. "I'm up for it if you are."

"I'm going. With or without you."

And he knew she was stating nothing but the whole truth.

McAllister sat at his borrowed desk keeping out of the way of the well-oiled machine that was a large daily newspaper. It would flow flawlessly, one edition to the next—unless another story broke minutes before deadline. Then it would be controlled panic.

Tomorrow's headline would declare the death murder. The article would remind readers of the horror of the fire, pontificate about the scourge of the gangs, and ask what the authorities were doing to control them.

There would be the usual comments from the police saying as little as possible, and the journalists attempting to write between the lines of what they knew and what they could write. Any comments from the Lord Provost's office would be full of all the usual platitudes about crime and punishment, and the safety of the citizens being paramount. And letters to the editor from "Outraged, Bearsden," or "Major (retired), Milngavie," would harp on about the iniquities of the heathen city, the solution being to bring back hanging for everything from theft to adultery.

McAllister used the time to make the call to Don McLeod.

"A week?" Don asked, a none-too-disguised reprimand in his voice. "You're the editor. Your decision."

McAllister knew Don was right. The *Gazette* could spare him, it was the silly season, after all, but he should not be taking a week away from home. Not now.

"I'm about to call Joanne. I know she has a lot of support, but would you keep an eye on her?"

"There's no need to ask." Don was clearly offended.

"I know, but . . ."

"Jenny McPhee was asking for you."

"I have a lead as to Jimmy's whereabouts, that's why I'm staying on. I don't want to get her hopes up, so best not say anything yet."

"Call me when you have information, then I'll let her know."

"I will." There was no more to be said, so they said their good-byes.

McAllister took a deep breath, picked up the phone, and gave the operator the number.

Granny Ross answered. "Joanne's asleep," she said. She listened as McAllister stumbled through his explanation before replying, "Aye, well, it can't be helped. Don't worry; we'll look after the lass. Telephone again later, but not too late."

He heard her sigh before she hung up, and could imagine her shaking her head, muttering one of her catchphrases—*Whatever next?* He felt like dashing to the station and booking the first train to the Highlands. But knew he wouldn't.

The phone rang not two minutes after he had hung up.

"Mr. McAllister?" It was the switchboard operator. "I have a trunk call for you. Putting you through."

It was Jenny McPhee. "Have you heard from Jimmy?"

"He sent me a message. I think he's in Millport—it's an island in the Firth of Clyde."

"I know where Millport is."

Now McAllister was attentive. Jenny McPhee knowing Millport, an obscure place except to Glaswegians, alerted him.

"I could be wrong," she said, "but there was this gagie living there, a friend o' ma late husband's, no' a tinker, but he came to all the horse fairs. He kept a horse or two, an' ponies . . . I think he's still alive."

"We're on the train first thing tomorrow, I'll find him . . ."

"We?"

"A crime reporter from the *Herald* who has a lot of contacts in Glasgow is helping."

"And helping hersel' to a good story an' all."

He was surprised Jenny knew it was a "she," then remembered Jenny McPhee never missed much. *She must be following the story in the* Herald.

And with that remark she was gone. No cheerio. No "look after yerself." No thank-you. But he expected none, as he had achieved nothing. Yet.

Eight

❧

Every gym McAllister had ever visited cried out poverty. Whether it was in Glasgow, or the east end of London, or one memorably seedy place in Berlin four years after the war had ended, they all smelled the same: disinfectant, iodine, and the sour smell of sweat-soaked ropes, punching bags, medicine balls, head protectors, and mitts. Overlaying the sweat was the faint stench of urine, whether from the lavatory or fear he didn't want to speculate.

And all the gyms he had ever visited were all painted the same institution-green, a color also favored by mental asylums and mortuaries. Disappointment and menace hung in the air like an early-morning haar over the North Sea. Posters lining the walls showing past and present champions who had never trained in boxing clubs as low down the evolutionary scale as this one were there to give hope to the hopeless.

Boxing, football, the army, or becoming a mercenary in whichever army would have Glasgow men—notoriously short in stature—were all the hope open to the boys of this city. Fighting was part of the streets and the alleys and back greens and school-yards. Fighting was bred in the bone.

Mary was looking around for someone to talk to. Everyone in the place was watching her, openly staring, particularly the two troglodytes guarding an office with a glass window. The glass looked tinted, but was more likely unwashed since the place had been built, in the twenties, and was speckled in one corner with a spray pattern that might have been sweat or blood.

"What do youse want?" Gog, or was it Magog, asked.

"The boss," Mary answered as fast as the fist of the man pummeling the punching bag in the corner.

"He's no' here," the second creature told them.

She and McAllister had already visited four boxing gyms that evening and had almost given up hope of finding anyone who would talk. Mary turned to peer through the office window when the twins, or brothers, or siblings hatched from the same shell, stepped in front of her.

She stepped back, hands help up in submission, when she noticed one particular poster. "Hey, McAllister. See this one? This was one of the matches my father took me to—before my mother found out and barred me from going to the boxing. It was a real ding-dong of a fight. But him here, he won fair and square even though his opponent was a total bruiser well above the supposed weight. The crowd went mental. The bookies were furious. My dad was delighted, he won quite a bit on that match."

"Did he now?" An old man, or a man who had been in too many fights—McAllister couldn't tell which—stepped out of the office. "And who might you be?"

"Mary Ballantyne. And this is McAllister."

"No' Colonel Ballantyne's lass?"

"Aye. Pleased to meet you." She stepped towards him holding out her hand. It was like a child greeting an ancient toothless bear, who seemed harmless if you were stupid enough to be fooled by his face.

There was a lull in the background noise of the gym as people paused to see what this novel encounter was about.

"Fancy a dram?" This time the question was addressed at McAllister.

"Seldom known to refuse," he said.

They went into the office. It was surprisingly neat and smelled more of surgical spirits than sweat. A first-aid cabinet was placed prominently on one wall. The back wall held a cabinet full of silverware: cups, trophies, and ribboned medals. A silver belt in the center had pride of place. It was then McAllister knew who this man was. And knew who the belt belonged to: Jimmy McPhee.

The whisky bottle appeared, then clean glasses. Mary declined water. None was offered to McAllister—only sissies and foreigners diluted the "water of life." They saluted each other.

"*Slàinte*," McAllister toasted.

"Here's tae us," the man who was known as Slugger, his second name being Slevin, saluted them.

Mary said nothing, only raised her glass in return, took a good sip, then put it down carefully; this was rotgut of the cheapest variety, and she was proud she hadn't choked.

McAllister sat back, giving Mary the floor. This was her show.

"My colleague here, he's from Dennistoun, but lives in the Highlands," she began. "He has an obligation to a man from up there—and the man's mother. Even though it's not his fight, he's honor bound to help."

McAllister watched the old man listening, showing nothing, except his eyes, which were alert, sizing up the challenge. He also noticed that Mary, for once, was asking no questions. *Telling it like it is*, he thought.

"See, the other night, late, I was still at work when the call came through . . ." She had an extensive network of firemen and policemen and ambulance staff on her list of contacts—even though it was illegal. She also had an informant in the mortuary. "Anyhow, when I got there the fire was all but over, it was that fierce. But my . . . friend, he helped rescue the body before it was burned to a crisp, and the victim . . ." Using the man's name was too personal, but she knew Mr. Slevin was well aware who the person she was talking about was. Maybe he'd been a friend. "He was tied up, he had fingers missing. Later I found out he had no teeth, and it seems he had a few left before the fire. He was alive when the fire was lit. And his death was horrible."

She left out the stench of burning flesh, the way the ambulance men, hardened from years of service during the wartime bombing, had to look away at the sight of the corpse. She left out the two shadowy figures hovering at the edge of the small crowd of onlookers, men gone before she could identify them.

"As for me"—she looked straight at the former boxer—"my interest is in getting a good story. I want to show those jumped-up snooty auld farts in the newspaper that a lassie can be as good as any man. I'll fight to get my story . . ."

"Like father, like daughter." Slevin was nodding.

". . . And if I destroy some evil bastards in the process, all the better," she finished.

"Another?" Slevin held up the bottle.

Mary covered her glass. McAllister held his out.

A sip or two later, McAllister took his turn. "I was admiring thon belt in the cabinet." His voice thickened to his pre-scholarship, pre-cadetship native Glasgow accent.

"Aye, one o' the stars o' Scotland." The old man was nodding but still not giving anything away. "Could've won a national title, no' just a Scottish one, if the war hadn't got in the way."

"Spoiled a great many things, the war," McAllister agreed. "The owner o' thon belt, I'd like to shake his hand. Or at least let his ma know the state o' things. After the fire an' that, she's worried."

Silence. But a silence punctuated by muffled shouts, groans, curses, the squeak of boots on canvas, gloves on leather, and a distant susurrus of heavy breathing from the two men competing to lift the heavy-duty weights outside the office window.

"We're thinking of going on a wee holiday tomorrow," Mary broke the silence. "They say Millport is right nice this time o' year."

"It is that," Mr. Slevin agreed. "An auld friend o' mine retired doon there. Jocky is his name. Right wild he was. But now, a quieter man you'll never meet." He grinned at this, and McAllister saw his top set of teeth was loose and the bottom set he hadn't bothered to put in.

"Let me give you the *Herald* phone number, in case . . ." Mary didn't get to finish.

"Now why would I be wanting a phone number?" he asked. Then stood. "It's been right nice to meet you, lass. You too, McAllister." They shook hands. "Right sorry about yer faither, Miss—a good man." He held open the door. Mary stepped out into the light and the smell.

As McAllister passed by, Slugger Slevin held his arm and muttered, "Tell Mrs. McPhee no' to worry too much, her lad's at least six o' his nine lives left."

"What was that about?" Mary asked as they waited for a bus to take them back across the Clyde to the city center. It might still be light, but a dim light. It was not a good idea to hang around the Gorbals at closing time on a Saturday night.

"Just wishing us well." McAllister had no idea why he lied, but the less Mary was caught up in this, the better, was his thinking.

"Time for a quick one before closing time?" she asked.

"It'll need to be a quick one, closing time in fifteen minutes."

"There's that pub on the corner." As she said this she stopped, looked around her, then stepped back towards a close entrance. It was impossible to see to the end but she went in a few steps and said, "McAllister, c'm 'ere. Listen."

When he joined her, he stood as she did, still, quiet, listening.

"There it is," she said. "Something's going on in there." It was a cheer, or at least a rising and falling sound, sound that seemed to be coming from a crowd.

"Probably an illegal drinking den," he said.

"Maybe." She started towards the end of the tunnel. Stone walls over and around them were funneling the noise. It sounded like a sports program coming from a neighbor's radio.

"Hey, where are youse goin'?" The voice resembled the growl of some big fierce dog.

Mary was quick, her accent matching that of the man who was no more than a shape silhouetted against the dark night at the end of the tunnel.

"Ah telt you this is no' place for a knee trembler," she was scolding McAllister, aggrieved, "an' us no' even engaged."

"Get away wi' youse."

They did just that.

Out on the pavement McAllister was doing his best not to laugh. "How does a well-brought-up lady know a phrase like that?"

She ignored him. She was trying to see if there was another way to find the source of the noise. "This way." She set off without waiting for him. "Here, down here." A narrow cobbled lane ran alongside the boxing gym. Fifty yards down, the buildings gave way to a high wall. There was a door, but it was locked. The voices were louder, rising in waves, then falling, hushed by someone saying, often, "Wheesht. Keep the noise down. Haud yer wheesh."

"Give me a leg up," Mary told McAllister. He obliged. Cupping his hands, he hoisted her up. She caught the top of the wall, balanced her feet on the narrow ledge of the door frame, and keeked over to see whatever was happening. He heard her mutter a profanity, and she peered down for a half a minute. He thought he heard her say "barbaric" before adding, "Help me down."

He did.

She was dusting the dirt and moss off her hands, saying, "You need to see this for yourself."

"What?"

"Bare-knuckle fighting. I want to get in there . . ."

"Whatever for? It's not our business."

"To see what we can see, McAllister. Where's your investigative spirit?" She knew this was not one of those occasions where she could just barge in. "Thon thug in the alley, he'll never let me in, but you . . . I know, quick, go buy a bottle. Then go back down the close, say Slugger sent you, and give him a bottle—a half will do."

He did as bidden, found himself in the dark almost bumping into the doorman cum watchdog.

"Slugger wants to know who's winning," was all he said as he handed over the door price—a bottle of McKinley.

"It's close. Been at it for a good whiley, near two hours, an' they're still standing."

The light came from three flaming torches set in the corners of what might once have been a stableyard. The smell of paraffin was strong, the flames unsteady. But there was enough light to see the blood-covered chests and torsos, and the bloodied, mashed-up faces and fists of the fighters. The men looked young, in their teens. Their legs and arms were skinny. One of the lads had prominent ribs, and had shaved his head to give him an advantage; it didn't seem to be helping, as he could barely stand.

McAllister knew this fight would end only with the loser unconscious at best. Severely injured, most likely. Deep flickering shadows cast the watchers' faces into gargoyle shapes, demon faces. Unlabeled bottles were being passed around. The referee was the only man in shirtsleeves—the traditional white, and he was wearing a bow tie. *How incongruous in a fight like this*, McAllister thought.

The bookie was in a corner taking bets, a sheaf of notes on a metal drum serving as a table.

The fighters were still staggering, bouncing off each other, gathering what strength they had left to swing a stray punch. In spite of the referee's warnings, they did not, could not, separate from a particularly long clinch. Then someone threw a bucket of water over them.

They separated, staggered back, falling into the crowd. Men, bloodlust up, pushed them back into the middle. They wanted more. They wanted broken bones, broken bodies, they wanted the bets paid out, no matter the damage done to the lads, both only one blow short of oblivion.

The fighters stumbled around, an occasional swing of an arm, missing the opponent, no more weaving and ducking, and no contact for over two minutes. Then a man, a wee bantam cockerel of a man, pushed one of the lads towards his opponent, saying, "Finish him."

"I'm away hame," one wag said, shaking his head, *hopefully in disgust*, McAllister thought. "This'll still be on in the morn."

"Break. I've telt youse, break. Now." The referee was almost pleading, as, once more, the fighters clung together, holding each other up in a semiconscious waltz, made all the more macabre by the blood dripping down the opponents' necks, backs, soaking into the waistbands of their trousers.

"If youse dinny break I'm calling it aff and all bets forfeit."

"Go on, Tommy, finish him," a voice called out.

There came a crack. No one saw where the punch came from. McAllister suspected the referee who was standing close, the sleeve of his shirt now dark with blood. One of the men-boys doubled over. Then collapsed. A cheer rose up. Other voices hissed. The referee held up the winner's arm long enough to declare victory before letting him drop to the dirt next to his unconscious opponent. "Wheest!" he hissed at the crowd. "Do you want the polis here?"

"They're paid aff," the man running the bets said as he was handing out money.

Time to leave, McAllister knew, but he could not help looking once more at the collapsed heap of flesh, the loser with a face that looked like it had been through a mincer. And no one was helping them.

"Are thon lads all right?" he asked no one in particular.

"What's it to you?" the doorman asked.

McAllister knew he'd made a mistake and, like some of the others, threw a ten-shilling note and some coins at the boxers, then left. Quickly.

The pub was shuttered and dark when he emerged into the street. He walked towards the bus stop with no hope of catching one.

"McAllister." Mary was beside him. She linked her arm in his. She was shivering, although it was not cold. "Was that what I think it was?"

"Aye, and as brutal."

"That's Glasgow for you. Much money floating around?"

"Probably." He was remembering the neat piles of cash, and paper, weighed down by stones, on the metal-drum table. "The fighters were no more than boys."

"Right. Tell me about it tomorrow, I'm knackered."

A taxi came by with the light out. But Mary stepped into the street. It stopped.

"Where to?"

"Blythswood Square."

"Jump in."

McAllister was no longer surprised at her ability to conjure taxis out of nowhere. The taxi took them to her flat first.

"Bright an' early tomorrow, McAllister. See you at Central Station. We can talk then."

"'Night." He did not look back as they drove away. He knew she would not wave. Or glance back. Or even think of him. *Mary Ballantyne is one driven young woman. And I am one ridiculous middle-aged man.*

NINE

~

McAllister had given Mary her ticket the night before and agreed to meet on the train.

"Go early," his mother had warned over breakfast. "It's right busy this time o' year."

He hadn't mentioned why he was going to Largs so as not to worry her. She held the view that taking a train for the sole purpose of walking up and down the seafront or along a pier was beneficial to the health and wished him a good day at the seaside.

"Take the ferry over to Millport for a few hours," she'd suggested. "Lovely place. We had great holidays there when you boys were wee."

When he agreed he might do that, he caught the brightness in her eyes, and was reminded he was all that remained of her family.

Once inside the train station, he looked up at the huge board displaying destinations, times, and platforms. Across the station concourse he saw a long line of people queuing up for the train to Largs. On closer inspection they looked like a line of refugees escaping the imminent demise of the city from an atomic bomb, or the Russians, or both.

Bulging suitcases were tied shut with rope—or perhaps clothesline. Sacks, and in some cases pillowcases, were hoisted up on shoulders, filled with what looked like rocks but was probably a week's supply of groceries, the prices on the holiday island being notoriously high.

Some of the women had sewn themselves new sundresses. Unfortunately these exposed whiter-than-white skin and chicken wings and rounded stomachs from too many children and too many potatoes. He knew that soon their city skin would take on the appearance of boiled lobster; every case of sunburn was a chance to show off to neighbors unable to afford a holiday.

And weaving in and out of the baggage, the couples, the grandparents, the church groups, or communities of neighbors who went on holiday together year after year from the first years of marriage to old age, children scampered, high on excitement and sugar-laden orange cordial. Playing chasie, they ran like rats in thrall to the Pied Piper, to the head of the queue, hoping to run under the barriers and be first on the train, dodging swipes and yells and distracted commands to *Get yersells o'er here right now.*

McAllister showed his ticket. It was duly punched and he was ushered through the first-class barrier. He joined a jolly bunch of people out for a holiday combined with a day trip to the races. This he deduced from their peculiar garb; like golfers, racegoers and racetrack bookmakers had a dress code all their own. Loud garish shirts, hats with bands that would soon be festooned with betting slips, they carried folding stick-stools, and, undoubtedly, flasks containing whisky.

Then there were the women. They were dressed for the winner's enclosure, or box seats in the stands—either that or the equivalent of the Queen's garden party at the Palace of Holyroodhouse. Overhearing their more subdued chatter, he picked up what was known as a Kelvinside accent—a mangled form of Glasgow English denoting their middle-class status. *We are not the hoi polloi*, proclaimed women in layers of pancake makeup, and flowery hats with brims worthy of a beekeeper.

It was only when the guard blew his whistle, loud and shrill, outside the carriage window that McAllister wondered if Mary was going to make the train. On the final whistle and with the groan and clunking as the carriages reluctantly let go their grip on the rails and began to inch forward and still no sign of her, he sighed a mixture of disappointment and relief. Meeting Jimmy on his own would be much easier. Turning up with Mary, well, he knew Jimmy would never pass judgment, but he would prefer it if he wasn't seen in her company.

The train was nearing Paisley when the carriage door slid open and Mary came in, plonked herself down in her seat, and grinned at him. "Thought you'd got rid of me, did you?"

The other four passengers in the carriage stared at her, the women with disapproval, the men otherwise. Mary was wearing a dirndl skirt in a bright abstract pattern, cinched in at the waist with a wide belt. Her sleeveless white shirt was buttoned within an inch of the brassiere, obviously lacy through the thin white material. With golden hoops in her ears, black around her eyes, and pale pink lipstick, hair tied up in a ponytail with a red chiffon scarf, she looked like a girl who'd borrowed, or stolen, her mother's clothes and makeup.

The man diagonally opposite McAllister winked. His wife, sitting across from him, kicked his foot and he looked away, but not before McAllister caught the you-are-one-lucky-bastard grin.

Mary took an apple from her shoulder-bag satchel and offered it to McAllister, who shook his head in refusal. She polished it on her skirt. When she bit into it, juice dripped down her chin. With a full mouth she mumbled, "breakfast," and continued to crunch on the apple until a slim core was all that was left. Then she stood, and on tiptoe, slid open the top window, threw out the core, and grinned at the five sets of eyes that had been watching her every move—and her legs, in the case of the henpecked husband. She sat back down and said, "That was a great night last night, McAllister," and she punched him on the arm before curling up like the proverbial cat, saying, "Wake me up when we get there."

McAllister looked out the window, carefully examining the flat stretch of moorland above Kilmarnock, trying not to laugh but unable to hide a tremor in his shoulders. *Mary Ballantyne, whatever next?*

The arrival of the train could have been as shambolic as the departure from Glasgow, but five minutes before Largs station, Mary woke and said, "I'll get us a taxi to the pier. But we'll have to be quick."

Quick she was. McAllister had to trot to keep up with her. Outside, she turned in the opposite direction of the queue already gathered at the taxi rank. Twenty yards on, she turned, stepped into the gutter, and whistled with two fingers, and with the other hand waved a ten-shilling note in the air. A taxi broke free from the herd and hurtled towards them.

"The pier," she said.

"But that's no distance!" the driver protested, looking back at the queue of porcine bookmakers, regretting not waiting for a better fare.

"Keep the change, but give me a receipt," she answered, waving the note. The driver grinned, said, "You're on," and drove them to the pier.

The ferryboat to Millport was waiting, swaying gently in the slight estuarine swell. Mary left McAllister to buy the tickets at the booth. At the head of the gangplank a man in uniform and cap held out a hand for her ticket.

She gestured back towards McAllister. "My uncle has them."

Seeing McAllister coming towards him and looking back at Mary as she ran up the ladder to the top deck, the man snorted to himself, "Uncle. That'll be right."

McAllister joined her in prime position on the prow of the top deck. They leaned on the polished brass railings and watched the holidaymakers boarding with as much ceremony as a herd of cattle being loaded. Eventually the boat let out a deafening blast, answered by a chorus of shrieks from the passengers. The engines rumbled, the ropes were cast off, and the ferry left for the short trip to Millport.

"This is nice," Mary said, hugging herself.

"Really?" McAllister answered. "If it wasn't that a man's life may be at stake, I'd agree with you. And we should talk about last night. I was thinking, maybe Jimmy . . ."

"McAllister, I've had six months of bad news and evil people. So I intend to enjoy every second of this journey." And with eyes half closed, she stretched her shoulders back as though pausing from the typewriter and a particularly fraught story, and took a slow deep breath of unpolluted salt-laden air.

He knew he was being churlish, spoiling the crossing. For himself. Not for Mary. Through deep dark water, the ferry chugged, leaving a dancing wake of parallel foam lines. The mountains of Arran to their left, the low hills of the Isle of Cumbrae to the fore, and the Isle of Bute to their right, a celestial blue heaven and bright sunshine completed the picture-postcard day. From the passengers came constant background of squeals of delight, murmurs of appreciation and excitement; the short trip was a magical time-out from a hard life in a hard city.

And McAllister was jealous of their ability to enjoy the moment; it felt like an eternity since he had been happy.

Mary was as quick off the boat as she was boarding, and she insisted on another taxi trip—*on expenses*, she told him.

They were deposited in the center of a town that was really a village strung along two adjoining crescent moon bays. Towards one end, a straggle of a cliff rose up to woodland. Below was a row of boardinghouses, many freshly whitewashed for the brief summer season, all with No Vacancy signs dangling from chains or handwritten and propped in the windows with unusually hideous holiday ornaments. The hoteliers might complain about the workload, but this was their chance to make money, as few came to the island outside of the brief Scottish summer.

On the south side were substantial homes for the smart people, built in Victorian or Edwardian times for the wealthy of Glasgow to escape the city. There was a pier halfway along this bay. As the tide went out, leaving the sea paddling-depth deep, and returned rapidly, only the locals who knew the tides berthed there.

McAllister thought they had about fifteen minutes before the hordes would descend from the buses bringing them from the ferry. "Let's ask at the local shop, find out if anyone has seen Jimmy."

"Breakfast first," Mary decided.

"I've already . . ." McAllister began.

But Mary was opening the tearoom door. A bell let off a loud ping. A young man with a very bad case of acne came out of the back, over to the window table, where Mary was examining the menu—one sheet of paper with four items. The waiter, probably a schoolboy forced to work in his mother's café in the long summer holidays, stood with pencil poised, receipt book open, waiting for Mary to order.

"Three bacon rolls, two mugs of tea," Mary told him.

The waiter wrote without speaking, without once looking at her, but managing a blush that matched the red scarf tying up her hair. He left with a grunt that might have been a thanks.

"Three bacon rolls?" McAllister asked.

"One's for you. I need two. Heaven knows what else there'll be to eat here, apart from fish and chips." She was staring around the room, up at the ceiling, and out the window, taking in everything and everyone. "Isn't it one of the rules of being a detective or a reporter? Eat when you can because you never know what might happen next?"

McAllister laughed, and when the food arrived, he discovered he was hungry. The bacon rolls were exceptional, and the tea came in a pot, with a hot water jug and cups and saucers.

"My mother would love this," he told Mary.

"Are you close?"

Close—not a word he associated with his mother. As for love—that was a word he was never certain of, except when it came to his beloved jazz. Some of the Latin nations and their almost worshipful attitude towards mothers mystified him. But having been brought up in the Roman Catholic faith, he reflected, he should understand the cult of the mother and of the Virgin Mary.

"I mystify her. I try my best, but I no longer fit in her world." He was aware that for many years he had not tried his best; he had neglected her as he tried to put distance between his up-bringing and his invented self. "She's my mother, and she is a good soul. You?"

Mary understood and told him, "I was my father's girl, and I was—okay, am—a wee know-it-all . . ." She grinned as she said this. "I drive my mother crazy. But I understand why only too well." She wiped the flour off the corners of her mouth with the back of her hand, leaned back, and said, "You need to give me a cigarette before I tell this story."

He was about to say *You don't smoke*, then realized she needed the cigarette for a prop as much as for the nicotine.

When they were both puffing away, she started. "My mother, since she was widowed, sees herself as half a woman. I get it, I really do, because I worshipped my father and miss him desperately. But it's been more than a decade. I once asked her if she was trying to emulate Queen Victoria and mourn him for the rest of her life." Mary laughed at herself, but McAllister could see her mouth tighten with regret. "My only excuse is that I was at university and thought I was the bee's knees.

"Anyhow, Mother rattles around in the far too big house, everything exactly as it was when Father was alive. We've even kept the castle, for heaven's sakes. All the furniture, the kitchens, even old jackets and wellie boots, are exactly as they were the last time we had a shoot on the estate. She's unable, or unwilling, to change anything. It's like a museum. The same in the city house. When I wanted to turn the basement into a flat, it was a huge battle. I won by threatening to move to London. So we continue to live together, in a distant kind of way."

She stubbed out the cigarette that had been sitting in the ashtray smoking away to itself. "Right. We haven't all day. Tell me quickly about McPhee. He must be important for you to be chasing after him like this . . . What does he look like, for a start? He was very young—we both were—when I saw him."

"What about last night? The fight?"

She wiped her mouth with the back of her hand. "Sorry, very unladylike," she said.

"You've flour on your cheek."

"Bare-knuckle boxing. Right." She took a sip of tea. "Very popular at the turn of the century, now mostly an Irish Traveler tradition of settling disputes . . ."

"Aye, I know all that, but what about now, in Glasgow?"

"McAllister, you know as well as me that anywhere there is poverty there is gambling. For some young men it's not a question of honor, it's hard cash, and, yes, I've heard of the fights, but it's not as huge as it used to be."

"I thought bare-knuckle boxing had died out. But," he reflected, "maybe this's why Jimmy is in trouble, he was in Barlinnie for fighting. And I've no idea if he was involved in that game when he was a youngster."

"It would make sense if he was the one organizing the matches, maybe stepping on someone else's turf. I'm assuming there's big money gambled on the fights."

"Jimmy is rumored to be involved in gambling in the Highlands. But I always thought it was small scale."

"Well, he's your friend. Don't you suspect this could be what's going on?"

"That fight last night was cruel. They'd've stopped a dog fight sooner." He did not like to think that a vendetta over bare-knuckle fighting was why he was helping Jimmy McPhee and his mother. "I have a friendship, of sorts, with Jimmy but . . ." It was as much the realization that he had few friends as trying to describe his relationship to Jimmy that had him grasping for words. "He's like me, a loner."

"You mentioned his mother?"

"A proud woman."

"I hope you're not a romantic, McAllister. Not one of those hopeless writers or academics who idealize the 'raggle-taggle Gypsies, oh.' "

He laughed. "The last thing I'd call myself is romantic."

"I told you I grew up near Blairgowrie," Mary continued. "I've seen the tinker camps, the bairns, the dogs, the carts and covered wagons. I know how the women struggle to feed everyone. I heard the men knocking on the kitchen door looking for work, chopping wood, mending fences, or kettles, anything for a couple o' bob. And yes, I've heard the songs, the stories, told around the campfire after a day picking raspberries. I've even seen a bare-knuckle fight. It was hard and fast and horrible. But the next day, it was as though nothing had happened between the families." She was picturing that night. Under stars, bonfire blazing, dogs barking, one minute they had been listening to singing, the next she was aware of shouts from a group of men on the edge of the campsite. She'd caught a glimpse of two men, naked to the waist, circling each other. When she saw what was happening, the gamekeeper's wife, who had come with Mary to enjoy the singing, whisked her charge back home, saying, "Never ever mention we were here, your mother will make sure ma husband loses his job if you do." Mary, at eleven, knew that even though her father wouldn't mind, her mother would never let the couple stay on at the estate.

"A Traveler's life is a hard hard life, McAllister. Never romantic. And it's changing."

"The twilight of the Celtic age," he agreed.

"Save us! You *are* a romantic."

McAllister did not want to discuss his lack of romanticism; it reminded him too much of how deficient he was around Joanne. And he was lost as to how to describe his Traveler friend. "Jimmy McPhee is small, but he's taller than a jockey."

"An average Glasgow size?"

"Aye." He smiled. "His skin is outdoors dark. Eyes dark— he's . . ." He was about to say "unmemorable"—which Jimmy McPhee was, unless you looked at him directly. That didn't happen often, as Jimmy had a way of avoiding your eye. "If he wants to hide, he can stay hidden. If he wants to be noticed, which is seldom, you'll know it."

"Clear as mud, McAllister." Mary was laughing as she stood and walked to the door, leaving him to settle the bill.

Once outside and into the bright of mid-morning, they found the beach and the pavements crowded.

"Hold on," Mary said, then dashed back into the café. He watched her as she spoke to the schoolboy waiter. He watched, saw her elicit at least half a dozen words from him, and what looked like a map drawn in the air with a pointing gesture to somewhere above the village.

That's why Mary Ballantyne is an ace reporter, he told himself.

"Right," she said when she came out. "First we try the beach."

McAllister shrugged, took off his jacket and slung it over his shoulders, then hurried to catch up with Mary. By the time he arrived she was deep in conversation with a woman who had been trying to ignore her, trying to sell rides on a raggle-taggle assortment of donkeys and ponies to passing families, and so far not succeeding.

"They're only just arrived," Mary reasoned with the woman, who looked like a man who'd seen hard times but wearing a dress. "They'll hire a pony when the bairns get bored."

"You trying to tell me ma job?" the woman snarled.

"If you help me, I'll get out o' yer hair . . ."

McAllister thought that a strange comment, as none of the woman's hair was visible under a floral scarf tied up turban-style.

"I'm looking for an auld pal o' my dad's, Jimmy McPhee . . ." Mary persisted.

"Never heard o' him."

She brushed past her, almost elbowing her out of the way. But this made no difference to Mary Ballantyne. "He'd good wi' horses . . . maybe he's looking for work . . ."

"Do these look like horses?" She was pulling a donkey's ears through the slits in a battered straw hat. The donkey didn't seem to mind; the hat and the placid creature looked so old, they had probably been a summer-holiday fixture for at least a decade.

McAllister, standing a short distance away, was enjoying himself, noticing how Mary thickened her accent, made herself smaller, younger, playing up the ingénue.

Sitting on a camping stool set up beside a sandwich board advertising the donkey rides was a man. *He's enjoying the conversation too*, McAllister thought as he noticed the old man's head swiveling like a spectator at a tennis match as the conversation went from woman to woman. Then McAllister saw the white stick lying beside the stool. He looked more closely. Under the shadow of the wide-brimmed hat dark around the band with sweat stains, the man's head, looking as wizened as a witch doctor's juju skull, held eyes that although open were empty of expression.

McAllister hesitated, then went towards the old man, hoping he would be more talkative than the vixen-woman.

Mary waylaid him first. "Come on, we don't have much time." She grabbed his elbow and steered him up the beach on to the esplanade and towards the west end of the town, where the rocky foreshore attracted fewer visitors.

"Where are we off to?" he asked as they reached a row of normal shops—a grocer, a butcher, a bakery. A newsagent with a display of plastic buckets and spades, and a stand of postcards in the entranceway, had a billboard out on the pavement. Huge headlines from down-market tabloid read, "City Gang Warfare."

Mary saw it and said, "Steal all my stories that lot do, too chicken to chase it up for themselves."

"What are we . . . ?"

"We're going to hire bikes and cycle around the island," she told him.

He stared. "Bikes? Me? On a bike?"

Seeing his dismay, she laughed. "Cumbrae's a wee place—four miles round at most, and we're only going to the top of the hill. On a day like this we can see forever, maybe spot horses in the fields. Jimmy has to be somewhere and the town is crowded, so maybe he's on a farm."

It was a ridiculous plan—so McAllister thought. But when

they reached the triangulation point at the top of the island, and when he managed to get his breath back, and they could see all across to the Isle of Arran and to Ailsa Craig, some forty miles distant, he appreciated the view. And appreciated how unfit he was.

"Well," Mary said, "I can see cows, but no horses. Come on, McAllister, we'll check out the farmhouses."

"We've only just got here . . ."

"It's downhill from here on." She was on her bike and off.

They checked out the farms, all five of them. No sign or knowledge of Jimmy McPhee.

"A tinker, ye say," one woman asked. On Mary's replying, "a Traveler," she looked as though she might set the dogs on them.

All day they searched. At farms, boardinghouses, pubs, tearooms, they asked after Jimmy, and discovered nothing.

Mid-evening, it was bright light still. McAllister was exhausted. He desperately wanted beer and whisky and a sit-down, but they had to catch the ferry back.

"We'd better find a taxi to get us to the pier," he told her as she sat licking an ice cream bought from the same newsagent that sold everything, and then some, as well as hiring out bicycles.

"Last ferry is long gone," she said, swinging her legs as she sat on a bench that was fractionally too high off the ground.

"Gone?"

"It left an hour ago." She looked at him and grinned. "Don't worry, we'll find somewhere to stay. I'll tell them you're my uncle to save your reputation."

Again he found himself discombobulated by her forget-me-not-blue eyes and could think of no quick or witty reply.

It took much asking before they found a place to stay. *No. Nae chance. You're kidding?* These were the polite answers to their pleading for a room. It was the stares and the frank looks implying *dirty auld man* that McAllister hated most.

Eventually, at the unfashionable end of town, up a narrow lane that smelled of a late-night city alleyway, in a house that was hidden behind another, taller, more respectable boardinghouse, a man wearing a string vest answered the door.

With a cigarette dangling off his bottom lip, he said, "Youse can have the attic for five pounds."

"Five pounds?" McAllister was outraged.

"We'll take it." Then she nudged McAllister. "Pay the man."

He was about to snap at her, *You pay*, and she saw it. "It's all on expenses," she said, but as he was still annoyed while he counted out the change, she said, with the landlord listening in, "Oh, I get it, you don't want to put in a claim in case some nosy parker in accounts starts wondering why we're sharing a room and spreads the gossip."

"Right," was all he replied. But that wasn't why he was annoyed. She was a rich girl; he knew how they behaved around money, always expecting someone else, someone as rich as herself, to pick up the bill. It was only in his twenties that he discovered the rich never paid cash; all bills, accounts from the butcher, the baker, the dressmaker, the department store, came in the mail, to be paid by a retainer. And in spite of her ability to change her accent, drink with her colleagues, and mix with the hoi polloi, she was still a rich girl. Still part of the Scottish aristocracy.

The entrance to the room in the eaves was off an outside flight of stairs, ending on a wide wooden landing, which McAllister suspected was unsafe. They found it was indeed an attic, the window a skylight, and the only other source of light a single bulb dangling from a long frayed chord. Behind them the cliff rose not two feet from the building's back wall. At the top, about fifteen feet higher than the rooftop, it gave way to a rocky ledge. Exposed tree roots clung to the damp rock formation, with ferns growing out of crevices. A smell of cave or cellar or mausoleum completed the sense that this was not a place to be in winter; even the brightness of high summer never touched this rock face.

"Leave the door open," Mary said. "It's warm enough."

There was one bed, single, with metal ends similar to a hospital bed. There was a sink. The tap dripped and had probably dripped for years, if the long rust-colored stain was any indication. There was a chair, large, leather, rounded arms, the bottom sagging, with a piece of fabric that looked like a horse blanket thrown across the back.

"You take the bed. I'm tiny. You're tall. And I can sleep anywhere, anytime," Mary said, flinging her bag on the chair. "Unless you want to share." Even in the dim light she could see his terror. She laughed. "I'll just think of you as one of my father's old pals."

He tried to not look offended but was taken aback.

"Sorry, I didn't mean . . . I'll think of you as my boss, and you know what they say about 'on your own doorstep.'" She took his cigarette from him, took a puff, then gave it back. "My father's pals, some of them were a right randy bunch. Oh so polite and respectable but leching at me, checking out how my breasts were developing. One man, a major, suggested I sit on his knee. I was all of sixteen, and he was visiting to pay his respects to my mother, who'd only heard a month previously that my father did not survive Hellfire Pass on the Burma railways."

She pulled off the scarf, shook out her hair, scratched her scalp with both hands, then twisted her head and stretched her neck, enjoying the release. She kicked off her shoes, then settled into the chair, turning this way and that to get comfortable.

McAllister was reminded of his soon-to-be-stepdaughter Jean's cat. He wouldn't have been surprised if Mary started purring.

He hung up his jacket and sat on the edge of the bed. It creaked. He took off his shoes. He had seldom felt so uncomfortable.

"Sandy Marshall says you're to be married soon. Tell me about your fiancée." Whether Mary said this because she was interested, or to distance them, he couldn't tell. But he began, "Joanne."

He swung his legs up and rested his back against the metal bed end. Then leaning forward, he pulled the pillow behind him. It was still horrendously uncomfortable; the smell of mildew didn't help. "Joanne worked—works—at the *Gazette*; she was there when I started as the new editor. Nearly three months ago she was hit on the head by a madwoman and kept prisoner for two and a half days and almost didn't make it."

"Aye, but she did make it. That's what counts."

"Yes. She did." McAllister considered Mary's comment. And was glad to be reminded. He had been dwelling on what-ifs for too long: *What if she doesn't recover? What if she's brain-damaged? What if I can't live with a ready-made family? What if I can't live in a small town any longer? What if? What if?*

"So what's she like?"

"She's kind. She's beautiful. She laughs a lot. She makes me a better person."

"That's a very sound basis for a marriage." Mary had pulled the blanket over her knees. The distance between the chair and the bed was not far enough for McAllister, and he was glad to be reminded of Joanne. Certainly he had occasional lustful thoughts towards Mary. But that was not it. It was her youth. Her intelligence. And, he admitted to himself, he was jealous; she had a future, he had a past.

"And you? Any plans for marriage?" He didn't know why he asked this. He knew women like Mary, knew them far better than a woman like Joanne.

"You disappoint me, McAllister. I wouldn't have taken you for one of those rare men who doesn't believe a woman has to have a husband—and children—to be complete."

"I'm not." But this sounded lame even to himself. "You should move to Paris. There are intellectuals there, not only women, who would agree with you."

"Maybe I will," Mary replied. "When I'm made a foreign correspondent for the *Manchester Guardian* I will do just that."

She let out a huge yawn. "Night-night, McAllister. Sleep tight."

It was that last phrase that did it. *Joanne says that*, he thought. *Night-night, sleep tight*. Sleep tight he did not. He lay awake. He dozed. He listened to her breath. He chastised himself for being an idiot—longing for what he couldn't have. His youth.

Ten

McAllister awoke to the dawn chorus and a cockerel crowing. His knees hurt, his thighs ached, mostly from the bicycle trip, but also from the bed that sagged in the middle and was too short, with the horsehair coming through the mattress in numerous patches.

The armchair was empty, the blanket discarded on the floor. After a wash in the bathroom out the back he felt better but, unable to shave, he saw himself in the cracked mirror looking like a crook in an Ealing Studios black-and-white crime film. When he came back he found Mary sitting outside on the wooden landing, leaning against the brick wall in a narrow shaft of sunshine.

"Tea"—she handed him a mug—"and rolls straight from the oven." She passed over a paper bag with two floury soft white buns. He sat on a step below her. "The baker wasn't open, but I went to the back door and used my feminine charm. They're buttered, but no bacon."

It was not yet six o'clock when, breakfast finished, they walked to the harbor. As yet there were no holidaymakers, but there was plenty of activity amongst the small fishing boats, and the wooden cobles with local men preparing lobster pots to lay along the rocky shoreline at the back of this and neighboring islands.

"Grand day," said one man, his skin weather-worn to the color of a native of India.

"It is that." Mary smiled back. She took a seat on a nearby bollard, watching as he mended his nets, the wooden shuttle wound with thin twine moving fast and sure along the tear.

McAllister leant on the seawall, leaving the conversation to her.

"I'm not going to spin you a line," she started. "I'm a journalist, and him over there"—she jerked her head in the direction of McAllister—"he's a colleague. We're looking for a man who's on the run from some pretty nasty Glasgow folk. This man's a Highlander, of the Gaeltacht, and bound to be noticed in a wee place like this. So we're wondering where he might hide out."

"There's some pretty rough folk in Glasgow," the fisherman agreed. "Not that I've been there, mind. No. You'll no' catch me in thon city." He tied off a piece of twine and cut it with a short deadly-looking blade, then started on the next tear in the net. "I've been to Buenos Aires, mind. Now that's a grand place. Stopped off there on the way back when we wiz at South Georgia for the whaling. I was the only one o' the crew who wasn't a Highlander, or an Islander. Mostly from Lewis and Harris the whaling boys, so I have a bit o' the Gaelic."

Mary knew to wait. Say nothing except an "aye" or "really?" and nod often.

McAllister offered a cigarette, which was accepted, his only contribution to the exchange.

Through a stream of smoke the fisherman kept working, then said, "There's no one much here the now. They'll come back from the fishing around mid-morning, around eleven, but I'll see what I can find out." He looked at Mary. "This Highlander, he's in trouble you say?"

"Big trouble."

The fisherman finished mending and began to pack up his tools into a folding layered wooden toolbox, with metal handles. "See you later."

Mary and McAllister said thanks and made their way to the promenade, Mary saying, "I hope to God the tearoom is open, I'm starving."

It was. The waiter was the same lad. His vocabulary hadn't improved, and the breakfast was excellent.

It felt like Sunday morning, which it was. From the Cathedral of the Isles, the smallest cathedral in Europe, according to the locals, a bell tolled. Neither Mary nor McAllister felt like moving, and they enjoyed an hour of calm. More tea. More cigarettes. Little conversation. But lots of people watching.

Families, laden with children, buckets and spades, tartan rugs, and wearing silly hats, were beginning to make their way to the sandy part of the seafront. A six-man Salvation Army band marched past, the trombone player marking out the beat with an oom-pah, oom-pah that McAllister always found comical. They were heading for a prime spot on the grassy strip above the sand to hold the Beachside Sunday school.

McAllister remembered them from his childhood holidays; "What a Friend We Have in Jesus" was a song he could never forget.

From the opposite direction, in procession, towards the small hut where they kept deck chairs for hire, came a man in a hat that from a distance seemed to match the hat on the donkey. He was leading a string of ponies and donkeys to the part of the beach with packed hard sand, where they would ply their trade for the rest of the day. With him was the blind man, but no sign of the woman.

McAllister's prayer was that the donkey would join in with the band. It was one of his favorite memories of another Sunday morning decades ago.

His mother and father were on deck chairs. He and his wee brother were playing in the sand. The Salvation Army band started up. One of the donkeys started to bray. His mother was shushing him and his brother. "Don't laugh," she was saying. But her hired deck chair was shaking.

The band kept playing. The donkey kept braying. His dad was laughing and eventually had to take the hankie, knotted at the four corners, off his head to wipe away the tears. It was the best holiday McAllister could remember. *I must remind Mother*, he thought.

"Come on, McAllister, time to go." Mary took his stillness, from being caught in the memories of that holiday, as reluctance. "You're here to find your pal. I'm here for a story. How else will we get our expenses past the editor?"

He had no intention of claiming expenses for a single room in a boardinghouse in Millport with Mary Ballantyne as his roommate. Not if he ever wanted to live down the teasing from Sandy Marshall.

Mary took her shoes off and began walking amongst the people on the sand, stopping now and then to ask questions. McAllister doubted she would find out anything useful. The whole trip was feeling like a waste of time. The sound of children singing to the beat of a tambourine drifted over him. "Jesus loves me, this I know, for the Bible tells me so . . ."

The squawk of seagulls as they fought for the crusts from the egg sandwiches that a wee lassie near him was throwing up in the air, was another evocative seaside sound reminding him of childhood.

He heard shouts. Then a scream. A donkey ran towards the line of sunbathers in deck chairs, then he saw Mary running towards the hut and the ponies.

Two men, with what looked like clubs raised above their heads, were hitting out at the ponies. *No*, McAllister saw, *they're attacking the man in charge of the pony ride.* He ran to help.

A pony broke loose, cantered over the grass, then galloped down the street. A third pony was bucking and kicking, reins loose, saddle askew. Its hind legs caught one of the men, who fell down in a ball, clutching himself and screaming like the women on the beach.

McAllister almost cheered. *That kick was right in the family jewels.*

More screams. And yells. The blind man was waving his stick in the air but keeping out of the fray, sheltering in the entrance to the hut.

Mary had grabbed hold of the bridle of a bucking pony. She was talking to it, trying to calm it down. The man in charge was struggling with another pony, trying to keep it between himself and the second gangster, who was trying to dodge between the terrified animals. His right hand held high, he didn't care that the razor was glinting in the sun. He was oblivious to all the onlookers and about to slash down and across the face of Jimmy McPhee, when McAllister yelled, "Watch out!"

A whistle blew; it was the woman in charge of the Sunday school. Everyone stopped, except the animals. But only for a moment. When no policeman appeared, the fight resumed.

Mary screamed a banshee wail and slapped a pony on the rump. She swung her satchel at its companion, shouting, "Shoo, shoo, get away with you." She hadn't realized they were tied together. Kicking and baring their teeth, eyes flaring, they pulled one way, then another, tangling the reins and stirring up the sand.

The second assailant became caught up between them in the tangle of reins and slipped. He fell, rolled into a ball, hands over his head to protect himself from flailing hooves.

Mary grabbed Jimmy's sleeve. "Jimmy?"

"Aye?" He was too surprised to ask more. But he had seen McAllister.

"I'm with McAllister. Come on! Run!"

They ran. And as they ran past a man with a Brownie camera pointed at the mêlée, she shouted, "Hey, mister! Get those pictures to the *Herald*, we'll pay for them."

They ran past the band, now playing a loud ferocious oom-pah-pah, hoping to keep the children distracted, and the woman with the tambourine kept banging away, yelling, "Jesus loves me, this I know . . ." The rest of the hymn was inaudible, as the distressed donkey kept running around in a circle, braying loudly and long, drowning out all but the tuba.

McAllister watched Mary and Jimmy running towards the harbor, dodging in and out of the startled pedestrians. He lost sight of them behind the seawall.

A trio of men, locals by the look of them, advanced on McAllister, all in a line. They called out to the blind man, "Aa' right, Jock?"

The blind man reached a hand out for McAllister's face. McAllister obliged. The man quickly patted it, and said, "He's wi' me."

The local men moved towards the fellow lying in a ball, hands over his crutch, rocking and moaning, "Mary, mother of God, help me, help me." The other fellow had vanished.

"Get up, ye bastard," a man in waterproof trousers and braces said. But the injured fellow couldn't stand. Not yet.

"Mrs. Cruickshank's tearoom would be best," the old man with the white stick said to McAllister.

"Aye," he agreed.

They made their way across the esplanade, McAllister holding his companion's elbow to guide him through the milling, chattering, excited crowd, leaving the injured man and the discarded weapons—razors and clubs—to the locals.

In the tearoom, McAllister and his companion sat in a window table.

"A pot of tea, please, Robert," the blind man called out.

"Coming up," the boy waiter replied.

McAllister was watching the beach over the lace half-curtain. A group of men were trying to untangle the ponies. Others were righting the deck chairs. Children, escaped from Sunday school, were darting around like flies in the aftermath of a battle. As the adrenaline drained, McAllister relaxed. Then he gave a half-smile. A small lobster boat was heading out to sea. Silhouetted against the silver horizon, he could make out three figures, perhaps two men and a child. *Two men and Mary*, he decided.

"Looks like Jimmy got away," McAllister said.

"Good," his companion replied.

"John McAllister," he said, wondering as he introduced himself what the protocol was. Did you lean over and take the man's hand to shake it, or wait? He waited.

"Jock McBride." The man held out his hand.

McAllister shook it. "Not Wee Jockie McBride?" This was a legendary name amongst boxing aficionados.

"The same."

Now it started to make sense. Of course Jimmy would hide out with friends from his time in Glasgow, and Wee Jockie was another of those boxing stars of the thirties—this time from the badlands of Govan.

"After I was injured I ended up here wi' ma daughter. A right miserable cratur she is, too, but I've nowhere else to go." He was looking around for his tea, which was slow in coming. He didn't see McAllister watching him but guessed. "I can see a wee bittie. Movement, shadows . . ."

"The referee should have stopped that fight." McAllister recalled the scandal of the match that was allowed to continue long past the point of safety.

"Aye, but the fight was fixed—I was meant to go down by round eight, only they forgot to tell me." The tea came. And scones, already buttered. "Thanks, lad." Jockie took a long noisy slurp of the tea and sighed, saying, "That's grand." He took a bite of scone and, satisfied, sat back. "So Jimmy tells me you're a friend." He said this with the amazement of a man hearing of a lamb lying down with a lion.

"Does he, now?" McAllister was pleased to hear it. This chase was costing him dearly. With Mary gone and obviously handling everything with little help from him, he knew he should be home. With Joanne. With her daughters. With the newspaper he was neglecting. But he was here. And he was curious. "One thing, Mr. McBride . . ."

"Jockie . . ."

"Aye, one thing puzzles me. This is a lot o' effort on someone's part to get at Jimmy McPhee. Why?"

"Ah dinny know and Ah didney ask. All I know is that after Kenny was murdered in thon fire . . ." He sensed McAllister's surprise. "I mayn't be able to read, but I keep up wi' the news. Anyhow, Jimmy arrived, asked if he could hide out here till it quietened down, so . . ." He reached for the remainder of the scone.

McAllister speculated, "Jimmy hasn't lived in the Lowlands for years. All his business dealings as far as I know are strictly Highland affairs."

"Some folk will nurse a grudge for years."

"'Nursing their wrath to keep it warm.'" McAllister misquoted a favorite line from "Tam o' Shanter."

"Dad, what the hell's goin' on? Where're the ponies?" The woman, an embodiment of the Burns quote, was standing in the doorway, her face as dark as an imminent thunderstorm.

There was no need to guess where the donkey was; although decreased in volume and frequency, the plaintive hee-haw could be heard from the beach, where a girl was holding the reins and trying to comfort the poor creature.

"I told you thon tinker'd bring trouble," she was yelling. There was no need to say whom she referred to. Not expecting a reply, she gave McAllister a death-wish glare, then left, banging the door shut, sending the bell clanging.

The tearoom was beginning to fill with families desperate to discuss the excitement or just thirsty for a decent cup of tea. McAllister looked up as a shadow appeared on the left side of the window. Outside, a big man, his hat pulled down shading his face, stared at him. Then shrugged. Then left. Gerry Dochery.

As though sensing the presence of the hard man, Jockie said, "Leave all this be. It's not your trouble. Jimmy'll sort it, and make his way home. Eventually."

McAllister wondered how much Jockie McBride knew. "Have you any idea who's behind all this?" he asked, not expecting an answer. "And why?"

"That's Jimmy's business." Jockie was turning his head around, listening. "You'd best be off afore the polis arrive. And afore ma daughter comes back. She'll want to blame someone, and you're handy, so . . ." He held out his hand. "Give Mrs. McPhee ma best when you see her."

McAllister shook the offered hand. He should have been surprised at him knowing Jenny McPhee, but he wasn't. Nothing surprised him when it came to Jenny. "I'll do that."

He settled the bill. He asked for the time of the next ferry. He took the bus to the pier, passing a police car racing towards the town. *A bit late*, he thought, and was pleased to have missed the policemen.

When the ferry docked on the mainland, he walked to the station, caught a train, this one almost empty. Emerging at St.

Enoch station, he debated whether to go home or go straight to the *Herald. Home first, a wash a shave clean clothes and a dram.*

The dram came first, then the wash, then a conversation with his mother. This made him pour a second dram.

"Wee Gerry came round here looking for me?"

"Yesterday. He said his father told him to make peace with you, and to tell you it was no' your business so you'd best go back home to your fiancée."

McAllister was so angry the whisky glass was shaking. *Coming to Mother's home? Mentioning Joanne?*

"Son, I'm right sorry. I know Wee Gerry is a criminal but I . . . I'm sorry. I told him you'd maybe gone to Millport." A single tear escaped.

Now McAllister was more than angry, he was scared. "Mother, I want you to pack a bag. You're coming home with me. We'll catch the early train tomorrow."

His mother did not argue. That was when he knew she too was scared. "I have to go in to the *Herald.* I need to explain to Sandy what happened . . ."

"Give him ma best . . ."

"Don't answer the door to anyone." He put his arm over her shoulder. "You'll love it in the Highlands, especially this time of year." It was all he could think to say. To tell her she might become caught up in this feud was unnecessary; his mother had been born and had lived all her life in one of the roughest parts of the roughest of cities, and they were Catholics in a Protestant stronghold. She knew.

Sandy Marshall was on the newsroom floor, a news conference in progress. "The man himself," he said as McAllister walked in. "You know about these?" He handed McAllister a contact sheet.

He stared. "Where on earth . . . ?"

"A holidaymaker walked in demanding money," explained one of the sub-editors who knew McAllister from his previous time on the *Herald*. "Mary promised him payment for the roll of film." He was squinting at the shots. "Canny use them, they're hopeless but ..."

"But from these, you get the gist of the story," McAllister finished.

"Backup for the copy Mary phoned in," Sandy said.

"Really? Where is she?"

"She didn't say, but it was a reverse charge call from a phone box. So we need you to write up your version, but tell us what happened first."

"Aye, we're all dying to know what great front-page scoop Mary Ballantyne has come up with this time." The failure of a man—Mary's description of her rival crime reporter—could not disguise his bitterness.

"Haven't you a weather report to write?" Sandy asked him. "Or is it an obituary?"

"His own, hopefully," the sub-editor muttered before looking at the clock. "McAllister, give us five hundred words. Mary's copy will lead; you can fill in the gaps. Then we'll repair to the Station Hotel for the juicy bits we canny publish. Then ..."

"Then I'm off home before the wife files for a divorce," said Sandy. "So let's put a humdinger of a front page together."

When McAllister left the *Herald* building at around 10 p.m., the streets were quiet. It was late for citizens to be out, but not for those working in newspapers. The evening light had dimmed to an almost-dark by the time he reached the entrance to his mother's flat, and the lightbulb at the foot of the staircase to the upper flats was out again.

As he searched his pockets for the keys, he cursed. He was exhausted and fumbling for the keyhole. He ignored a faint noise a few steps along the passage leading to the back green; rats were common here. He felt before he saw the movement behind, and instinct made him swing his right arm around backwards, his hand clutching the keys between his fingers. He struck something. Someone. Him being so tall, he struck a face. There was a clatter of metal dropping on the slate floor.

"Ma eyes," a man bellowed. McAllister turned and in the streetlight saw the outline of a small man, scuttling backwards into the street, a hand on his forehead.

McAllister trod on whatever had fallen. He struck a match. As he was bending to pick it up—razor—a second man came at him. McAllister dropped the match. His eyes couldn't adjust quickly enough and a weapon, a short stick maybe, or a cosh, landed on his right shoulder. It hurt—badly—but no bones broke.

"You bastard," McAllister yelled, his voice echoing up the close stairwell.

"Is that you, John?" His mother's voice came from behind the door.

"Stay inside!"

Again his attacker launched himself at McAllister, landing on his back, clinging to him, hands around his throat.

"Mr. McAllister? Is that you?" Another voice called out, this time from the second-floor landing. The neighbor looked down the stairwell. Although he couldn't make out what was happening, the neighbor retreated. And slammed his door.

The man dropped to the ground. A sharp blow landed on McAllister's left elbow. Pain shot up his left arm, leaving it useless. All he had, apart from his height and longer reach, was his keys, with the larger iron key protruding from his clenched fist.

When this assailant came close enough, McAllister's right fist shot out and connected with the man in the region of his neck. He fell forward against McAllister's arms. An explosion of breath burst hot in McAllister's ear. He dropped the man to the ground, stepping back to protect himself and land a kick on the still body. But he was too slow. His attacker scuttled on all fours, reached the bottom of the stairs, and began to climb.

McAllister followed. He knew he was being stupid. He knew he should run for home. Bolt the door. Count himself lucky to have escaped, to live, to fight, or write about, another day.

The man was fast. One floor. Two, three. On the fourth-and-final-floor landing the man was waiting. Legs akimbo. Razor held out.

"Nae need for aa' this." The voice sounded that of someone young, sure of himself, and, although breathing fast, he was not out of breath—unlike McAllister. He couldn't know how angry McAllister was, couldn't see the white-hot rage, the buildup of days of frustration, guilt, fury at being an onlooker, unable to help Jenny bring her son home, and bested by a girl. Mary.

McAllister tripped and had to scrabble up the last two steps. The figure looming above him, his hand gripping the railings, giving himself purchase to launch a kick. But too slow. McAllister saw the kick coming. He dodged to one side. The kick missed. Still on his hands and knees, he launched himself towards his attacker and caught an ankle.

"Let go, you fucker," the man screamed. "Let go." He was thrashing about and his free foot caught McAllister on a shoulder, narrowly missing his head.

"You've no idea who you're messing wi'." The voice was lower, trying to squeeze menace, not fear, through his vocal cords. "Get off a' me." He was writhing, kicking.

McAllister's hand slipped from the ankle, but he managed to grab the other leg by the trouser cuff. The man was leaning too far back. He was bent backwards from the waist, in danger of toppling over. His arms were flailing like a wind-up toy. All that was between him and a four-floor drop onto slate flagstones was McAllister, holding him by a trouser leg.

And McAllister was tempted: if he suddenly let go the man would fall. He wanted to let go, but in that second, illuminated by the moon shining through the skylight above, he caught a glimpse of a face. A boy's face. But a man in these parts, where the streets and the gangs and the poverty made a man of a fifteen-year-old. He jerked at his assailant's legs, pulling him in and down. The man-boy swiveled around. Holding onto the railings, he doubled over and was sick, the vomit falling down the depths of the dark well, to the floor that might have been his death place had McAllister not seen the terrified boy rather than a hardened hard man.

Halfway down the stairs, the second-floor door opened again. The neighbor looked down. Then up. He took in the boy. He took in McAllister. He retreated. The sound of bolts being slammed shut echoed through the hallway.

"Go home to your ma," McAllister told the heap of bones sitting sobbing on the landing.

He then walked down four flights, calling out to his mother, "It's me," so as not to scare her, before letting himself in.

She was sitting in the kitchen, her arms wrapped around herself. She looked tiny.

"Fetch your bag," was all he said. She scuttled off. More dormouse than rat.

He went to the sitting room, poured a substantial dram. Waited.

When she emerged, holding a small cardboard suitcase in one hand, her handbag in the other, he went out to check there was no one waiting to attack a second time. The close was empty but for the smell of vomit. The street too. He locked up, took her arm and the suitcase, and they walked down the hill to Duke Street.

There were no buses or trams, and few taxis cruised the East End of Glasgow, especially this late. They walked to the station. It took awhile; his mother had not walked much in recent years.

He knew the milk train would be leaving in a few hours. He phoned the night desk on the *Herald* from the station, spoke to a former colleague, who promised to pass on a message to the editor. His call was then transferred to a copy taker. He quickly dictated a short account of the attack. *Sandy can use it in the late edition. I want it known I'm alive and well and will be looking for revenge.*

He and his mother sat in the waiting room, saying little, never once mentioning why they were there. She let him hold her hand.

"I wonder why they call it the milk train?" he said after an hour or so. "Why not the newspaper train? I mean, that's how the papers get distributed . . ."

"No' everybody's that interested in newspapers," she said.

And he almost laughed. It was not meant with malice. It was only the way she saw it. Give her a wireless and the cool calm voice of the BBC newsreader and she was happy.

"Mind you," she added a good ten minutes later, "they're handy for lighting the fire."

This time he laughed. He wanted to hug her. But they didn't do hugs. "And good for keeping your fish supper warm."

"Aye. That, too."

Right up until the penultimate whistle and the answering blast from the engine, Mrs. McAllister kept sneaking looks around the station, in case criminals wielding open cutthroat razors were to come into the waiting room and attack them—even though it was the first-class waiting room, an unlikely place for gangsters, to her mind. But no one came.

Perth was the last major station before the climb up the foothills of the Grampians. There they would have a long wait to change to the train for the Highlands. Better than hanging around in the city, McAllister thought, and although he hadn't asked, he knew his mother would agree.

Even though no one he knew boarded the train at Perth, he was remembering her antics on the train to Largs and kept up a distant hope that Mary would appear. He found himself looking out the window at the River Tay, half hoping she, or Jimmy, would materialize in the compartment and they would joke about their adventures before dozing all across the high plateau. But nothing happened. And no one appeared.

As the train climbed through the narrow gorges deep in bracken and birch and pine, towards Pitlochery, and after heather and boulders the size of small houses, and tumbles of rocks, and white streaks of falling water began to replace the woodland, he gave up hope.

Throughout the journey over the Grampians, through the empty moorland and stark bare rounded mounds of mountains, with many lochs, large and small, breaking up the boggy vista of the high plateau, two thoughts kept nagging at him. Were Mary and Jimmy safe? And how did Gerry Dochery know he had a fiancée?

ELEVEN

The taxi driver dropped them off at the house with a cheery "Welcome to the Highlands, Mrs. McAllister."

"Is he a friend o' yours, John?" she asked her son.

"It's a small town," he explained. "Most people know me from the *Gazette*." He picked up her suitcase and his bag, looking around, expecting something to have changed. He had had a tumultuous few days; here the lawn had grown a fraction of an inch.

He could see his mother examining the polish on the brass door knocker and on the red doorstep, in judgment of the woman of the house. He was glad Joanne had the excuse of being unwell—*not herself*. A polished doorstep had never been one of her priorities, the garden taking up most of her attention. Even that would not pass the scrutiny of most gardeners, as Joanne hated uniform rows of dahlias and chrysanthemum. She loved wildflowers, she loved flowers in amongst the vegetables, she loved flowers and shrubs that attracted birds and butterflies and bees and would never complain if most of the fruit vanished before she'd gathered the crop—much to her mother-in-law's chagrin. "There's no strawberries left for the jam," Mrs. Ross would complain.

Joanne would laugh. "Och, well, the birds are happy."

As McAllister reached out for the doorknob, the door opened.

"Mr. McAllister," Granny Ross said. "And you must be Mrs.

McAllister." She had her pinny off, was in a twinset, and her hair had that recently permed look, with not a single crimped curl out of place. "Mr. McLeod said you'd be coming." She glared at McAllister, letting him know it should have been him who telephoned.

"Take yourselves into the sitting room, and I'll fetch the tea. Or would you like to see your room first?" Mrs. Ross then gave Mrs. McAllister a none too subtle countrywoman-meets-suspicious-city-person look. Mrs. McAllister returned the instant appraisal. McAllister had to look away in case they caught him smiling.

"Thank you, Mrs. Ross," he said. "Tea would be lovely."

"I'll bring it into the sitting room." This was another declaration of territorial rights; the kitchen was for family, the sitting room for guests.

The room was tidy. Barren even. The usual pile of discarded books and newspapers covering sofas and side table or in piles next to his armchair were gone. *All to impress my mother, no doubt.* "Where's Joanne?" he asked Granny Ross.

"Monday is the girls' piano lessons. Joanne's gone to talk to the teacher, find out how they're doing." It came out almost as a reprimand. *You've been gone less than a week and forgotten already,* she was implying.

"My John's been right worried about his fiancée. And the children." Mrs. McAllister was immediately on her son's defense. "It's good to hear Mrs. Ross is well enough to be out and about."

"I'll get the tea," Granny Ross replied.

"Don't go to any trouble on my behalf."

And I thought the McPhee situation was fraught, McAllister was thinking as he took his mother's suitcase up to the spare bedroom. He was about to remove his own clothes and books from the room but saw it had already been done. He knew Mrs. Ross had been told of his homecoming by Don. *Via Sandy, no doubt,* he thought, but somehow tidying up of his personal items felt intrusive.

"Joanne cleared out your books and things," Mrs. Ross told him when he came downstairs. "Annie is sharing with Joanne, so you are in her room."

Again he felt a frisson of disapproval. As his relationship with Joanne was yet unblessed by a legal, or religious, ceremony, they could not possibly be in a *shared* room. Not with Granny Ross there to safeguard their morals.

He heard the front door open. Jean arrived first. She ran up to him. Then stopped. Mrs. McAllister was struggling to rise from the armchair.

"Hello, dear. What's your name?"

"Jean." She was blushing. "My name is Jean Ross. I'm pleased to meet you." She gave a little bob of a curtsy.

Joanne came in, brushing past McAllister, her hair and skin smelling of fresh air. She went straight to his mother, took both her hands in hers and said, "Mrs. McAllister. How lovely to meet you at long last. John's told me so much about you."

Annie Ross had sidled up behind him. Though no one else heard her, he did. "John. Doesn't suit you, McAllister."

Joanne turned. "McAllister." She smiled. Then looked around, aware everyone was being formal. Suddenly, as often happened since her release from hospital, she looked ill at ease, shifting from one foot to the other. "Isn't this nice?" Her hand strayed to her hair. She pulled down a lock over her forehead, as though this would hide the scar from the wound, and the thin spot where her head had been shaved.

McAllister moved beside her and squeezed her hand. She squeezed back. Briefly. Then she went to the sideboard. "I picked some roses from the garden for your room." She brought over a vase with seven roses of mixed colors and presented them to Mrs.

McAllister. "Some people don't like flowers in a bedroom, so I thought I'd ask you first."

She's thinking of her own mother. McAllister knew this because on the long drive back to the Highlands after her father's funeral, Joanne had listed the many offenses she had committed as a child.

"Once, on my mother's birthday, I put flowers in their room. My father made me throw them out. He said everyone knew flowers in your bedroom stopped you sleeping properly."

It had broken his heart then, as it did now, to hear her talk like that. He hated that shame was an emotion she accepted as her due: shame her marriage had failed through no fault of hers; shame that she was weak and ill and suffering after a vicious attack that had left her barely alive; shame that she was the person she was—never quite good enough.

"They're lovely, dear," his mother said. "And what a lovely thought." She smiled up at her future daughter-in-law. "I'm ever so pleased to be here."

And Joanne smiled back. And McAllister was glad.

Over the next half hour, over tea and a chat, they relaxed. Annie spoke to his mother, told her she loved reading more than anything, and was going to be a writer.

"Like my son," Mrs. McAllister said.

"And my mum," Annie added.

"And I'm going to be a nurse," Jean told her.

They had supper in the dining room. Granny Ross had cleared away the girls' toys and drawing materials and set the table. Her glare at her eldest granddaughter stopped Annie from protesting at a peremptory clearing up of the room that had become a de facto study for her and an art studio for her sister. Annie was as fussy as McAllister when it came to her papers and books.

McAllister was wondering when he could have his first

whisky of the day when two incidents further inflamed what he later thought of as the guerrilla battle of the grannies.

"That was delicious, Mrs. Ross," he said as he finished the last spoonful of an elaborate trifle, normally served on Sundays.

"Thank you, Mr. McAllister." Granny Ross stood. "Annie, Jean, help me with the dishes."

"Let me help." His mother stood also.

"Not at all, you're our guest." Mrs. Ross senior instantly realized her mistake. As did Mrs. McAllister; in the status stakes, this was her son's house. Granny Ross busied herself stacking plates. "It's a long journey you've had . . ."

Then Jean, all of nine and a few months old, and with a sweetness that would serve her well should she become a nurse, said, "Granny McAllister, you have a rest. Then maybe later we could read a story together."

"A good idea. *Mrs.* McAllister must be tired." Granny Ross put full emphasis on the *Mrs.*

"I'm fine," Mrs. McAllister replied. "But thank you, Mrs. Ross. If we can have tea in the sitting room, Joanne and I can talk. We should get to know each other better, me and my soon-to-be daughter-in-law."

And I will definitely have that whisky, McAllister didn't say.

When Granny Ross had gone home for the night, when his mother and the girls were in bed, and with a whisky in one hand, a cigarette in the other, McAllister looked across at Joanne and said, "It's good to be home."

"Is it?"

Her reply was said lightly, with no malice, no agenda, but it pained him. It was as though she sensed his restlessness, his almost disloyalty. The excitement of the pursuit of a story was one thing, his questioning of a future life at a small newspaper in a small town another. His fascination with Mary Ballantyne he knew was bordering on improper.

"I'm glad you're back, McAllister." Joanne patted the space on the sofa beside her. "Come and sit here. Tell me about your adventures."

So he did. He told her of the ferry crossing to Millport, the fight on the beach, and the front-page headlines. He made it all fun. He had her laughing, marveling, at hearing it all firsthand.

"So Jimmy is fine?" she asked.

"Last I heard," he answered. He had left out the fire in the gym, the man's death. He did not tell her about the bare-knuckle fight he'd witnessed, the brutality of the scene. There was no mention of the attack in the close outside his mother's flat and their flight, just the evening before, on the milk train. No need to worry her, he decided.

"I'd liked to have had a career like this Mary," she said, "but . . ." She shrugged.

"Aye, she has a future ahead of her," he agreed.

"My future is here." She looked around as though puzzled as to how she'd arrived at this place.

"Mine too."

He hadn't meant to convey any doubt, but she intuited his hesitancy and shivered slightly. It was not a conversation she wanted, not now. "Sorry. It's past my bedtime." She leaned over and kissed him lightly. "Night-night, sleep tight."

"You too."

He was hoping she hadn't sensed the tremor her parting words sent though his conscience. *Night-night, sleep tight*—Mary's words, Mary's benediction.

As he heard her close the bedroom door, the clock in the hallway chimed. *Ten. They'll be putting the finishing touches to the first edition of the* Herald. *I wonder if Sandy has anything fresh on this story.*

He wanted to phone him. He wanted to talk to Mary. He needed to be there, on the newsroom floor, hearing the constant tap of typewriter keys, the ping of the return carriage, the shouts of "copy" and the copyboys darting between desks, fetching the articles, dropping them into the sub-editor's tray, running for tea, for cigarettes, back-chatting with the reporters, laughing as they learned their trade, relishing the fast and furious chase towards another deadline on the best newspaper in the country.

Next morning on the walk to the *Gazette* office, McAllister was looking forward to talking to someone, anyone, about his adventures—for that is how they seemed in retrospect. In the city, he and his colleagues would have finished the shift, gone to the pub, where he would retell the story, in language that would have been ripe, in a dialect incomprehensible to outsiders. They would share details and opinions that the libel laws would never allow them to publish. Much laughter and mocking later, he would sleep deeply, ready to chase the excitement of the next breaking story. And in that city there were many.

"Morning, all," he said as he walked into the reporters' room.

"Just in time." Don McLeod squinted up at him. "I need you to finish this report on the redevelopment of Bridge Street." He shoved some typed pages at the editor.

Rob McLean laughed. "Serves you right for coming back early, McAllister."

"I didn't notice you were away until yesterday," Hector Bain, the photographer, said.

McAllister grinned at Hector, who was not known for

noticing much, unless it was through a lens. "Glad to hear I've been missed," he replied.

"So did you find what you were looking for?" Rob asked.

"Later," Don told them. "Let's get some work done, and we can talk later."

"You could come over to my house . . ." McAllister thought of the two grannies, the two girls, and Joanne, and wasn't sure their usual gathering place was such a good idea.

"We will, but tonight," Don told him. "How about nine?" He had a shrewd idea what was happening in McAllister's life.

"Nine it is," he replied, knowing most of his household would be off to bed.

It was mid-afternoon when the call came through. McAllister was alone in his office, staring out the window, unable to concentrate on the editorial, thinking of Mary, Jimmy, their escapade in Millport, wondering if they were safe, wondering if . . . The telephone bell startled him.

"There's a lady on the line for you," came Fiona's voice, with the emphasis on *lady*. "Putting you through."

It was only a moment before he heard the click on the line as the trunk call was connected. And he was unaware of his mouth stretching into a grin. "Mary, where . . ."

"Mr. McAllister. This is Jane Ballantyne. Mary's mother." The cool tone, the way her words sounded—a micropause between every syllable—conveyed her disapproval. "I have a message from my daughter . . ."

"Where is she? Is she okay?"

"Mr. McAllister. Even if I knew exactly where Mary is, I would not tell you—a man who put my daughter's life in danger . . ."

One of those women whose every wish is a command, he surmised.

"As for the company to whom you have introduced her . . ."

So Jimmy was with Mary. "I'm sorry you feel that way, but it is Mary's job to associate with—" He was no match for Jane Ballantyne. She cut off his sentence with as much emotion as one of the High Court judges in her family sentencing a man to the scaffold.

"Mary has asked me to tell you that they are well. She has borrowed my car and has taken Mr. McPhee"—she managed to imbue the name McPhee with all the distaste and venom of a woman mentioning the serial killer Peter Manuel—"to a place of safety. She strongly advised that you return home, but I surmise you have already done so."

"So where are—"

"I have no wish to engage in a conversation. Goodbye, Mr. McAllister."

He was left holding the receiver, listening to the dial tone, and feeling like cursing the woman. "Where are you, Mary Ballantyne? And why couldn't you call me yourself?" But no one answered.

McAllister was not looking forward to the evening.

After Don McLeod arrived—his mother had stayed up long enough to be introduced before excusing herself, saying it was past her bedtime—and after Rob arrived on his motorbike, making enough noise to alert the neighborhood, and after Annie came downstairs in her pajamas to inspect everyone, say hello, then go back upstairs satisfied she knew what was happening, they settled down to talk.

McAllister and Don attacked the whisky decanter. Rob had wine, Joanne a cup of tea. And the conversation began.

"There will be a major story in tomorrow's *Herald*. No names mentioned—this time—but I was there on the Isle of Cumbrae and have written an article about the fracas."

Joanne had been listening to the first part of McAllister's tale, then decided it was not a conversation she wanted to hear more of. "My bedtime," she said, and came across, laid a hand on McAllister's sleeve, smiling at Rob and Don and saying, "It's lovely to have the old crew together again."

"Aye, it is," Don replied.

Rob stood. Hugged her. "Sleep tight," he said.

She smiled. "With these pills the doctor gave me, I'm out like a light."

It was a reminder to them all of her condition. And Rob's. When he and McAllister had gone to Joanne's rescue, he had inadvertently killed a woman. That memory was not gone, though it was well buried.

Hearing the sound of the bedroom door shutting, McAllister relaxed. He refilled Don's glass and his own. Rob helped himself to more wine. The alcohol worked its magic.

"There might also be a small piece on an attack on me outside my mother's flat," McAllister added.

"Jings," Rob said, "you've been busy."

"You'd better fill us in," Don told him.

McAllister gave a quick description of the crime scene in Glasgow, the turf wars over protection rackets, loan-sharking, illegal bookmaking, and illegal boxing matches.

"I thought thon fights had died out long since," Don said. "Except in Ireland."

Giving Don and Rob the details about the boxing club fire and about the retired boxer who hid Jimmy McPhee and paid with his life, he then told them of the ex-boxer Jock McBride on the island.

"I remember reading about him," Don commented. "He was good."

"Jimmy's old friends are doing their best to help Jimmy. Whether all this ties in with the bare-knuckle matches or not, we don't know."

Don noted the "we" but said nothing.

McAllister then described the fight in Millport, and Jimmy's escape on the fishing coble with Mary Ballantyne.

Rob was enjoying the tale. "It's like the plot of *Kidnapped!*"

McAllister left out the part about the donkey. It all seemed surreal enough without the donkey, and that was a story he wanted to laugh about with Glasgow friends, friends who knew and understood the city. And Mary.

To outsiders, it would sound bizarre: a fight with cutthroat razors, in front of at least seventy witnesses and a Salvation Army band, and no one intervening. In the city, in the impoverished, overcrowded, insanitary streets and alleyways and closes, when fights broke out—even fights to the death—if they took place in public in the daylight, everyone would look the other way, and say nothing. Everyone, the police included, accepted this as the code of the streets.

No wonder the city fathers want to clear the slums and move people out to the new high-rise schemes on the fringes of the city, McAllister had heard more than once from nice respectable middle-class professionals in their nice respectable tree-filled suburbs.

"As to who is after Jimmy," McAllister continued, "no one knows—"

"Except your old pal Gerry Dochery—" Don said.

"And he's not likely to tell, is he?" Rob asked.

"I know." McAllister sighed. He didn't want to think about Gerry Dochery. The trip to Millport had reminded him of the good times. After winning his scholarship to Glasgow High School he had seen Gerry only twice—at his father's funeral, and at the funeral of his younger brother. Nothing of that funeral had registered, so even if he had talked to Gerry, he would not remember. But he was glad Gerry had come—for his mother's sake.

"Although it seems to connect with boxing, and it's most

likely about money, I can't find any reason for someone wanting to kill—harm—Jimmy." He changed the word when he registered the shock on Rob's face.

"Not a good idea if you're wanting your money," Don said, staring at his hands, which seemed to be moving with a life of their own. Something was bothering him and he couldn't fathom what.

"Kill him?" Rob asked, his voice low, flat, his stare somewhere beyond the cypress tree outside the bay window.

"I'm sure it's only threats." McAllister saw that Rob was not reassured.

By now the light had dimmed, and the first stars were beginning to pop up in the washed-out navy-blue sky. Don sighed and stretched his shoulders. "Time to be off to ma bed. You'll speak to Jenny McPhee, will you?"

"Tomorrow," McAllister promised.

He saw them out. He watched them walk out into the street, Rob to his motorbike, Don towards the hill and his house in Church Street.

He went back to the sitting room to clear up the glasses. But once again he was waylaid by a final dram, a book, and a record. With the volume low, the piano player reached him in a way nothing else could. Thelonious Monk, "'Round Midnight." It was a tune of loneliness, of aloneness, a tune that, on first hearing, had become McAllister's theme song.

Past three o'clock, nearer to four, he awoke. His back and neck were stiff from sleeping in the armchair. The book had fallen to the floor and the bookmark had fallen out—something he hated—the whisky decanter was empty, and dawn was sending out the hesitant glow over the northern hills enveloping the town.

He stood, then changed his mind; instead of heading

upstairs, he made for the sofa, pulled down the multicolored blanket Granny Ross had crocheted, and went back to sleep.

Next evening, after supper, he excused himself, telling his mother and Joanne and the girls that he had to meet with Jenny McPhee.

"Can I come?" Annie asked.

McAllister looked surprised.

"I heard she's a witch and I want to talk to her because I'm writing a composition about witches for history," Annie explained.

His mother's eyebrows were raised. Joanne was trying not to laugh. And seeing that Annie was completely earnest, he said, "Maybe another time." He saw she was about to argue and held up his hand. "Not tonight, Annie. But I will mention it. Promise."

As he was walking into the hallway to fetch his hat, he overheard his mother say to Joanne, "She's quite a character, your eldest." But her tone was not disapproving.

Out of the mouths of babes and sucklings, he thought as he left, not at all looking forward to the encounter with Jenny McPhee.

"So you've no idea where our Jimmy is," Jenny stated, coming straight to the point, letting McAllister know her displeasure before he'd had a chance to take off his hat, greet her, or order a drink.

"I was told he is safe," he said. Then he sat down, asked after her health, inquired if she wanted a drink, then ordered. Since their meeting last week, he thought he could detect extra lines on the map on her forehead.

"Don't worry, McAllister." She'd been letting him squirm before telling him, "I know where ma Jimmy is, or at least in what part o' the world."

"Perthshire?"

"Aye, and in a castle, no less."

McAllister began to laugh. He had guessed a tinker's camp. He had no idea Mary would put Jimmy in the family castle. But it made sense. Whoever was looking for him was obviously intelligent, would know where the Traveling clans gathered, and might even risk an attack there. Who would guess that a McPhee of the road would be hiding in a castle owned by one of the most illustrious families of the land, a family with more lawyers than the Nuremberg Trials?

"So how did you find out where Jimmy is?"

Jenny glared at him. "My Jimmy knows his letters. And I can read." *A wee bit, anyhow,* she was thinking. "And there's such a thing as the Royal Mail even in Muir of Ord."

"Is he coming home?"

"That's where you come in," said Jenny. "He needs to know it's safe. Jimmy says thon lass Mary told him you're the only one who can find out."

Thanks, Mary, he thought.

"All this would never have come to our door if Jimmy hadn't . . ." She downed her whisky, obviously a Laphroaig, in one swallow.

"So you do know what's going on."

"No I don't. I'm only guessing."

Or it's the legendary second sight. Then he remembered Annie's request. "Annie, Joanne's daughter, wants to ask you about witches."

It was Jenny's turn to laugh. "Does she now? Well, tell her I'll call round one day, see how her mother is doing, and we can all have a right good chat."

The thought of Jenny McPhee, Granny Ross, and his mother in the same house made him think of cats in a sack. "That would be grand, Jenny. I'll let Annie know."

When he left, Jenny McPhee called through the hatch to

the main bar for another dram. Then she sat back to think. She well knew why all the trouble was happening. But it was now clear McAllister knew nothing. *Should I tell him?* She considered the price her son was paying to be well beyond his obligation to Joanne Ross. But Jimmy had told her it had been his choice to help Joanne, then and now. His parting words to his mother, *and not a word to McAllister*, she remembered well.

"What's done is done," Jenny muttered to herself, pulling her coat tight as though an evil wind had somehow managed to penetrate the thick walls of the small room, in the drear bar, in an insalubrious district, in the small Highland town.

"Where's thon whisky?" she shouted.

"Haud your horses, it's coming."

She looked up, saw her second son standing in the doorway. She nodded.

"Took your time, Jimmy lad." Her hand was trembling as she accepted the glass.

TWELVE

Breakfast was chaotic with two grandmothers vying for the cooker and the frying pan, two children arguing over whose turn it was to set the table, and Joanne in the sitting room, practicing scales on the piano.

"I have some work to catch up on," McAllister said and left for the peace and quiet at the *Gazette*.

On the staircase to his office he smelled carbolic soap. It must have been strong, as his sense of smell was not the best, being a smoker of long standing. As he opened the door he was greeted with a curt "I haven't finished here" from the cleaner whom he had inherited when he became the first outsider appointed as editor. He didn't know her name; he seldom arrived in the office at the ungodly hour—for a journalist—of eight o'clock in the morning.

He walked back down to the High Street. He stood at the top of Bridge Street, looking down towards the stone arches of the bridge.

Soon to be demolished, he remembered. Although he knew how inconvenient the old bridge was, the newfangled plans to demolish the bridge and replace it with another of no architectural merit whatsoever pained him, as did the plans to destroy the lovely but inconvenient rows of eighteenth- and nineteenth-century houses and offices and shops, and replace them with hideous, to his mind, boxes.

It will soon be the nineteen-sixties, the planners were quoted as saying, we have to move with the times.

Aye, McAllister thought, *but at what cost to our heritage, our history?*

He turned back once more, making for the office. Once more he climbed the stairs and went into the reporters' room. The smell here was of stale tobacco, but that he didn't notice.

He sat. He rolled a sheet of paper into a typewriter and stared at it for minutes. He was lost. He felt he was neither here nor in Glasgow, not at the *Gazette* or the *Herald.* His home was no longer the refuge he looked forward to at the end of a day, where excitement was a book and music. He was not sleeping well, not even sure which bed was his. And he dared not think about Joanne. The thought he couldn't rid himself of—*she's not herself*—was even stronger after a trip away.

Thoughts of Mary Ballantyne made his stomach curdle. "For God's sakes, McAllister, grow up," he muttered to himself.

"Talking to yourself, first sign of madness, you know." Rob McLean was also in early.

McAllister looked at him. The cheery, handsome former boy-reporter was now a fully qualified journalist. And a man. *And he is no longer the old Rob either.* McAllister saw how thin he was, how his cheekbones had hollowed out, how his eyes seemed less blue, his hair less yellow, and, most of all, he was smoking.

"It's early for you," was all McAllister said.

"We weren't expecting you back so soon, so lots to do."

Don McLeod ambled in. "McAllister," he said. Now three cigarettes were contaminating the air of the narrow high-ceilinged room. "You heard about Jimmy McPhee?"

"I heard he's safe."

"Aye, he was telling us a wee bit about his adventures," Don said.

"Jimmy's here?" McAllister was astounded. "I thought he was in Perthshire."

"He was. Now he's here. I saw him last night—down the pub with Jenny. Said you an' thon lass Mary saved his life—"

"Where is he? I want a word with him." McAllister was not happy. He'd sacrificed a lot to help Jimmy McPhee and felt he was owed at least an explanation.

"They'll be long gone by now." Don was looking at the big clock high on the wall, the clock they lived by on deadline day. "Off to the wilds before daybreak, so they said."

"You'll have to talk to me instead." Mary Ballantyne stood in the doorway, grinning. In wine-colored corduroy trousers and Aertex sports top with a faded school emblem embroidered on the pocket, she looked like a heroine from the Chalet School books.

"Take a seat, lass," Don said.

McAllister was nonplussed at seeing Mary Ballantyne in the *Gazette* office. "I wasn't expecting you here." It sounded begrudging. And it was. She was his Glasgow friend. She had no place in the Highlands.

Rob was captivated. Mary Ballantyne, legendary crime reporter on the *Herald*, was here, in their office, and much younger than he'd expected from her reputation. He recovered enough to say, "Hello, I'm Rob McLean," and hold out his hand.

She took it. "I enjoyed the articles you've been sending the *Herald*," she said. "I was sorry to hear about you and Joanne Ross. It must have been traumatic."

"It was," Rob said as he fell in love.

"So," Don interrupted—he had a newspaper to assemble. "How much of Jimmy's story can we publish?"

"None of it," Mary answered.

"How no?" Don asked.

A long conversation began, with interruptions—from Fiona on reception putting through essential phone inquiries; from Frankie Urquhart, the advertising manager, about the layout; from Hector Bain, delivering photographs; and from Rob or Don breaking off to attend to an article that needed correcting.

When the numerous clocks around town rang out twelve o'clock, Mary announced, "I'm starving."

"Me too," Rob said. "I'll take you to my favorite café." He meant the one with the new jukebox. "We can have a sandwich there."

"Brilliant."

"Before you young things escape, let's sum this up," Don said. He nodded toward McAllister, knowing that with his sense of drama, and knack for summary, the editor was best at this.

McAllister held up his left hand. Pointing upwards with his pinkie finger, he said, "Jimmy is safe—"

"For now," Mary interrupted.

McAllister nodded. "Maybe. But he's a hard man to track down on his home turf."

Next he held up his ring finger. "We still don't know who is after him . . ." He watched Mary shrug her shoulders in a "search-me" gesture. He raised his middle finger. "Or why." He missed the glance between Don and Mary, as neither of them moved their heads, only their eyes meeting across the table.

"As well as being a Queensberry boxer, Jimmy McPhee was once reputed to be a bare-knuckle fighter. When I asked him, he didn't answer." Mary seemed hesitant and, seeing McAllister's eyebrows shoot heavenwards, laughed. "Actually, he did answer. He told me to mind my own business—or words to that effect."

She would never admit it to anyone, but Jimmy McPhee intimidated her. In their time together she'd been uncomfortable, not with the long silences but by the way, when she asked what she thought were legitimate questions, he would turn with his whole body, stare at her, say nothing, then turn away again. Once—and that was enough to silence her—he'd said, "Ask no questions, Miss Ballantyne, an' you'll never be disappointed."

"It's my job," she'd replied.

"Aye, but me an' ma family, don't you be using us to make a name for yersel'."

Don broke into her recollections. "There was big money in bare-knuckle boxing, but to my knowledge, it's rare now."

"Do you know if Gerry Dochery is involved in those fights?" Mary asked McAllister.

"No idea." She gave him a look that he took to mean, *Haven't you asked?* He felt completely out of touch. Which he was.

"I'd no idea those fights were still being staged." Using his forefinger he continued, "So, point four. Jimmy is safe, so is it still our business?"

"You mean, is there still a story in it?" As ever, Mary went straight to the point.

"I'm glad I'm not involved," Rob said. "I don't think I can cope with any more drama. His voice was low. They all heard.

"You're right, it is not *your* business," Mary told them. "But it is mine. I have a job to do, and this story is too good to drop."

The phone rang. Don answered. He handed the receiver to McAllister. It was Joanne.

"Will you be home soon?" she asked. "Granny Ross wants to know how many to cook for."

"I'm really sorry, I've too much to do," he said, hating himself for being so cowardly. "But I'll be home by five. Let's go for a walk before supper, just you and me."

"I'd like that." Her breathing was distinct, as though she was making the call at the end of a march across moorland. "See you later then."

"That was Joanne," he said to an almost empty office. Rob

and Mary's chatter was echoing up the stone staircase. He felt excluded. He wanted to hear about the escape with Jimmy, the boat ride, Perthshire. He wanted the companionship of Mary, the excitement. He tipped back on the stool, holding onto the table. *No fool like an auld fool.* He was furious with himself. He considered changing his mind and going home. Then he remembered the grannies. "Let's you and me get a beer," he said to Don.

"My kind of lunch," Don replied.

Later in the bright afternoon, and after rewriting the editorial twice, McAllister finished off the mundane stories that made up that week's newspaper. His thoughts were constantly wandering; trying to find an explanation as to who was so desperate to find Jimmy. And why.

Mary appeared.

"So how's the Highlands?" Don asked.

"A foreign country," Mary answered.

"Aye, we are that." He was not in the least offended; indeed, was proud of the schism between Highlanders and Lowlanders. "Different race, too."

"Stubborn Celts!" Mary laughed. "I've been to the Highlands as a child, staying with friends near Beauly." She didn't elaborate, *In a castle.* "I love it. Here it's not pretty like Perthshire. There is grandeur in the glens. I love the emptiness, but it feels forbidding the way the mountains rear up like monsters in nightmares. I remember one holiday, our family friends took us out on a picnic. It was a glorious morning and terrifying by mid-afternoon. I've never seen such rain and mist, everything dripping, trees, rocks, and rushing burns turned into waterfalls. We could barely get across and back to the Land Rover. As for these Highland sheep standing, staring, giving you the evil eye, I was terrified of them. Still don't like them, nasty beasts."

"Great Sunday roast, though, specially with mint sauce." Rob was grinning. He was smitten with Mary and didn't mind who knew it. "And your escapade with the infamous Jimmy McPhee?" he asked. "What happened?"

"Now, that is a long story." She suddenly looked tired. Younger.

McAllister was glad Rob had asked, as he had been working out how to broach the subject himself.

"Let's go to your place, McAllister," Rob said. Turning to Mary, he explained, "That's where we usually convene when we need to—"

"Plot?" She grinned.

"Be off with you, young Mary, I need these two to concentrate for one more hour," Don told her. "We can hear of your adventures later." It was not that Don took the threats to Jimmy's life lightly, more that he wanted McAllister back in the Highlands, safe, and married. He was unable to say why, but he sensed an undercurrent between Miss Mary Ballantyne and the editor. He did not blame Mary. Nor McAllister. But he thought there was nothing more foolish than a middle-aged man enthralled with a young woman.

"See you back here later," Mary said and left them to put the finishing touches to a newspaper that, although she could see was above the ordinary, held no interest for her.

McAllister was home by five o'clock as promised. The girls were surprised. Annie looked at him, saying, "What are you doing home so early?" She sounded so much like a mother-in-law, he nearly laughed out loud.

"I'm going for a walk with your mother."

"Can I come too?"

"Not this time, we—"

He was saved by *his* mother. "I thought we were going to make a rhubarb crumble together."

"Goodie!" Jean said, and the girls followed their new granny to the kitchen.

Joanne suggested to her mother-in-law that she go home early. "Thanks, Granny Ross, we'll manage to get supper tonight." She smiled.

The reply was a harrumph and a muttered, "I can see when I'm not wanted."

Again McAllister felt like laughing, but the frown from Joanne made him behave himself.

At the garden gate, they instinctively turned to the street that led to the river. He offered her his arm. She accepted. Keeping close, they walked slowly, taking in the smell of gardens—roses, wallflowers, annual flowers McAllister could not identify but, he was certain, Joanne would know the names of.

"Did you find Jimmy?" Joanne asked.

"He's back here, so I heard, but I haven't seen him."

"Jenny will be pleased."

They came to the steep street leading to the steps that would take them down the side of St. Columba's church to the river, and the gentle stroll along the banks to the Islands.

They chatted about the girls, the grannies, and all the small events that made up ordinary safe lives. No mention was made of Joanne's trauma. When asked, all she said was, "The doctors say I'm doing fine."

McAllister kept to himself his brush with the darkness of the city and the gangs. Then Joanne reminded him of the one event he hadn't forgotten about, yet hadn't remembered—the wedding.

"It's only six weeks away," she said. "And thank goodness we're having a quiet wedding. I couldn't cope with too many people. Granny Ross was insisting on having a party at your house. I told her thanks, but Chiara has already offered and I've accepted. She was not best pleased." Joanne was frowning. She hadn't meant to offend, but she was finding the busyness and the fussing weari-some.

"Then, as it was a wee white lie saying she'd offered, I had to telephone Chiara and tell her she was doing the catering. She was delighted. 'That's what best friends are for,' Chiara said. Think of it, McAllister, wonderful Italian food—and wine. And our closest friends and your mother, it will be lovely." She was smiling, eyes bright. He could feel her happiness coming through her hand, which was holding on lightly to his, could feel the heat, her flesh on his flesh.

He was stunned. *Six weeks?* He struggled for words. "Marvel-ous." He'd known the date of the wedding—the thirty-first of July. If he'd thought about it he'd have known that was six weeks away—dates were hard to avoid when you were a newspaper edi-tor. But only six weeks away? "Weddings can be stressful. Are you sure you're well enough?" he asked.

"Getting cold feet?" she teased.

"Never," he answered.

Yet somehow the rest of the walk through the Islands, under tunnels of trees, over the river shimmering in the late sun like the breast feathers on a golden eagle, over swaying suspension bridges and along the opposite bank, felt like a fantasy. *This is not my life*, was the phrase that kept popping up, that he kept trying to sup-press.

Passing the cathedral, the sun low in the west, he knew. *You have no choice. You can't let her down.*

Seeing a taxi, he hailed it. She smiled as he helped her in. "Thanks, I was dreading the climb up St. Stephen's Brae."

As he opened the front door, the smell of cooking and the chatter of voices came echoing down the hallway. He heard laugh-ter. Mary Ballantyne. The sound disturbed him in ways he did not want to think about.

"There you are, we've just been talking about you." Rob came up to Joanne, put his arm around her shoulder, then made the introduction as though showing off a new girlfriend.

"Joanne—Mary Ballantyne," Rob said. "Mary is the star crime reporter on the *Herald*."

"I've heard so much about you." She smiled up at Joanne, who was a good six inches taller.

McAllister stepped back into the recess in the hallway. He could not bear to see Mary with the others. *She doesn't belong here, she's . . .* By the umbrella stand, with coats hanging each side, in the long narrow mirror, he saw his reflection and was ashamed. *Why shouldn't they meet? Why do I want Mary Ballantyne locked away in another, separate part of my life?*

"Welcome to the Highlands," he heard Joanne say.

"I'm only here for two nights," Mary said, "but I walked around town this afternoon, really bonnie."

"I smell pudding, I hope there's enough for me." Don McLeod came in to join them. He made straight for Mrs. McAllister, taking her hand, saying, "Donal McLeod. I've the honor of working with your son."

McAllister was momentarily distracted as he wondered at Don. From his mother's shy smile he could see she had made a friend, a rare occurrence in her life. *But they are contemporaries, Don is my father's age,* he reminded himself.

That Don McLeod also took to Mary Ballantyne made McAllister admire her all the more. And he could see what she had done for Rob; in the morning's discussion she had briefly acknowledged the shadow he, they, were living with, the consequences of the attack on Joanne. But Don's bringing her to his house to meet Joanne made him more than uncomfortable; he was jealous, and confused, and annoyed with himself. *Grow up,* he was thinking.

Supper of ham and salad and new potatoes, followed by the rhubarb crumble and egg custard, disappeared fast, and was much appreciated. Especially the crumble.

Mary and Joanne talked comfortably, easily. They asked which schools they'd gone to. They discovered they could have played each other at hockey, if not for the five-year age difference.

McAllister did not join in the conversation; his working-class socialist prejudices he kept in check. *What school did you go to? Who asked questions like that except the privileged?*

He hadn't noticed when the new subject came up, but when he looked across at Joanne he saw her laughing—the first time in a long time.

"Now you've discovered our guilty secret, McAllister," Mary said. She was looking at him, seeing in him something she couldn't quite fathom. It was as though she was reappraising him, seeing him differently in this setting of domesticity. *Or maybe it's my paranoia.* "A passion for the love stories in the *People's Friend*."

Mary turned her spotlight back on Joanne. "I have to hide my copies from my mother, else she gives them to our housekeeper—before I've even read them."

"I pretend I buy them for the recipes," Joanne said.

How do women do that? As soon as they get together it becomes a conspiracy.

The girls disappeared, happy to be put to bed by Mrs. McAllister, but not before Annie reminded Mary of her promise to write to her. "Promise. Guides' honor," Mary said, and gave Annie the Girl Guides salute, which Annie returned.

When they went into the sitting room, Joanne said, "That's me for the night. Can't keep my eyes open a minute longer." She walked over to McAllister, kissed him on the head. She looked at the others. "Night, all. And Mary, let's keep in touch."

"Love to," Mary replied. They both knew that was unlikely

and if asked why, neither would be able to answer. "I'm happy we met," Mary added.

The summer night was dimming and the whisky bottle diminished by three-quarters as Mary continued the conversation, filling them in on her "big adventure" with Jimmy McPhee—a phrase she used deliberately, trying to diminish the fear. Mostly her fear.

Later, when the gloaming had truly set in, and just before McAllister switched on the standard lamp and table lights, Mary admitted being terrified by the realization that the men on the beach were willing to pull out open razors in front of dozens of spectators, if not a hundred, showing no fear of the consequences. "But we were saved by the ponies—and McAllister, remember that poor donkey?"

Rob enjoyed the account of the braying donkey, the furious Shetland ponies, laughing at her account of the gangster being kicked in the family jewels.

"We were lucky the fisherman had enough fuel to get us to the mainland. And we were really lucky there was a train leaving two minutes after we got to Largs," she continued, leaving out the pain in her side, the sweating terror of the race for the harbor, and the train, and safety.

"When we got to Glasgow, I borrowed my mother's car and immediately left for Perthshire."

She left out the description of her mother's reaction when she introduced Jimmy McPhee. But she could recall every syllable of the icy upper-class voice saying, "McPhee. Are you related to the McPhees of Blairgowrie?"

"Ma couseens," Jimmy replied, hardening his Muir of Ord accent, staring at her, defying her to show him the door, as she ordinarily would when a tinker came calling.

"We need the car," Mary said.

"And if I require the use of the car?"

"There's a bus stop outside out door," Mary replied. She did not add that it was she who paid the road tax and for the petrol and the servicing of the old Jaguar—her late father's pride and joy.

Mary continued, not relating how fast she'd flung the heavy car around the bends on the road to the foothills of the Grampians. "When we arrived, Jimmy looked up and saw the turrets. He asked if this was Colonel Ballantyne's place. I said it was. *Used to steal apples from the orchard when we were bairns*, he said."

"That's tinkers for ye," Don quipped.

"I asked him about his family, his life on the road," Mary continued, "but he didn't say much."

"That's Jimmy for you," Rob added, grinning at Don.

"But did he say why these men are after him?" McAllister asked. "And who they are?"

"He did say he knows the man who wants him—"

"Wants him hurt? Maimed? Killed? And for what?" He watched her considering her reply.

"It's a debt, goes back a few years . . ."

"You mean we might have been killed over money?" McAllister was furious. "If that's all it is, I can pay."

"I pay ma own debts, thanks all the same." Jimmy had come in.

If it had been a ghost McAllister would have been less surprised. The others were smiling. Jimmy helped himself to the decanter, then gestured to Mary to move over, and sat on the sofa beside her. From the chair directly opposite Jimmy, Rob nodded. "Good to see you alive." Although somewhat afraid of Jimmy, he was always glad to see him.

McAllister now remembered how, on more than one occasion, Jimmy had startled him with a sudden silent appearance in this house. In a bar, in open countryside, or down a dark alley, he had a specter-like ability to turn up when least expected, sometimes wanted, sometimes not. This time his face was also specter-like, his usual working-outdoors-in-all-weathers tan now grey. His cheekbones were more prominent, and he looked leaner, smaller, more whippet than greyhound.

"I'm not stopping long," Jimmy began. "I've only come to thank you." His eyes met McAllister's, and, giving him the prison-yard stare, he said, "And to tell you it's over as far as you're concerned. You too," he said to Mary but still looking at McAllister.

McAllister stared back. "First you want my help, now—"

"Ma *mother*—she was one who asked. No me." It was clear from the way he rolled the "r" at the end of "mother" that was unhappy with her decision.

Don felt the tension and broke in. "Maybe you should settle this wi' a round o' bare-knuckle boxing." When McAllister looked away he continued, "So, Jimmy, I hear your mother has gone?"

"Aye, she's taken to the road."

"Fine time o' year to be out on the open road," Don said. "I envy her the freedom, the nights around the campfire, sleeping under the stars."

Jimmy dropped his hard-man persona. He was tired. He wanted to be with his mother, his people. "Aye, me too. But she'll be back for the Black Isle Show. Never missed one yet."

"And back for the wedding. Joanne has asked her to sing," Don said.

McAllister let the remark go, even though this was news to him. He was watching Mary watching Jimmy, noticing how quiet she was. *Perhaps she learned on the trip north that Jimmy doesn't do conversation.*

He'd known Jimmy McPhee three years. But he would never say he knew him. He knew his reputation as a hard man, sergeant-at-arms to his mother, who was matriarch of the McPhees of the North East of Scotland and related to most of the other Traveler families of Scotland through ancient and convoluted marriage bonds.

Jimmy knocked back the generous dram he'd poured himself. "I'm sorry ma ma involved you, McAllister. But I thank you all the same."

He turned his eyes on Mary, and she flinched slightly. "Miss Ballantyne, I owe you, so I'll tell you straight. This man who's after me has no respect. Makes no difference to him you're a woman, a wee scrap o' a thing. If you keep on writing about his business, he'll go for you." What the man's business was he wouldn't say.

When Mary tried to speak, Jimmy held up his hand. "Naw, he'll no' have you killed, he's no' that stupid, but rearranging yer bonny face wi' a razor, or chopping off yer fingers so ye canny write no more, that's his style."

He stood. "Night, McAllister. Mr. McLeod. Thanks again, Miss Ballantyne." As he walked past Rob he stopped and said quietly, "You an' all. You've had enough troubles lately, so no getting ideas in yer head about investigating or whatever you ca' it." He squeezed Rob's shoulder. It hurt, a reminder to Rob that Jimmy was not a man to cross.

Then Jimmy McPhee of the Highland McPhees was gone, as silently as he had arrived. Only the sound of an engine starting broke the hush of the evening.

"I'm away home an' all," Don said. "Good to meet you, lass. If you're ever in need o' a job . . ."

"I'm way too ambitious, and expensive, for you, Mr. McLeod." She smiled as she said it.

He laughed. "Right enough."

Mary turned to Rob. "We should be getting back, too," she said.

"Mary's staying at our house tonight," Rob explained.

"Then first thing in the morning"—she grinned—"that's journalists' time, so maybe nine o'clock, I'm driving back to Glasgow." She shook McAllister's hand. "It's been fun."

He wanted to say, *Stay*. He wanted to hear more. He needed an explanation—of Jimmy's troubles, yes, but also of what had passed between her and Jimmy McPhee. What would happen next? Would they remain friends? Would he count in her life? So many questions. And no answers; it was no longer his business.

As Mary and Rob walked down the path to the car, in the still night their voices were clear. McAllister could hear her chatting as happily as a child who'd been to a birthday party. "My mother will be having hysterics if she's without the car any longer. Not that she needs it . . ."

McAllister was left with the remains of the evening and the remains of his fantasies. And, as he shut the front door, he hated himself for being such a fool, *and an old fool at that*.

THIRTEEN

Domesticity and routine returned to McAllister's household. For a day.

Joanne was distracted but in a loving, smiling, vague way.

"Now, where did I put the scissors?" she'd ask. Or "McAllister, have you any idea if we invited your colleague Sandy Marshall to the wedding?" He didn't want to remind her that she had been the one to insist he ask Sandy to be his best man and that Sandy had agreed.

Jean was being her sweet and smiling self, sometimes too eager to please everyone, including her cat, but there was a touch of anxiety in the child's unwillingness to leave her mother's side, her nervousness every time the district nurse visited.

Annie read. Constantly. But McAllister was occasionally disconcerted by the way she would look over her book, examining him as though expecting the worst. On one occasion, when he had to attend an evening function with the bigwigs of the County Council, and when Joanne did not feel up to accompanying him, Annie had asked, "Do you have to go?"

Joanne had said, "It's McAllister's job—he's the newspaper's editor." And Annie shot him a glare of disapproval and contempt—a look that said, *What's more important than my mum?* A look he had seen before from children trapped in war zones. *She is a child of domestic violence,* he reminded himself, *and recently, she saw her mother in hospital, badly injured.*

That his mother and Granny Ross were waging a guerrilla campaign over the kitchen he found amusing, in very small doses. And his mother, who neither approved nor disapproved of her son, kept to her room mostly. "I'm right tired," she said. But he knew it was shock. She would never tell him that he was a stranger to her, having lost him when, after he started at Glasgow High School, he denied he was from Dennistoun, and refused to wear the jumpers or socks she knitted, wanting only shop-bought clothing they could ill afford. They did not have a relationship where, if she told him what a petty tyrant he had been as a thirteen-year-old, they would laugh, he would tell her he was ashamed and apologize, and Joanne would tease him and tell his mother how much he would love hand-knitted socks now, especially if they were black.

And McAllister was unable to admit how much he was missing the peace of his bachelor days, the excitement of the city, the loss of his youth. No, these were not issues that affected him, John McAllister, former war correspondent, former big shot, or so he told himself. Most of all, he was unable to see that he was scared.

The *Gazette* office became his refuge. But even there he was restless. With Mary gone and Jimmy who knew where, the Technicolor of the past weeks had dimmed to sepia. He stayed late at work, especially on Wednesday, deadline night. *Wanting to see the paper to bed* was his explanation.

"I can manage fine," Don told him. "You spend time with Joanne. She's still recovering from . . ." He could not finish the sentence, for once not having the words to describe Joanne's ordeal. And Rob's.

"The doctor says she's making progress." McAllister was curt. He needed no one to remind him of his responsibilities. "And we have an appointment with the specialist at Raigmore Hospital on Friday morning."

"Aye, she's better than she was," Don agreed, yet there was something about Joanne that bothered him. She was bright, could walk, cook, see to the garden—all this he knew from Granny Ross, but when he saw her—he called by about twice a week, usually when McAllister was otherwise occupied—he felt an absence, a difference from the Joanne he knew well.

"It's perpetual pandemonium in our house," McAllister continued. "Not much peace to convalesce. Mrs. Ross and Annie are forever at each other, and now Mrs. Ross and my mother are at daggers drawn. Joanne doesn't seem to notice; she leaves the moment an argument starts, sits down at the piano, and plays loudly, drowning out everything."

"Wise woman."

"I wish I could do the same. An old bachelor like me, it takes some getting used to, all these people." McAllister hated himself for sounding so self-pitying.

"Aye," Don agreed, "that's why I stay single." But, observing his colleague, he didn't like the look of defeat in McAllister's eyes, the slump of his shoulders, nor his chain-smoking—and this from a forty-a-day man.

Although he was typing, McAllister could sense the silent examination. That he couldn't sleep, that wanting to be back on the chase for a story, any story, was haunting him, that the longing to be in a pub in Glasgow, with colleagues, with Mary, laughing, plotting, being his old self, the successful journalist, acknowledged by his peers, admired by readers, he would never admit.

Don half guessed. And he knew there was nothing to be done. And that saddened him.

Next afternoon, Thursday, a quiet after-deadline day, when five o'clock struck, Don said to McAllister, "I've invited myself to your place for tea. I'll finish up some business wi' the father of the chapel, then we can walk there together."

"Am I invited too?" Rob asked.

"Not a chance," Don told him as he went out the door.

Rob laughed. "Just as well, I'm playing doubles with Frankie Urquhart at the billiard hall. Want a small wager on us?"

"No," McAllister said. Then looked at Rob. *He seems to be recovering from his ordeal,* he thought, *but he wasn't hit on the head.* "Och, go on then, five bob for you two to win."

"Great." Rob took out his reporter's notebook, marked it in, and McAllister put two half crowns on the table. If they won they would make a tidy sum; all in the print room had placed a bet on the *Gazette* team.

Granny Ross was still there when the two journalists arrived at McAllister's house.

"My, my, Elsie," Don said, "your man is a right saint. Six o'clock and his tea no' on the table. He must be starving away to nothing by now." He said this in his best joking manner, knowing that Granddad Ross was more than happy that his wife was looking after his beloved grandchildren. "And I did hear say that the flower display in the church is no' the same wi'out your special touch."

This was a sore point with Granny Ross. Her archrival in the flower stakes, Mrs. Colquhoun, was attempting to take over and push Granny Ross off the flower arrangement roster.

Standing with her feet shoulder-width apart, her soup ladle held like a cudgel, she told him, "Joanne and the bairns need me."

Joanne went to sooth her mother-in-law. Laying a hand on her wrist she said, "Granny Ross, you've done so much for us. But tonight I'd like to impress my future husband with my cooking." She grinned at Don, then added, "Make sure he doesn't get cold feet—you know what they say about the best way to a man's heart ..."

That swung it—that and the church flower arrangements.

Mrs. Ross relented. "Aye, well, I need to see what flowers can be found for Sunday," she said, taking off her pinny, and left Joanne in control of the kitchen.

Mrs. and Mr. Ross senior, Granny and Granddad, they too had their secret worries—secret even from each other; with their former daughter-in-law remarrying, and their only son about to depart for Australia with his new wife and baby son, they were terrified of losing their granddaughters. *Not that Joanne would ever do that,* Granny Ross told herself over and over, *but what if Mr. McAllister decides to return to the city?* She sensed his restlessness, but hadn't the capacity to see that it was being alone and quiet he missed. To her, being alone equated to loneliness, a fate worse than death.

After supper, when Don was about to leave, he took Joanne's hand. "Lass, that was a smashing fish pie. Best I've tasted in a long time." He winked. "But don't tell Elsie I said so. Thanks for a lovely evening. It's right good to see you looking so well."

"I'm spending every minute in the garden," she replied. "Never know when this weather will break."

"Aye, you're right, it's right strange for Scotland to have so much sunshine." He turned to Mrs. McAllister. "Thanks for the pudding, missus. Fair enjoyed it."

"Thank you, Mr. McLeod," was all Mrs. McAllister said, before excusing herself and going to bed at the same time as the girls.

McAllister knew his mother's exhaustion was a consequence of their flight, but also stemmed from her unease at being away from her flat and sleeping in a strange bed, something she had never done since the few nights they had slept in an air-raid shelter in the bombing, and a week's occasional holiday in Millport when her husband was alive. And he was proud of her.

He had posted a letter from her to Mrs. Crawford, the

neighbor who had the spare key. He included a note from himself saying that his mother was getting to know her future daughter-in-law. He did not want her to know, and worry over, the truth. "You can trust Mrs. Crawford," McAllister had said. "She's a right sensible woman."

As the house quieted and the last of the evening filled the deep bow windows with a soft pink light, Joanne and McAllister sat together, listening once again to the *Pastoral* Symphony.

"Soothes me," Joanne said. Then once again, she went to bed before the darkness arrived, leaving him with a kiss to the forehead and a "Night-night."

He tried to read. He smoked. He drank. He worried. Most of all he was irritated. He had gone to the aid of Jimmy McPhee. He had put his life in danger for him. Now it was over. Jimmy had said so. Mary said so. But Mary had her scoop. Her career. A future.

He poured another dram. He needed it to sleep, and to escape the face of the young man he had wanted to kill that night in the close, knowing he had been a moment away from murder.

"I'll take the car this morning," McAllister told Joanne over breakfast, which for him consisted of two aspirins and two cups of tea. "Pick you up at eleven."

"The appointment's at eleven," she reminded him.

"Half past ten, then."

"I'll be ready. See you then."

He kissed her hair, drove to the office, left the car in the castle car park. Three-quarters of the way up the steep stairs leading to Castle Wynd he was short of breath and his knees ached. *Maybe the doctor is right about cutting back on smoking.* He was one of those who believed the alternative medical opinion, that smoking was good for you. Continuing on to the *Gazette*, he justified his smoking, telling himself that, when accosted by the more belligerent of the *Gazette*'s readers, who, often, would tell him how to run a newspaper, a cigarette would prevent him running amok with an axe.

"Mr. McAllister." He was surprised to see Detective Inspector Dunne. And worried. Standing beside the local police inspector were two men. From their buttoned-up overcoats and faces that suggested they suffered from constipation, McAllister guessed they were policemen.

One of the men stepped forward. "John McAllister, I'm—"

"Not here." DI Dunne stepped in front of the man, practically pushing him to one side. "Mr. McAllister, would you care to come to the police station, we'd like a wee word."

McAllister nodded, grateful for the local man's courtesy. Glancing over the heads of the visitors, he saw Fiona the receptionist staring, her normally ruddy cheeks pale.

"Phone Angus McLean, the solicitor," he told her. "Tell him—" One of the men gripped his elbow, turning him towards the doors. Fiona was nodding, too shocked to speak. Now with a man on each side of him, the one slighted by DI Dunne gripping his other arm tightly, he called over his shoulder, "Tell Don Joanne has an appointment—"

"That's enough," the second policeman interrupted.

"What?" Fiona was doing her best not to panic.

"This is my jurisdiction," DI Dunne intervened.

McAllister was through the doors, out into the deserted lane, when a sly shove in his back made him stumble on the last step.

"Joanne has an appointment at Raigmore at eleven," he repeated, as he was marched over the cobblestones the short distance to the police station.

"I'll let someone know," DI Dunne promised.

And in the space of fifty yards the weather changed, a cloud as black as the bruises on a boxer covering the sun. The temperature dropped. McAllister shivered. Not from cold—*someone stepping on ma grave*, his mother would have said.

And the nightmare began.

Fiona called the solicitor. She knew nothing of the law. Had no idea that a phone call to Angus McLean meant nothing; Scots law indulged no rights of representation after a charge was made. Then she ran up the stairs to tell Don McLeod. "Mr. McAllister said Mrs. Ross has an appointment—"

The phone rang. "*Gazette*," Don said, holding up his hand in a "one minute" gesture. He listened, saying nothing, but his body slowly uncurled from his usual stoop until his spine was straight and his face beetroot-red. "Thanks, Sergeant Patience, right good o' you." He slammed down the phone. "Rob, where does McAllister keep his spare car keys?"

"Why, has he lost his again?"

"Shut up and listen." Don was almost shouting. "McAllister has been . . ." *Charged* was what he was about to say, but he didn't know that, so he quoted Sergeant Patience. "McAllister is being questioned by the police over an incident in Glasgow."

That got Rob's attention.

"You take Joanne for her appointment at the hospital. Make up an excuse for McAllister, and make sure Joanne doesn't realize . . ." He guessed from the way Rob turned away how fragile the reporter still was. "Your father is onto it, so it will all work out."

Lightning flashed directly overhead. Thunder boomed out seconds later. Fiona squealed. Then burst into tears. "I hate thunder," she lied. Another burst of thunder. Again right above them, rattling the high window, darkening the room.

"That fair set ma fillings a'rattlin'." Don smiled at Fiona. "Rob, call McAllister's house, speak to Mrs. Ross, ask her what time Joanne is due at Raigmore, say . . ."

"I'll say the press room is flooding, so it's all hands to the pump, so to speak." Rob followed this with a grin, but his heart wasn't in it and his mouth looked like a stretched, deflated balloon.

Don cocked his head, listening to the rain drumming louder than a Boys' Brigade band kettledrum. "Aye, that'll do." He saw Rob was more than nervous. *Fear*, Don realized. *He'd had enough of hospitals.* "On second thoughts, ask your mother to take Joanne. A woman's touch," he explained.

"My mother is good with doctors. She understands their gobbledy-gook."

As Rob dialed home, Don turned to Fiona. "You mind the front desk, lass. And if anyone should hear of this—"

"I'll no' let on anything to anyone, Mr. McLeod."

"Good girl." He patted her as though she was his favorite puppy. Then he looked at the two juniors; their joint ages wouldn't add up to forty, yet he knew he could rely on them, trust them. "Like the storm, this'll all blow over soon."

None of them was sure of that, but chose to believe it anyway.

In the interview room at the police station, when asked about "an incident" outside his mother's flat on Sunday night, McAllister said, "I've no idea what you're talking about."

The policemen kept up a barrage of questions and threats. "Where were you on Sunday night?"

"At the *Herald*, then home," he replied.

"Who did you meet in the close outside your home?"

"No one."

"We have witnesses who say different."

If the inspector in charge, Detective Inspector Willkie, had said "witness," singular, McAllister would have worried. It was the plural that made him suspect the detective had nothing, no one.

When the inspector said a name, describing him as a "close acquaintance of leaders of the criminal fraternity," asking, "Why was he outside your mother's house?" again McAllister answered, "I've no idea, why don't you ask him?" The inspector replied, "I'm the one who asks the questions."

So he wasn't the boy I thought he was. From the way the inspector was questioning him, McAllister considered the possibility that the inspector had been tipped off. *But why? And by whom?* He knew he would eventually find out.

Who did you meet? Why were you meeting him? I know you know this man. I have witnesses. Of course your mother will back you up. But who'd believe your mother? He continued to threaten McAllister, threaten the *Herald*, promising to come back with a warrant, promising to lock McAllister up and throw away the key. He made it clear he hated journalists. *Scum* was one of his less profane words for the profession.

McAllister knew DI Willkie was enjoying himself and he kept refusing to answer, except to say, "I don't know. I was at work. I came home. I saw no one." He knew his refusal to say more meant the interview would continue until he, or the inspector, gave in. It might also mean time in a police holding cell. Without a cigarette.

The only bright spot was DI Dunne's refusal to leave the room. "My station, my jurisdiction," he repeated.

Finally, when the policemen realized there would be no answers, particularly with DI Dunne insisting everything be done following police regulations, they told McAllister he had to come back to Glasgow with them.

"Do you have a warrant?" he asked.

"It would be regarded favorably if you helped the police in their inquiries." DI Willkie was attempting to appear conciliatory.

The effort to hold his temper in strangled his voice and made his already red nose—a boozer's nose, McAllister noted—turn a color worthy of Rudolph.

"We'll be needing to talk to your mother to back up your story that you were at home that evening." This was Willkie's last stab at threatening the editor. "So where can we find her so she can give a statement?"

"She's visiting relatives," McAllister said. "I'll let you know when she is home and she can go round to the local police station, make a statement there." He had no intension of letting DI Willkie anywhere near his mother. Or letting his mother anywhere near a police station.

Inspector Willkie was sitting back in his chair, arms folded. "Oh, really?" He smirked. "It'd be better for you if she does that sooner than later."

McAllister knew this was the policeman's trump card, and he had no choice but to ask, "Why is that?"

For the first time, the second policeman spoke—McAllister had forgotten his name but knew he was a detective constable. He could see the decency in the man, and the embarrassment; wouldn't last long as a Glasgow detective, had been McAllister's initial impression, he'll be posted to Auchtermuchty or some other tiny place if he doesn't harden up.

"Unfortunately there's been a break-in at your mother's house. It would be a good idea if she came back and listed what was stolen."

"Not much stolen, but the whole place was trashed." DI Willkie was enjoying himself. "So when your mother gets home to clear up, she can give us a statement as to your whereabouts Sunday night."

McAllister was gripping the edge of the table. He saw his knuckles white, felt his jaw tight, and saw DI Willkie willing him on. It was the malevolence in the man's eyes, the unsaid, *Come on,* *hit me,* that stopped him.

"Thank you, Inspector, for coming all this way to let me know, but a phone call would have sufficed." McAllister's' voice was deliberately conciliatory and the satisfaction of the fury on the detective's face was the only good moment of the three-and-a-half-hour interview.

"I think that covers everything, don't you, Inspector?" DI Dunne had had enough. He stood. "If the Glasgow police visit my jurisdiction again, I will need the professional courtesy of a phone warning." "My chief constable should be notified as well," he added.

"Oh, I don't think there will be any problem with your chief constable. Not when we come back to charge McAllister wi' murder."

"Murder?" McAllister stood, catching the chair before it fell over. "What murder?"

"Can't say anything that might prejudice our investigation." The inspector was not about to explain. Seeing McAllister's shock, he smiled, satisfied. "We'll see ourselves out, Dunne."

DI Dunne ignored the deliberate lack of courtesy to a fellow officer. He was too busy making sure McAllister stayed silent. And didn't move within striking distance of the inspector.

"Not at all, Willkie, I'll see you out."

When DI Dunne came back he took the seat opposite McAllister, offering him an ashtray as an invitation to smoke, something denied by the visiting officers. He was examining the man he had known for two and something years. "We've seen a lot together, Mr. McAllister. I respect you and your judgment. So what's this about murder?"

"I have no idea. Well, maybe an inkling, but nothing I can share. Not yet."

DI Dunne nodded. "I don't like this. Not one bit."

"Neither do I."

"Mrs. Ross doesn't deserve any more trouble."

"My mother neither," McAllister replied. His hand was shaking as he tried to strike a match. And failed. DI Dunne took the matchbox and did it for him.

McAllister thought of the man he'd encountered in the close. *Could he be dead? How? Why?*

Then he thought of his mother's home. Her possessions that meant so much to her: the shrine to his brother, photographs, the cabinet with his brother's boxing trophies, the album he didn't know existed until recently, with articles where McAllister had a byline, cut out and pasted in over the years, the only physical record of his career. He thought of her everyday teapot and hoped it had been spared. He remembered her best china tea service—collected cup by cup, plate by plate, since she never had enough money to buy a complete set and always refused his offer to purchase one for her, telling him it gave her pleasure to collect the items this way—and he feared for it.

"I trust you'll sort this out." The way the inspector spoke—calm, mild, serious, certain—reminded McAllister that the policeman was destined for the church before the war changed everything.

"I'll do my best."

The inspector accepted McAllister's assurance. But the slight shake of his head and the grim set of his mouth were saying to McAllister, *Good intentions are not always enough.*

Fourteen

～

It was nearing two o'clock when McAllister arrived back at the office.

Don was waiting. "Margaret McLean wants to talk to you."

"I haven't time—"

"She had a conversation with the consultant at the hospital." He saw McAllister's cigarette shake. "Nothing bad, so she said. And your mother called, she's in a right state, something about a burglary." Don didn't mention that he knew the Glasgow police had come all this way to question him, he was waiting for McAllister to tell him.

"I know. That's why the police were here."

"Oh, aye?" Don knew this was not all, but continued, "Mary Ballantyne phoned, says you have to call back. Urgently." He was looking at McAllister as though measuring him for his coffin. "This can't go on—"

"I know."

"You'd better tell me what's what. Someone has to mind your back."

"Later. I have to go home."

"Mary—"

"You talk to her." McAllister said this as he grabbed his hat. "And find Jimmy McPhee. Urgently." He hurried down the stairs.

Fiona was about to say something, but seeing his face, she

hesitated. "Mr. McAllister," she called out to the retreating figure. "An urgent message from a Mr. Dochery. He said—"

Too late, he was out the door and didn't hear.

He drove home. He went into the kitchen and found Mrs. Ross but no Joanne. *If looks could kill . . .* he remembered his mother's expression as he asked where Joanne was.

"Resting," Granny Ross replied.

"Thank you, Mrs. Ross, you can go home. We'll see you tomorrow."

She took off her pinny, muttering, *I know when I'm not wanted,* and as she left, she slammed the door behind her, shaking the glass in the kitchen windows.

He was tempted to pour a whisky but put on the kettle instead. When the whistle rose to a piercing shriek, he poured the bubbling water first to warm the pot, then a second time to make the tea—even in a crisis he never cut the steps in making a good pot of tea. He didn't hear Joanne come in but felt an arm sneak around his waist, her head nestle on his shoulder.

"Granny Ross gone home?" she asked.

"I told her to," he said.

"How's the flooding?"

"Flooding?" The morning's summer storm had vanished as quickly as it arrived. Coming home, a blue summer's day with the wind balmy, clouds nonexistent, and the smell of roses around the front porch overpowering had returned.

"Coward. I knew it was an excuse to get out of coming to the hospital." She was smiling. "But it was great to have Margaret McLean's company. She insisted on seeing the doctor with me. And she badgered the consultant to explain all thon gobbledygook he spouts. The Big Panjandrum, Margaret called him." She giggled.

"What did he say?"

"Oh you know—making progress, that kind of thing . . . That tea, it's ready." She poured the milk and he poured the tea.

"My mother . . ."

"She's in her room. She's tired, not used to change, she said, so let's leave her for now." Joanne had two mugs of tea and was leading the way out the kitchen door to the bench McAllister had had made by a local carpenter and placed next to the one apple tree that still produced fruit.

"I heard about the burglary. You need to go to Glasgow to sort it out. Your mother is really upset, so I think she should stay here. Take a few days—but no more." She said this as a statement. Then looked up into his eyes, making sure he understood.

He looked back. He saw the old Joanne in there. Part of him was relieved, part of him disconcerted; this Joanne saw much, forgave much, but was seldom deceived.

"Jimmy McPhee . . . I know you feel obliged, but it's not your business." She was taking her time. Choosing her sentences carefully. "You need to make a choice. If you've changed your mind about us, you need to tell me."

She shook her head when he attempted a protest, "I'd never—"

"One week. Agreed?"

It was the longest speech, and the most coherent, since the attack had left her with a possibility she would never recover from the damage to her brain. Not completely.

All he could say was, "The consultant is right, you are recovering."

"Slowly. But I still have a problem with . . ." She didn't finish the sentence. Mrs. McAllister was standing in the kitchen doorway, a hand to her brow, peering into the light. Her voice, distant, weak, calling, "John? Is that you?"

He went to her, offering to make fresh tea.

She said, "That'd be nice," then handed him a letter. "This came this morning from Mrs. Crawford."

He read it while Joanne made a fresh pot of tea. "I'm so sorry, Mother."

"Aye, well, it's never been a safe place, the East End."

He could not express his anger, could not tell her that her stoicism made it worse. She was the same when his father had been killed in the Clydeside Blitz, accepting that as he was a fireman, and it was wartime, death was to be accepted. When his brother died she had retreated into a private hell of emptiness. But looking at her as she looked away, he saw that she was protecting him, not wanting to lay the blame, which was surely his, on his already burdened shoulders.

Although she didn't know the how or the why of what had happened in Glasgow, Joanne wanted it all to end. "Don't worry," she told the older woman, all the while looking at McAllister. "John's leaving for Glasgow first thing tomorrow, and he'll have it all sorted out in no time." She looked at him, challenging him, "Won't you?"

Don called around mid-afternoon.

He and McAllister were in the sitting room, the women in the garden, the girls out riding their bicycles.

"I've never been so proud of my mother as now," he was telling his deputy. "All she said was, *Go back, Son, and sort it all out, I'll stay here wi' ma new daughter*. "Two good women, Joanne and my mother."

"Glad to hear you appreciate them," Don said. He was a great believer in the nothing-is-perfect philosophy. "It takes a whiley before we recognize the grass is always greener an' all that, so enjoy what you have is my advice."

McAllister didn't have time to respond.

The front doorbell rang, the door opened, a voice called out, "McAllister, I know you're here. No use avoiding me." It was Margaret McLean.

"I'll come straight to the point, then I must dash." She did not sit down or remove her hat, only took off the sunglasses. "Did Joanne tell you what the consultant said?" She didn't wait for an answer. Joanne had asked her to explain it. For a reason that was beyond Margaret's comprehension, Joanne was ashamed of her condition. "No? Well. The optic nerve is damaged. Joanne has difficulty seeing properly, and she has a problem reading."

"So that's why—"

"Yes, McAllister. That's why she hasn't read any of the books you so kindly bought her. That's why she won't look at you directly, in case the damage is visible, which it isn't. But the good news is that an operation can probably fix it. It can't be done up here, an eye specialist is needed, but he is reasonably optimistic . . ." She'd made that bit up; the man was unreasonably gloomy, in her estimation. When she pressed him, in private, on the chances of success, the specialist had said "fifty-fifty." "In the meantime Joanne will have to wear glasses with one lens covered over and—"

"Men seldom make passes at girls who wear glasses." Joanne was standing in the doorway.

"No man could not make a pass at you," Don said, "unless he was half blind."

"Like me," she answered.

They laughed, and McAllister said, "You should have told me," and smiled.

She said, "I know, but I can play the piano without looking, and knit."

Don said, "And type."

Joanne said, "No, I'm not coming into work, not yet."

And both McAllister and Don said, "Quite right."

Margaret McLean said, "Well, my dears, I must be off, I've lots of shopping to do. I'm taking a camping holiday in Portmahomack."

McAllister took in her sin-red nail varnish, her white open high-heeled shoes, the cartwheel-size sunhat, and was unable to imagine her sleeping in a tent. "Don't look at me like that, McAllister. I love an adventure. And Rob will be with me to pitch the tent, as Angus refuses point blank to join us."

McAllister was of the opinion that camping was for Boy Scouts only. And Girl Guides. So he had every sympathy with Angus McLean.

"Can we come with you?" Joanne asked.

McAllister looked at Joanne. "But . . ."

"Wonderful." Margaret clapped her hands, laughing. "You can squeeze the lemons for the gin."

"Are you sure?" McAllister was struggling as to how to mention medical considerations, doctors, emergencies, all the disasters that can happen when under canvas in remote villages.

"I'm sure." Joanne had the same look her daughters gave him when he asked if they were old enough to light fires, walk miles, stay up late.

Annie had come in on the last part of the conversation. "Camping. Goodie. Jean, we're going camping."

Her sister came running. "Camping? Really? Really, Mum?"

"Uncle Rob is coming too," Margaret told them.

Annie was even more delighted. "We'll have great fun. Uncle Rob can make a bonfire."

"And I shall cook marshmallows," Margaret added.

"You're off to Glasgow to sort out your mother's flat, aren't you?" Joanne was looking at McAllister, daring him to object. "And last I heard, Ross-shire isn't on the moon."

"All right"—he threw up his arms—"I surrender." And the girls laughed and Jean clapped her hands and they followed Margaret to her car asking questions about the holiday, the first coming from Jean, "Can I bring Snowy?"

When Margaret and Don left, for the first time in a long time McAllister put his arms around his future wife and held her, tightly. He was distressed she hadn't told him about her sight. Never once had she said anything other than "thank you" when he bought her books, magazines, new sheet music.

"Joanne, I'm so sorry. I know I've been neglecting you—"

"Shush," she said, putting a finger to his lips.

He was about to kiss her, when Annie came in. "Yuck, kissing," she said.

And they laughed, and all was lighter, and McAllister knew happiness could be his. If he could accept it.

Fifteen

~

McAllister had arranged to meet Sandy Marshall, and Mary, at the *Herald*. He told them of the visit from DI Willkie.

"I wonder what he's up to?" Sandy asked.

"Knowing him, nothing good," Mary replied. "We'll just have to wait and see."

Waiting was not McAllister's forte; the threat of further business with a detective of Willkie's reputation perturbed him. When he said he had to leave to check up on his mother's flat, Mary insisted on joining him.

It was mid-evening by the time they arrived. The door was open a fraction. He pushed it. He froze. The devastation in the hallway made him cold with anger. "The bastards! Absolute and utter bastards!"

A voice called down the stairwell, "Is that you, Mr. McAllister?"

"Aye, Mrs. Crawford. I'm here with a friend to see what's what, and get it sorted."

The sound of a door being double-locked, then footsteps and Mrs. Crawford came down the stairs. She was small, *a fierce wee woman*, as he remembered. She was wringing her hands, trying to wash away all the trouble that had visited their close, and so obviously scared that he was at a loss as to how to reassure her. He had brought the violence. He should banish it.

But Mary knew; she was patting the neighbor's arm, saying,

"You put the kettle on. We'll come up as soon as we've had a look at Mrs. McAllister's place. We'll be needing a cup of tea by then." She was gesturing to the broken pictures, smashed mirror, and scattered clothing. The smell of urine was strong, but no one commented on that.

The woman scuttled off like a sand crab to its hole.

"The bastards," McAllister muttered over and over as he opened each door in the flat, leaving the sitting room till last. In there it was worst. Not only were the photograph frames broken, but the photos themselves had been torn into bits. The silver trophy cups had been stomped on, the thin metal twisted out of shape. The glass in the china cabinet and all contents were scattered on the carpet like a damaged mosaic.

Mary knelt, trying to piece together a photograph.

"Leave it!" McAllister barked. It was a portrait of his brother he'd had a *Herald* photographer take on his fifteenth birthday, and had been his mother's favorite.

"If we take these to the boys in the photo lab they might be able to—"

"Leave it. I need to do this on my own." His voice was almost a sob; he wanted to be the one to gather the fragments of his mother and father's marriage, his brother's brief life, the mementos and the memories that made his family.

"It's late. Come back in the daylight. We'll bring buckets and mops." She knew the strong smell of urine was coming from the sofa. She saw that the carpets were thick with jam and treacle and a substance she dared not guess at. She took the front door keys from him and, taking his wrist, pulled him towards the door. In the dim of the close she tried to lock the door, but the lock was smashed.

"A bit late for that," he said, leaning again the wall, breathing the anger out in loud long sounds. At first she couldn't quite decipher the words, only hearing the repeated cursing, and a name, *Gerry*. Then he whispered, like a vow made before the altar, "If this is you, Gerry Dochery, I'll get you."

That Mary heard. And it scared her. She pushed him towards the stairs. On the first-floor landing, she knocked on Mrs. Crawford's door. "It's Mr. McAllister and me, Mary Ballantyne."

The kitchen—a mirror image of his mother's, had almost the same teapot, tea cozy, and cups. From the washing on the pulley above there came a strong smell of carbolic soap.

Mrs. Crawford glanced up. "I took in some o' your mother's things. Gave them a wash," she explained.

But McAllister wasn't hearing her. How would he tell his mother? How would she cope? Her world was her photographs and silver trophies and tea service and ornaments. Even her statue of the Virgin, and the vial of holy water that McAllister had brought back from Lourdes when on an assignment there after the war, had been smashed.

Mary said, "Mrs. McAllister's lucky having a friend like you."

Mrs. Crawford sighed. "Aye, we've been through a lot together. The polis asked if I could say if anything was missing, but . . ." A tear plopped into the blue-and-white-striped milk jug. "The council, they sent a man to board up the windows . . ." Another tear, this time hitting the mock tartan oilcloth. "Ah always said to her I couldn't be doing wi' living on the ground floor. Much safer one floor up. Not that we've had trouble before now, no' even in the war . . ." She dropped into her chair and picked up the edge of her pinny to wipe her eyes. "Poor Mrs. McAllister."

"Did you see or hear anyone?" Mary asked.

"I'm no' sure but . . ." Now her eyes were darting around, searching for some invisible assistance. She found it—the crucifix above the door.

"If he finds out I've said anything . . ." she began again. "But the McAllisters were always right good to him when he was wee . . ."

McAllister looked at Mary. She nodded.

"Not that he went into the flat—that was two others. I never saw them, I only heard the crashing an' . . . But him, he was knocking on doors, went to everyone in the close . . . and all that racket and everything going on—smashing glass and china . . . it was terrible." She was trembling.

"What did Wee Gerry say?" McAllister wanted her to know he already guessed.

"Aye, Wee Gerry Dochery, he was asking about last Sunday night." She was blowing her nose. "Something about an accident. I telt him I knew nothing. An' I telt him I heard nothing because I sleep in here." She pointed out a truckle bed with curtains across, the old-fashioned kind built into the wall for the many children of previous generations. But her face said different.

She knows, Mary thought.

McAllister remembered that after her sons had been killed in the war, Mrs. Crawford had taken to living in one room. "Did the police come around any time this week? I mean, before Mother's place was . . ." He couldn't find a word for the deliberate destruction of his mother's life. Bombing, earthquakes, hurricanes people could eventually accept, but wanton vandalism brought an evil hard to eradicate.

"No, there was no polis until after your mother's place was . . ." She too was unable to find a word for the desecration. And it upset her that she had done nothing, too afraid to open her door until the next morning.

"So no police came on Sunday night?" he persisted. "Or in the wee hours of Monday morning?"

"I ken you and your mother left. I found your note saying you were takin' a wee holiday, but I never heard you leave."

"So who called the police?"

"No me," she said apologetically.

"Quite right," he said, "no need for you to get involved." He knew this was the way of it. No matter what happened, it was not the bystanders' role to report to the police, not if they cared for their own and their family's safety. "You say Gerry Dochery called on everyone in the close?"

"Aye, I think so." Her voice was weary, but McAllister wanted more.

"And nothing was mentioned about . . ." He had no idea how to ask without giving himself away. The less said about his fight with the man-boy the better. *But if the police had not been there on Sunday night, only turning up for the vandalism?* "Can you think of anything else?"

"The only person I've spoken wi' is the newsagent. He was right concerned about me, me being on ma' own. No one else has said a word."

The neighbor upstairs, McAllister was thinking, *could he be the informant?*

Mary stood. She leaned over and took the old woman's hand. "Is there anyone you can go to for a wee break?"

"Ma sister lives in Shawlands. She's always on at me to go and bide wi' her. Maybe I should . . ."

"I'll drive you there if you like," Mary offered.

"I'd like that."

As the women were making arrangements for the next day, McAllister remembered that Mrs. Crawford had never liked her sister. Seeing how miserable she looked, and vulnerable, and her agreeing to Mary's suggestion without the usual polite protestations of *I couldn't put you to all that trouble,* it sank in how frightened she must be.

When they left for the *Herald,* Mary to work, McAllister to pick up the overnight bag he'd left there, Mary asked, "What is it you're not telling me?"

"Nothing."

The denial was so outright she knew she was right. "Where are you staying?"

"I'll find a B&B. There's plenty of them in the squares off Bath Street," he said.

"Stay with me. I have a spare room. But you'll have to share with Jimmy."

"Jimmy? He's here again?" McAllister was not expecting that.

"Aye. But he says it's his business, nothing for you or me to be concerned about."

He was not fooled; there was nothing Mary would not be interested in when it came to Jimmy McPhee. Plus the chance of a good story.

"I couldn't possibly . . ."

"Yes you can." She was smiling. "It will give my mother something more to complain about."

He could see the offer meant nothing more to her than a practical solution to his need for accommodation. Through the shock, through the pain—and the guilt—he knew he wanted company. Yet he knew that staying with Mary Ballantyne was not a good idea. He said, "That would be great. But for one night only. Then I'll find a boardinghouse."

"As you like," she said, and stepped forward to signal to the oncoming bus.

As Mary opened the iron gate to the steps leading down to the basement flat, Mary's mother opened her door, the main one on the floor above. She must have been watching, waiting.

"Your tinker friend has gone. He gave me the keys and a message. 'I'm off to see a man about a horse,' he said."

Mary laughed. "Thank you." She didn't move from the lower steps. Speaking upwards to the equally small and equally formidable woman, she said, "Mother, this is John McAllister. I believe you've spoken on the telephone."

"Mr. McAllister." Mrs. Ballantyne examined him. He could see the distaste in the shadows on her face. Or maybe it was the light from the streetlamp distorting her features. "I asked you not to involve my daughter in your sordid and dangerous affairs."

No, you didn't ask, you ordered. In the lamplight flickering through the leaves of a wild gean tree, he saw how angry she was. *A mother's anger*, he realized. *And fear.*

"Mother. Not now." Mary ran up the steps, took the keys from her, and ran back down to the basement.

McAllister followed, saying, "Good night, Mrs. Ballantyne." There was no reply.

As she shut and locked the door Mary said, "Don't mind my mother, we've been arguing since ever I can remember."

McAllister put down his bag, helped himself to a dram, knocked it back, then said, "Right, I want to know what Jimmy is doing back here, and how you are involved."

"Jimmy hasn't told me his reasons for returning. All I can guess is that he needs to finish what was started, perhaps to feel safe."

McAllister knew Jimmy had to respond to the attacks, or lose respect. In a rat-eat-rat place like the Glasgow slums, and in the Travelers' culture, where your name and reputation were everything, Jimmy would never back down. He would stand up to the person who had put a price on his head until he was defeated, perhaps killed.

"Do you think this is about bare-knuckle fighting?" he asked.

Mary said, "I've been told organized fights died out a long time ago. But if there's lucrative prize money . . ." She turned her palms outwards.

McAllister saw a bruise of carbon ink at the base of one thumb. He wanted to rub it clean.

"It's a deep part of Traveler culture, those fights won't disappear entirely."

"I know. But Travelers fighting to decide a dispute, that's different."

"Jimmy said he gave up fighting when he returned to the Highlands. I *think* I believe him." From her voice, not knowing was clearly frustrating her. "Also, I've been hearing names, Jimmy McPhee and Gerry Dochery obviously, but I heard another name again recently—the Big Man, or the Heid Yin, a man so protected no one knows, or is saying, what he's up to, where he's from. I do know everyone is terrified of him. But is he the one after Jimmy? Is Gerry working with him? For him? And why? I've no idea." She covered her mouth to stifle a yawn. "If I can break a story on a big crime boss, it could make my career."

McAllister did not think less of her for admitting it. But for him it was personal; involving his mother had ensured that. And again the questions haunted him. *Why? And why involve me?*

He awoke in a strange room with a different light and the sound of a telephone trilling. The phone stopped. He became aware of buses, cars, bicycle bells, a horse clopping by. He checked his watch. Twenty past eight. He'd slept in. When he went into the small galley kitchen he found Mary, looking half asleep but awake enough to have the kettle on and the teapot readied.

"That was the *Herald*. The police are looking for you. But no one knows where you are, so . . ."

It was his turn to yawn. "It'll be about my mother's flat." He tried to sound more confident than he felt.

"Oh, aye," she said, but there was a tinge of *and what else* in the upturned inflection on the *aye*. "I've work to do," she said. "May as well go in now I'm awake."

"I'll join you."

They didn't wait for the bus. Walking down the long decline to the *Herald* office, not saying much, there was no tension in the silence between them. It was another particular about Mary he liked.

A woman behind the reception desk recognized McAllister. "Good morning, Mr. McAllister. I have a message from Detective Inspector Willkie. He asked you to call him. He said it's urgent." She handed him a note with a phone number neatly typed.

"Willkie?" Mary said. "That nasty wee shite?"

The receptionist smiled. The detective had been nasty and bullying when he called at reception looking for McAllister. He wouldn't believe the woman didn't know McAllister's whereabouts. He threatened to go upstairs to check and to charge her with obstructing the police. She decided that even if she did know where McAllister was, without his permission she'd deny it.

When they reached the reporters' floor, Mary saw there was half an hour until the news conference. "I think you should talk to our esteemed editor," she said. "DI Willkie is not good news."

Sandy Marshall heard the brief knock on his door and shouted, "Later," but Mary was in his office and taking a chair, with McAllister on her heels.

"DI Willkie is after McAllister," she said.

"Is he, now?" Sandy Marshall pushed his papers aside. He knew he would be unable to work until Mary had his attention.

"It's probably about the burglary at my mother's flat." McAllister was lighting his third cigarette of the day. His mouth felt dry, a mild headache was starting, and he looked dreadful.

Mary said, "A detective inspector in the murder squad involved in a burglary? I don't think so."

"So who have you murdered?" It was a joke, but Sandy saw the flicker in his old friend's eyes. Mary didn't.

"If curses killed anyone, then guilty as charged." McAllister was looking up at the ceiling and watching a spiral of smoke, not risking the stare of a man he had known since they were copy boys starting their careers together over twenty-five years ago.

"So Mary, have you more on the story?" The editor was looking at the layout for the next edition.

She began, "I'm hearing whispers of the Heid Yin." She had no need to explain the vernacular; the Glasgow terminology for head man, boss, *capo dei capi*, was clear. She saw the editor focus his attention on her, and wished she had more than whispers. "He must be involved in something big. He must be more than nasty." She shook her head in frustration, hair escaping from the hastily tied ponytail. "Mention him and my contacts are suddenly dumbstruck."

Sandy thought about it, then said, "Let's see if we can cobble together a follow-up on the fight in Millport, keep the story alive for another edition. Maybe you could help." He nodded at McAllister.

Mary grinned. McAllister looked doubtful.

"But if nothing turns up," the editor was speaking to Mary, "I need you to help Keith. The story on council building tenders being awarded to favored businesses is important and—"

"I'd rather cut off my right hand than work with thon useless piece of sh—"

"You're still a junior around here."

"I'll be off." Hearing the steel in Sandy's voice, McAllister was reminded why his friend was editor of a prestigious newspaper, not stuck in a backwater like him.

"Prepare yourself for a long hard session with Willkie—that's his style, so get a good breakfast down you before you go," Mary advised. "Come back here after. With any luck there might be a story in it for me, and Mr. Keith, the so-called crime reporter, can do his own research." She was grinning, any animosity with the editor forgiven and forgotten.

"Good luck," Sandy said.

"Thanks, I hope I won't need it." McAllister made for the door.

"McAllister, a moment . . ." Sandy went into the corridor with him, shutting his office door before asking, "Is there anything you need to tell me?"

"No."

There was a silence. Sandy sighed. "This is not your fight."

"It wasn't, but it is now."

"Aye, I know. Give your mother my regards," he replied. He knew the destruction of his mother's flat was a breach of the un-written gangland code. He knew the betrayal by Gerry Dochery called for revenge. He hoped it could be talked out. But he was not hopeful. "If I can help at all . . ."

"In return for a cracking front-page story . . ."

"If it's publishable." The editor grinned, held out his hand. "Good luck and be careful. There's a wedding invitation sitting on the mantelpiece at home, and the wife's decided we'll have a wee holiday up north after the wedding. So . . ."

"And you're my best man—"

"So make sure Willkie doesn't get up your nose."

Or worse, McAllister was thinking.

McAllister walked to the Turnbull Street entrance of the Central Police Office. On a corner, the building, taking up two streetfronts, was a large redbrick construction, with red sandstone detailing around the windows. McAllister noted a bay window on the second floor with a strange cupola above. He imagined the chief constable with a brass telescope, surveying his command, much as a sea captain surveys the oceans. *More likely a cramped office with too many desks, and too many workers in a fug of cigarette smoke. A detective is as valiant a smoker as a journalist.*

He told the constable at reception he was here at the bidding of DI Willkie. A second or two later a sergeant appeared from the back office.

He was expected. "If you'll just come this way, Mr. McAllister."

It happened so fast McAllister couldn't take it in. Five minutes earlier he'd been in a café on West Sauchiehall Street having bacon, eggs, black pudding, and tattie scones; the next he was in a cell.

He was left there for what seemed an hour but was only forty minutes. Next he was walked through the detectives' room, everyone turning to stare, and pushed into an interview room. He knew to listen and say as little as possible.

DI Willkie was alone. That alerted McAllister, but he had no idea as to what.

Licking his lips like a fox about to seize a fat duck, the detective announced, "You are being questioned over the murder of one William Stuart Smith."

McAllister was stunned. He denied knowing this person—true. He denied ever meeting the man—not true, perhaps. He denied causing his death—absolutely true. But all his answers were discarded as lies.

McAllister knew that if this William Stuart Smith was indeed the person he had grappled with in the close—and he had no way of knowing this unless he admitted to their encounter—the man probably had a few bruises, but was otherwise alive, and fine, when McAllister last saw him.

Throughout the interview, McAllister kept calm, listening between the lines. Half an hour into the interview, he felt there was something he was missing, another agenda.

DI Willkie repeated over and over as though it was a football chant. "We have witnesses." Said in varying tones, varying rhythms, but always in glee, "We. Have. Witnesses."

Then McAllister began to make sense of the questions. *Witnesses? Plural? The other man, the one who had scuttled away in the first minutes of the attack, he would lie. But his companion? Surely not. Then again, Gerry Dochery is a man to be feared.* Then there was the neighbor upstairs. He didn't know the man other than to nod to, but again, he doubted the man would talk—especially since Gerry Dochery had visited everyone in the close.

Willkie declared a break. McAllister was locked up in the holding cell. He knew the timing would be too close for Sandy or Mary to drum up a lawyer to argue for bail. So he resigned himself to a night in the cells. He took comfort from DI Willkie so obviously having nothing other than the doubtful witnesses. But he did not look forward to a night with the drunks and the desperate of the city streets.

What happened next he did not find out until later. When he did, all lingering loyalties to Gerry Dochery, to the City of Glasgow police force, to his colleagues at other newspapers, vanished.

The late-afternoon edition of a rival tabloid newspaper ran with a screamer of a headline.

JOURNALIST QUESTIONED OVER GANGLAND MURDER

How the rival obtained the news in time to run it, given that the *Herald* heard about it after deadline, was remarked on. But no one was surprised. "Willkie!" Mary shouted across the reporters' floor when the hot-off-the press edition was delivered to the *Herald* office.

◆　◆　◆

The revelation made Scottish Television evening news, and the wireless bulletins.

Joanne heard the story from the wireless broadcast.

She was in the kitchen, having supper, and thinking about what to take on the camping trip. The background of Scottish country dance music did not register, but the sound of the pips leading to the news caught her attention. The lead story was on political unrest over the nuclear stalemate. Next came a story of a politician involved in a scandal in London. Then the Scottish segment of the news began.

"Glasgow journalist John McAllister, forty-six years old, is being held on suspicion of murder. The deceased, William Stuart Smith, was found on waste ground near . . ."

Joanne jumped up. She switched the wireless off. She and Mrs. McAllister and Granny Ross stared at one another. Annie was too frightened to say anything. Jean was in the sitting room with her cat and hadn't heard. It all sounded much worse because it was announced in the posh news reader's voice into the homes of everyone who knew them. Or didn't.

"Whatever they're saying, he's innocent," his mother said. It didn't help.

"I know. John would never do anything wrong," Joanne told them all, working hard to keep the terror out of her voice and off her face and to steady her hands. And knees. "There's been a terrible mistake. It will all work out."

Annie saw through her mother's reassurances. "Nothing ever works out in our family," Annie muttered. No one contradicted her.

Sixteen

It was left to Sandy Marshall to coordinate the legal help for McAllister. Which he did: he set the newspaper's legal team to work on the bail application; he himself worked the phone calling in every favor owed. But all his contacts warned that as it was the weekend, little could be done until Monday.

"Probably a deliberate strategy on the part of DI Willkie, a trick the inspector is very fond of," the *Herald*'s solicitor explained. "But we'll do our best."

There was nothing more Sandy could do on that front. Next he telephoned Joanne and explained it was all a piece of mischief on the part of corrupt policemen. He did everything to reassure her.

"Thank you for letting me know." He could hear her take a breath to calm her voice. "It's taken me a while to accept that this is part of his job, and his nature, and I accept that McAllister can't stop himself getting involved . . ." *But it doesn't make it any easier*, she didn't say.

Sandy was impressed at how calm, how accepting, she sounded. And before he hung up, he added, "We're doing everything we can to get him out and send him home."

Aye, she thought, as she thanked him for his kindness, *but where is home?*

•   •   •

Mary Ballantyne hadn't forgotten the promise to drive Mrs. Crawford to her sister's in Shawlands. She was pursuing the same goal but with a different strategy; she had an idea that Mr. Gerry Dochery senior would lead her to Gerry Dochery junior and to help for McAllister. Or trouble for herself.

On Saturday, Mary picked up Mrs. McAllister's neighbor, calculating that the distance from Dennistoun to the suburb of Shawlands was long enough to establish a rapport with the terrified old lady and ask questions. As they were crossing the River Clyde towards the Kilmarnock Road, she began questioning her. "Do you know old Mr. Dochery?"

"Aye. A nice man . . . he did his best, but Wee Gerry . . ." She hesitated. Then, remembering his visit, said no more.

"Did you hear that McAllister is being held on suspicion of murder?" Mary knew she was being ruthless, upsetting an already frightened old lady.

"I saw in this morn's paper . . ."

"He's innocent, of course, but how to prove it . . ." Mary left the question dangling in the middle space on the leather bench seat that was a feature of her mother's car.

"I might have heard something in the close that night, but I didney look. Kept ma door firm shut."

"Wise," Mary replied. "What time was this?"

"Late. Almost ten o'clock. It's hard to sleep sometimes and . . . I heard the neighbor above's clock strike ten . . ." *Then I pulled the blankets over ma head,* she didn't say. *As I didn't want to hear what was going on in the close.* "Next day, when Wee Gerry came around . . ." She was clutching her handbag tight, holding on to it in case even here, in the safety of the car, the bad men might come for her next.

"The police were saying a body was found in your close. It's a wonder none of them came and asked you about it." Mary kept her tone conversational. But the implication was there—something was not right.

"The police did come. But no' that night. Next day, the man above me, a right nice man he is, too, even though he's a Rangers supporter, he went with them. Came back a good while later, four hours or more. He's gone, though. I heard he canceled his milk an' I never seen him since."

"Do you know where he went?"

"No idea. He has a daughter over the Maryhill Road way. But he doesn't get along wi' her husband."

They arrived in Shawlands, a district of respectable homes and row upon row of red sandstone terraces. Her sister's flat was in one such row, three hundred yards from the main road. It curved up a slight hill, and every flat looked as though the curtains were made from a job lot of the same lace.

"Thanks for bringing me over," Mrs. Crawford said as she sat staring at the front door but not moving.

Mary sensed her reluctance. She pulled out her notebook. Scribbled two numbers. "If you need anything, call me. This is work, this is home."

"I'll make sure I have pennies for the phone—just in case." The old woman nodded and reached for the door handle.

"I was thinking of going to see old Mr. Dochery, but I don't have an address for him."

"He should have disciplined thon son o' his years ago, but he didn't have the heart." The old lady tutted, then explained. "The wife died in childbirth, leaving him to bring up the bairn wi' the help of his old mother. Mr. and Mrs. McAllister, they were the soul o' kindness to Wee Gerry and look where that got them." With the look of a thunderhead about to burst, she turned to Mary. "Lend me yon wee book an' the pencil." She wrote down an address. "He's living in Govan. I'm not sure he'll help, Gerry's his only bairn, after all."

"Thank you," Mary said. "And if anyone threatens you . . ."

"I'm too old to be feart o' the likes o' Wee Gerry Dochery. And if I can help Mrs. McAllister, I will." She was out of the car, carrying what looked like a full laundry bag. She paused on the steps and gave a wave before ringing the doorbell.

Mary sat thinking over what Mrs. Crawford had told her, scribbling down notes as the questions piled up.

The absence of a full police search, especially in a murder case, was odd. What was most strange was the nonappearance of the full panoply of photographers, fingerprint team, detectives, and constables on door-to-door inquiries—all the paraphernalia of a murder scene was missing. Plus there was no indication of a body. She thought about the neighbor taken in for questioning and his subsequent disappearance.

"Something not right about all this," Mary muttered as she did a three-point turn to take her back to the *Herald* office. And to herself only, she could not hide the satisfaction, and the thrill, of chasing another potential front-page scoop.

In a cell, in a row of cells filled with the night's refuse gathered up from the streets and the tenements and the public houses of Glasgow, McAllister considered how he would survive if it all went wrong and he was convicted. Thinking about the deprivations of prison, he knew what he could not tolerate: sharing a cell. Bad food, constant noise, the smell, the despair, he could cope with. No books? He lived inside his own head for much of the time, he knew he could endure that. Lack of solitude, that was his idea of hell. *Ah, well, I could always punch DI Willkie, that might earn me time in solitary.*

It was seventeen hours from his arrival at the police station before the *Herald* lawyers achieved his release. When the door of the custody cell was unlocked and he was told to go, he asked, "What's happening?"

"Just go," said a large round sergeant with the complexion of a man who'd eaten one too many pies. "Think yourself lucky."

McAllister made straight for the newspaper. There was nowhere else he could think to go.

Even though it was Saturday afternoon, Mary was at her desk. She looked up when he came in, grinned, but didn't look surprised.

"I'll call our esteemed editor. You look in need of good feed, so go down to the canteen." She waved him away and picked up the phone.

They had to wait nearly an hour, as the editor was at home. He had been looking for an excuse to escape, since his wife's brother and family were visiting and they had four children, all boys. Sandy's wife had a soft spot for McAllister, so all she said was, "Give him my best."

The whole argument for McAllister's release had hinged on the time of death.

Even Sandy Marshall was amazed. "Our solicitors were tipped off that even though the postmortem has yet to be done, the time of death was at the earliest five in the morning . . ."

"And I can prove I was on a train," McAllister said.

"So why on earth did Willkie, and the procurator fiscal, charge you?" Mary asked.

"They say they have witnesses," McAllister said.

"DI Willkie must have known the time of death. It's the first thing you ask." The editor was so puzzled by the police actions, and nonactions, he hadn't noticed that McAllister bore a close resemblance to a gentleman of the road. But Mary did.

"Phew! McAllister! You stink," she said, fanning herself with her notebook.

"Thanks." McAllister smiled. He didn't care. He was out.

"How did you know the estimated time of death?" Sandy was pointing a finger at Mary.

She shrugged. "Contacts."

Sandy left it at that; he knew how unreasonable she became when anyone tried to discover her sources of information. She would never tell the whole truth, never admit to using her late father's circle of friends and relatives in what she referred to as the Auld Boy's Club, emphasis on Boys, too conscious of her rival Keith's accusations that that was what helped her get ahead. *If you have the contacts, use them—discreetly*, was her motto.

"Thank Mrs. Crawford for tipping me off . . ." Mary started.

"Mary, what happened?" Sandy was exasperated. It was his day off. He wanted a drink. He wanted to hear the football results. "How did you find out?"

Mary ignored him; she would tell the story her own way. "Mrs. Crawford, Mrs. McAllister's friend and neighbor, it was something she said." She moved her chair away from McAllister. "She said she'd heard scuffling, and shouting, in the close around ten that night. So I asked the other neighbors in the close, and the newsagent—a nice man—and they had no idea there'd been a fight, or a commotion of any kind, and no police came around asking questions. The man had been reported dead in the early morning, according to Willkie, so how come the circus of a murder inquiry didn't start until the next day?" She tossed two packets at McAllister. "Here, the newsagent gave me the cigarettes you ordered."

"Thanks." Exhaustion had descended and he was hearing the conversation as though the voices were coming from inside an old-fashioned record player's horn. And for the first time he was scared; if DI Willkie could behave so arbitrarily, locking up a journalist with no good cause, what else might he do?

"The story was leaked to our rivals, probably by Willkie, minutes after your interview ended and you were taken into custody."

"What do you mean?" McAllister didn't yet know about the front-page splash.

"A story ran saying you were being held for questioning over the suspicious death of the man," Sandy explained. "And it was on the wireless and the telly news."

"God in heaven." Exhaustion drained out, replaced by fury. "Does Joanne know?"

"Aye, I spoke to her and to your deputy, Don McLeod," Sandy said. "He called around to your house and said to give him a bell as soon as you can."

"I spoke to Joanne," Mary said. "She was calm." *Joanne Ross is stronger than McAllister realizes.* "The lawyers are on the case, making certain there is no reason for Willkie to interview you again. Then you can go home."

McAllister looked down at his hands. Seeing the grime on his shirt cuffs, remembering the smell of vomit and fear in the cells, going home was tempting. But he knew this had to end—lest it come back to haunt them. "The man who was killed, what did you find out about him?"

"Not much," Mary answered. "Maybe you should ask Wee Gerry."

McAllister shook his head. "The lad was fine when—"

Two separate hands shot into the air. "Don't want to know!" Sandy said for both of them.

"I found the name of the examining police doctor . . ." Mary didn't say that he was a retired military doctor in the same regiment as her father. "I asked for an estimated time of death. He wouldn't tell me, so I watched him closely and gave out times . . . One a.m.? Three a.m.? On six a.m., he looked away. Then . . . nah, I won't tell you the rest, might compromise you both." Her shoulders shook—a tiny shudder. "Anyhow, there is no way this Smith character was killed before three in the morning."

"And I have an alibi for three a.m.," McAllister added. "How did the lad die?"

"This person you never met, remember? He was beaten to death. Won't know until after the official postmortem report which of his multiple injuries killed him." She wasn't going to elaborate on the visit to the mortuary, next door to the High Court, in the Saltmarket area, which had been gruesome.

She paid five pounds to see the body plus a keek at the attending doctor's report—a very expensive bribe in a city where five shillings went a long way. The man had been beaten so badly he was unrecognizable. She also read that a prison tattoo—MUM, with roses around the letters, badly inked in red and purple—was noticed by a constable who had arrested the young man numerous times. This led to an interim identification, later confirmed by his mother.

When Mary left the mortuary, she had focused on inventive ways to invoice the *Herald* for the five pounds, the accounts department being wise to Mary's sometimes bizarre expense claims. But it was hard to put the horror of the broken, twisted body behind her.

"So who killed him?" Sandy Marshall brought her back to the here and now.

"Or ordered him killed?" Mary threw out the question, knowing they were all thinking the same thing. Gerry Dochery. Mary shrugged. "Your guess is as good as mine."

"I can't run a story on guesses. Anything else?"

"Last night, I saw Jimmy McPhee," Mary replied. "He's not saying much. But he looks frightened. Coming from him, that's scary. The reward Gerry Dochery offered for information on Jimmy is still out there. Then there's the puzzle as to why McAllister was attacked—Gerry said he wouldn't come after *him*, only Jimmy. So we're back to the same question—who killed the man?"

"And why, and how, was McAllister set up?"

They were silent for a second or so thinking through the question. Finally Mary said, "Let's hope we find out before someone else dies."

At Mary's last sentence, McAllister rocked back in his chair and looked upwards in a silent plea to the Wee Man or one of His ministering angels. *If you discount the stone angels in the Necropolis*, he thought, *in Glasgow it's mostly fallen angels.*

Mary asked, "Boss, can we ask the paper's legal eagle about raising a malicious prosecution charge against the police at Central? 'Harmed the reputation of one of our journalists, hence the newspaper.' That would make a good story."

"Maybe."

"There is one piece of good news . . ."

McAllister was looking like he'd lost a sovereign and found a sixpence. "Good news? I doubt that's possible."

"Listen to this. The *Herald* lawyers dragged a sheriff away from a game of golf. He was not happy. He took it out on DI Willkie, made him look an idiot at the bail hearing. He told him there was no case against you. He reprimanded him for wasting police resources, and the sheriff's time, and said he was submitting a report to Willkie's superiors." Her informant was the custody sergeant who had had scant time for DI Willkie.

She put her hands together in prayer and said, "So please, Mr. Editor, can I write that up?"

Sandy laughed. "Discreetly. I don't want our solicitor having to bail you out an' all."

She was swinging her legs beneath the too-high chair, enjoying herself. "Me?"

"And be careful." The way she rolled her eyes reminded Sandy of his eight-year-old daughter.

"I'll need help with the research," she continued, "a bright young cadet, preferably one who is street-smart . . . No, don't even suggest Mr. Sleazy." The very thought of Keith, her colleague on the crime desk, a man she described as "an all-round sleaze," gave her goose bumps.

"Anything else?" Sandy asked, glancing up at the clock.

"Him. McAllister. I can't stand it a minute longer." Mary handed over a set of keys. "Go to my place and have a bath."

"Okay, okay, I'll be off." McAllister stood.

"Phone Joanne first," Mary said.

"Yes, Mother," McAllister replied.

"Looks like he had a hell of an ordeal," Sandy said when they were alone.

"Aye," was all Mary could say. Being jailed was something that terrified her; she knew how fellow inmates would treat a woman of her class. But it didn't stop her from taking liberties with the law if she thought it might lead to a story.

Sandy could see she was furious. Mary's anger had many shades: loud-shouting-gesticulating-racecourse-bookie anger; fast-talking-multiple-cursing-unladylike anger; cold-white-eye-piercing anger that he had witnessed only once when she was told by a relic-from-the-Jurassic-age journalist that the crime desk was no place for a woman—and this after he'd stolen her story and written it under his own byline.

The editor was equally angry, but he would channel his anger into protecting his journalists by legal means. He finished the conversation with, "I have to get back to the family. See you tomorrow afternoon?"

"I'll be in early. I have a potential story for Monday and I need it to be watertight."

The editor, aware of how much she hated being treated differently from the males, knew not to tell her again to be careful. He sent up a prayer instead.

Seventeen

~

McAllister was exhausted. And dirty. And distressed. And he hadn't called home.

Opening the gate to Mary's basement flat, he noted that the drop from the trefoil-topped iron railings was just right if you should feel like hanging yourself.

A flicker of movement in the upstairs bay window made him glance up, then look down. He hadn't the patience for a confrontation with Mary's mother.

He stood in the hallway, undecided whether to have a bath first, or a drink, when the decision was made for him.

"I've poured you a dram."

Jimmy McPhee.

McAllister remembered Mary had given him a spare key, but Jimmy had vanished that same night. When was it? Thursday? Friday? *Whenever it was, it seemed a lifetime ago.*

"I stayed here last night," Jimmy said, handing him a crystal tumbler of amber liquid. "Mary told me what was going on." He was looking as tired as McAllister, and thinner than his usual skinny self.

They held their glasses up in a silent toast. McAllister saw the tremor in his hand. Jimmy didn't ask about his night in the Glasgow Central Police cells, about the hours of questions and verbal abuse. McAllister was grateful and felt a bond with Jimmy, understanding that here was a man who surely knew what those hours had been like, hours when time seemed suspended.

"I need a bath," McAllister said after he had downed the whisky in one gulp, "then we need to talk."

"Aye," was all Jimmy said.

When McAllister emerged, he was cleaner, but no matter how much he had scrubbed himself, he felt the reek of the police cell lingering in his hair and skin and under his nails.

Jimmy was in the kitchen. He pushed a plate with two pies towards McAllister. His plate had the same, except his pies were covered in bright red tomato sauce. McAllister felt queasy at the sight, but the smell of the lamb mincemeat and a taste of the crust reminded him how hungry he was. They finished their meal with a cigarette. Then talked.

Jimmy began, "You know Gerry Dochery might have had this lad killed."

"I can't believe that."

"Suit yerself. But who else knows where you live? Who else would have sent the lad round?"

"And buy off DI Willkie."

"Aye. I hear thon bastard can be bought easily, but no' cheaply. And Dochery is flush."

They talked, but not for long. McAllister didn't ask the question that was eating him up. He knew there would be no answer. Perhaps not even a lie. *What is this about, Jimmy McPhee?*

"Joanne gave me one week," he said, leaving out that the week was to clear up the so-called burglary at his mother's flat. "So . . ."

Jimmy interrupted. "You're on the night train back. This is my fight."

"Wrecking my mother's place . . . it's personal now." He ignored the growl coming from Jimmy's throat. "Besides, I can probably find Wee Gerry and . . ."

"And what? Remind him of holidays in Millport? Appeal to his decency? Involve his father?"

McAllister knew it was about living with himself if he did nothing. "Old Mr. Dochery lives in Govan. I'm paying him a visit."

Jimmy knew McAllister would do just that, with or without him. "I've the keys to Mary's mother's car."

McAllister gave a half grin. After two pies and tea and whisky, and with Jimmy on his side, optimism had returned. "We should ask Mrs. Ballantyne if it's okay."

"You do it. She'd have me hanged, drawn, and quartered, if she could."

Ten minutes later McAllister was ringing the doorbell of the main house. When she answered he gave her no time to speak. "Mrs. Ballantyne, I'm letting you know Mary has given us the keys to the car. We'd like to borrow it for a day or so."

"Have I a choice?" She was hugging herself as though a non-existent north wind was attacking her bones. She had an aristocratic thinness that reminded McAllister of a highly bred whippet: wrists that he could wrap a forefinger and thumb around; collarbones prominent above the vee of a bone-colored silk blouse with a shade lighter strand of pearls; hair an indeterminate shade of gray-blond and so thin that even a spectacularly expensive haircut could not hide the pink scalp. Her long thin nose reminded him of a whippet, and of another of his mother's sayings, "Who does she think she is—looking down her nose at folk?"

"I'm sorry, Mrs. Ballantyne. We need the car."

"And I need my daughter, Mr. McAllister. She is all I have left." She shut the door, leaving him standing on the step. Feeling guilty, again, he reminded himself, *She is a widow. Mary is her only child.*

McAllister drove. Jimmy slumped down in the passenger seat, a flat-cap disguise working well; he looked like any other Glasgow man, small, defeated, and if anyone caught his eye, ready for a fight. McAllister was wondering what it was about Jimmy McPhee that made him risk his own, and now his mother's, safety. *Friends* was too shallow and too intimate a word to explain their relationship. Yet their oft-times-wordless communication was something McAllister had with no other—not even Joanne. And Jenny McPhee? Why did he come when she called? He had no answer. But the Traveling people, enigmatic, outsiders, remnants of a Celtic past that was sometimes romanticized when the reality was hardship and prejudice, fascinated him. *Perhaps it is the bonds that tie them, bonds I'm scared of, especially with women.* He didn't want to think this was true. He was a man who thought his inability to engage emotionally was a mark of intellect. *Wee Gerry said my going to the high school cut me off forever from ordinary folk. Maybe he was right.*

A horse and cart delivering coal stopped on his side of the street, blocking the way. He could not overtake it for a few minutes. When he did he saw that they were only a few streets from Mr. Dochery's flat.

Once again, it was a tall, soot-blackened tenement block, one that had survived the carpet bombing of Clydeside. They parked in front of an empty block, bright with fireweed and broken glass, which had not been so lucky. Shipyard cranes filled the skyline to the right. And litter and dust and empty dreams tumbled in a wind coming off the river. The bright sun made it all the more drab.

The shipyards were silent, it being late on a Saturday, none of the usual pulse of industrial noise echoing between buildings. And there were few men around, most being at the pub, celebrating a win or recovering from the loss of their football team. Whichever it was, the public houses would be full.

There were no numbers on the buildings. Jimmy asked a wee boy, and the boy asked for sixpence. McAllister gave it to him. Then another boy asked for sixpence to "mind the car." Jimmy was about to refuse, but McAllister handed over the silver coin.

The old man lived in a single end unit on the top floor. It took awhile for him to answer the door. McAllister could see that the worn steps and the four flights would discourage anyone, especially a man in his seventies, from going out much.

"I've been expecting you," he said when he eventually answered the door. He nodded to Jimmy. They had not been introduced, but Mr. Dochery could guess who the man with the red hair was.

"I read about your troubles," Mr. Dochery said after the men had refused a cup of tea.

"That's not what this is about," McAllister began. "My mother's flat was broken into. Your Gerry was there, questioning the neighbors, whilst his friends were smashing up the place."

"That's no' right . . . no' right at all." The old man was shaking his head slowly, his eyes swimming with old people's tears.

McAllister wanted to comfort him. But didn't. "They smashed her best china, they tore up all her pictures of ma dad, ma brother, even their wedding photos were ripped in half." McAllister felt sick at being so relentless. "He tried to pin a murder on me. He might have . . ." This was going too far; it was only a guess that Gerry Docherty was involved in the lad's death. "I want this ended so I need to talk to your Gerry."

"Is your mother safe?"

McAllister could see the old man's eyes filling up again. "She's away on a wee holiday." He was reluctant to name the place his mother was; there was no safety anywhere until this was over.

The old man started muttering, "Why? Why?" He looked like a puff of wind would break him in half.

McAllister remembered the strong laughing man in his fireman's uniform, lifting him up into the driver's seat of the bright red engine. "I'm sorry," he said. "It's no' your fault."

"Why Mrs. McAllister? She always looked out for Gerry. She was always right good to him."

McAllister could barely hear the words, but Jimmy did. "Was

your Gerry working for them bookies that ran the boxing before the war?" he asked.

It was McAllister's turn to be surprised. *Did this whole saga go that far back?* And he noted that Jimmy did not specify what type of boxing.

"Bookies?" Mr. Dochery was shaking his head as though this might shake loose a memory. "Aa've no idea."

They saw he needed to talk, and they listened.

"After he turned eleven, maybe twelve, our Gerry was always in trouble." It began not long after his son started secondary school. The truant officer was always at the door. His son always had cash in his pocket, a florin here, a ten-shilling note there—a lot of money in those days. "Gerry never knew his mother. An' I was always working. Then his granny, ma mother, she died, 'n' there was no one to look out for him, except Mrs. McAllister . . . so for our Gerry to hurt her? That's no' right." He sighed long and slow; years of accumulated sadness were in that breath. Years of disappointment. And helplessness.

"Women, their wee bits o' things meant so much to them . . ." Mr. Dochery looked up at the shelf above the china cabinet. There was a china shepherdess, the kind bought at the Barrows or won at the fairground. There was a mug saying *Souvenir of Largs,* and three framed photographs. One was a small faded wedding portrait, the bride in a simple tailored dress, looking away from the camera at the man in uniform perhaps a foot taller than his bride. The second picture was of a group of men in uniform posed in front of a fire engine, a replica of the one McAllister's mother had in a similar silver frame, now destroyed. The third was a holiday snap in a cheap wooden frame, the varnish cracked and peeling. It was taken at the seaside. McAllister looked at it again. It was a picture of McAllister, his mother, his father, his brother, and Wee Gerry. They were all smiling.

Millport, that summer I won my scholarship and everything changed. The thought hurt. The old man muttered again, "Poor Mrs. McAllister, that's no' right." McAllister thought, *He's right, Gerry's abandoned all decency and honor.*

With a turn of his head, Jimmy gestured to the door, *Time to go.*

McAllister nodded. "Mr. Dochery, if you can tell us where we might find Gerry, we'll be gone."

"There's this warehouse across the river, he says he works in a building business there." The old man sounded skeptical; nothing he knew of his son's affairs was as harmless as a building business. "If you open yon drawer, third one down, pass me paper and a pencil, I'll draw a map." He drew the map. In a simple drawing he betrayed his son.

The warehouse was off South Street in Whiteinch at the far end of the Broomielaw, an area of stone-built warehouses and demolition yards, and run-down wharves, unattractive and dirty. They took the ferry from Linthouse across the Clyde. The giant cranes and gantries of Fairfield shipyard hung over the thick dark water of the river, dwarfing the small vehicular drive-on drive-off boat.

It had been years since McAllister had been in Partick, the original home of Partick Thistle football club, and a district he remembered well from his time as a cadet reporter.

On an early evening on a Saturday, it should have been shut. But through the iron railings and across the large cobbled yard in front of the long low warehouse, Jimmy and McAllister could see men loading and unloading two lorries, one van, and a horse and cart with bricks, planks of timber, and other building materials.

They stayed in the car, watching the scene for about five minutes. McAllister said, "No use making ourselves obvious." He started the car and began to drive off towards the city center. "We can come back after dark."

Jimmy grunted. He'd been thinking the same, but he had been planning to visit without an amateur like McAllister in tow, or in such an obviously expensive car. "Sure you're up for it? Your night in the lock-up was hardly a doddle."

"The sooner I have it out with Gerry Dochery, the sooner I get home."

They didn't take the car. After leaving it outside the house on Blythswood Square they returned by bus, then went to a pub near the warehouse to wait for darkness, hoping whoever had been at the yard earlier would be long gone. When the warning bell rang signaling five minutes to closing time, Jimmy McPhee and McAllister finished their beer and walked around the back streets, waiting for the last of the drinkers to stumble home. Then they went to work.

The high stone wall around the property was old, the mortar crumbling, but Jimmy was up and astride the wall with ease. McAllister was balanced halfway up, unable to find further toeholds. With surprising strength for such a small man, Jimmy put a hand down, gripped McAllister, and hauled him up the last two feet. The drop to the other side was into soft ground but thick with stinging nettles. McAllister hissed on an in-breath, trying not to curse, as he felt the sharp pain on the palms of his hands.

In front of the warehouse, the cobblestoned area the size of a narrow football pitch was open and empty and anyone crossing it would be easily seen. They snuck around to the riverside at the back of the building. On this side, the warehouse doors were large enough to admit cargoes of cotton or coal or timber or iron girders. Overhead three gantries reached out over the dock. At the end of them hung a block and tackle. Resembling an oversized scaffold, the dangling noose was high-tension wire, not hemp rope, and the hook—a huge curve silhouetted against the night sky—looked large enough to execute an elephant.

The dock was empty; likewise the short jetty. No sign of

movement, no craft alongside, nothing tied to the substantial py-lons large enough to accommodate a coastal tramp or sailing ship or a barge or three. The flow of the Clyde was imperceptible. On the flat surface a mirror image of winking red lights at the top of the high gantries of the shipyard looked romantic. But it was all a deception; the menace of that oily black stretch of water, now underused and overpolluted, but still deep enough to launch an ocean liner, was branded into McAllister's psyche. This was the river that had claimed his brother.

Jimmy was examining an outside stone staircase leading to the level first floor, then up to a door leading to the attic space above, looking for access. They tried the door. A substantial wooden af-fair with iron crossbraces, it wouldn't budge. Jimmy looked up at a long line of dormers, about seven feet apart, running the length of the steep slate-tiled roof. Some were windows, some doors leading out onto gantries. He gestured upwards and murmured, "You wait below. If anyone should come along, do nothing." He saw McAl-lister shake his head. "I can look out for maself."

McAllister had to acknowledge the truth of that. Never had he felt so clumsy as after the climb over the wall when he had skinned his knuckles and torn fingernails. The nettle stings were throbbing, his right hand swollen as the poison spread.

He was edgy. He dared not pace. He dared not smoke. It was a long wait.

A scrabbling sound from above alerted him. He stepped out of the shadow of the staircase but could see nothing. Around the river-side, indeed in the entire city, rats as big as the proverbial cat were rife. So he stepped back into the shadows again. A minute later he heard a creak directly above him, a rubbing sound, timber on timber. He looked up. Out on the end of a gantry a figure—it could have been a monkey if they were on the Hooghly, not the Clyde—was clinging to the beam, lying as low as possible, inching its way to the end.

It had to be Jimmy.

The sound of metal hitting metal at high velocity rang out, the sound amplified by the water. *Ping, ping.* And a *phut* sound.

An air rifle. McAllister remembered a neighbor shooting at rats with the gun. *Ping.* He ran out. "Jimmy," he yelled, and instantly knew his mistake. But his yell distracted the shooter. He heard a patter of shots hit the cobblestones next to him. He ran back into the shadows of the warehouse wall. Shocked, scared, he could not think how to help Jimmy. All he could do was hide and watch.

The creature, *definitely Jimmy,* McAllister thought as he watched him clamber over the edge of the wooden arm and cling to the wire. The shooter was firing again, aiming for the dangling figure, maybe missing him, maybe not, as Jimmy made no sound. His feet on the hook, he was trying to swing the wire to give himself momentum so as to reach the water.

The wire moved, but not enough. At the high point of the arc, Jimmy launched himself into midair. There was a sharp crack as his body hit the edge of the jetty. A piercing yell cut through the night air, cut off by a splash.

McAllister began to run. "Jimmy! Jimmy! Over here!"

Not caring who was shooting, not caring he would surely be seen, he dropped to his knees at the edge of the jetty, one kneecap hitting a piece of metal bolted to the timber. Pain shot up his leg. He lay flat and peered underneath, searching amongst the wooden pillars and crossbeams for Jimmy's face. For his grin.

"Jimmy!" he was screaming. The name echoed back at him. Mocking him. *Jimmy!* He tried again. Same taunting echo. He pushed himself up and stumbled some yards further down. Shouted again. No one. Nothing. Except the gurgle of water sucking around the pilings. Except the hum of a sleeping city.

The tide had turned and was retreating. Now the river was running fast. Black night merged with black water. In the rain that had begun a few minutes earlier, a hard steady rain arriving with no warning, no thunder, no lightning, drumming on the water, and visibility was down to a fraction above zero.

McAllister patrolled the riverbank until stopped by a wall with a protruding iron security railing covered in barbed wire. His breathing harsh, his chest tight, he whispered Jimmy's name. He sank down, falling on the painful knee. He didn't care. He put a hand up to his face, finger and thumb into his eyelids, holding back the choking sobs racking his body. To lose another person, another brother of sorts, to this river, that he was unable to bear.

The man above the gantry was watching. He, too, was waiting for Jimmy to surface. When he could no longer see through the dark and the rain, he pulled the door shut, walked down the stairs, let himself out by a small door cut into a main door, and snuck into the empty streets of Whiteinch, confident he had done the job, confident McAllister would not follow him. Nor find him. Or find Jimmy McPhee.

Mary heard the scrabbling at the door. She was scared, but not too scared to take a keek through a chink in the curtains, the windows being securely barred.

McAllister. She sighed. *What is it about drunk men that they can't manage to put a key in the lock and turn it?*

"I am not your mother but I feel like saying, two o'clock in the morning, what time's this to be out?" She was talking as she walked down the hallway, turned the key, and opened the door.

He stumbled in. He leaned against the wall and slid down.

Not that she wanted to—she felt like leaving him to sleep it off in a heap in the hallway—but she bent over him to pull him upright in case he choked. He was soaking wet. There was no smell of alcohol. She felt the heaving of his chest and thought he might be crying. She stepped back and switched on the light. He brought an arm up to cover his eyes but not before she saw the red rims, and a pain in his eyes that shocked her.

"What's wrong?"

He sobbed.

"McAllister! What's happened?"

"Jimmy's gone. He's gone."

She turned out the light, then sat on the floor beside him. She pulled him towards her.

"Jimmy. He fell . . ." He was shaking, his teeth chattering. "I couldn't help."

She was worried about his wet clothes. But he needed to talk. She listened. The sequence of the story confused her. It started with his brother, went via his childhood, his father, his mother, and Gerry Dochery. It started and ended in the Clyde.

She forced him to stand and helped him to bed. Her bed. And for the rest of the night, all four hours of it, she held him close, spooning into his back, warming him, whispering into his ear when he wrestled with the bedcovers and nightmares.

And in the morning, when the noise of the milkman delivering the bottles to her mother above, and the buses, and the cars, and the early pedestrians, filtered through the window and curtains into her dim lit room and her big bed, he turned to her. He pulled her to him. She did not want this to happen. But knew it was inevitable. They barely kissed. He penetrated her. And it felt right. But wrong. They made love with a ferocity that astonished them. Breathless, they lay conjoined just long enough to understand it was a mistake. Then he rolled over. Exhaustion, and release, and the heat of her coursed through his veins. And he fell asleep.

She didn't. Later she went to work, leaving him still asleep.

When reason returned they would acknowledge it shouldn't have happened but accepted it for what it was—comfort, love even. Neither of them ever mentioned it. And they would never forget.

EIGHTEEN

How many times do I have to say it? There is no story. You and the McPhee fellow were on private property. Around midnight. You heard an air rifle. But you saw no one. With McPhee gone, you have no witnesses." Sandy Marshall held up a hand when he saw McAllister about to interrupt. "And, not half a day earlier, you were in lockup on suspicion of murder. So, who's going to believe you and a tinker?"

Mary added, "You can't go to the police. DI Willkie holds a grudge. He could still be out to get you."

"You too, Mary. And the *Herald*," Sandy added. "I'm not unsympathetic, but I'm not about to publish an article on the illegal activities of one of our journalists."

It had been three days since Jimmy had fallen into the Clyde. There were no sightings of him, alive or dead. McAllister had contacted the river police, the ferrymen, shipyard workers, asking the likely whereabouts of a man coming ashore—dead or alive—with no result. He'd hunted throughout the Broomielaw, he'd been into pubs and shops, he'd questioned the tramps congregating under the railways arches. Not even the offer of cash had worked; no one had seen anyone or anything.

He's fine, he kept telling himself. *He's Jimmy McPhee, a man with nine lives.* He hadn't yet told Jenny McPhee her son was missing. The only ones who knew of that night were himself, Mary, Sandy, Jimmy, and whoever fired the rifle.

He was staying at Mary's flat. She had moved upstairs to be with her mother. What she didn't tell him was that her mother, with a mother's radar, suspected the relationship had changed and had ordered Mary upstairs. "For propriety's sake." For once she took her mother's advice.

He wasn't sleeping well; any movement of wind or tree or footsteps on the pavement above startled him into thinking it was Jimmy returning. And in the night, thinking of Mary, he knew he should be ashamed, yet he knew what had passed between them for what it was: a gesture of life in death, a gift of comfort and affection, a single episode never destined to be more than it was.

"Do I have to?" Mary was wriggling in her seat. "I mean, if I do have to I might strangle the man even though he's three times my weight."

Mary's protests brought him back to the editor's desk, back to the argument.

"It's potentially a good story, Mary. And much as you dislike the man, he's a thorough journalist, just doesn't have your connections."

"Was. Was a half-decent journalist. Past tense. He's living on his former reputation . . ." She could see she'd gone too far. "All right, all right, you're the editor, but the moment anything comes up about Jimmy . . ."

"You can put the City Corporation investigation to one side."

"I'm off first thing tomorrow," McAllister told them. "I promised to be back . . ."

"We'll let you know the minute we hear anything," Mary promised.

"Aye," Sandy said. "Get away home. Your mother and your sweetheart need you." He did not add that his friend was bruised and battered—and that was only his body—and having him here was like hosting the proverbial specter at the feast.

"I'm off to Edinburgh in an hour, researching in the companies register. I may stay with friends there tonight," Mary told McAllister. "So post the spare keys through the letterbox."

He looked at her.

But all she did was gather her notes and, with a grin and a sigh, say, "Maybe I'll get a pay rise for putting up with Mr. Sleazy."

Sandy was smiling. "Cheeky bissom," he said as she left, and winked at McAllister.

But there was no response.

McAllister spent that evening searching the public houses around the Trongate. He checked into billiard halls, he went to the pub he knew the boxing aficionados frequented. No one knew anything. Or at least said they knew nothing. Back in Mary's flat he spent the remains of the evening listening to the wind in the trees in the park in the square. Mary did not return. Nor Jimmy. Eventually he slept.

The clink of milk bottles being delivered to upstairs woke him. When he reached the station, early for the train, he realized he hadn't checked at his mother's flat. *Maybe Jimmy went there. No. Unlikely.* He reached the newsagent's kiosk. Searching in his pockets for change for a copy of the *Spectator* the thought came, *the mess at the flat, I've done nothing to tidy up at least the worst of the damage.* He turned back. Then Joanne's face came clear through the fog of indecision, *I made her a promise.* And again he went towards the platform. He was so tangled up in a fankle of anxiety he nearly missed the train he had been three-quarters of an hour early for.

The final whistle from the guard saw him leaping into the carriage, hurtling into a man who was hauling a cabin trunk large enough to contain a body. He almost asked if Jimmy was inside.

The long journey stretched even longer. The dining carriage running out of kippers for breakfast made him furious. "Bloody tourists," he complained, not quite quietly enough for an obviously English couple sitting behind to miss hearing.

The empty stretch of moorland on the Cairngorm plateau depressed him; not seeing the flashes of loch and lochan, the running peat-brown burns, a solitary golden eagle hovering above the heather, the rowan and birch and pine around Aviemore, he took no comfort in the grandeur of the landscape. A delay at the water tower at Carrbridge made him seethe. And when the train finally drew into the station he found he had crushed the ticket so tightly the inspector told him off. The man recognized McAllister and had been joking. But glimpsing the Grim Reaper countenance only partially obscured by the brim of the hat, he said no more and waved the passenger through.

It was late afternoon when the taxi dropped him home.

Leaving his bag in the hallway, he made for the kitchen.

"You made it." Joanne was smiling.

"I said I would." It came out shorter than he intended, but he reached for her hand to soften the hurt he saw flit across her face.

"I'll put the kettle on," Granny Ross said.

"I'll butter some o' my new gingerbread," his mother said.

"Did you bring me a present?" Jean asked.

"Jean!" her mother chastised her.

Annie, standing back from the fuss, was examining him in an *I'm not examining you* way. She was gauging his mood, looking for change, for damage, not knowing it was her own behavior that betrayed damage.

The front doorbell rang. Mrs. Ross went to answer it.

His mother was shooing a kitten off the table away from the butter.

Surely that cat is new, he was thinking as he sat at the table trying to ignore the girls, who were squabbling like seagulls over whose turn it was to clean out the rabbit's cage.

"Outside, both of you!" Joanne said loudly, and for the second time.

Mrs. Ross came back.

"Who was at the door?" Joanne asked.

"Mrs. McPhee, the tinker woman," her mother-in-law answered. "I sent her to the back door. The cheek o' the woman coming to the front . . ."

"You did what?" His shout echoed off the ceiling, bounced down to the table. Everyone stood still like a game of statues in the schoolyard.

Granny Ross's mouth took on the texture of a prune. "She's a tinker," she said. "You can't let her in through the house."

"Scared I'll steal the silver, are ye?" Jenny McPhee stood on the kitchen doorstep, the door being wide open in the unusual summer warmth.

"This is my house. Mrs. McPhee is my visitor. She is to be treated with respect." McAllister's voice was harsher than intended.

"Why is she here? Why is she getting you to run thither and yon at her bidding, risking your life—aye, I've heard it all. She's no' even family. But here you both are, upsetting my daughter-in-law . . ." Her voice trailed off. Then Mrs. Ross undid her apron, took her handbag off the dresser, and left by the front door.

Silence.

Mrs. McAllister could sense there were to be no answers to the questions she too had been puzzling over. So she said, "I'll see to the rabbit," and went into the garden, nodding at Jenny McPhee on her way out.

Annie took her sister's hand, and they followed.

Joanne said to Jenny McPhee, "Mrs. McPhee, can I offer you tea? Or maybe something stronger?"

McAllister looked at the tinker woman. He saw what Joanne

had seen. Jenny McPhee knew. What, he didn't know. A tremor ran through him, terrified there was more news. Worse than the news he had come back to break to her.

In the sitting room, after fetching a glass of whisky for McAllister and Jenny, Joanne sat on the piano stool, hesitating. "Do you want me to leave you together?" She was looking at Jenny, one eye squinting through her new spectacles, the damaged eye hidden behind a horrid piece of flesh-colored sticking plaster, roughly cut to black out the lens.

Jenny was shaking her head. "Up to you. But maybe you're no needing bad news after all you've been through."

"I'll stay," Joanne said, and crossed the room to sit on the sofa with the old woman.

"I've just arrived back. I was coming to tell you," McAllister said. "Jimmy is missing, but I'm sure he's fine. You know your son, nine lives and all that." He was forcing a cheerfulness he did not feel, and neither woman was fooled.

"I couldney sense him," Jenny said. "A was lookin', listenin', right feart he's gone."

McAllister did not understand. "He's missing, hiding out somewhere. He'll be fine."

"If he's gone," she continued, "I want his body. I need to see ma son buried the old way. That's what he'd have wanted. The old way."

"You can't be sure he's gone, maybe he's . . ." He stopped. He'd asked himself the same questions over and over. And come up with no answers.

Joanne knew that reassurances were only words. She looked at Jenny. "Mrs. McPhee, McAllister will do all he can to see Jimmy is returned to you." *One way or another*, she was thinking as she frowned at him, willing him to say no more.

"Good enough." Jenny was nodding, almost rocking, as though in prayer. Then she gathered her shawl around her, put her bag over her arm, and with an effort akin to that of an invalid, she unbent and stood. "Thank you, Mr. McAllister. Thank you, lass."

"I'll let you know the minute I hear anything," McAllister promised.

But she only nodded.

Joanne saw Jenny McPhee to the front door. She was gone a few minutes. When she came back she stood on one side of the empty fireplace. The light was behind her, but directly on him, and it did not flatter. She examined him. Slowly. She saw his dark blue eyes, now nearer black. He was looking at the box of Passing Clouds as though they were a precious artifact. She took in his hands, which were unsteady when he struck a match for another cigarette. She felt there was a difference to him, something she would not have been able to describe if asked, something that, after a second of panic, she put down to fear. And she knew, no matter how much she did not want to, she should listen.

"I have to deal with the real world sometime. When you hide things from me my imagination makes it far worse." She said this quietly but he heard what he took to be anger in her voice.

But it was not anger, it was frustration—utter infuriating frustration upon frustration: the headache behind the eyes which came and went in waves that she could not control; the fantasies that overpowered her—one in particular—when she opened a book, it only happened when it was a novel, she fancied the pages damp with a colorless blood, sticky, with a hint of a smell, a sweet cloying presence that would never leave her fingers if it touched her; and the air, in every room in the house, anywhere indoors, she felt a pressure on her skin, her throat in particular, so the only place safe was outdoors, amongst flowers, in a breeze or a wind. She shared this with no one, especially not the doctors. The mass of Craig Dunain, filling the western corner of the horizon in the hills above the town, the place of so-called asylum but to her mind imprisonment—why else were there bars on the windows?—terrified her.

"Tell me what happened. All of it."

"How could Jenny think Jimmy was gone? No one knows what happened, so why . . ."

He gestured to her to sit down. With a generous measure of whisky in his glass, he began. He told her of the destruction of his mother's home. He told her of his struggle with the young man, now deceased. He glossed over his night in the cells, saying it was no more than DI Willkie going on a fishing expedition. He described the visit to Mr. Dochery. He left out the bare-knuckle fight. Then there was nowhere to go but the dark night at the warehouse down by the Clyde. When she heard him describe the splash and the water and the tide and his fear, she knew he had been searching for two people—Jimmy and his brother.

That week McAllister went to work for a few hours each day. Mostly he stayed at home, in a dwam. The others in the household, but not Granny Ross, who had not been seen since he'd asked her to leave, kept clear of him. Even Annie knew not to pester him with questions. She was longing to know what was happening and gathered it was serious and was scared; the wedding meant more to her than she knew.

Passing the hours by attempting to read until it was time to sit down with his best friend, the whisky bottle, McAllister was desolate at his failure. He recalled every visit to every pub and dive and sleaze pit and boxing club. He counted the money he'd paid out and the favors he'd pulled in.

Mary had done the same. And she had put out the word to her vast network of informants that she'd pay ten pounds for information—an unheard-of amount of money where five pounds or less would pay for a kneecapping. Or worse. So far, no news.

The extended McPhee clan, Jenny's eldest son, her younger sons, and her cousins—who were legion—they were all searching for Jimmy.

No news.

Mary rang daily, talking mostly to Don McLeod. *Thankfully*, McAllister thought, as he did not want a conversation with Mary lest he was tempted to return to his city.

No news.

And every time the telephone rang, at home, at work, every time the postman delivered the mail, his heart began to pound, until he heard the news—no news. The days passed, a week passed, nearly two weeks; McAllister finally gave up hope of ever seeing Jimmy McPhee alive.

The river took him, just like it took my brother, he thought. Then changed his mind. *No, it was that bastard Gerry Dochery.* But he didn't know it was Gerry. *Whoever it was, I'll get you.* And he vowed, just as he had when he discovered who had driven his brother to take his own life, *I'll get you. Maybe not now, maybe not next week or next year, but I'll get you.*

Five more days elapsed. It was Thursday morning, the day after deadline, so a late morning for McAllister. He was sitting at the kitchen table, enjoying the morning quiet that had descended since Granny Ross no longer came around when he was at home; no more muttering when he refused a cooked breakfast, preferring his usual coffee and cigarette. No more arguments between Annie and her grandmother over what she was wearing—too scruffy; what she was reading—too adult; how she was sitting—slouching in her chair; her reading and eating toast—getting crumbs everywhere.

And no longer came the whine of the vacuum cleaner weaving in and around his feet when all McAllister wanted on the morning after deadline was to sit quietly and read the national newspapers, with his second cup of coffee. Sitting around reading was not an occupation Granny Ross approved of, her being convinced it was bad for you. "Gives you headaches," she said. *Makes you too big for your boots, all thon ideas,* she thought.

McAllister read the *Herald* first, glanced through the *Scotsman* next, read the headlines of the Aberdeen newspaper, and ignored the *Gazette.* He was on page five, reading the follow-up article to the front-page headline story written by Mary Ballantyne. Although there was no byline, he recognized her style, and was interested in, but not surprised by, the exposé of City Council corruption.

Joanne was sitting opposite him reading the *Gazette.* She glanced up at the headlines in the *Herald.* With her one-lens glasses she couldn't see clearly, but the headline jumped out at her. She squinted at the picture, but even with her weak vision, she recognized the man. "McAllister," she whispered.

"Mm-hmm?" he replied.

"McAllister . . ." The color in her face, which had only just returned to her cheeks, had drained to a pale corpselike pallor.

"Joanne, what is it? Is it your eyes?"

"That man . . ." She pointed to the newspaper. "Don said it was all over . . ."

Her cup shattered on the tiled floor. Joanne slumped sideways. He raced to her, his chair clattering to the floor, gripping her under the arms. "Here, put your head on the table. I've got you. It's fine, I have you."

"The newspaper, it's getting wet, it's . . ." She was reaching for the newspaper, trying to rescue it from the pool of spilt tea.

"What's happened?" Annie rushed in, still in her nightie.

"What's wrong?" His mother was in the doorway, bringing with her the scent of warm bread.

"What have you done to her this time?" Granny Ross had

come in the front door, having forgotten this was McAllister's late morning.

"Annie, call the doctor." The grannies he ignored. "Here, my love, let's get you onto the sofa. Can you stand? Here, lean on me."

They stumbled into the sitting room. She lay down. Annie came back. "The doctor will be fifteen minutes."

She came over, sat beside her mother, calm, scared, in charge. "McAllister, bring the pills from the kitchen dresser. And water."

"Are you sure?" An almost-twelve-year-old had more presence of mind than himself, and he did as he was told.

The grannies were at the kitchen table, cleaning up the spilt tea, picking up the shattered teacup. They looked up as he came in. He saw how old they were, and how frightened.

"She's had a turn, she's tired that's all." He knew that to be untrue; something she saw in the newspaper had shocked her. What, he didn't know. But he would find out. He reached for the bottle of pills, then poured a glass of water. Remembering the *Herald*, he quickly folded it, putting it in the dresser drawer. "Don't worry. The doctor will be here soon."

When her son had gone, Mrs. McAllister went to the stove and lifted the kettle. "Tea, Elsie?" she asked.

"That'd be grand," came the reply from Mrs. Ross. They nodded at each other. Truce.

The doorbell rang. Annie answered, saying, "Hello, Dr. Matheson, you were quick." She showed him into the sitting room and at a glance from McAllister she left.

Annie went to the kitchen. "Mum's fine. She just fainted," she said. Then she went upstairs, because she felt like crying and didn't want anyone to see her.

After the doctor left, and after Joanne went to bed to sleep, and after his mother left with Granny Ross to visit her house, he telephoned the *Gazette* and spoke briefly to Don McLeod.

"Buy the *Herald*," he told his deputy, "and when you've read it, come over to my house. I want an explanation." He hung up without the usual courtesies. For the next half hour he read and reread the article and was none the wiser.

When Don arrived he was faced with a man he did not recognize, a man in such a fury Don was afraid the editor might have a heart attack.

"This"—he was holding up a tea-stained, crumpled newspaper—"something about this picture or headline made Joanne faint in shock."

"Is she a' right?"

"No, she's not. But the doctor gave her a sedative, and she's asleep." His hand and the pages and his knee were shaking. He had shut the sitting room door, not wanting the children and Joanne and whoever else might appear to overhear the conversation.

"Joanne's read it?" Don asked.

"No. It was the picture. She recognized the man." He tapped the front page with his finger, but there was no need, Don had already seen it.

"It was a couple of years ago . . ." Don began.

"A couple of years ago? So I was here?" He was staring at Don, doing his best to suppress his anger. But the fierceness in his eyes and the tap of his fingers on the newspaper made it clear; he was furious.

"Aye. But you'd only been here—maybe nearly a year . . ." The deputy editor didn't know how to lessen the guilt he was feeling. Not at deceiving McAllister—they had not known him well at that time, but he needed to lessen his own guilt, his sense that by not connecting the past with the present, he had let Joanne down.

"If you knew, and Jimmy . . . ?" A thought hit him. "So Jenny must have known about whatever it was and that's why she asked me to help Jimmy." He was shaking his head. "So something went down up here in the Highlands, no one told me, and I'm expected to clear it up for you? So heaven's sakes! Tell me!"

Don couldn't look at him. The accusation was fair. As calmly as he could he lit another cigarette from the glowing butt of the previous one and started. "It was a while ago, all sorted out and . . ."

"How was Joanne involved? And Jimmy?"

"He was the one who fixed it." Don didn't add, *At my request.* "It all started with Bill Ross . . ." Then he stopped. If he involved Joanne's former husband, he guessed that McAllister might find him, and violence would follow. "Look, I'm not at all sure there's a connection with recent events."

"What happened?" McAllister asked as though the words were in capital letters. "How does Joanne know this man? Why did she faint at the sight of his picture?" The sense of betrayal was what hurt the most. The sense he had been kept in the dark. And used. "People have died. I've put my mother and myself at risk— and Jimmy said nothing. And you, I thought we were friends but . . ."

McAllister began pacing, wearing a path from fireplace to bookcase on the already threadbare Turkish carpet. "I want to hear everything, because if I later find out you've deceived me . . ."

Don let the threat go. He could understand that McAllister might feel betrayed and had a fleeting thought that perhaps one of Joanne's calm pills might be needed. "Sit down, man. I canny talk when you're all over the place like a madwoman's custard."

McAllister sat. The fury had drained him, too drained to even offer a dram, or take one himself. He smoked throughout the time it took for Don to explain. As did Don. Although the front door opened and closed twice, no one interrupted.

"It was Bill Ross. His business was in trouble. He borrowed from a loan shark who was new to town, and trying to set up shop here. Then Bill Ross couldn't pay the loan back—one o' those compound interest scams. These men, they came after him. They threatened Joanne, and the girls. And she told me."

He took a deep breath. That time, when Joanne was at her most vulnerable, when she regularly had to hide the bruises, to hide what was happening to her and her children, when friends and family knew but did nothing, Don had not intervened. He had not supported her because, like most people of this time and place, he saw it as horrible, but not unusual, something women had to bear, separation and divorce being completely unacceptable. *Till death us do part*, he knew that was, is, what everyone believes.

"Then it turned out these people, men, wanted more than Bill Ross's debt, they wanted his building business. What with all the new road building contracts, a new bridge, and council housing schemes, there's a lot to be made up here in the Highlands, if you're in the building trade. These people from Glasgow, that's their trade, amongst other things—not that we knew that at the time—and this was a way to expand their business. I told Jimmy. He knew them, said he'd had dealings with them in the past. He never told me the details. He saw them off. And as far as I know, Bill Ross's debt was never repaid."

That was the bare bones of it. Don couldn't bear to remember how terrified Joanne had been, how crushed by domestic violence. When it was over, when she began to make a life for herself in her wee prefab house, earning her own living, taking care of her children without the shadow of violence, he'd watched her change, blossom into the beautiful confident woman she was, until once again attacked, this last time by a violently insane woman. In Don's estimation, apart from the physical injuries, the last attack was easier to recover from than the long insidious undermining violence of a husband ready to settle any perceived slight with his hands.

"How much was the debt?"

"A thousand pounds."

"That's a fortune!"

"It is."

"And where is Bill Ross?" McAllister asked.

"I'm no' sure," Don replied.

"Betsy, his new wife, is still in town. I saw her last week."

"Aye, but what with a new baby an' all, Bill Ross was planning to leave for Australia first, to start work, find a house, and she's joining him when he's settled."

"Granny Ross hasn't mentioned it." McAllister now understood the woman's heartache, but that didn't excuse her son. "And if Bill Ross has gone, he didn't bother to say goodbye to his daughters."

Don McLeod shrugged. He thought so little of Joanne's former husband, that didn't surprise him.

"So with Jimmy stymieing a lucrative link between the building business in Glasgow and potential new contracts up here . . ."

"And Jimmy showing the man up in front o' his brothers . . ." Don thought loss of face was a much more likely cause for revenge.

McAllister stubbed out a cigarette. His mouth felt raw and dry, and he was weary of the whole drama. "Will you call Mary from the office?" he asked. "Fill her in. It's hard to make a private phone call here." It was another matter about sharing a house that frustrated him; any other reason for not calling Mary himself he could not admit to.

It was mid-afternoon when Joanne came into the sitting room. "I'm sorry about today."

He hadn't heard her; he was writing in a notebook, trying to decide which recording of Sidney Bechet he would order from the stockists in London, anything to stop himself agonizing over the perceived betrayal by Don and Jenny McPhee. And Jimmy. When he looked up and saw her, as insubstantial as a wraith half glimpsed across a lochan in the gloaming, McAllister felt sick.

"Don told me what happened between Bill Ross and that man. You have every reason to be upset." He could not use the word *husband*. Even *ex-husband* was too intimate.

"So have you."

She took the armchair on the other side of the empty fireplace, opposite him. She took a deep breath, and the scent of the pinecones in the empty grate, pinecones she and the girls had collected from the forest around Craig Padraig, the ancient vitrified fort on the eastern flanks of the town, filled her with the memory of shadows and sunbeams piercing the gloom of the dense woodland, and the dark scent of the sticky pine secretions she loved to pick off and roll into balls, staining her fingers, and the shouts and laughter from the children echoing around the bowl of the fort. The memory tugged at the corners of her mouth and she smiled.

It was quiet. She had the unpleasant feeling of having slept too much. She had a metallic taste in her mouth of the pills the doctor insisted she take. "Something to help you sleep." She'd agreed, even knowing how much she hated the woozy afterfeeling. But sleep was preferable to the terrors swirling around her brain.

"I'd really like a cup of tea."

He took her hand. "A cure for almost everything, a good cup of tea."

She wished he meant it; whisky was not her favorite form of comfort. *One drunken husband was enough*, she thought.

The kitchen was empty. And the garden. He had no idea where all the women had gone. But he was grateful they'd left him alone with Joanne.

After the tea, and after the shortbread had taken away the medicinal aftertaste, Joanne began, "That man in the newspaper, he and his brothers threatened me. And my girls . . ."

"Forget them. You're safe now."

"Don't patronize me. I might not be fully well, but I'm not stupid."

The sharpness in her voice, the flash in her eyes, startled him. "I'm sorry, I—"

"McAllister, we need to talk."

If it were anyone other than Joanne who had said this, he would shut down. He hated the phrase *we need to talk*. It made him think of endings—end of a love affair, a friendship, a job. *We need to talk* rang as clearly as the tolling of a funeral bell.

"It takes time to recover from an operation on the brain," she began.

He was listening and watching, and her opening remark forced him to see that underneath the pallor, the dull hair, the thin body, Joanne, the Joanne he loved, was still there, mostly intact.

"My optic nerve was damaged but hopefully will mend. I need rest. I need to eat more. Worry is the bad for me, but trying not to worry when you don't fully comprehend what is going on is impossible." She said nothing about the headaches so incapacitating that she could not see, or stand. The hallucinations she put down to the tranquilizers she hated but depended on.

He was nodding, waiting for her to say what she needed to say.

"At the time, we—Don and I—had no idea what to do. Bill couldn't pay. He said they wanted to take over his business, and he would never let that happen." *He'd put me and my girls in danger rather than let go of his precious business.* "So we asked Jimmy to help. And he did. After they left, I tried to deny it, but there was always a possibility they would return. It's an awful lot of money." She stopped. This was the most she had spoken in a continuous stream since the operation, and she was exhausted.

McAllister nodded. "This is not just about the money. I've been thinking about it and I'm sure there is more."

"Meaning they want revenge on Jimmy?" When McAllister said nothing, she answered her own question. "Maybe this will only end when they kill Jimmy. Or he . . . She couldn't complete the thought it so horrified her. "I met that man. He came to my house. He is pure evil."

They were quieted by that thought. Then the tick of the carriage clock and the groan of the oak tree across the street as the night wind rose and the faintly nautical sound of an old house, the sounds of minutely shifting windows and floorboards and roof slates and ill-fitting doors, surrounded them, unheard yet there, comforting them.

"Would you like more tea?" he asked eventually.

"I'd love some," she replied.

When he returned she asked, "What now?"

"Sandy Marshall has Mary Ballantyne and a colleague at the *Herald* searching for details of Councilor James Gordon's businesses. They think he's involved in corruption with council contracts." He knew he had to be honest. "But no word of Jimmy."

"You need to find him." She saw him about to protest. "No. Listen to me. If I could, I'd be in Glasgow searching for him myself. You need to do this for Jimmy. For his mother. And for me."

"I can't risk leaving you alone."

"I won't be here. Don't worry"—she was smiling at his reaction—"we loved our few days camping so much, Margaret suggested we take a cottage in Portmahomack for a week or so—the girls don't go back to school until mid-August, and your mother can come with us."

"You've thought this through." He didn't ask about their wedding scheduled for the thirty-first of July, three weeks away. He knew nothing about the preparations, or lack of preparations—that was women's business. He knew he would be there. Knew he could not, would not, let Joanne down.

"I have. No one will know where we are, so we'll be safe. And the girls will love it."

He could see it was settled and he was relieved. But the thought of Glasgow was no longer enticing: His mother's flat, he needed to clear out; Jimmy, he needed to find; Councilor Gordon, that was a *Herald* investigation; and Mary Ballantyne, he was embarrassed to face. But he had no choice. He was now even more obligated to help Jimmy McPhee, whether Jimmy wanted his help or not.

"Find Jimmy," Joanne said.

"I'll try." He did not say what they were both thinking—*alive or dead.*

"Start with your old pal Gerry." She saw his wonderfully expressive eyebrows shoot heavenwards—something that usually made her laugh. Not this time. "I know he's a criminal, but there is a history between you. Your mother told me about the holiday in Millport when you were boys, your fathers working together, so start with him. Then come home when it's over."

He would never know how terrified she was that he wouldn't return. Never know how clearly she saw his doubts, his ambivalence about marriage, this town, this life. She knew he loved her, so she was prepared to wait. Fight for him if necessary.

"When this is over, we will talk about our future. In the meantime, all I want is for my hair to grow back over my scars."

She was proud of her thick nut-brown hair. "And I do not want to wear glasses." She stood, came over and kissed him lightly on his head, saying, "I really need to eat. My tummy is grumbling something rotten."

Her kiss was a benediction, a release, a kiss of thanks. And trust. He felt unworthy.

When she left the room, he stood, looked around the room, thought about this house, a house he owned. And he made a decision; when he went back to Glasgow to make one last effort to find Jimmy, he would repay the debt. He was not a rich man, but without quite knowing how, he had money. Over the years, when he had only himself to support, his salary had accumulated, and his flat in Glasgow had sold for much more than he'd paid for it. It would almost empty his bank account, but it was not in his nature to resent the loss of cash, not if it protected Joanne. And assuaged his conscience.

Nineteen

This time he drove to Glasgow. His mother was with him. Nothing he'd said could dissuade her.

"I need to see my home," she said. "It'll need a good clean."

More than that, he thought. "I can see to it," he protested.

She'd rolled her eyes at that suggestion. It was not so much her son she distrusted; in her way of thinking, no man knew how to properly scrub a floor.

"Mother, it's a mess, it's . . ." *Heartbreaking* was the word he wanted to use, but daren't.

"I know. Mrs. Crawford told me. Besides, I'm coming with you to talk to Mr. Dochery—and I've an idea where to find Wee Gerry."

As the road south unwound, he was glad his mother was with him. She revealed the familiar landscape anew, pointing out landmarks that in his anxiety at returning he would have driven past without noticing. And with his mother in the front seat, he daren't speed.

Along the Great Glen; past Loch Ness, Loch Lochie, and Loch Oich; under Ben Wyvis; through and over the Pass of Glencoe, as they waited for Ballahulish ferry, finally reaching Ben Lomond and the "bonnie, bonnie banks." Along the loch, familiar territory for Glaswegian day-trippers, she had commented, "It's right bonnie" so many times, he had stopped responding. For it was, this sparsely populated Highland landscape, this Scotland of history, of clans, and battles, and clearances, of mountain, river, loch, and glen, it was indeed bonnie.

They arrived in the outskirts of the city in the early evening.

"You can't stay in the flat until it's cleared," he said. "So we'll stay in a wee hotel near St. Enoch's Station."

"You do that, Son. I'm staying wi' Mrs. Crawford. Then her and me, we're going to make an early start on the cleaning." He had seen the letters arrive, but had no idea the old friends had everything planned. "She was biding wi' her sister but couldn't stand it, so now she's home."

Since his mother's visit to the Highlands, and the time spent with Joanne and the girls, he had commented on how much more outgoing she had become.

"It's the children," Joanne explained.

And adversity, he thought. *My mother knows how to deal with adversity. It's only afterwards she falls apart.*

McAllister took the first boardinghouse he could find. It was near Kelvingrove Park, deliberately away from Blythswood Square. Next morning he was at the *Herald* early—nine in the morning—hoping Mary would not be there. He knew he would have to meet her sometime, *but not yet*, he told himself as he walked in the big doors and past reception.

An older woman whom he'd known from his time on the newspaper smiled and said, "Mr. McAllister, there's a message for you," and handed him a folded piece of lined paper.

For a moment his heart raced as he thought, *Jimmy*. Then he saw another scrawl, another uneducated hand. *Stop being such a snob*, he told himself as he read the bad grammar with little punctuation.

> Its nothing to do with me. So call off the Mary woman or
> it will get bad for you and him A frend

He was engrossed in the note. It was from Gerry Dochery, of that he was certain. The *its nothing to do with me* he took to be a denial. *Of what, though? Call off Mary* . . . that was clear. But how? If anyone knew Mary they would know it was impossible. *For you and him?* Did that mean Jimmy was alive?

"Hello, stranger." Mary had come up behind him.

He jumped. Then quickly put the note in his pocket. She was grinning. He smiled back. But a faint sweat broke out on his lower back.

"How's Joanne?" she asked.

So that's how it's going to be, he thought, and was immensely grateful to Mary Ballantyne.

"She's well. She and the girls are going on holiday with Rob McLean's mother, Margaret."

"I know, Don McLeod told me." She turned and they went upstairs to the end of the reporters' floor. "Come on, McAllister, our esteemed editor can't wait to hear all about Councilor James Gordon and his shady deeds in the Highlands."

Her good sense touched him. What had happened between them was an episode of that moment, that night of terror, and never to be repeated. Or spoken of.

"Can't get rid of you," Sandy Marshall said when they came into his office. They settled down to thrash out what they knew, and what they could print.

"I now know the background, and it may explain everything," McAllister told them.

Both journalists noted the "may."

"Don McLeod told me the gist of Councilor Gordon's visit to the Highlands," Mary said. "So I've been trawling through the company records of the building business in Whiteinch. Not that I've found much, as yet. But Gordon's trying to take over a Highland building company is interesting."

"Everything about Councilor Gordon was hearsay until your deputy tipped Mary off," Sandy Marshall added.

"I've been researching company records, building tenders, contracts, building suppliers, employment contracts, everything and everywhere there might be a paper trail," Mary continued. "The trouble is, it's mostly cash in the building trade, and the union officials I've spoken to know very little about this company. The father registered it under the name *Gordon Brothers* thirty years ago. Now another Gordon is director with two brothers, but Councilor James Gordon's name is *not* registered with Company House . . . What? What are you two grinning at?"

"Do you ever come up for air?" Sandy asked her. "You've spoken all that in one breath."

"Eff off." Mary shook her head at him. "However, I do have some other leads—"

"I'm only joking," Sandy said. "This is one of the news stories of the decade . . . if we can prove it."

"That's what I'm trying to do. Only Mr. Sleazy, who is too busy filling in his football pools, is worse than useless, and accounts are after me as my taxi fares are astronomical. I need help. So, McAllister?"

"I'm here to find Jimmy and bring him home." That stopped the flow of words.

"McAllister, everyone's concerned about Jimmy McPhee, but . . ." Sandy couldn't bring himself to say what he believed.

McAllister could see they thought Jimmy was dead. "This was left for me at the front desk." He gave the note to Sandy and watched as he and Mary read it.

Mary shrugged, saying, "This won't stop me, I've had far worse threats than that." She looked at the note again. "'And him'? Does that mean he knows where Jimmy is?"

"Does 'him' mean Jimmy?" was Sandy's question.

"I don't know but I think it does." McAllister hoped it implied Gerry knew where he was. As for Jimmy being alive, and well, that he could only hope for.

"What do you propose?" Sandy asked McAllister.

"Find Gerry Dochery."

"I'm coming with you," Mary said.

"No."

From the way he said no, she knew McAllister meant it.

"Best you follow up the contracts angle."

She shrugged. He was right, that was what she did best. But being ordered to stay away from the action, that she did not like. "I want an interview with Gerry Docherty as soon as you find him. I want to know if he knows about the Gordon brothers' business dealings."

"And ask Gerry if he knows about the one thousand pounds," Sandy added. "That's a small fortune."

"I did hear Councilor Gordon has a great big place on a lochan in Milngavie." Mary was certain this was a good lead.

Milngavie was a rich suburb on the outskirts of Glasgow where Lanarkshire became Stirlingshire. There was a large reservoir, and in some areas views to the Campsie Fells. Amongst the more recent post–World War I semidetached houses of solicitors and civil servants, there were a good number of large Victorian homes inhabited by citizens whose wealth had been passed down through generations of merchants, many in the East India trade. The best of these backed on to a large pond or small loch, depending on your aspirations, and it was a place of beauty. Not a place for a Gordon of Partick Cross notoriety.

"You find out whose name the house is in," McAllister told her. "My mother said Gerry Dochery might be hiding out in his late grandmother's house in Strathblane. That's only fifteen miles further on from Milngavie, so I'll drive past and check it out."

"Drive by. That's all," Sandy warned. "No confrontations, no letting Gordon know you're on to him."

"I'll look but won't stop," McAllister promised.

He left Sandy and Mary to their discussion about how to continue with the story. He had a late breakfast at the canteen. He went to the big department store on George Street. Then drove to his mother's flat.

Not including his mother, there were four women there, with mops and scrubbing brushes. The fumes from the bleach and disinfectant made his eyes water. His mother was sitting in a cleaned kitchen drinking tea out of the one surviving cup from her wedding tea service.

"Thon nice man Mr. Gillespie from upstairs is going to repaint the hall for me," she said. He could see the effort it was taking her to keep bright. "Then on Sunday me and Mrs. Crawford are going to the Barrows to shop for more dishes."

"I've got a wee present to start you off." He handed her a box. Watching her as she opened it, he was expecting the usual protests of *you shouldn't*, or *you have to take it back, it's too expensive*. He was wrong. His mother lifted out the teapot first, then the milk jug, then the sugar bowl.

"The cups and saucers are in this other box," he said, waiting for a reaction.

Mrs. Crawford came in smelling of furniture polish. *Lavender*, he thought.

"Mrs. McAllister, that's right lovely. A new tea service exactly the same as your other one."

"It's right good of ma John to think of it," his mother said proudly. "And I have a spare cup." She held up the one she was drinking from and toasted, "*Slainte*."

Mrs. Crawford began to laugh. The other ladies came in to see what was happening.

McAllister smiled. Patting his mother on the shoulder, he whispered, "I'll be back later." He left to the sound of billing and cooing from the old ladies as they unwrapped and admired the Crown Derby half tea service, a replacement for the one that represented the decades of Mrs. McAllister's married life. And his mother could show it off to her friends, proving what a good son she had.

He did not need a map. Nor, he decided, did he need to visit old Mr. Dochery. Not that he distrusted the old man, but he didn't want Wee Gerry Dochery to suspect that McAllister knew of his possible bolthole in the countryside.

Maybe he'll be there, he thought as he started the engine and drove out of the East End towards the main arterial road north.

He'd been to the village once before and remembered a swift-flowing burn and the steep escarpment of the ridge that rose only a scant mile from the village. On that one visit, someone, he couldn't remember who, had pointed out a waterfall that to his child's eyes was only a long white scar on the face of the cliff. Then a few minutes later he saw what the adults were looking at. The waterfall was streaming upwards, in reverse direction, and throwing off rainbows into the bright sky. He was a wee boy, and he'd thought it was magic, water traveling upwards. "It's the wind," someone had explained. "It blows the water up through the chimney in the cliff." The explanation had puzzled him, for he saw no chimney, and as every child knew, adults couldn't see magic, so he decided magic was the real explanation.

The main road north to the Trossachs ran out through Maryhill and Anniesland and was busy, but not as busy as later when returning workers would commute to the more desirable suburbs on buses and trams and, more and more, by motorcar. He passed the new Roman Catholic church, an inverted V shape, appreciated by architects, and not much loved by the parishioners. He took the right turn to Milngavie, then, towards the northwest of the suburb, he turned into the street that wound around the circumference of the loch, which was more a large pond, and could be glimpsed only in occasional gaps between substantial gardens, and trees, some being magnificent specimens of copper beech.

He was looking for house number 73. He was driving slowly, but not too slowly. This was a street with gardeners and house-keepers, or nannies pushing prams and women walking dogs; a slow-moving car would attract attention. "Sixty-five, -seven, -nine . . ." he muttered as he read the number plates on houses and gates.

There it was; the number 73 was entwined in an intricate wrought-iron faux art nouveau design. The gates and a semi-circular, gravel-filled driveway, were wide enough to accommodate a coach and horses of royal magnitude. The house was set well back and looked deserted. McAllister found it hard to believe that this was the home of Councilor James Gordon, born in the slums of Glasgow.

He drove around the road once more. Seeing nothing of interest, he returned to the main road and continued onwards past the high banks of what he knew was a reservoir, for it said so on a large sign, towards the high ridge of the Campsie Fells and Strathblane.

When he arrived, it came back to him. Gerry Dochery's grandmother's house was on the other side of the village and semi-isolated. Of a different ilk than Councilor Gordon's supposed home, it was in a row of perhaps twelve dwellings, separate flats upstairs and down, the outside stone stairs to the upper flats doubling back and bordered with black metal railings. The building seemed lifted from a city or outside a colliery, and dropped into the green and pleasant countryside. A burn flowing by added to the rural idyll.

The football pitch was as he remembered from the visit many years since. The road also; unsealed, it was a walking track about three hundred yards long, running alongside the burn, past the block of flats, and continuing on to the next village, Blanefield.

McAllister knew that if Gerry was there, there was no chance of a surreptitious entrance. It being the school holidays, there were girls skipping over a long rope, chanting out the rhymes, boys kicking balls. It being an unusual summer of long warm days, women were sitting on stone steps or hanging over railings, chatting, drinking tea, all curious as to what a well-dressed stranger was doing walking down the track towards them.

As he approached a group of women of different ages, sitting and standing at the foot of a staircase, he started, "I came here when I was a boy. Not much changed."

One of the younger ones laughed, a mother, he deduced, from the nappy pins stuck in her overall cum apron, in one of the ubiquitous floral prints beloved of housewives everywhere. "Aye, you're right there, nothing changes in this place."

"Except more bairns," her companion added, and they both laughed.

"Does the waterfall still blow skywards in the right kind of wind?"

"Aye, it does." The woman who answered was pretty, with freckles and brown curly hair falling into tight ringlets at the back and sides. A stray strand kept falling into her eyes and, in a gesture that reminded him of Joanne, she blew it out of her face, only for it to fall back.

"Fancy you remembering that," her friend said.

"I came with my dad and his friend," McAllister said. "We

visited the grandmother of a boy I was at school with. Gerry Dochery is his name."

It was as though he had cast a spell.

"I need to be getting the dinner on. The bairns'll be starving," one woman said.

"The washing'll surely be dry in this sun. Best get it in and ironed," said another.

They were all gone before he could say another word, and he knew it was highly unlikely they would return.

He walked back to his car. Then thought he would try the village shop. This was a general store that served also as news-agent and sub–post office, and outside there was a large round red postbox on the edge of the pavement. Next door was a butcher's shop. He tried the newsagent first.

"No, I don't know any Mrs. Dochery."

"Not Mrs. Dochery. I don't remember her name, but she was Mr. Gerry Dochery senior's mother-in-law," he tried explaining. The same hard shut-down faces looked at him. He knew better than to press his luck.

As McAllister returned to his car, about to give up, an old man who had been lingering in the corner of the shop watching the exchange, spoke.

"You'll no' find Gerry Dochery here."

"Has he been here recently?"

"Maybe. You have a cigarette to spare?"

They lit up. The old man looked again at the oval-shaped cig-arette and said, "I haven't had one o' these since I was in the Black and Tans. An Irishman we captured smoked them." *Took them off him before we shot him*, he remembered, but didn't say.

"Gerry Dochery," McAllister reminded him as they leant against his car, enjoying the smoke.

"The flat's no' his anymore. He visits from time to time, but no' recently. He keeps his *friend* there—if you take my meaning. Nice lass, though."

"Do you know where she is?"

"Naw." He grinned. His top teeth dropped, so he pushed them back with a nicotine-stained forefinger. "An' if I did, I wouldn't be telling."

McAllister handed him a ten-shilling note. "Here, get yourself some cigarettes." He had the key in the car door and was about to open it when he heard the parting bombshell.

"Aye, she's right nice, Gerry Dochery's girlfriend. And the wee lass an' all. Her faither dotes on her."

McAllister turned to ask more, but all he got were two raised hands and a shaking head and "That's all I'm saying. Even that's too much." And he was gone, back into the newsagents, *to buy cigarettes*, McAllister thought. *I should be off too.* But he changed his mind and drove to the local hotel for a beer and a think. When no plans as to how to find Gerry came to him, he drove home. But he knew he now had a hold on his old friend.

He has a girlfriend. And a daughter. That is information Gerry Dochery will want kept quiet. Not once did he feel guilt that he might use this to threaten Gerry; Jimmy's disappearance, the trashing of his mother's flat, and Gerry's complicity in both cases had changed the unwritten rules. He also felt he would not have to wait. Word of his visit would reach Gerry. And Gerry would come looking for him.

TWENTY

~

Arriving back at his mother's flat, he found neat piles of broken furniture and cardboard boxes of smashed crockery on the pavement waiting for the council scaffies, or for those in need, to help themselves—broken did not matter when you were desperate.

Inside the difference was remarkable. The place had been cleaned, giving the impression that the tenant had packed up, ready to leave for another place of residence. Only the gouges near the skirting board on the left side of the hallway betrayed the vandalism inflicted on his mother's sanctuary. It was enough of a reminder that he would, somehow, anyhow, have revenge on whoever did it. Or ordered it done.

In the kitchen his mother and Mrs. Crawford were sitting at the table making a black-and-white jigsaw puzzle from scraps of photographs, the result more a modern abstract from an art college student than a family photograph.

His wee brother's silver boxing trophies were lined up on the kitchen cabinet and, in spite of the bashes and the twists in the thin metal, they were gleaming.

Mrs. Crawford saw him smile. "Ach," she said, "may as well clean them afore we take them to yon man down the Trongate. A right good silverworker he is. I'm sure he'll make them as good as new."

"And when you've pieced the photos together I'll take them

to the *Herald*. The photographic department might be able to do something with them," he offered.

"Maybe," Mrs. McAllister said, "but I found an old envelope wi' the negatives for most o' them. Mind you, they're old . . ."

"The lads in photographic are brilliant with old stuff and can at least give it a go."

At that news everyone cheered up. They had a cup of tea together. Then he left them to finish what needed finishing, his mother telling him that the beds were made, the borrowed sheets and pillows ready for use.

"Not yet," Mrs. Crawford said. "You're stopping wi' me till this is all over."

Again his mother surprised him by agreeing.

"Soon," he promised. "It will all be over soon."

She nodded. "Do your best, Son."

It was what she always said when, at school, he struggled with his arithmetic and mathematics. And again his guilt at involving her angered him. He could only nod in reply.

At the *Herald* reception desk, the same woman greeted him and gave him a similar sheet of cheap notepaper, the writing in the same hand. As he read it, he pursed his lips, nodding to himself. *Just short of three hours and already Wee Gerry's heard. Maybe told by the man I was speaking with.* McAllister had noticed the phone box across from the newsagent and was convinced this was what had happened.

The huge clock above the reception desk showed it was nearing six o'clock. The note read, *Meet me at seven* and named a pub. He took a bus to the well-known Celtic supporters' pub in the Gallowgate, next to Barrowland, the huge covered market beloved by Glaswegians searching for bargains, secondhand goods, and items that "fell off o' the back o' a lorry."

He took off his tie and stuffed it into his pocket before he went in. There was nothing he could do about his twenty-guinea suit. Ditto his hat, old but expensive from a hatter's in London. He took a seat in a corner as far as possible from the door to the lavatory, where the smell, on another warm summer's evening, was noticeable, though not enough to deter the hardened drinkers that frequented the place. *Gerry has chosen this place well*, he thought as he ordered a Guinness, eyeing the shamrock etched into the mirror above the bar. *Home turf.* McAllister may have escaped a Christian Brothers education but he knew the etiquette. And the songs.

Gerry Dochery too was early. As he came in, most eyes in the pub acknowledged him. The barman went to pour his Guinness without being asked. He took a seat next to McAllister, knowing the porter would be delivered to the table once it had settled and the foam the perfect depth.

Gerry was angry—almost as angry as McAllister had been when he'd learned of James Gordon and his brothers terrifying Joanne. His face was red, his voice almost a squeak and, speaking with his lips barely moving, the intensity of his words made McAllister reappraise his old pal—for the better.

"You had no right seeking out ma family," Gerry said.

"You started it," McAllister replied. "It was appalling what you had done to my mother's place, an old woman who never harmed a soul."

Gerry didn't look at him. "I'm sorry. It was that or something much worse."

McAllister half believed him, remembering the man beaten to death and dumped, as a warning, maybe, and wondered if that should have been his fate. "Picking on me, fair enough. But my mother? How come women are now a fair target?" He knew Gerry would know he meant his girlfriend.

"You can't tell anyone about Sheena. Or about Wee Sheena. Not even ma faither knows. And them, if they found out . . ."

"I won't. I know how it feels. So the same goes for me and mine."

"He already knew about *your* family."

"He?"

There was silence between them. But not in the bar. Conversation was loud, but not inebriated loud, convivial conversation loud. A wireless was playing faintly in the background. Someone started on a halfhearted version of "The Minstrel Boy." As yet no other singers were drunk enough to join in, and the song tapered off.

"He?" McAllister repeated. This was what he'd come for. This was what he needed to know. But Gerry wasn't answering, and McAllister saw he never would—at least not to a direct question, for that would make him an informer.

"How did it all go wrong, Ger? We were pals. An' you were always as bright as me, just not at book learning."

"Wrang? Wrang?" Gerry was furious.

His answer, almost shouted he was so angry, made the barman look over, reach for the already broken chair he kept to deal with any troubles, then leave it at a signal from Gerry. He brought over two fresh pints. Back at the bar, he watched the two men sip their Guinness. They had dropped their hackles—or at least their shoulders. But he kept the chair handy.

"It never went right." Gerry lit a cigarette without offering McAllister one. "I hated you in those days."

But not now? McAllister thought, lighting a cigarette of his own, understanding that Gerry Dochery was not being rude, just remembering McAllister's taste in cigarettes. That bond between them, knowing each other's tastes in beer and cigarettes and football teams, pleased him. *He was—is—my oldest friend.*

"Your mother, she was always ready wi' 'the poor soul,' always showing me up as the boy to be pitied, always showing you aff as the boy who done good. An' them holidays when she made me wear your auld clothes, us being the same size. And her chiding me on ma manners—'What's the magic word, Gerald?' It was all, 'Please, Mrs. McAllister. Thank you, Mrs. McAllister. Yes, missus, no, missus, three bags full, Mrs. McAllister.'"

McAllister laughed.

Gerry glared.

"Sorry Ger, that's ma mother to a tee. She's a right stickler for manners, but she was no different to me and ma brother."

"Aye. I know. An' I'm sure I'll be the same to ma wee one."

Good, McAllister thought, *now we're really talking.* "How old is she?"

"Three. No one knows about her. I'm right sorry I can't take ma faither to meet her. If thon man, or his psycho brother, finds out . . ."

"You still work for him?"

"I've never worked *for* him. Never. When the word was put out that whoever found the tinker could collect the one thousand pounds, well, no one could turn down that much money."

One thousand pounds. That made McAllister think. *Same amount, same debt?* "Jimmy? Is he a . . . around?" *Alive,* was what he wanted to ask.

"No idea."

"He was shot at with an air rifle."

"Was he now?" Gerry's expression gave away nothing.

"At the warehouse in Whiteinch, he went into the river and no sight nor sound o' him since."

McAllister kept watching Gerry. Nothing. He kept going. "The lad that died, the death DI Willkie tried to fit me up for, what was that about? I know the boy was sent to duff me up, and it was more luck than any skill on my part that he didn't do worse damage, but why was he beaten to a pulp?"

This time Gerry reacted. "Beaten, you say?"

"A colleague saw the body. She said whoever did it was a right sadist."

"Mary Ballantyne?"

"It was bad, Gerry. He was tortured."

"Thon maniac," Gerry muttered and looked away, but not before McAllister caught his distress.

Their glasses were empty. McAllister was about to return to the bar to order again when he saw the men come in. Two of them. Obviously brothers. One was wearing a Rangers football scarf.

Outright provocation, McAllister was thinking, *and enough to get a man glassed in a bar in the Gallowgate.*

From the way the room went quiet and no one heckled them over their colors, they were obviously known. McAllister guessed the barman and customers were waiting for the signal from Gerry, who gave a wave of his forefinger, and conversation resumed. But everyone was watching, and this time the barman had not only a chair within reach but also a loaded sawn-off shotgun, under the till.

"Who's yer friend, Ger?" One of the men was standing too close to their table, so close McAllister imagined he could feel his breath.

Gerry Dochery showed no emotion. As though he was inquiring the time of the next bus, he asked, "What do youse want?"

Then McAllister guessed who they were. The family resemblance was strong but these two looked like factory rejects, blurred, slightly unformed. He introduced himself. "John McAllister. Gerry and me, we were at school thegether."

"John McAllister, eh?" the shorter, rounder one said, making a play of scratching his head in puzzlement. "No' *the* John McAllister, big-shot newspaperman." He pronounced *John* the Glasgow way—*Joan.* His brother was giggling and grinning like a Halloween lantern.

At the high-pitched-hysterical-wee-girl sound, McAllister looked more closely at the second brother. Only slightly taller, he had that look Scots would call glaichit—glazed, blank, lights on but no one home. And evil with it.

The man giggled again. "I ken who you are," he was saying to McAllister, "an Ah ken your Hieland friend." He made a gun with his right forefinger. "Ping! Pop! Ping! Splash! The tinkie's deid."

"Wheesht!" His brother poked him in the ribs. It did no good, and he kept pointing his forefinger but was now mouthing the sounds.

McAllister was forcing himself not to move. As was the barman. And the customers. But how long Gerry could contain them was uncertain.

Brother number one sensed it. "Right, we'll be off. Good to meet you at last, Mr. McAllister. We'll see *you* later, Ger." He was all business. Polite. McAllister sensed that he was the brain—and, he decided, one between them was possibly all the brothers had. McAllister also surmised that the articulate brother was keeping his reputation for being the reasonable one intact, by using his sibling as a human Gatling gun.

"You'd better leave an' all," Gerry told McAllister after the brothers had left and the swing doors finally stopped, and the murmur in the bar resumed.

"That was the one who killed Jimmy." McAllister was too shaken to be angry.

"He's the psycho in the Gordon family. Keep well away from him."

"James Gordon? As in the Gordon Brothers? Is that who you're working for?"

"I work for no one!" But Gerry saw McAllister's eyebrows reaching up to his hairline. "I take contracts now and then and . . ."

"And one thousand pounds is an awful lot of money," McAllister finished. He was not passing judgment. He knew how it was. *And better Gerry is involved than some unknown gangster.* "Gerry, if anyone comes near my mother again, or my fiancée, or her daughters, I'll—"

"You'll what, McAllister? Get your hands dirty? Get someone else to do it for you? You have no idea what you are dealing with here. Thon manny . . ." He gestured towards the door where the brothers had left. "He's no' right in the head—a complete and absolute nutter, so he is."

"He shot at Jimmy."

"I believe you. Look what they done to the lad at your mother's flat."

For the first time McAllister wondered if the young man was dead from a beating in order to implicate *him*. They had almost succeeded. And it had revealed the extent of the Gordon brothers' influence—the police, perhaps the procurator fiscal's office, and from what Mary was discovering, perhaps the City Council.

"You knew the dead man?"

"Aye, I did. A good lad." Gerry fumbled with his cigarettes but didn't light up. "And that, that is one more thing between me and . . . and a Gordon." The finality in his voice, the way he slammed the box of matches onto the table, spilling them into a puddle of beer, made McAllister back off with the questions.

Gerry took up the empty pint glass. Not wanting to look directly at McAllister, he was staring at the dark dregs and dirty foam flecks as though preparing to make his case to Saint Peter. "If you want to protect your missus, call off Mary Ballantyne. The rest is nothing to do wi' you—it's between him and the McPhee fellow." He caught the question in McAllister's eyebrows. "If he's alive," Gerry added.

"It's too late for me to back off."

Gerry nodded. Then sighed. "We *were* friends, weren't we? Long ago?"

McAllister understood the change of subject; Gerry Dochery would never rat on anyone, no matter how evil. "We were. I hope we still are."

"Sheena took to you."

Again it was McAllister's eyebrows that asked the question.

"The lass wi' the bonnie brown curls."

McAllister nodded. "I took to her, too."

"If anything happens, would you see her right? Her and Wee Sheena? And tell ma da?"

Gerry looked straight at McAllister as he asked this, and McAllister could detect no fear, only resignation. He knew not to spout empty assurances that all would be well because, likely as not, it wouldn't. Maybe not this time, but some time, Gerry Dochery's life would catch up with him. One way or another.

"If Sheena should ever need anything, tell her to contact me at the *Herald*. Or the *Gazette*, the newspaper I edit in the High-lands. And Gerry, tell your father. He's old and alone. Knowing about Wee Sheena would make his life worth living."

"And make up for having a son like me," Gerry added.

The conversation was over. Gerry held out his hand. They shook. Gerry left. McAllister left a minute later. He knew he should go to the *Herald* and tell Mary and Sandy Marshall what had passed between him and Gerry and the brothers Gordon. But he couldn't.

He walked back to the *Herald*, collected his car, drove to his boardinghouse. Parked. Was surprised it was not yet nine o'clock. Time to catch the late showing at the Curzon art cinema on the steep brae off Sauchiehall Street that led up to Garnethill.

It was a French film, *Et Dieu . . . créa la femme*. He had no need of the subtitles. And the film, starring Brigitte Bardot, was not to his taste. It was the language he wanted hear, to remind him of another country, other times. The audience of students and the bohemian set of Glasgow were appreciative and respectful to the film, but not to the national anthem played at the end.

As he and they strolled out into a balmy night, some discussing the film, some discussing where might be open for a late night drink, stars and planets and a half-moon lit the dim backstreets with a beauty that should have been a salve to his fear.

Reaching the damp room in the dank boardinghouse, which even a long warm summer had been unable to make charming, he realized he had seen little of the film, little of the supposed charms of BB, and had no idea of the plot, if there had been one. All he could feel was a dread that the whisky he'd brought in his overnight bag could do nothing to dissolve. And fear.

Remembering the talk of their childhood, his mother's insistence on manners, on their washing hands and brushing teeth, her inspection of their necks and behind their ears, checking they had done it all properly, he remembered her insistence on bedtime prayers.

He could almost feel the hard floorboards; himself and Gerry in the attic bedroom in the boardinghouse in Millport, kneeling side by side, his mother standing in the doorway saying the lines, and he and Gerry repeating them. And the intimacy of that summer, of two boys, closer than brothers could ever be, that he would never forget.

Not being a religious man, having no faith in a God he couldn't bring himself to believe in, nevertheless the prayer ran around his brain, and he couldn't dismiss it. "Now I lay me down to sleep. Pray the Lord my—our—souls to keep . . ."

TWENTY-ONE

McAllister needed to return to the Highlands. He needed to know if Jimmy McPhee was alive. He needed his mother safe. And he needed a friend. He was a walking bag of needs.

He was in reception in the *Herald* building and phoned upstairs to ask Sandy Marshall, "Have you time for a pint anytime soon?"

"I'll have the newspaper shout us lunch. We deserve it."

They met at Guy's restaurant in Hope Street. It was busy, but the power of the *Herald* name secured them a table in a quiet corner.

Sandy told the waiter to hold off on the menu but ordered a bottle of wine. Glasses filled, he listened to McAllister say his mother was fine, Joanne was fine, everything was fine. So, being McAllister's friend, his conclusion was, *Everything is definitely not fine.*

McAllister told him of last evening's encounter with the Gordon brothers, his fears for Gerry Dochery's safety—this surprised Sandy, but he made no comment. McAllister told him there were no hospital admissions that might have been Jimmy, no unidentified bodies in the mortuary, and no sightings from the river police.

"So looks like there's nothing else to do but return to the Highlands having achieved nothing."

After a sip of white wine, which hadn't been chilled enough in the first place and was now warm, Sandy said, "Seems to me your life is a catalogue of misery."

McAllister flushed in anger, and for a second Sandy thought

he would fling down the overlarge linen napkin and stalk out in high dudgeon. He quickly raised his glass and said, "So, let's hope it's onwards and upwards from here."

McAllister had the good grace to laugh. "Aye, here's hoping."

They ordered. The food was good. This was one of the few restaurants in the city up to London standards. They finished with coffee and cigarettes. Then Sandy said his piece.

"I can't help you with Jimmy McPhee. He turns up or he doesn't. Gerry Dochery, he's chosen his life and it can be a short one in his game. Your mother is tough; you can't protect her forever. And she has friends—she's a 'guidwife' if ever there was one."

McAllister snorted at this description of his mother; it was a righteous Scottish word, and it summed up the indomitable women of the city, women who kept going under the yoke of poverty and too many children and not enough of anything, except friends and the pride of being Glaswegian.

"On your personal life I have only this to say: you are bloody lucky."

McAllister nodded an *I know*.

"From what Mary told me, your Joanne Ross is not only a good woman, she is beautiful and smart and a real catch. Don't lose her." Sandy said the last words slowly, carefully, his eyes fixed on McAllister's face.

They were good enough friends he could say this, but still, McAllister felt a momentary surge of anger. But he knew Sandy was right. His neglect of Joanne was a mystery even to him. "I can't give up, not yet," he said. "Gordon and his brothers, they won't give up. If they don't get Jimmy, they'll go for Joanne."

"Threatening Joanne is Gordon's way of finding Jimmy. But face it, man, McPhee may no longer be alive." Sandy wasn't being cruel, just realistic. "If your family need protection, go to the police—and no, don't give me that look. Apart from DI Willkie and a few like him, there are many decent policemen around. Go home, McAllister. Tell your local police. You must have friends there."

McAllister immediately thought of DI Dunne. "I do."

"Mary's in Edinburgh. She says she's found documents in Company House that might shed light on Councilor Gordon's business activities." Sandy was rubbing the back of his head as he spoke.

A sure sign he's uncomfortable.

Sandy Marshall didn't know if there was anything between McAllister and Mary Ballantyne, but suspected there was something. "I'm not counting chickens, and you know fine well that whatever we publish needs checking and double-checking and vetting by the lawyers. But maybe, just maybe, we might have something on the councilor. From what you told me about his house in Milngavie, he didn't get that from a wee three-brother building business."

He signaled for the bill. "Go home, McAllister. Get married. Me and the family are looking forward to the wedding—I've dusted off ma kilt, and the wife's new hat cost a fortune, plus I've promised the bairns a holiday in Nairn, so . . ."

McAllister wanted to say, *Don't count on there being a wedding*, but he knew it was too late to back out. He wanted Joanne. But marriage? He was not at all sure he could be a husband. "I hope Joanne will be well enough . . ." he started, but Sandy cut him off.

"There you go again, incurable pessimist." He was remembering his own wedding, how terrified he'd been. Not of the marriage, but of the relatives, the well-wishers, the pressure to settle down when he, like McAllister, had considered himself above all the conventional rot. They were young journalists going places, not potential husbands and fathers and property owners with enormous bank loans.

If Sandy Marshall could have run away to Gretna Green he

would have. He'd offered but his fiancée had laughed. "Elope?" she'd said. "Then my dad would have to come after you wi' a shotgun." They had laughed so much, and he loved her so much, he'd willingly walked down the aisle, McAllister his best man, with his inoffensive five-foot-four of a father-in-law bursting with pride.

And now, Sandy thought, *we are middle-aged men.* "Life is a compromise, McAllister. Cliché I know, but that's how it is. And from where I'm sitting you don't look much of a catch . . ." It was true, his friend was disheveled, needed a haircut, and his fingers were so stained with nicotine they were the color of a kipper. "Middle-aged, obstinate, with a weird taste in music, be grateful someone is willing to have you."

McAllister had the grace to laugh.

Five minutes later, they parted outside the restaurant and McAllister walked down Hope Street wondering whether to go back to his mother's flat or drive to Govan to see Gerry Dochery senior. He did neither. It was past 2 p.m., public house closing time. He went to the Station Hotel. As he wasn't a guest, he flashed his press card, which persuaded the barman to serve him. "Double Glenlivet and a pint of bitter."

McAllister took his drinks to the saloon bar. He thought over his conversation with Sandy. Between the steps of the restaurant and the steps of the hotel, the good cheer he had felt in the editor's company had vanished. He'd told Sandy most of what was bothering him, just not the extent of his fears. And guilt. He'd said nothing about Gerry Dochery's girlfriend, Sheena. Nothing about his absolute certainty that there would be, or had been, a confrontation between Gerry and one or all of the Gordon brothers.

And he'd lost Jimmy and failed Jenny McPhee and was waiting for a body, or bodies, to turn up.

What he didn't know was how lost he himself was.

◆ ◆ ◆

A body turned up.

It was early, only a few minutes past eight o'clock, but the boardinghouse breakfast was so dire, watery porridge and plastic hard eggs, that McAllister bought fresh hot rolls and drove to his mother's for a real fry-up. He was also hoping to persuade her to return to the Highlands with him.

"A note was delivered not half an hour ago from the *Herald*," his mother said as soon as she saw him. "I couldn't mind the name o' the place you were staying, so I told them to leave it here." Her bottom lip was twitching in anxiety; telegrams, messages delivered by courier, were never good news.

He ripped open the envelope, read the note, pushed it back into the envelope and into his pocket. "No, it's fine, Mother, just Sandy asking me to drop by." He looked around. Although the flat was sparsely furnished, and clean, the tea service was in use, the frying pan at the ready, and there were some sweet peas in a jam jar filling the air with summer.

The flowers reminded him of Joanne. His throat tightened. It was hard to swallow. He missed her.

"Mother, I'm driving back up north tomorrow. I'd like you to come back with me."

"I'll take the train up maybe the day before the wedding. I hope you don't mind, but I've asked Mrs. Crawford to come with me. Not that I asked her to the wedding, mind, I would never be that forward . . ."

"I'd be delighted if Mrs. Crawford came to the wedding," he said, thinking, *Another old woman in the house? I'd better book a B&B.* "The more the merrier." And he meant it. Just not in his house.

He went straight to the editor's office. Sandy was with Mary and the chief sub-editor. He waved McAllister to the visitor's chair. "Two minutes," he said.

McAllister listened as they argued over a story. He heard the

274 • A. D. Scott

name Gordon repeatedly. He caught the gist of the dilemma: was the story watertight? Mary thought so. Her colleagues didn't.

Mary was furious. "There is enough there to damn the man, look." She pointed to a document. "The company had four share-holders—four Gordon brothers. Here is a list of the council contracts they were awarded . . ."

"None were directly awarded to Gordon & Sons, Ltd.," Sandy repeated. "Gordon & Sons were the subcontractors twice removed."

"Aye, but with Councilor James Gordon being on the planning committee . . ."

"Mary, Councilor Gordon signed over his shares to two of his brothers after he was elected to the council . . ."

"What does Derrick Keith say?" the sub-editor asked. McAllister had worked with the man and knew him to be one of the best in the country and the reason the *Herald*'s legal bills were so small.

"Derrick Keith?" Mary asked. "Mr. Useless? I knew he was sleazy, now I know he's useless with it."

"You mean you haven't consulted him?" Sandy said. "I told you to work together. So now, you and him, together, go over all the documents again. If you find corroborating evidence that Gordon was influencing the bidding process, and it's watertight, and passes the legal boys, then and only then might I publish."

"Gordon is on the planning committee. They oversee the sealed bids. Contracts end up with his brothers' company . . ."

"Very indirectly." Sandy was fed up with again and again discussing, arguing, the same points. "I need more or we won't publish." He was firm. Discussion over.

"Fine." She walked out. She hadn't even said hello or good-bye to McAllister, only a glare as though he too was one of the older overcautious males preventing her publishing a front-page scoop.

"One determined young lady that one," the sub-editor said as he gathered up his papers. "Mind you, it's a good story if we can prove it. McAllister. Sandy. Catch you later."

"A body?" McAllister asked when they were alone.

"Aye." Sandy sighed. "I'm sorry, McAllister."

"Jimmy." The way McAllister said the name it came out as a moan from a person in torment.

"Gerry Dochery." Sandy knew that in spite of everything, a childhood friend, a boy you had grown up with, kicked a ball with, gone fishing with, spent holidays with—that person mattered.

McAllister, looking up at the ceiling, for he didn't trust himself to look directly at his friend, asked, "What happened?"

"Not sure. Late last night, Dochery was found in a lane out the back of the warehouse in Whiteinch. This detective I know—no, not Willkie—gave me a tip-off."

For cash, McAllister guessed.

"He'd been tied up, beaten right badly, then his throat cut. The body was dumped there and two, maybe three people, were involved, so the police think."

"Aye, it would take more than one to handle Gerry."

"Some anonymous caller phoned for an ambulance. When they got there he was dead."

"Murdered, then."

"Aye."

They let that hang in the air for a moment.

"Does Mr. Dochery know?" McAllister asked.

"He identified the body."

"How come Mary is not chasing this? It's a big story."

"I'm about to tell her. I wanted you to know first. Give you time to do whatever you need to."

He meant visit Mr. Gerald Dochery senior.

"This is big news, it will placate Mary for the corruption story not running." McAllister sounded bitter. He knew he had no right to be, but he was irked that Mary was keeping her distance.

He drove to Govan. As he locked the car he could see that the news of Gerry Dochery's death had spread. Most of the curtains of the flats on the communal close were closed. A group, some with arms folded as though protecting themselves from the bad luck of a violent death, was gathered tightly together, listening to an older woman. He overheard her say, "I'll take him his dinner. Sadie, you make his tea."

As he climbed the stairs, McAllister knew he too was grieving. He accepted he had to be here but as to how to comfort a man whose only child had been killed, his throat cut, dying slowly as the blood ran out into the gutter of a back close in a foreign part of the city, Rangers territory, Protestant land, alone, McAllister was at a loss. Then he reminded himself, *We parted friends, I'll tell the old man that.*

He knocked on the door. "Who is it?" a voice called out. It was coming from the kitchen, and McAllister didn't recognize the voice, but grief could twist the vocal cords.

When the door opened and he peered into the dim of the entrance, the curtains being closed, he thought it was a ghost.

McAllister stared. He began to shake. It was as though through some cruel trick of light, and his grief, and exhaustion, were deceiving him. When the apparition said, in a voice that would have been appropriate if they had parted the day or a week before, "McAllister. We've been expecting you," he knew it was real.

"Where the hell have you been? Why the hell didn't you contact me?" He was furious. His trembling turned to anger, to the edge of violence. "Your mother, everyone, we've been looking for you."

"That's why we kept Jimmy here," Old Mr. Dochery said. He shuffled towards McAllister, held out his hand. "It's good of you to come over," he said.

"We? Who's we?" He was still furious, and thinking furiously also. *We? Gerry? His father? How? Why?*

The story came out. It did them all good—the three men— to tell it, to listen to it; the talking kept the remembrance of Gerry Dochery, now lying on a mortuary slab, at bay.

"Ma collarbone snapped and my arm broke, when I hit the edge o' the dock," Jimmy began. "Not that I haven't had broken bones before, but the current took me. I went with it and kept maself at the edge o' the river, came ashore, not too far down, on some big wooden steps. A night watchman found me. Wanted to get me to hospital. I said no. He gave me tea and whisky and made me sit by his fire. I must have passed out. Next thing I knew, Gerry was there. The watchman manny, he'd heard of the reward and thought I might be the person wanted. A whiley later Gerry turned up. He brought me to his father, then sent for a doctor to strap up ma bones, so here I am."

"Aye," the old man said. "No one would think o' looking for Jimmy here."

"No, they wouldn't." McAllister was turning it over in his mind, trying to make sense of it all. And couldn't. Why would Gerry Dochery protect Jimmy? Was that why he was killed?

"He was a fine lad when you and he were wee laddies together." Mr. Dochery was looking at McAllister seeking confirmation that his son was not all bad.

"He was," McAllister agreed.

"I did ma best to bring him up right, but he was lost to me a long time since. Now . . ." He was staring into his teacup hoping to find better fortune in the leaves.

"Mr. Dochery," McAllister said, remembering that at one time he would have called him Uncle Gerald, "Gerry told me that if anything should happen, I was to tell you about this lass Sheena." He went on to explain about Sheena, her daughter and Mr. Dochery's granddaughter, where they lived, and how he had met them. As he spoke he saw the old man's shoulders rise, his head lift.

Scarcely believing what McAllister was saying, his voice a bare whisper, the old man asked, "I have family?"

"You do. And from what I've seen of this Sheena, she'll be happy to meet you." McAllister watched as the news sank in. His only son was dead; all McAllister could do was to tell him of a granddaughter he never knew of. And much as he didn't want to, he knew he had to be the one to tell Sheena, tell her before she read about it in the next day's newspaper, maybe even in today's late edition of the tabloids. He looked at his watch. "Sorry, it's getting on, and I have to drive to Strathblane . . ."

"I'm coming with you."

"Mr. Dochery, it might not be for the best. Maybe later when—"

"I don't want to meet her over ma son's coffin."

McAllister was hoping Sheena would have the sense to miss the funeral but thought that was unlikely.

"If you don't take me wi' you, I'll take the bus. I know how to get to Strathblane." Mr. Dochery's voice and his right hand were trembling. "Besides, if it's the Sheena I'm thinking of, I ken her mother."

"An' I'll be hitting the road," Jimmy said.

"Wait till dark," the old man advised.

"Where will you go?" McAllister asked.

"Best you don't know. But I've relatives all over." Jimmy gave McAllister a grin that did not reach his eyes. "We're tinkers. Haven't you heard? We're as countless an' as aggravating as the fleas on an auld dog."

"Take the boat to Ireland like I telt you," Mr. Dochery said.

"Maybe I will at that." Jimmy turned to McAllister, shook his hand, and again McAllister felt he was communicating with a wraith, so slight was the hand, and no strength in the arm from the yet-to-heal breaks. "Look out for Ma, will you?"

"I'll do my best," McAllister promised. "But I don't seem to be much use to anyone these days."

"Stop being so maudlin, man." Jimmy had no time for self pity. "You're alive, aren't you?"

On the drive to Strathblane, McAllister thought how he'd done more driving in the past few weeks than he had in two years. It surprised him how much he enjoyed how his instinct would kick in, taking him easily through the traffic, through the turns and twists of the narrow country road, then up and over the steep braes, leaving his mind free for thinking.

As they passed through Milngavie, he thought again about Councilor Gordon and his brothers. *So much violence and for what? Money? Pride? Revenge?*

The old man was silent most of the journey, but when they came out into open moorland, to the sight of the Campsie Fells, passing a lochan on the right where the water, ruffled by a strong breeze, seemed to be dancing, Mr. Dochery remarked, "Right bonnie."

McAllister glanced to left and right, saw the light in the clumps of birch trees and hawthorn, beech and oak, saw the shades of green and rust and the darker smudges of conifers on the lower slopes of the high ridge ahead, and agreed, "Aye, it is." He was distracted on the why of it all. Something had been nagging at him—*four brothers.* He asked, "Mr. Dochery, what do you know about the Gordon brothers?"

"Not much. And if you don't mind, I don't want to know more."

"I'm really sorry. That was completely thoughtless of me."

"I have a granddaughter, you say?" The old man was saying the words to himself as though learning a foreign language. *I have a granddaughter. I am a grandfather.* "This Sheena was no more than a baby when we came here on visits to ma mother-in-law. The mother, she was called Sheena an' all, was a neighbor, and as I recall, a nice woman."

"She still lives in the village," McAllister told him as he did his sums. *That would make Sheena in her early thirties. She looks younger.* He remembered the friendly freckled face, the large brown eyes, and knew her visitors were about to break her heart.

"What'll I say to them? Maybe they won't want to know me?"

McAllister replied, "Be yourself, Mr. Dochery, that will be enough."

The meeting was as difficult as McAllister had feared, but also better. He was left with the impression that Sheena took the news as inevitable; there was a stoicism about her that he knew would see her through tough times. He was reminded of the widows of firemen and police officers and miners and, yes, criminals, all those whose husbands were in dangerous occupations. Women who, when he was a cub reporter and sent to doorstop, to interview in the first moments of grief, had broken down, but also shown a dignity, if only to protect their children.

Sheena thanked McAllister for driving out to the country to tell her in person. She thanked him for bringing the old man. She thanked him for his concern for her welfare, saying, "My mother is here, and my sister. The eyes were still big, still brown, but the sparkle had gone.

Wee Sheena was outside, playing on the step with her new grandfather. She'd been shy at first, but they had walked to the shop for sweeties and he had given her a piggyback ride and she had taken to the old man with a child's open and unguarded delight in a person who gave undivided attention.

When it was time to leave, McAllister asked, "Is there anything I can do for you?"

"Wait a moment." Sheena stood and, brushing a curl off her forehead, gathered herself together as countless women from time immemorial did when having to deal with a husband's death, a child's survival. "Gerry left something for you."

She went into the house, returned with a box about the size of the one they used to store files in at the *Gazette*. She handed it over. It was heavy. "I've no idea what's in it, and I don't want to know, but Gerry made me promise if anything happened, it would go to you."

Sure enough, it had his name printed boldly across the brown wrapping paper, which was tied with string, the knots secured with red sealing wax.

"Since Wee Sheena was born, he changed. But he was trapped, said he couldn't get out of the life even though he wanted to. He knew what might happen, and he told me to trust you."

She didn't mention the one thousand pounds Gerry had left with her only a week ago. *In case anything happens*, was all he'd said. It was so much money she was terrified to keep it, guilty at knowing it probably came from somewhere bad, but it was a future for her and her daughter, and she would keep it, not even telling her mother of the legacy.

They said their goodbyes.

"Mr. Dochery," Sheena said as she took her daughter from him, "I'm not going to bring Wee Sheena to Glasgow, or Govan, I've no good memories of the city. But you can visit us whenever you want. Now, if you don't mind, I need to see my mother."

McAllister nodded. Mr. Dochery said, "Cheerio, lass. Be well." He said, "See you soon, ma wee pet," to the little girl wriggling in her mother's arms.

They walked the track alongside the burn in silence. It was early evening, still a good three hours of light left, and as they drove through the ninety-degree turn in the road at the top of the village, heading back towards the lochan and the city, McAllister said, "Best not to visit until this is all over."

"I know," Mr. Dochery replied. "But when will that be?"

TWENTY-TWO

~~~

M<span>cAllister</span> delivered the box of papers to the editor. After sifting through the first twenty or so documents, Sandy whistled and said, "This is sensational. Looks like the Gordon & Sons accounts are in here. Wait till Mary reads them." He was laughing. "She's still furious about the press conference. We couldn't run her article after Gordon preempted us."

In a folder, separate from the files, Sandy found lists of names and dates and amounts of monies paid for "Services Rendered." There were five pages, handwritten, and the payments, large and small, seemed to be regular. What was astounding were some of the names. The one that immediately jumped out was DI Willkie.

McAllister smoked in silence as Sandy read the documents. He was not uninterested in the contents of the box, he was just exhausted. And he knew he'd find out soon enough.

It took only fifteen minutes for Sandy to realize the documents were dangerous, illegal, and electrifying. He called his secretary and asked her to set up an appointment with the newspaper's legal department first thing in the morning.

When Mary walked in, she said, "McAllister, I heard you were here. What did you find out?"

"And hello to you too, Mary." Sandy was joking, used to Mary appearing whenever there was a story in the wind. "McAllister has just gone and delivered the coup of the decade—looks like the accounts of Gordon & Sons, but the real ones, not the ones tidied up for the tax man.

"Read these," he said. "We're off to the canteen to recover. And Mary, lock the door and don't open it for anyone except me."

"Fantastic," she said when her colleagues returned. "More than fantastic! Where did these come from?" The sums of money, the sheer depth and length of the trickery—going back at least ten years—this was a scandal on a scale she had never before encountered.

McAllister didn't answer the question. "Jimmy McPhee is alive. He's—"

"I know. He's back at my place," Mary said.

"You and Jimmy seem to be great pals."

Mary gave no indication she'd picked up on his sarcasm. "He needed a bed for a few days."

"Happy to hear McPhee made it," Sandy intervened. "How is he?"

"Broken bones, but alive. That man has nine lives." She was leafing through the documents. She couldn't stop herself.

"What about these? Looks like a list of kickbacks—they're dynamite." Sandy handed her the pages.

Mary said, "I know, they'll blow the council and the police to kingdom come."

"I hope you get Councilor Gordon this time." McAllister's voice was flat, empty, and he had a headache, not something that normally happened without alcohol.

"We'll have to inform the police," Sandy warned.

Mary replied, "Aye, but not yet."

"I'm meeting the legal department tomorrow to see what we can publish, and I'll ask them to lodge the documents high enough up the chain so no one can say they weren't received."

"Publish first. Then give them to our Member of Parliament. Or is he compromised too?"

"Don't know, but it's worth a try."

"McAllister, how long can you stay?" Mary asked. "There's heaps of work here, we should get started—"

"I can't."

McAllister saw Sandy watching him. He knew he should explain but couldn't. He couldn't tell his friend, perhaps his only real friend, that a woman he hardly knew, and her daughter, had made the decision for him. The extinguishing of the light in Sheena's eyes at the loss of a man they both knew was a criminal, whose life was always in danger of being foreshortened, had affected him deeply. "I need to go home."

Sandy heard the word *home*. *That's a first*, he thought. He didn't like what he saw in his friend's eyes, didn't like the black shadows under them. He knew nothing of Gerry Dochery's family and he never would, but whatever made McAllister realize that the Highlands were his home, he was glad of it. "Thanks for delivering these." He gestured at the papers. "I'll see you at the wedding, if not before."

"Yeah, see you, McAllister," Mary said. "Say hello to Joanne. And Don McLeod." And she went back to the accounts, engrossed in the columns of figures and the final sums at the bottom of each column that, although she was no accountant, even she could see were staggering.

As McAllister walked down the steps of the *Herald* building, hoping it was for the last time in a long time, he was glad Sandy Marshall hadn't told him he was doing the right thing, hadn't spouted a list of clichés about married life and happily ever after.

He told his mother about Gerry, about seeing old Mr. Dochery. She listened quietly, and with tears in her eyes, but none shed, she shook her head, saying, "It was bound to happen sometime." He knew she was not being unfeeling, but the inevitability of death was as obvious to outsiders as it was, McAllister suspected, to Gerry himself. The news of a granddaughter pleased her.

"Just what Mr. Dochery needs, someone to care for."

She did not mention, and never would, her own feelings about grandchildren—something she'd given up hope of long since. As for McAllister, he had always rejected the idea of having children of his own. *And always will*, he had stated, often, when the subject was raised by the well-meaning—interfering busybodies, in his parlance. He had never raised this subject with Joanne, presuming that, in the same way she knew he took coffee black, no sugar, she knew that children, for him, were not a necessity.

After again trying to persuade her to come north with him, unsuccessfully, he bid his mother cheerio, and she said, "I'll be up north a day or two before the wedding."

Taking the A9 road north, as he knew the Ballahulish ferry would be closed until the morning, he drove through the night. Cigarettes and coffee from the thermos flask his mother had packed for him, along with some ham sandwiches liberally plastered with mustard that he consumed in a lay-by at the Pass of Killiecrankie, kept him awake most of the journey. But in that hour before dawn, on the high plateau, on the homeward stretch some ten miles short of Aviemore, he stopped again in a lay-by for the last of the coffee. In this summertime predawn, a tall post with red-painted markings, a snow marker, struck him as unnecessarily high. Then he remembered winters up here; the *Gazette* had published enough road closure notices for him to guess that this was the stretch of road where unwary travelers lost their lives.

He relieved himself into a running burn. A faint smudge of silver was creeping over the hilltops. The sound of a bird, a solitary cry in an emptiness that formerly he would have cherished, hung in the air, a falling note, a cry that made him think that a spirit, someone he knew, was calling out for help. And he could do nothing. He wanted to cry. And he couldn't. A sob escaped. He shook himself. He took off his jacket. He wrapped his arms around himself in the cold. Cold he welcomed. He had left the car door open. After starting the engine, he wound down the window. He wanted, needed the cold, the discomfort, anything to rid himself of a fear, a terror that that bird had implanted in his soul.

"Big bairn." He spoke out loud. "There's no such thing as ghosties." This he said in an exact echo of his father, a man he no longer remembered well, only seeing him in fragments, in small scenes, no longer as a whole complete man.

In the days after his homecoming, there was a quiet busyness in the house.

"Chiara is organizing a small party at her house after the wedding," Joanne told him.

"That sounds good," was all he said. But he was pleased. Chiara was Joanne's best friend. Peter, her husband, was McAllister's chess partner. They were good people. They wouldn't make a fuss. And Chiara and her father, Gino Corelli, and more important, the aunt who lived with them, were wonderful cooks.

"I asked Mary Ballantyne if she could come, but she says she can't get away from work."

"The story she's working on is potentially huge," he told her, hoping she would not see how relieved he felt.

"Do you miss it?" Joanne had her sewing basket at her side, and was sewing buttons on what looked like a new blouse, which it was, as she had started sewing again.

He didn't know the answer to that. Not completely. "I did . . ." He put down the magazine he'd been reading and considered his answer. "I did. Then, when I thought Jimmy was dead, and then Gerry was killed, and when I saw how much you have to sacrifice to chase a story . . ." Here he was thinking of Mary, a woman with no life other than her work. "I knew it was a young person's game."

"There are other jobs in a newspaper. Editor, for instance."

"I don't think I could live in the city again." That part he was not certain of.

"I'm not from here either," she began. "I'm only here through marriage. I was, am, will always be an outsider. I am a divorced woman. I have been living in sin. My girls will have to live with that stigma too. One day they will hear the gossip—you know how cruel people can be."

"Do you want to leave?"

"I've never really considered it before now, but . . ." What she meant was, *Where else can I go?* This was the only place she had family and friends. She had been looking out the window as she thought this. Then she turned her gaze back on him, seeing a man diminished by the last weeks, months even. She loved him. She wanted this marriage. But in quiet moments, when she felt his uncertainty, she had considered if she could continue with the present arrangement—living in sin as his permanent "fiancée"— another word for "fancy-woman."

She could not.

She and her children needed the respectability of marriage. And the financial stability. Never again did she want to be searching down the back of armchairs for lost coins to pay the milkman, or having to tell her daughter they had no money for a day out at the seaside in the long summer school holidays, or money for new shoes, new coats, all the necessities for growing children.

She had struggled with her conscience and hated that she had even considered marriage as security, as protection. But she would always be a mother first.

And she knew she could make it work. But she knew it had

to be said. "If you want out of this wedding, this . . . us . . . it's not too late."

"I don't."

"You've not been yourself lately . . ."

He almost told her he'd been thinking the same of her. But, he reasoned, Joanne was horribly injured. *No such excuses for me.*

"This is a huge step for both of us. I will never again tolerate years in an unhappy marriage. So be certain this is what you want."

He surprised himself. "I am." He stared at her. She blushed. "I am certain."

"Good. Now go and make us a cup of tea." She waved him away when he looked about to come over and touch her, as she knew she would cry, and she had had enough of crying.

"Yes, Mrs. McAllister to be." And in the kitchen as he filled the kettle, warmed the teapot, then measured out the tea leaves, he knew he was happy. And content. *I'm too old for blissful happiness,* he thought, *and content is good.*

TWENTY-THREE

Mary was trying to piece together what promised to be a sensational exposé of Councilor James Gordon. To keep the documents secret until publication was hard, as they had to be checked, double-checked, names and dates verified. Knowing how news leaked out in a newspaper building, and suspecting that the police had their contacts, and vice versa, she also had to work fast. Her offsider—Derrick, the former Mr. Sleazy, now Mr. Hopeless, Helpless, and Useless—was of no help, often missing, often at the pub. When she received the invitation to a press conference in the City Council chambers, the seat of her investigation, and courtesy of the councilor she was investigating, she was unhappy.

"What the hell is Gordon up to?" she asked the editor.

Sandy shrugged, saying, "Search me."

The event was well attended.

"Who does he think he is?" Mary said to a friend and rival, and the only other female journalist in the room. "Press conferences are for the chief constable and the provost."

"Maybe he's on his way to being provost," Mary's friend Maureen answered.

Not if I have anything to do with it, Mary thought.

He was ten minutes late. Not late enough for the reporters to leave, just late enough to emphasize that he, Councilor James Gordon, was calling the shots.

"Firstly I want to thank you all for coming." Councilor

Gordon cleared his throat, made a drama out of adjusting his glasses, then began to read from his notes. "It has come to my attention that one of my brothers is implicated in some questionable activity re council building contracts."

A swarm of bees seemed to have been dislodged from the rafters of the high-ceilinged room. James Gordon waited. When the buzz quieted, he continued. Mary shook her head, muttering to herself, "Got us all in the palms of his sticky hands."

"Unfortunately for me and my family, this brother was in trouble before. But he paid the price."

"Three years in Barlinnie," Mary's friend said. "Got out in two for good behavior." They both snorted at that. Someone behind them hissed, "Wheesht."

"My solicitor informed me that there is a possibility—yet to be proven, I must stress—that this brother might also be involved in a matter of tax fraud." Gordon had been reading from the sheaf of notes. At this statement he looked directly at his audience, his face composed in pain and sorrow, just right for a photograph, and the photographers suitably complied. "Now, these are very minor matters, and none of it involves me. However, some members of the press"—he searched the crowd for Mary—"Good morning Miss Ballantyne." He grinned. "Some journalists from of our esteemed broadsheets could perhaps misinterpret this unhappy state of affairs, but, as they say, you can't choose your family."

That brought a laugh and glances from her colleagues.

"Pompous wee shite of man, who's been giving him elocution lessons?" Maureen commented. Receiving no reply, she looked at Mary, saw her bright red face, saw she was trying to control her breathing, and said, "Quite right, hen, say nothing. The cheek o' that man will be his downfall."

"As I said," Gordon continued, "these activities of my brother could, very indirectly, be seen as compromising my position as a city councilor. Therefore, to maintain my good name, and that of the City Council, I have resigned from all committees relating to building and planning matters, but will continue to serve my constituency, unless the voters decide otherwise at the next election."

There came a roar of questions, and the flashes of many cameras. It took some minutes for Gordon to quieten the crowd.

"I will be happy to answer written questions. Thank you for being here today."

Mary despaired that she was the only one not fooled. All read from a script, his grammar was English, his accent cleaned up. She understood Gordon's strategy and thought he and his solicitors had been clever. And forewarned.

Councilor Gordon stuffed his notes into his jacket pocket, taking his time with the gesture, and, with his face artfully composed to show gravitas, he made his way down from the podium, two burly henchmen on either side. They cleared a path through the reporters and photographers, making sure no one came too close. Somehow Mary managed to dodge them and planted herself in front of the councilor, so he would have to push her to squeeze past her. Her head came as high as his shoulder.

She looked up, saw his fury and his smile, and loudly and clearly asked, "Who told you?"

"Miss Ballantyne, please excuse me, but written questions only."

"You're a disgrace of a man, Councilor Gordon. Who told you?" The councilor's men grabbed hold of her. One thug had one arm, a second one her other, and they were pulling her to one side. Mary kicked out, catching an ankle. A hand tightened on her wrist. She knew she would have a bruise, but thought it worth it.

"Hey, leave her be." Maureen pushed at the bullyboy, but he wouldn't let go.

"Aye, leave the lassie be, she's only doing her job," another journalist, someone Mary didn't recognize, said.

"Aye, leave her." Gordon smiled. He reminded her of a gargoyle high up in the cathedral parapets. "Miss Ballantyne is a respected journalist—when she's not entertaining gentlemen friends." This he said mostly to entertain the crowd, but also to imply that he knew who her friends were, whom she drank with, who had visited her basement flat. It was enough to make her step aside.

"Telephone my office for an appointment, Miss Ballantyne. Always happy to cooperate with the *Herald*."

There was little she could do but watch him leave with a posse of newsmen and photographers in his wake.

"You owe me," Maureen said. "One o' thon bruisers deliberately stepped on my foot, and it hurts like hell. So share. Who told Gordon what? And what do you know that I don't?"

"I'll share," Mary said, "promise. But later. First I have to strangle someone."

Mary told the editor about the press conference. Then she told him there had to be a leak at the *Herald*.

"Maybe," Sandy said. "It's too good a story to keep quiet, and journalists are the biggest gossips ever. Bring me proof, and I'll make sure whoever it was never works on a decent newspaper again."

"I'll bring you your proof," she said. "Then I want him fired. He's a disgrace to the profession."

Neither said who "he" was, but they both guessed his identity. Next she had to think of a way of making her colleague incriminate himself. It took her the rest of the morning to come up with a plan. Then she commandeered a cadet who was not unhappy at helping the star crime reporter, even when it meant retyping fifteen pages of single-spaced documents, most of it figures, and all of it comprehensible. She told him to use a type-writer in the features department, hoping no one would discover what she was up to.

She then went to a corner shop near the Renfrew Street bus station where they sold everything from groceries to hardware to small bags of coal. Next stop was the *Herald* stationery cupboard. She then took the purchases to the toilet and prepared a large heavy-duty envelope, one that closed by wrapping string around a circle of cardboard. For the next step she put on the pink rubber gloves she'd bought at the general store. Working over the toilet bowl, she tipped the contents of a mimeograph machine ink refill into a small plastic bag, and tied it loosely with an elastic band.

Her desk was within talking distance of the sub-editors' table, if you raised your voice, and definitely within hearing range of Derrick Keith—formally known as Mr. Sleazy.

"Hey, Lachie," she called out, "those documents I showed you earlier, surely there's something there we can use to get Gordon."

"You heard what the editor said, he's off the hook. Printing something now would seem like sour grapes." The man was busy, but looking up at Mary he gave her a fierce glare. "Weren't you supposed to hand them documents in to the polis? Don't want you up on a charge of withholding evidence."

Mary had briefed the cadet earlier. He had no idea what she was up to, only that she was out to get Derrick, a man he had no time for.

"They're in my locker. I'll take it over to Central when I've finished this." She started to type furiously. Ten minutes later she rolled the article out of the typewriter, saying, loudly to Lachie on the subs' desk, "Right, better get this to the editor to approve before I waste your time."

As she left she winked at the cadet. He was as baffled as Lachie but, intrigued, he was ready to play his part in Mary's scheme.

She waited fifteen minutes. When she came back, she was told Derrick had left on a break.

The cadet said, "I followed him like you asked. I saw him go into your locker—" He saw the question on her face. "No, he didn't see me." He started to laugh. "He's in the gents', scrubbing his hands wi' the lavvy brush."

Mary marched down the corridor, ran down one flight of stairs, and went into the gents'. The cadet followed.

"Hey, you can't come in here!" a man shouted as he turned his back to her to button up his fly.

She ignored him, marching up to the washbasins, where Derrick, seeing her in the mirror, snarled, "I'll get you for this!"

She looked at the ink-stained basin, looked at his blue-black hands, and said, "So are you going to tell me what you were doing in my locker? Or do you want to complain about me to the editor?"

In the mirror she could see the cadet with the borrowed camera.

"Watch the birdie," he called out.

Derrick Keith half turned, giving a clear view of the ink-stained sink, the right hand dark to the wrist, the left hand also marked. A flash bounced off the mirror. A second flash followed. Derrick rushed towards him, inky water dripping over the black and white tiles. He was grabbing at the young man, at the camera, shouting, "Give me that! You've no right—"

"You had no right to go into my locker." Mary was leaning

against the wall, grinning. "I can guess what you were up to—stealing the documents to pass on to your pal Councilor Gordon."

"They were stolen from him in the first place."

Mary grinned. "No denials? No excuses?"

A man came in, saw her, did a double take worthy of a music hall comedian, and said, "Whatever's going on will you please finish coz I'm desperate." And he held his knees together miming a wee boy about to pee his pants.

"He's desperate too." Mary pointed at Derrick. "And finished."

Later the cadet reporter confessed to Mary that there was no film in the camera. "I didn't have time to load it," he apologized.

"Never mind," she said. "It did the trick."

"What about the documents I typed up?" the cadet asked.

"Sorry, I didn't give you the real ones, I . . ." She didn't want to say she trusted no one. "They were my mother's estate accounts for nineteen forty-seven to forty-eight," she told him.

"It's okay, I get it."

That did it. He was now, at least in Mary's mind, the new journalist on the crime desk.

"D'you fancy a job on the crime desk to replace Mr. Sleazy?"

"You're kidding. I want nothing more." His grin was as wide as a basking shark's, basking. "But what about Derrick?"

"He's resigned, apparently to take up a senior post on the *Kirkudbright Courier.*"

And they laughed. More than necessary. He said, "A drink later?" and she looked at him. Saw a good-looking bright man maybe a couple of years younger than her and was tempted. "Aye, a drink. But colleagues."

She took in the flash of disappointment and was flattered. And pleased. Then told herself, *Good decision, no episodes with colleagues. Ever.*

That night, alone in the flat—Jimmy having disappeared yet again—Mary considered her alternatives. More and more, even one of the best newspapers in the country was beginning to feel parochial. She was twenty-eight. Her birthday had passed, forgotten by her but not by her mother, ten days ago.

I vowed I'd be an internationally respected journalist by thirty, she reminded herself. *Maybe it's time to make a move.*

Six months back, she'd sent her curriculum vitae to one newspaper only. She knew where she wanted to be; it was either the *Manchester Guardian* or else she'd take time off, go abroad for a year. *France*, she was thinking, *a complete change of scene*, but she wanted to be there on assignment, with a salary.

Next morning the reporter newly on the crime desk unearthed a new twist in the brothers Gordon saga. Trying to impress Mary and the editor, he'd come in early to study the documents bequeathed by Gerry Docherty via Sheena his girlfriend.

Calum—his name was Calum Sangster of the Oban Sangsters two generations back—told her. "Those documents you came across" (he hadn't been told how they came into the *Herald*'s possession). "It shows here . . ." He held up two or three sheets of aging paper, as the *Herald* had kept the originals and sent copies to the police. *Just in case they get lost*, Mary had argued.

"The Gordon & Sons company," Calum continued, "was started by one Mr. James Gordon, grandfather of Councilor Gordon. There's not much information because it was a wee family operation. Then his son, father of the Gordon brothers, joined the firm, developed the business, and turned Gordon & Sons into a limited liability company. That was when they bought the warehouse in Whiteinch." He laid down a separate document detailing the purchase.

He was being pedantic. Mary didn't mind. It showed he was good at research and careful with the facts.

"Then he, the father of Councilor Gordon, was killed in the war, a bomb landed on his house, and the business went to his four sons."

"Four sons?" She got it instantly. "So where is number four?"

"Actually he was a twin—to Alasdair Gordon . . ."

"The psycho?"

"Aye, but we canny call him that in the *Herald*." He grinned at her through a thick lock of hair falling over his left eye, and she saw again how attractive he was. *No more men, right?* She chided herself. *Besides, he's far too young.* A few years was no age difference when it was the man who was older. *But if it's a woman?* It was another of those prejudices that infuriated her.

"I searched 'Births, Deaths and Marriages.' It seems he is still alive. But I can find no trace of him, which is strange, as he's registered as a director of the building company, and his name and signature are on most of the documents. Then I found this. It was on the wall of a boxing club I visited."

He unrolled a small poster, the type that would have been mimeographed and stuck on lampposts. She knew the format, had seen them often enough around the city. It was for a match in a small venue in Paisley, a formerly prosperous town, southwest of Glasgow, now a shabby place, the Victorian Era weaving mills long since closed down.

"A fight between Jimmy McPhee and Smart Alec Gordon? Right. But what does this have to do with anything?" Mary asked as she studied the poster.

He caught Mary's look of inquiry. "I don't follow boxing. I'm a film buff."

"That explains why you look so peely-wally."

They laughed.

"Look at the bottom line." *No-holds-barred contest to follow the main events.* It was in bold but small type. Mary knew what that meant.

"Bare-knuckle boxing," she said. "Again, where does it get us?"

"It establishes a connection."

"So?" Mary shook her long hair in frustration.

Calum had no answer to that, so he quickly turned to the next page in his notebook. "The youngest Gordon brother, I *have* found information on him. His name is on many of the contracts and accounts, and he's surprisingly well educated." There was no need to tell Mary why it was surprising that a man coming from a family like the Gordons, had an education. "He's a qualified chartered accountant."

"That explains why the books were so well kept. Calum, this is great research, but where is the story?"

"No idea," Calum said.

She later thought that the research on the brothers Gordon *was* interesting and definitely a good career move on Calum's part, but what next?

With no ideas of her own, Mary decided to ask her mother's cousin, another stuffed shirt. Mary remembered him from family gatherings. His redeeming feature was his obsession with the American War of Independence and most things American. As she picked up the phone, she had the good grace to smile, knowing she was doing what Sleazy Derrick had accused her of, *using yer friends and family in high places.*

"Taxes," her second cousin said over the telephone after she explained her quest. "That's how they got Al Capone."

"If I send you a copy of the second set of accounts, could you give me an opinion?"

"Only if you promise to come to dinner; it's been so long, my children refuse to believe they are related to the famous Mary Ballantyne."

She laughed. "Infamous, according to my mother."

Dinner agreed to, she sent over the accounts books. A day

later he called. "Plenty to intrigue Her Majesty's Inspector of Taxes," he said. "I've written a brief overview, and whoever did the accounts, I'd offer him a position in my firm if he'd turn legitimate. A real Meyer Lansky."

A phone call the next afternoon cheered her immensely.

"I believe the tax man has made a surprise visit to Gordon & Sons. And to Councilor Gordon," her second cousin told her. "I've no idea if they will be able to prosecute, but it will certainly be uncomfortable for them."

"That was quick," she replied, meaning the move by the notoriously slow tax department, except when they were collecting money.

"I did hear that someone else has come forward with information."

"Who?"

"First, promise you'll come to Sunday luncheon? And bring your mother?"

"Promise."

When he told her, her jaw dropped. *Catching flies*, her housemistress at her former smart school for girls had called it.

"And Councilor Gordon?"

"No doubt he will be asked to answer, and pay, and probably be charged with fraud and tax evasion. I told you he was our very own version of Al Capone." The smugness of his voice reminded Mary how excruciatingly painful Sunday lunch was going to be.

When she put down the phone, Mary knew that in leaving this city, she would be out on her own for the first time in her career, no longer able to pick up a telephone and inveigle distant and not-so-distant relatives, and friends of her late father, to help her winkle out information, by legal means, or otherwise.

Then she remembered the poster. And she thought of another friend of her father's, a fellow boxing aficionado. *He will know surely*, she thought as she leafed through her "wee black book," her contact bible.

"Shuggy? It's Mary Ballantyne. How about I buy you a drink?" She listened. Then laughed. "Aye. You know me too well. But it will be great to see you and, aye, you're right, I need to pick your brain. Six? Thon pub at the bottom of Garnethill? You're on."

"Aye, I kent him," Shuggy said when Mary showed him the poster. "A right maniac, but no boxing brain. In fact no brain at all." He chortled into his pint.

Mary had noted the past tense—*kent*. "So what happened? I can't find any trace of the man."

"Adding a wee bit o' color to your Councilor Gordon story, are ye?" Not much went past Shuggy. He might have cauliflower ears and a nose that resembled a volcanic eruption, but *his* brain was all working. "See, I'd like to tell you, you being your father's daughter, but with thon tink still around it's best I keep ma mouth shut."

"Jimmy McPhee?"

"From what I heard, you're right good pals wi' him." He winked. She didn't mind. Her being single, being teased about any man she came into contact with was fair game. "Anyhow, thon Gordon twin, last I knew he was in the loony bin out at Gartnavel. You know, indeterminate sentence 'at Her Majesty's pleasure.'"

"Thanks, Shuggy."

Mary ordered and paid for more drinks. She was comfortable in the pub, one of many in Glasgow with the long dark wood bar-counter, brass rail along the bottom, spittoons still positioned at intervals. Hopefully no longer in use, she thought, but avoided them nonetheless.

As he sipped carefully on his beer, careful not to disturb the sediment on the bottom of the lukewarm hop-scented Bass stout, she listened to the reminiscences of his and her father's outings to boxing matches at the Kelvin Hall. Shuggy was more than a contact; he was formerly Corporal Hugh McPherson, inveterate fighter, and proud soldier in her father's regiment. *A fine fellow to have on your side in a dark corner* was her father's description of him.

They parted with Mary promising to meet up again but as friends, not journalist and informant.

"Maybe we could go to the boxing, like auld times," he said.

She wasn't sure she liked boxing anymore but said, "I'd like that."

As she walked home, thinking through the whole debacle, Mary became convinced that the brother who was incarcerated in the Glasgow Mental Hospital, the section for the criminally insane, was important. How, she didn't know. *Maybe he was released. Jimmy will know.* But she had no idea where to find him. When she and Jimmy had parted, she assumed he went back to his Highland home.

It's unlikely he'll come to Gerry Dochery's funeral, she thought. *But McAllister will surely return for the service. He might know how to contact Jimmy.*

McAllister. She asked herself if she cared for him as more than a friend. *No,* she decided. *He was—is—a friend. But also a distraction. An about-to-be-married distraction.*

Early evening the next day, Mary was at home. Two men came to the flat. When she keeked through the curtains to see who it was, she recognized Shuggy. The other man she didn't know.

"You're coming wi' us," the stranger told her when she opened the door to see Shuggy, shuffling on the doorstep, cap twisting and turning in his hands.

"Who's goin' make me?" She stepped back, ready to slam the door shut on his foot.

"You'll be safe. You're under the protection o' your wee tinker friend."

"Jimmy asked for me?"

"No skin aff o' ma nose if you don't come." He climbed the steps.

She grabbed her bag and locked up. In the car she could feel Shuggy's agitation and knew he was scared.

"I'm right sorry about this," he whispered as they sat in the back of the car.

"Jimmy sent for me, we'll be fine," she whispered back. She was scared. But never scared enough. Her position on the newspaper, her upbringing as daughter of an illustrious soldier and ancient family, had bred into her a sense of invincibility.

The drive went through the streets along the north side of the Clyde, an area of warehouses and elaborate buildings with statues and cornices and mock Greek columns, former counting houses of the nineteenth-century "tobacco lairds" of the Merchant City. Other buildings, no longer holding the tea and cotton and plunder of empire, were dark dirty and desolate, echoing Mary's feeling that this outing was not about to turn pleasant.

At first Mary had thought their destination might be the warehouse McAllister had told her about. But a few miles further on, the car turned northwest towards countryside, and after another four or so miles, turned in to a track leading to a farmyard. Parked along the lane, making passing difficult, were cars and vans; in the farmyard itself, more parked vehicles.

Quite a crowd, she thought.

Low stone byres surrounded a cobblestoned square, with grass and weeds sprouting around the perimeter. Only one of the buildings seemed to be in use. The driver pulled up alongside open doors wide enough and high enough to accommodate a laden hay cart, and turned off the engine. She could hear the grumble of a crowd waiting for a spectacle, preferably bloody, to begin.

It was dusk—the gloaming, in Scottish parlance. Across the yard, Mary's eye was drawn to a circle of men, seeing and feeling an anticipation in the swaying bodies.

The man turned. He pointed a finger at her. His almost joined-up eyebrows remained steady, his voice calm.

"You've been asked to be here as a witness. When it's over, someone will take you home. If it goes wrong for the Highlander, you're to get news back to his mother. And however it works out, there's to be no more bad blood. Understood?"

She nodded. "Aye, understood."

He continued, "If you write one word 'bout this, someone might come for you. Or your mother. Same goes if you tell the police." He looked at her carefully.

Again she said, "Understood."

"I'm here to make sure it's a fair fight, an' Ah'm about to do ma best, so let's get this over wi'." He was clearly not happy about the bout as he strode towards the cleared area.

She did not doubt the man's integrity, but if, as she suspected, it involved the Gordons, nothing was guaranteed. And the man had made it clear that this could be a fight to the death.

"He's the referee," Shuggy explained.

"Aye, I gathered that," Mary said. "So was it you who told them where to find me?"

"Never." He sounded aggrieved that she had even suggested it. "They picked me up, said I wiz to look out for you, and yer man over there, I know him. And he already knew where to find you."

"Sorry."

Mary followed behind Shuggy. When the men turned to see who was trying to push their way through the crowd and saw

Shuggy with what looked like a wee girl in his wake, they parted like the biblical Red Sea.

Once at the edge of the circle, Mary could see Jimmy and the Neanderthal she knew to be James Gordon's brother. But no sign of Councilor Gordon, or any Gordon other than one of the twins—Alexander or Alasdair, she didn't know.

The light was low, and on the horizon Mary spotted the evening star. Its appearance seemed to be a signal for the fight to step up.

Both contestants wore ordinary trousers and were stripped down to their vests; Jimmy's was new white, Gordon's unwashed and stained. Both men had their knuckles and wrists wrapped in white bandages. No gloves.

Jimmy looked across the open space towards her and Shuggy and nodded. She nodded back. The driver walked into the middle. At his side were two men, both in shirtsleeves. One took his place at Jimmy's side. The other stood near but not too near the Gordon brother, obviously a reluctant second.

They were waiting for nothing Mary could see. Shuggy explained, "No' all the bets are in yet."

"Never knew they'd let him out o' the asylum," a spectator behind them said to his friends.

"It's no' him, it's his twin," another added.

"The other wan, he wiz detained at Her Majesty's pleasure, as they ca' it, but I heard he wiz dead," someone behind said.

"Good riddance if he is, he wiz a right maniac."

Another spectator cautioned, "Dinny let any o' Gordon's lot hear you say that."

There were nods and murmurs of agreement.

A man in a wide-brimmed hat appeared at the opposite edge of the circle. He held up a handful of papers.

The driver cum referee nodded. Then he stepped forward. "Boys, we need a fair fight," he called out.

"Aye, that'll be right wi' thon nutcase," the same voice, coming from behind Mary, muttered.

"No holding, no biting, no kicking. When I say break, you break, else I stop the fight." Then the referee blew the whistle.

Jimmy stepped forward. In his sand shoes, compared to Gordon, who was lumbering towards him like a man about to toss the caber, it was clear how much shorter and skinnier Jimmy was. And with much less of a reach. But after they'd circled each other a few times, and as he danced inwards and outwards, it was obvious the Traveler was quicker.

Jimmy got in the first two lightning-quick left-right jabs. His blows landed on his opponent's substantial belly. It was as though he was attacking blubber. Gordon was aiming for the head. His arms were swinging. Jimmy's hands kept jabbing. So far Gordon kept missing his target. Jimmy found his, and it made no impact.

A man yelled out, "C'mon, Jimmy!"

Mary looked across and could see a group of men apart from the rest of the crowd.

"Tinkers," Shuggy explained. Unnecessarily. Mary would never have been able to say exactly why, but she too had been certain they were Traveling people and was glad Jimmy had support.

The dancing, the jiving, went on for a fast-slow twenty minutes or so. But a blow landed here and there. A clinch or two was broken up. But no damage was done.

Jimmy let off a flurry of punches to the big man's guts. A blow landed on his left ear sending him staggering backwards, almost losing his footing on the still-dry cobblestones. Mary was worried; as the temperature dropped, she knew the dew could leave them as slippery as black ice.

Once more the big man waded in, invigorated by the dark swelling that was spreading from Jimmy's ear to his face. But

Jimmy kept up the attack to the stomach. One rapid flight of blows made the big man bend forwards. He dropped his guard to clutch his belly. Jimmy landed two hard blows to the face. Blood flew. The crowd cheered. Gordon bellowed. From a distance the noise could be mistaken for the roar of an incensed bull. And, like the big dumb creature he was, this Gordon brother was most dangerous when injured.

He grabbed Jimmy in a clinch, wrapped his arms around him, and squeezed. With his chin he was drumming on Jimmy's skull. The referee stepped in. "Break. Break!"

Both men's seconds stepped in, trying to grab their charges and pull them apart.

Gordon shook off his second as though the man was no more than a flea and kept up the attack on Jimmy's head. All Jimmy could do was wriggle, move his head from side to side, and try to slip down from the clinch. When his opponent lifted him off the ground, his incongruously white sand shoes dangling a couple of inches above the ground, Jimmy was unable to save himself. Gordon tossed him across the cobblestones, and when he did not move, Gordon was immediately on him, kicking and punching at his ribs, his groin, bending down to pummel his head.

Mary saw blood from the big man's nose spraying out in a halo as he shook from the effort of repeatedly kicking and stamping as though trying to squash a giant and dangerous insect.

The two seconds tried all they could but could not stop him; Gordon was a man possessed. The baying from the crowd grew louder and louder. Three Travelers were trying to fight their way towards Jimmy but were being held back by some in the crowd. Another fight broke out to Mary's left.

The referee was blowing his whistle, splitting the evening air. In between shrills he was shouting, "Stop the fight! Stop the fight!"

Now a group of men, Travelers, were clambering onto Gordon as though he were a rock face, and he was pulled away.

Half stooping with exhaustion, he was snorting and panting, trying to get his breath back, still shaking his head from side to side as if recovering from a fugue, a blackout. The blood from his nose splattered the cobbles, and the red stains on the front of his vest were spreading into Rorschach blots.

Gordon slowly straightened. He raised his right hand, then his left, and clasped them together. He shook them above his head and let out a triumphant roar. Then he spotted Mary and grinned right at her; she felt her stomach lurch, and if it were not for the crowd surging forward, pushing and shoving, patting Gordon, trying to see what had happened, trying to get a glimpse of the casualty, she would have found some way of scratching his eyes out with her bare hands.

Jimmy too was surrounded by onlookers four or five deep, and nothing could be seen.

Shuggy had had an arm around Mary's shoulder for most of the fight. And she had been glad of the protection. Now he was pulling her back. And she was resisting. "Jimmy," she was saying, "Jimmy . . ."

For all that Shuggy was skinny, he was tall and had seen what was happening. "C'mon, hen, we're off out o' here."

"But Jimmy needs—"

"His people are here. They'll look out for him." He was surprisingly strong. Mary remembered he had been a well-thought-of welterweight. Holding her by the arm, almost lifting her, he pulled her towards the parked cars. A few others had seen the way the fight was heading, didn't want to become involved, and were making for their vehicles.

"Hey, Alec, any chance o' a lift?" Shuggy called out.

"No!" Mary was wriggling, batting Shuggy's wrist. "I have to stay, I have to see Jimmy—"

"No. You're coming wi' me." He pushed her into the back of his friend's van and climbed in after her. She stumbled over a box of carpentry tools and fell onto a paint-stained tarpaulin.

As they rode down the farm track, Mary realized Shuggy was trembling.

"It's a bad do," the driver said. On the journey back to the city not another word was spoken until he dropped Shuggy and Mary off at a pub near Partick Cross.

Shuggy said, "Thanks for the lift, Alec."

He replied, "Nae problem," and drove off without making eye contact with Mary but shaking his head at the sight of a woman. *A wee lassie*, he later called her when he lectured Shuggy on bringing a woman to a bare-knuckle fight, a fight that quickly went down in the legends of bare-knuckle fighting, especially since it resulted in a death.

Twenty-four

~

Next morning Don McLeod took a phone call. "*Gazette*."

Mary spoke with no emotion in her voice, telling it as though she were dictating to a copy taker. When he heard the news, Don understood her need to protect herself; journalists, ambulance crews, the police, all those dealing with the extremities of human behavior had to insulate themselves to survive.

She had been up all night, waiting, listening, praying even, that the telephone would ring and Jimmy would, once again, be on another of his nine lives. When the call came, the speaker did not identify himself, but from the voice she knew he was the driver and referee.

"Do as he asked, would you? Let his mother know."

"Is he . . ." She knew the answer. But needed to hear the words.

"He's gone."

Thinking she was about to be sick, she doubled over, dropping the phone. The dial tone seemed to be coming from a dark space beyond the stars. Then silence.

She hurt more than she thought possible. "Daddy," she whispered, "help me."

She waited until nine o'clock, knowing no one would be at the *Gazette* office until then. She called Don McLeod. Why him and not McAllister she wouldn't have been able to articulate.

It was a long phone call.

After she had assured him she would be fine, and he hadn't

believed her, yet knew he could do nothing to help from his eyrie in the *Gazette* building in the Highlands, they said their farewells.

He drove to McAllister's house.

McAllister answered the doorbell. Don spoke to him on the porch, not wanting to bring more news of death into Joanne's household. McAllister leaned on the wall in the hallway. Then his legs gave way and he slid down to the black-and-white-checkered tiles.

Don sat beside him, ignoring the creak in his knees as he lowered himself to the floor. He took out his cigarettes, lit one for himself and one for McAllister, and they smoked in silence.

Ten minutes later Joanne found them there. She stared. Then she too leant against the wall, knowing that whatever it was, it was bad.

"Jimmy's dead," Don told her.

"Right," she said as though he had just announced the late arrival of a train.

She was numb. It was too much to take in. So she said, "I'll make the tea," and they got up and followed her into the kitchen. She wanted to cry but couldn't. That would come later. She put the tea mugs in front of them but neither man picked one up—not that she minded, making tea was what you did when news—good, bad, or life-changing—visited.

"Does Jenny know?" she asked.

"I don't know," Don replied. He was looking his age—ancient. And Jenny being Jenny with her way of knowing, seeing, had already divined that her second son, the one she was closest to, was gone.

"Does this have to do with Bill's, my, debt? Was Jimmy killed for helping me and for threatening the Gordon brothers if they started business up here?" Her voice was flat. Trying to hide how sick she felt, she was staring at the wallpaper she had always hated and couldn't wait to tear down after they married. *If we marry,* she was thinking. That she might be responsible for the events that led to Jimmy's death were constantly on her mind and was only partly dulled by the tranquilizers the doctor insisted she still needed when she'd protested she wanted to come off them.

"No, this had nothing to do with the debt," Don told them. "Mary explained it was all about the past, a leftover from Jimmy's boxing days." He nodded gratefully as McAllister added a dash of whisky to the tea. "Years ago, before the war, Jimmy was a fighter on the bare-knuckle fight circuit. One o' the Gordon brothers was his opponent and Jimmy knocked him out and he never really recovered. He died a few months back in the asylum in Glasgow. Attacked by another inmate, apparently. His twin was out for revenge. It was him who killed Jimmy."

"How do you know? Maybe this Councilor Gordon will come back for me . . . it's an awful lot of money."

"Mary was told no, all debts end with Jimmy's death. She was there at the fight," Don added.

"Is she all right?" Joanne put a hand on McAllister's arm as Don said this and through the shirtsleeve, through the palm of her hand, she felt how the news had hit him. Hard. She had a fleeting moment of apprehension. Mary means more to him than he's admitting. *But she knew Mary would never settle for a man like McAllister.*

"Right." Don stood. "I'm away to find Jenny McPhee."

"I'm coming with you."

Neither Joanne nor Don contradicted McAllister. They knew he needed to do this.

"We'll be a few hours, lass," Don said. "And I'll bring him back safe."

McAllister was not fit to drive his car. So, with Don at the wheel, they were now on the upward climb at the top of the glen leading past Strathpeffer on the Ullapool road.

"You knew from the beginning that all this trouble concerned Joanne, and you didn't tell me." McAllister spoke quietly in a flat calm voice, but neither of the men was fooled. His anger was so deep, so profound, they could feel the chill across the short distance between their seats.

"No, I had no idea, not until the photo of James Gordon appeared in the *Herald*. Jimmy, all the Travelers, keep their business to themselves." Don spoke quietly, concentrating on the road. He was a slow driver, and there was a buildup of traffic behind him desperate to pass. At one point on the narrow winding roads leading to the glens, he pulled over to let the cars and lorries pass.

"Maybe I should have guessed, but I didn't." He took the car back onto the road and continued, "This whole business wi' Bill Ross, and later Joanne, started three years ago. When it became desperate, she came to me asking where she could borrow money. It was then I found out the whole story of her husband's debts and these people up from Glasgow wanting to take over her man's contracting company when he couldn't pay. The accountant brother, he hoodwinked Bill Ross wi' the compound interest tricks. There was never any way he would be able to repay a debt that size.

"When Bill Ross refused to sign over his business, they came to Joanne's house, threatened her and her girls. I told Jimmy. I thought he was willing to sort it out coz it suited him not to have the Gordons in town taking over his own loan-sharking and such-like."

McAllister knew Jimmy operated outside the law but hadn't wanted to know the details.

"It was only in these last weeks I heard Jimmy had a grudge wi' the Gordons going back years."

"And Jimmy's grudge?"

Don thought for a moment. He'd known Jenny McPhee for

over forty years, and although divided by birth, they were both of the Gaidhealtacht. They had witnessed each other's lives, knew many of each other's secrets. And although he could never say he knew her, Don understood that all Travelers were secretive, Jimmy especially. He was never one to blether about the past—or the present and future. But Jimmy was dead.

"It was before the war," Don began, "another bare-knuckle fight, wi' this Gordon brother, the twin. The fight was supposed to be fair—but Jimmy was set up. An' this manny, the Gordon twin, was huge, but raw, never been in a real fight. Jimmy won and the lad was injured real bad. Never quite right in the head even before the fight, he was a lot worse after, always in trouble fighting people, unprovoked I heard. He ended up in the asylum in Rutherglen on manslaughter charges, pleaded diminished responsibility, and was detained for life. He died recently in a fight wi' another loony. His twin, he's as mental as anything too, and he blamed Jimmy. The fight that got Jimmy locked up in Barlinnie, that was the start o' all this mess, and that same twin has now ended it just as he promised."

"And Bill's debt? And the twin, the killer, what happens now?" McAllister knew, but he needed to ask.

"It's over," Don said. "Them's the rules. Everything is settled. Over . . ."

"Like Jimmy's life?"

"Aye. That too."

They reached the camp at the west side of Ben Wyvis and saw a van and a car already there.

When Don and McAllister approached, a dog ran out and began barking and snarling and darting in, trying to nip at their ankles. They stopped. Stood. Waited.

A man in a suit and white shirt came to the caravan door, spotted them, went back inside, then came out and gestured towards the ring of boulders around a burnt-out campfire. It hurt McAllister to look at it. He remembered the spot well, remembered other conversations, late on a star-strewn night, with Jenny McPhee. And Jimmy. The sound of the burn was the same, and the sighing of larch and the rustling of birch and rowan. But the conversation would never be the same, not without Jimmy.

They stood waiting. Jenny came towards them. She had shrunk.

"Thank you for coming," she said. "The cousins told me. But I knew anyway." She turned away, and spoke with Don in Gaelic.

McAllister waited. He watched Don take both her hands in his. Lean forward and say something, again in Gaelic. She nodded. She turned towards McAllister.

"This is Travelers' business, you're no' welcome here right now."

It wasn't meant to hurt. But it did. He knew all she meant was that the mourning, the funeral, were for her and her remaining sons, and her family, and kin.

"Go home and marry that lass o' yours. Look after her well." She looked up, and only for an instant did their eyes meet, and he had to look away lest the pain and the grief wound him more than he already was.

She pulled her shawl tight around her even though up here in the clear summer's air, it was a bumblebee-humming, bird-singing warm. Her journey back to the caravan seemed to take a long time.

The man in the white shirt was watching everything. At the caravan steps he helped her up, and went in after her. And with no eye contact, no acknowledgment, never a word said, he shut the door.

McAllister followed Don back to the car. Don made a three-point turn, and they were back on the road to town not fifteen minutes after arriving. They said nothing on the journey, both contemplating funerals.

McAllister speculated on who would attend the death ceremony for Wee Gerry Dochery, a man mostly feared in his lifetime.

Don McLeod was thinking that when Jimmy was returned to his homeland, the funeral for the son of the matriarch of the McPhees was certain to be conducted in the old way. A wake would be held with drinking, stories, reminiscences, the body never left alone. They would walk to the burying place, the family carrying the coffin. And in that coffin would be placed a candle and matches to light his way, a silver sixpence to pay the ferryman, and a hammer to knock on the door. There would be no music, no singing, and the death of Jimmy McPhee would hit them all hard—especially his mother, Jenny. That Don did not want to see. But knew he must.

Only on reaching Clachnaharry, the strip of a fishing village between the shore and the railway line, did McAllister break the silence.

"What did Jenny say to you?"

"She asked that I come to the funeral, but that you and your kind stay away."

"Right." He eyes smarted. His jaw was tight. "Right."

When Don stopped outside McAllister's house and they got out of the car, he said, "Jenny meant what she said about you and Joanne. Marry the lass. Put everything you have into it, and it will work."

"I'll do my best."

Don nodded, knowing this was as much as he could expect. But still it pained him. He wanted more for Joanne. "I have things to do, I'll see you at the wedding." He walked away, hands deep in his pockets, head down, completely drained.

"See you at the wedding." McAllister watched, but felt unable to help Don, or himself. He walked up the path, and when he heard the piano being played, badly, and as he listened to Joanne laugh and one of the girls join in, he knew Jenny was right. He knew Don was right. He would marry Joanne.

But first he had a funeral to attend.

Once again McAllister made the long drive to the city. With his wedding date nine days away, he was anxious to spend as little time as possible in the Lowlands. He left before dawn, drove seven hours without stopping.

McAllister was meeting his mother in Strathblane, and planned to return to the Highlands that same day, driving through the night again, if necessary. He hoped, almost prayed, that it would be the last visit for a long time to come.

The funeral was at two o'clock and Mrs. McAllister was coming with old Mr. Dochery, to be with him as his only child was interred next to his mother and grandmother. Mrs. McAllister had buried a son. Mr. Dochery had been at the graveside. The old acquaintances were aware their connection was now only in times of sorrow and that one or other might not be able to meet again in this life, but would attend the survivor's funeral.

At the service McAllister was struck by what a good person Sheena seemed. And by what a waste it all was. With her at his side it might have been different for Gerry, he thought. Then rejected the idea. His father was right; he was too deep into that life. He watched his mother comfort Mr. Dochery. He watched the neighbors gather around the old man and take time shaking his hand, offering condolences.

Turning away from the graveside, refusing the request to come to Sheena's mother's house for the funeral high tea, saying he had a long drive ahead, McAllister had the notion that with Gerry's death, Sheena would not have to endure years of anxiety for herself and her daughter. She would not have to fear every stranger in the village, every knock at her door. Nor would she watch the man she loved become harder and more violent, simply to stay alive. Her daughter would not grow up with an absent dad who dared only visit at night, never coming to her school events or visiting on her birthday, for fear of who might recognize him, who or what he might bring in his wake. And he was guiltily glad for her.

Gerry Dochery had chosen his life and had left it the only way possible; he had been too deeply entangled in the evil of the gangs and the killers and the robbers ever to escape. And he'd known it.

Mary Ballantyne came to the funeral service but left shortly after the burial was over. She and McAllister noted the presence of two plainclothes policemen, one of them DI Willkie, whom they chose to ignore. She shook the old man's hand. She looked curiously at Sheena and her mother, who were introduced as neighbors.

She greeted McAllister, saying, "This is a depressing sight," gesturing at the open grave with the coffin out of sight and the sound of earth upon wood accompanying their brief conversation.

They looked at each other, neither wanting to be the first to say his name.

"I'm sorry about Jimmy," she got in first and he was grateful.

"Aye." Raw, simple, a word that contained everything Scottish: acceptance, agreement, doubt, inability to express emotions, said in differing inflections, all, and more, could be contained in that one word—*aye*.

"I have to get back," she said. "The lawyers are meeting, and once we get the go-ahead, we'll publish what we can. Is it enough to destroy Councilor Gordon?" It was a rhetorical question. "We can only hope."

He gestured around the kirkyard. "I've been following the news. You've done well out of all this."

"I have. Thanks again for passing on the documents." He shrugged. "McAllister, don't tell me you've lost your journalistic instincts? Don't you want to know the details of what we found?"

"Company accounts."

"Aye, a double set of accounts—one clean, the other jiggered with to hide Councilor Gordon's direct involvement in Gordon & Sons, building and supply company."

He was longing to know if he meant anything to her. He knew it was stupid. No, worse than that, it was disloyal. "So how did Gerry come by those company documents?" he asked.

She wanted, needed, to be away from this kirkyard, this death, from DI Willkie, who was hovering in a far corner watching them. And she wanted to be away from McAllister. Being with him, standing so close, she wanted his arms around her, holding her close. She needed him to say her name. Over and over. Instead, speaking quickly, she asked, "Remember there were four brothers?"

"Aye."

"Councilor James Gordon, the twins, Alasdair and Alexander, the fourth one, the youngest . . ."

"The accountant?"

"The accountant . . ." She glanced towards Willkie and his colleague, a policeman with an overcoat to hide his uniform, and failing. They were walking towards the arched gate leading out of the cemetery, unacknowledged by Mr. Dochery, the minister, and the mourners. "A falling-out amongst thieves best expresses it."

"It was him who—"

"Gave the company accounts to Gerry? Aye, seems so."

McAllister tried to interrupt but Mary held up a hand. "I have no idea of the exact charges as yet, corruption, falsifying tenders and bids, all that sort of thing, and the tax inspector is involved. The accountant brother is pleading complete innocence and had provided my . . . someone I know . . . with everything to convict his oldest brother. Councilor Gordon won't escape this time." She laughed. It was a strange grim sound.

It was then he saw, in her eyes, in her movements, her grief. "Jimmy, he always makes me think of the old Scottish saying, 'We'll never see his likes again.'"

She turned away to leave.

But he couldn't let her go, certain this was the last time he would see her. "And the list of corrupt officials?"

"I've handed that to the police. And I forgot to keep a copy."

"Not like you, Mary." It came out more bitter than he intended.

"Our esteemed editor said the exact same thing." That she did have a copy she would never disclose; three names on the list were relatives. Another was a former colleague of her late father, a gentleman she'd always called Uncle, and still a regular dinner guest at her mother's table. He was also her source within the Lanarkshire police force. The revelation had saddened her, and reinforced her decision that it was time to move out into the big wide world.

"I have to go." She didn't know how to say goodbye. "Thanks, McAllister."

He looked up at the escarpment, seeing the clouds scudding over, but no sign of rain. He could see she wanted to flee. He was suddenly angry; a mere thanks demeaned what he felt they'd meant to each other. "Don't thank me, thank Gerry. Without him you wouldn't have Councilor Gordon as your front-page scoop."

"A wee bit late to thank him, don't you think?" She jerked her head in the direction of the grave. She wasn't being cruel; gallows humor was what saw a journalist through the worst of times. "Give my best to Joanne."

She stepped forward. She reached up. She pulled his head down. She kissed him on the cheek. "Have a good life, yeah?"

He wanted to reply, to say something, anything, but she was striding away in her private-schoolgirl-hockey-playing lope.

All he could mutter was, "Bloody Jimmy McPhee, why did you have to die on me?" Then he shuddered. "Someone stepping on ma grave," his mother would say. *Sorry, Jimmy, Joanne would never be safe if it wasn't for you.* He looked heavenwards at the clouds building up above the ridge of the Campsies and spoke out loud, "And I'm bloody furious you won't be at my wedding."

His mother stayed to keep old Mr. Dochery company. As he said goodbye, Mr. Dochery told him, "I'm sorry about your pal Jimmy. He was a good man."

McAllister could only say, "He was."

His mother squeezed his hand. "It's none o' it your fault, Son."

She knows me too well, he thought as he said goodbye. "I'll be seeing you in the Highlands."

"Aye, I'll be there for your wedding." Her voice, and eyes, daring to hope, was saying "your wedding" as though it were a miracle on a par with the visions in Lourdes.

On the now familiar drive home, he drove fast. But not dangerously so.

Along the shores of Loch Lomond, through the twists in the road, through the tunnels of the dense summer foliage, and flickering light, and in the reflections in the loch, and on the slopes of Ben Lomond, the song seemed to hover, crying the tune and the words, "Oh ye'll take the high road and I'll take the low road . . ."

He started to speak. Alone in the car he said all he needed to say.

"You were my friend. We never said it, but I knew. You were my friend."

He made the last ferry across the loch at Ballahulish. He reached the top of the pass of Glencoe. The piper was there as always in the same lay-by.

McAllister stopped the car. The Traveler, renowned for his piping skills, was in full dress kilt. In a kilt sock, a sgian-dubh with an amber Cairngorm stone set into the hilt was winking in the last of the evening light as the man paced, piping the haunting laments for the dead of the glens.

And for Jimmy, McAllister thought.

A wee boy collecting the donations in an empty tin ran up to him. He stared at the ten-shilling note and said, "Thanks mister, thank you very much," and gave McAllister a sprig of lucky white heather in return.

On the downward drive past the series of lochs, McAllister nodded. *Only the home straight now.* On the outskirts of the town, passing over the canal bridge, he told himself, *home to be married.*

It came over like a freezing tsunami. He watched for a lay-by. When he found one, sheltering under a rock face with ferns stuck in crevices all the way up to an overhang with tree roots dangling in the air, and a trickle of an almost waterfall that would be a torrent in the rain, he stopped, got out of the car, and breathed deeply. He breathed in the water and earth and air—the scent of his homeland. Lungs full of oxygen, the tension, the worry, the pain began to dissolve. His skin and his hair and the saliva in his mouth felt fresh. New.

Without Joanne he knew he could have a fulfilling life—a middle-aged eccentric bachelor, alone with his books, his music, and an occasional game of chess. He would be invited to all the social occasions that befitted the editor of the local newspaper.

There would be flirtations with the widows, the lonely, and the daughters of the impoverished gentry of the county would be pushed at him by their desperate mothers.

And he could see that over time, he would dry up and become not so much a man, more a character.

Even in illness, Joanne radiated a life force, making everything brighter, lighter. He was never certain what she thought, what she wanted, and was often surprised by the little things—like birdsong, or a well-shaped seashell—that made her exclaim in delight.

He looked at the loch, a dark deep stain in a crevasse created millennia ago in an ice age beyond time beyond the Highlands and the Highlanders. Beneath the neat chaos of the dry-stane dyke he read the marker stone. Twenty-seven miles. He was light-headed. Exhausted. He needed food. He needed coffee. He needed his own bed.

As he looked around one last time before continuing onwards, he smiled. *Saint Paul on the road to Damascus—I know how he felt.*

At the next stone, marking fifteen miles to town, he started to hum. He was unable to hold a tune. He knew this, and sang only in the solitude of his car. Stuck in his head was the tune the piper had begun to play as he had driven off.

He began to hum. Then sing in his fledgling-crow bass.

> *Step we gaily on we go,*
> *Heel for heel and toe for toe,*
> *Arm in arm and row on row,*
> *All for Mairi's wedding.*

Only he changed it to "Joanne's wedding."

EPILOGUE

~

Glasgow Herald
12 September 1959

On the 9th of September the body of a man was recovered from the River Clyde. It was found trapped in the pilings of a dock outside a warehouse in Whiteinch.

The man has been identified as Alexander Malcolm Gordon. His brother James Gordon, a former Glasgow city councilor, was unavailable for comment as he is currently on remand in Barlinnie Prison awaiting trial on corruption charges. No one else in the family could be contacted to comment on the death.

Sergeant John Dick, 47, of Partick Cross police station, said in a statement to the *Herald* reporter, "The body was spotted by a passing tugboat crew member. The deceased had been in the water some time. The report to the procurator fiscal's office stated that the throat had been cut and the city police have set up a murder inquiry. Any witnesses are asked to contact this station or their local police."

CALUM SINCLAIR

McAllister read the article and was uncertain whether to make the call. In the end, curiosity overcame doubt.

"*Glasgow Herald.*"

"Can you put me through to Sandy Marshall?"

"Sorry, Mr. Marshall is out of the office this week."

He had forgotten the dates but remembered Sandy saying that he would be playing in a golf tournament on Turnberry Links. He hesitated. "Put me through to Mary Ballantyne, please."

"Miss Ballantyne no longer works at the *Herald*," the voice, a woman's, said. "Shall I put you through to Calum Sinclair on the crime desk?"

"No. Thanks."

He hung up. He lit a cigarette. He called Mary's home telephone. It rang out. His phone book still open on his desk, he saw Mary's mother's number scribbled in pencil under her number. He remembered Mary had put it there when they were on the island, in Millport. "Emergencies only, McAllister," she'd said.

He dialed.

"Ballantyne residence." In her tone, and in her accent of privilege and wealth, Mrs. Ballantyne's voice conveyed a disappointment with life as obvious as her status.

"Mrs. Ballantyne, this is John McAllister, a former colleague of your daughter."

"I remember who you are, Mr. McAllister, and I cannot believe you have the audacity to telephone. What you have done to my daughter is unforgivable. And you a married man. You are beyond despicable."

He thought she might be crying but dismissed the notion as ridiculous. *Can't cry if you're made of stone.*

"Would you ask Mary to call?"

"Mary is no longer in the country. When she left, she gave me specific instructions to tell no one of her whereabouts. Please do not call again." She hung up.

"Nasty auld bag," he muttered.

"Who?" Don asked as he came in with the dummy for the next edition.

"Mary Ballantyne's mother. I wanted to ask about this." He pushed the article towards Don.

"Aye, I saw that. Justice, if you ask me."

McAllister was staring at the dummy for the next edition. *What had her mother said? What I have done? Unforgivable? Married?*

Don didn't notice. He was in a hurry to finish then get to the pub for a beer with an old friend from Fort William.

"Don, do you know where Mary—"

"McAllister." Joanne was standing in the doorway wearing the white summer frock printed with poppies that he loved. "Ta-raa!" She was waving a small piece of paper. "Look, a check for twelve guineas." She was laughing. "Don, congratulate me, I've sold my very first story."

"Congratulations, lass. Well done." He took her hand and was pumping it up and down. "Your first story—must be a great feeling."

"It is."

McAllister took the check his wife offered and saw it was from a well-known publisher of women's magazines. "This is marvelous. Absolutely wonderful. I had no idea. Why didn't you tell me you were writing stories?" He was grinning, thrilled at her laugh, her smile, her pleasure.

"It was my secret escape. And as this is my very first payment for my very first story, I'm taking you out to lunch."

Don looked at them, saw what he saw, and left them alone. They didn't notice.

"Mrs. McAllister," McAllister began, "I can't begin to tell you how proud I am of you."

"Tell me over lunch," she replied. "I'm starving."

* * *

Over the rest of the year and into the next, McAllister would wonder occasionally where Mary was. That she would be a successful career woman he had no doubts.

Sandy Marshall, when he recovered from his initial anger at Mary's walking out with only one week's notice, was also curious but, he later told McAllister, no one had heard from her. "Perhaps she's locked herself away to write a novel."

They laughed, knowing that that was the fantasy of many a journalist, and knowing the crossover from reporter to novelist was seldom successful.

Rumors reached them that she was at the *Manchester Guardian*, but that proved to be untrue. Someone said she'd been seen in Paris. One woman insisted Mary was in London. But no one spoke to her, or read her work, and life moved on.

She became a person McAllister remembered fondly but did not want to think of much as it reminded him of Jimmy McPhee. And he needed to forget he had come close to losing his reason over Mary Ballantyne.

ACKNOWLEDGMENTS

To Cat Wheeler, author, raconteur, environmentalist, and a key founder of Growing Old Disgracefully (Ubud, Bali chapter). Thank you for showing me another side of Ubud and Bali.

To John and Barbara Orme, thank you for your many kindnesses, and thank you Barbara for allowing me to stay in your lovely home whilst I wrote.

As ever to Tran Duc and Ly Le for the wonderful food and the love without which I doubt I could ever write.

To Pete, for the L.O.V.E.

I thank my agents Sheila Drummond and Peter McGuigan. I know, I know, it's your job. But the effort and enthusiasm and dedication you both put into representing your authors is truly appreciated.

To all at Atria Books, a publishing team that makes authors feel part of a family, thank you for your continuing faith in the folk at the *Highland Gazette*.

Thank you once again to a woman whom I have never met, Anne Cherry, the copy editor on my books. Her eagle eye, her comments and suggestions, her patience, are truly appreciated.

No book of mine would ever be complete without the encouragement, the wisdom, and the intelligence of Sarah Durand. Thank you.

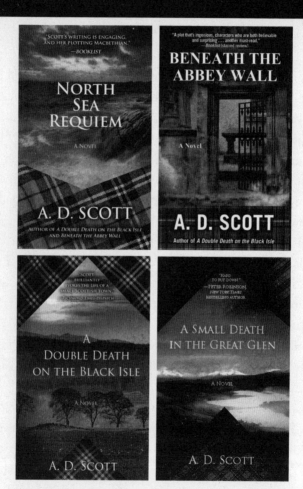